Nigel Lampard was a Lieutenant-Colonel in the British Army and after thirty-nine years of active service he retired in 1999. Trained as an ammunition and explosives expert, he travelled the world and was appointed an Order of the British Empire for services to his country.

As a second career he helped British Forces personnel with their transition to civilian life, and finally retired in 2007, when he and his wife Jane moved to Leigh-on-Sea in Essex. Married for over forty years, they have two sons and four grandchildren.

Nigel started writing after a tour in Berlin in the early 1980s – he fell in love with what was then a walled and divided city. After leaving Berlin, the only way he could continue this love was to write about it. By the time he completed the draft for his first novel he was already in love with writing.

Also by Nigel Lampard

Naked Slaughter
Obsession
In Denial
Pooh Bridge
Subliminal

The Loser Has To Fall

Nigel Lampard

A Bardel Publication

Published by Bardel 2015
© Nigel Lampard 2007

First Edition
The Loser Has To Fall

Cover designed by Bardel
Images provided by www.123RF.com

I dedicate this story to the two groups of marvellous people
Firstly, to the Iban people of Sarawak – I hope I have done you justice.
Secondly, to the men, women and children who experienced the horrors of internment during World War 2.

Acknowledgements

I acknowledge Datuk Michael Buma, the author of Iban Customs and Traditions, who gave me such a tremendous insight into his people.
I also acknowledge Julitta Lim, the author of 'Pussy in the Well', who described the horrors of internment in Batu Lintang POW Camp in Kuching, during World War 2.

Sarawak, Borneo June 1963

Chapter One

The young man watched the Malayan Airways Vickers Viscount turn for its final run into Kuching International Airport. The sun glinted on the plane's wings and fuselage, its flat passage belying the anxiety that he knew some of its passengers would be feeling. The plane's passage looked so smooth but his own experiences told him that the hot tropical air created changes in the currents that could buffet even the largest of aircraft.

Although he had his feet firmly on the ground there were butterflies in the young man's stomach too. He wasn't concerned about the onward flight the following day from Kuching to Brunei Darussalam: his nervousness was because of the person he was due to meet. Even though he had never met her before, it wasn't as if he didn't know the young woman he was meeting. They had exchanged so many letters and photographs over the years they knew everything there was to know, or perhaps what they needed to know. Starting when she was eight and he was seven, the exchange went on for thirteen years and hardly a month had gone by without each receiving a letter from the other.

On the flight, and trying not to look down at the jungle beneath her, the young woman who was meeting the young man was also anxious, but she would admit that part of her anxiety was flying. She was quite happy once they were above the clouds, or even when she could see the sea or land thousands of feet below, but taking off and landing always scared her. As she gripped the armrests, an elderly lady sitting next to her covered the young woman's hand with hers.

"We'll be on mother earth in a few minutes, my dear," she said. "Is this your first time in Kuching?" she asked, trying to be of help.

"No," the young woman said, her eyes closed. "I was born here and spent the first three years of my life in Kuching."

The lady turned her head so that she could get a better look at the young woman's face.

"May I be rude and ask how old you are?" she said.

Opening her eyes the young woman replied: "Yes, of course, I am

9

twenty-one. I have just finished university and I am taking a year off before I start work."

"But your age means that you were born here during the war?" the lady suggested.

"My mother was interned by the Japanese. I was born in a place called Kampong Punkit and then we were transferred to a camp in Kuching called Batu Lintang."

The young woman felt the other woman's grip on her hand tighten.

"It can't be," the other woman said. She nudged her husband who was still fast asleep across the aisle. "Peter, wake up," she commanded. Turning back to the young woman, she said, "Your name is Angelique Lefévre, isn't it?"

"How on earth do you know that?" the young woman asked as her eyes opened wide in astonishment.

"I ... I was with you and your mother in Kampong Punkit, and Peter and I were in Batu Lintang. This is our first time back."

The older woman was staring at her.

"What's your name?" Angelique Lefévre asked.

"Marjory Field," the other woman said.

Sarawak, Borneo December 1941
Colin's and Rachel's Stories

Chapter Two

The pain was excruciating.

He had never experienced anything like it before. He wanted to scream but to make a noise, to move, to do anything other than lie there would tell them where he was. If they found him, interrogation, torture and imprisonment would follow if he were lucky, if not he would be shot or beheaded.

However, at that moment he would welcome a quick death by any means. Being tortured was his biggest fear. Torture scared him because he knew his pain threshold was low. Without any training on how to withstand pain, he did not stand a chance: that is why he wanted to die now. He wanted his injuries to kill him: he did not want to die at the hands of some sadistic torturer. But he did want the pain to stop. He might die anyway: he could be only minutes away from dying. The pain he was currently experiencing made him wish his death was seconds away rather than minutes.

But he was giving up and he mustn't. While he was still breathing there was hope. There always had to be hope. A bullet in the back of the head, a bayonet thrust into his chest and stomach meant all hope could be abandoned, and swiftly. But even that would be preferable to torture. He had to keep his head as clear as possible. He must think and his thoughts needed to be logical. Should there be so much pain? It was so intense.

He was running and didn't feel anything at first. His right leg just stopped functioning. Running with just one leg was not possible. As he fell, he was either hit again or fell heavily on his shoulder. He wondered if he should feel so much pain if he were going to die anyway.

Surely, God would show mercy on him. If a main artery had been severed, it would all be over soon. As he lay there trying not to make a noise, was his life's blood pumping out of his body? Was it soaking into the earth beneath him? There was no way of knowing. Was this where he was going to die? If he were losing so much blood, he would begin to feel weak, he might start to hallucinate but

11

maybe that would be a Godsend. Maybe as he lost his strength the pain would ease.

So if the pain began to ease, would it mean he was dying? Is that what he really wanted? What did he have to live for? Not having the faintest idea what still existed out there and who controlled it, did not seem to matter. He could hear shots and men were shouting in the distance. The distance, where was that? Where he was now lying did not let him gauge distance, but the shouting could be close … then again it could be … wherever. He had no idea. Other than being in the jungle, he didn't know where he was. After he was shot, he lost all sense of direction. He stumbled and fell – he could be anywhere. It would be better if he just closed his eyes and thought of Rachel. At least thinking of her masked the pain a little

Would she be told? He was being an idiot. If he died where he was, his body might go undiscovered. If captured, tortured and executed, his enemies would not notify anybody: his body would be dumped and forgotten. Even if not told hopefully she would never forget. He would never forget. She could have gone with him but she said she would not leave. She had responsibilities – it was her choice.

He was pleased now that she had stayed where she was. It was safer there.

He hoped … no, he prayed … she was safe wherever she was now.

If she had gone with him ... well, he would not have been able to protect her.

How could he protect her when he could not even protect himself?

Chapter Three

Rachel looked about her.

Initially her mind would not let her accept what had happened and was now happening to her and all those around her. Her aching and bruised legs moved automatically. Her whole body hurt. But her mind was active and she couldn't be punished for what she was thinking. If only she could put her thoughts into some semblance of order – they were all over the place. It was proving difficult to bring everything she had experienced together and come up with a laudable explanation. The silence of the group, their hanging heads and their shuffling feet told of their shared hopelessness and despair. They were no different to her: they too were scared witless and unable to explain what was happening ... maybe more importantly what was going to happen ... to them.

Every now and again, she heard a baby whimper or cry out and when she turned her head in its direction she saw its mother cover the baby's mouth to stifle any further noise. No one cried because like her, no one dare cry. Even those that had been on the earth for so short a time seemed to sense the danger they were in: there would be plenty of time for them to cry, for them all to cry – tears now would gain nothing other than advertise their misery.

As with the others, she had gone from relative comfort to this in a matter of days: if it weren't so frightening it would be incredible and equally unbelievable. Had she known it was coming? Of course she had, she could not be that stupid. So why had escape eluded her at the first opportunity? She had stupid, misguided responsibilities, that is why. She decided that those who told her she must leave were scaremongers. The finest army in the world protected her: didn't they? How wrong she and many others had been. She should have gone when she had been told to go. There was nothing so important to keep her there ... but Colin. She was told to go long before Colin left without her. Colin had wanted her to go with him but she had refused. If only she had listened to him. She would be safe now. She would be with him and she would be safe.

Colin was now far away and without her. He and his Sammy escaped in time. Were they safe? Were they still together? Rachel prayed so on both counts. But for now she just wanted Colin and

13

Sammy to be safe. Sammy would help him escape to wherever she took him. It had to be wherever because nowhere was safe – not now.

Maybe some places were less dangerous than others were.

It had been her duty to stay where she was. Now, she didn't know where she was and where she and the others would finish up. Where were the men? She had searched the group for faces she recognised and there were so many. But no one spoke. There was a telling look, an attempt at a helpful smile, but no words. Speaking to each other was forbidden.

The faces she recognised meant so much to her. Seeing a face she recognised was comforting … if comforting were the right word.

Would she ever see Colin again? Rachel fought back the tears she must not shed. She would cry later. She and the others would all cry later. They would cry together. Her tears would replace her numbness and would bring her closer to him.

She wished she knew what the future held for her and all the other women and children who moved with her.

There would be plenty of time for her to cry. Tears were currently for the weak. If she cried now it would be because of her ignorance and shame, she would not know why she was crying. If she did cry, then punishment or worse would follow. Now was not the time for crying, that would come later.

If there was going to be a later.

Chapter Four

There had been two females in his life. He wished there still were two.

Sammy's back was broken. There was no way he could be with her when she died. She could not have survived what had happened to her. Her injuries were too severe. She was as dead as he was going to be shortly. He wished now they had died together. But as he left her, survival had still been an option ... but only for him. If he was going to escape, he had little choice but to leave her. She would lie alone in the middle of the field, her back broken, her body mutilated and her skin burned to a cinder – her blackened skeleton would be all that was left of her. She would be unrecognisable now.

Being with Sammy for three years was now unbelievable. She had proven to be everything he expected. But like all females she had her moods, but even when he got to know her so well, there were times when he didn't see her mood changes coming. Her moods apart she usually did as he told her. She responded to his touch: there were even times when he believed she pre-empted what he was going to ask her to do. Three years ... in some ways, it seemed longer. Maybe because he was with Sammy for most of the time made it seem a lot longer. For every hour he was with Sammy he probably spent a minute, if not less, with Rachel.

It was when he was about to leave yet again that he saw the resentment in Rachel's eyes. She never said anything. But the resentment was always there, in her eyes, telling him she didn't want him to go. She hated sharing him. He loved them both. Perhaps now he had lost them both. One was dead and the other was God knows where. Hopefully Rachel was safe. He knew Sammy's fate. He had tried to save her but he had failed.

He met Rachel only a few days after his introduction to Sammy. They were so different. Sammy thrilled him unlike any female before her. She was responsive to his touch and yet every now and again she would do something that made him really appreciate what he had been given. She took him to emotional heights, played with him for as long as he and sometimes she wanted, before she – and only she – guided him back down to earth as gently as a feather. She had never failed him ... but he had failed her.

15

Rachel on the other hand kept his feet well and truly on the ground. She was a realist. When they looked at each other across the bar the attraction was mutually instantaneous, or so he thought. After the first few weeks of heady excitement, she put her foot down. He thought there would be an ultimatum. It would have to be either Sammy or her. It was his choice. He could not have both of them.

Although in her eyes the ultimatum accompanied the resentment, her words never mirrored her thoughts. He loved her for that. He loved the way they were able to communicate without saying anything. A look in her eyes, a touch from her fingers, the unspoken word – they all told him so much.

"You be careful and tell Sammy from me that I want you back in one piece," she always said, tears in her eyes, her arms on his shoulders. "You're no good to me in bits and pieces … or dead."

Whenever he was with Sammy, he knew Rachel believed that Sammy had this hold on him that she would never have. She also believed that if he ever had to choose Sammy would win. He always smiled when he was with Sammy as his thoughts drifted back to the last time he was with Rachel. There were times when he felt Sammy shudder beneath him and he was sure it was because she knew what he was thinking. Was she jealous?

No, Rachel could never replace her. Nevertheless, in other ways, Sammy could never replace Rachel. Now, though, he would never have to make that choice … there were no winners.

Just losers … there were only losers.

Chapter Five

At least as she walked the noise was no longer there. It was peaceful by comparison. The bombings had stopped, as had the shootings. The noise and heat from the raging fires had been so intense. There had been shouting, screams, wailing and sobbing: noises that previously had not been part of her life. Yes, it was peaceful now.

Peaceful? Poor choice of words, Rachel told herself without being able to summon even the most ironic of smiles. Yes, the bombs, the shootings, the fires, the screams, the blood and the killings had been awful and the noise had been horrific, but that did not mean the cause had gone away. It was still there, the evidence was guarding them.

She had watched unbelievingly as one man was executed on the spot because he did not react as quickly as the soldiers required. She would never, ever forget the look of total astonishment on the man's face as the bayonet was driven into his stomach, the bayonet's point appearing momentarily out of his back before being withdrawn followed by a spout of red blood. Another thrust brought realisation and a scream, the third death. And silence. His bloody and contorted body was left where it fell. His murderer just smiled before moving on as though nothing had happened.

That poor man had been the first killing – murder – she had ever witnessed. The first dead body she had ever seen. There were and would be many others. She witnessed what they were capable of: the brutality, the sadistic enjoyment they seemed to get out of unwarranted and unnecessary death. She would never have believed that one human being could be so barbaric towards another, especially when there was no justification.

What could ever justify such barbaric behaviour? The others had seen the horrors as well. That is why she was being so compliant. That is why she had already walked so far from her home, so far from what she knew. At least her father was not there, he was safe in England. The others had left fathers, brothers and husbands to their unknown fates. That is why she and the others hung their heads. Simple eye contact could be misinterpreted and an eighteen-inch steel bayonet thrust into the body was an easy answer, an easy way of disposing of a complication. Compliance was the only response.

Perhaps as each minute passed her hopes and her courage would grow. But she doubted it.

There had been so little time for her to pack and take anything with her. She was carrying a small bundle of clothes. Nothing else was allowed. She had hidden a couple of treasured items that hadn't been found during the search.

The incongruity of the summer dresses and hats the women wore, their bare arms and legs – dirty now from the dust, the heat, the humidity and submissiveness – was not lost on her. The way the children walked by their mothers' sides, the looks of total bewilderment summing up how she and the others felt. She may have lost her dignity but she still had her private thoughts. Such thoughts were hers, nobody else's. With her thoughts came lots of questions to which she had no answers. How could she have answers when she had never experienced anything like it before? Now was not the time to ask questions, not the time to speak.

When they reached their final destination, it might be her final resting place.

Was mass slaughter the aim of their captors? She and the others were an inconvenience. They would need feeding, watering, housing and guarding. The alternative would not need any of those things. A bullet in the back of the head or a bayonet thrust into the body would cost so little by comparison. Life was cheap. The look of astonishment on the bayoneted man's face leapt into her mind. What would it feel like?

She had only ever cut her finger before … while peeling potatoes.

The man had looked surprised at first.

Chapter Six

He sensed movement.

Where he lay was moving. There was a swirling sensation, a buffeting and a rocking. His face was in the shade and he couldn't relate what his senses were now telling him. Had he passed out? If he had, how did he get to where he was now?

Having no idea where he might be, did not seem to matter.

Where was the pain? The pain had been almost unbearable before but although the pain was still there, it was tolerable now. There was just a dull ache, a throbbing. Was he dead? Surely if he were dead he would no longer feel any pain. Was he hallucinating? Was he somewhere between near-death and whatever lay on the other side? He'd never believed in such things so why was he thinking that?

His shoulder throbbed and his leg throbbed. But there was much less pain: not as it was before. He tried to move. He could move his toes, his fingers. He tried again – everything seemed to be in working order. He lifted his head and twisted it a little, a bone in his neck clicked. He moved it again – more clicking. That was perfectly normal.

He heard a noise. It was a recognisable noise, but his brain would not tell him what it was. He concentrated on the noise. Suddenly his brain did tell him what it was. It was an engine, not a powerful engine but it was definitely an engine. It was running smoothly, its pitch changing every now and again, but it was a controlled change.

Did that mean he was with somebody else? Slowly, he opened his eyes. His blurred vision slowly cleared. He could see legs – dark brown legs and bare feet. There were four legs. He tried to tilt his head backwards so he could see who he was with, but something behind his neck restricted any attempt at movement.

The noise of the engine, the swirling, the buffeting and the rocking – he was in a boat and it was moving at speed. The buffeting came each time the boat hit a wave. The rocking, as the boat changed direction.

It was a narrow, wooden boat. He could smell fish and he could smell oil.

The engine he could hear must be an outboard motor. The owner of the pair of legs furthest away would be controlling the engine and the boat's direction.

He was on a river. He could see the trees whooshing by either side of the semi-translucent canopy that was above his head. He could see the sun almost directly above him, its brilliance masked intermittently as the boat passed under an overhanging branch. Every now and again he could feel the spray from the river cooling his body.

Why was there less pain?

He may not be dead but was he dreaming?

Over the steady throb of the outboard motor, he heard voices. The words – which he did not understand – suggested uncertainty. There were two voices, men's voices, young voices. How they spoke was not threatening, the words spoken softly almost in a whisper. They were debating something, not arguing.

He heard two words he did understand: '*Orang puteh!*' – a white man.

The two men with him were not orang putehs: their skins were dark brown.

Where was he? Why was he there?

How did he get to wherever he was?

He closed his eyes, his questions unanswered.

The noises lessened.

Suddenly they stopped altogether.

Chapter Seven

Passing through a *kampong* for the first time since leaving the town, Rachel thought that maybe it was their destination. She didn't care what the name of the village was, but she did need to rest and go to the toilet. She looked about her hoping for some sort of sign that their ordeal was finally over. But as the group of bedraggled women and children moved on it became obvious this village was not their final destination.

Reaching the last few huts in the village, she saw that a small crowd of local Malays had gathered and the men, women and children were staring at her and the others. Seeing so many white and Asian women and their children as they were herded by armed soldiers through what was normally a peaceful existence, would be strange for them.

The locals gawped in silence.

She caught the eye of one woman who was about her age. On seeing the woman frown and shake her head slightly, Rachel guessed she was asking what was going on. Rachel averted her eyes because there was nothing to tell.

The prisoners moved on and Rachel bowed her head once again. A few seconds of hope dashed.

She saw a child in front of her – he was about eight or nine – returning the crowd's stares as he wondered why he was such an attraction. He didn't understand their plight.

Just beyond the kampong, two lorries were parked on the side of the track. The women and children in front of her shuffled on and she did the same, the significance of the lorries – if indeed there was any significance – not registering. It was hot, humid and she was tired. The sweat was running down her back, between her breasts and her face felt on fire.

"*Shuushi!*" She didn't understand the shouted command but it startled her. The order came from the junior officer who was in charge of the prisoners. "*Kissuru!*" he shouted this time. She certainly didn't understand and she doubted if any of the other women understood Japanese. The officer ran to the front of the shuffling column. He waved his arms in the direction of the lorries. "*Shuushi!*" he shouted again. "*Shuushi!*" When no-one responded he

21

drew his Samurai sword and stood his ground in front of the head of the column.

The lead women stopped, lifting their forlorn heads slightly to look at him. The officer pointed at the lorries. "*Kissuru!*" he shouted. The women looked at the lorries. They were obviously army lorries, and the drivers were standing by their cabs smoking and staring at the women in the same way the villagers had stared … although this time Rachel sensed amusement.

"I think he wants us to go over there," Liz Coultard said to nobody in particular. Rachel knew Liz Coultard, not particularly well but they were members of the same tennis club and had played against each other a couple of times. "Why?" somebody else said. "We'll find out when we get there," said another.

The women dropped their heads again but changed direction slightly so they were heading for the lorries. The column moved forward. "*Kissuru!*" the officer, who had raced ahead of them, shouted.

Rachel was a few rows back but could not believe her eyes when she saw the women in front of her drinking. The lorries were carrying water and it was there for them as well as their guards. The water generated much excitement. Children were handed from adult to adult so that they could get to the water first. She hadn't realised how dehydrated she had become since leaving Kuching, and when it was her turn, she gulped the water down as quickly as she could. She didn't care about its cleanliness. For the first time the women started talking.

If allowed to drink water perhaps they would not be raped, mutilated, shot, bayoneted or beheaded. Perhaps there was a ray of hope, after all.

Chapter Eight

The fever lasted for five days. At the time, he was oblivious to what was happening to him. Once told he began to understand.

For every hour of every day when his temperature soared, there was somebody with him. His carer checked him regularly, cleansed and treated his wounds, washed his body and dried it, and changed the rudimentary bedding. As the fever tried to consume him, she wiped his brow while the sweat flowed from every pore. Then when he curled up with the shivers racking his body, his helper lay with him, letting her body heat do what it could to lessen the depths to which he tumbled.

Until told, he was completely unaware of how caring his helper was, as she tried to keep him alive. He was delirious as well as oblivious. He remembered nothing after waking up in the boat as it raced along the river.

Once his temperature began to drop, he did have fleeting moments of lucidity. Every now and again, he opened his eyes: he could hear noises, strange noises. He could smell something musty and slightly perfumed. He was in darkness. Once again, he did not know where he was but he was aware of his head lifting as water dribbled between his lips. He felt the dryness abating slightly before falling back into a fitful sleep.

His mind was as gripped by the fever as the rest of his body.

As his temperature soared and then dropped so suddenly, his mind took him back to his childhood. Once he was better, this time he could recall his imaginings quite clearly and they made sense. He heard laughter: he could see his mother and father and they looked so young. They were playing with him. It was Christmas. There was a big fir tree with what seemed like thousands of twinkling lights, colourful baubles and bangles. On the top was a feathery fairy. How he longed for the day when he was tall enough to put the fairy on top of the tree himself.

There was a baby.

It was the same tree, the same room, his mother and father were no different but now there were four of them. His mother held the baby on her knees and both of his parents were laughing as the baby gurgled.

The baby was his sister but not for long because she died from meningitis before she was three-months old. As a young boy of only five the memories and so his dreams were vivid, the house was in mourning for months. He lay in bed listening to his mother sobbing and his father doing his best to console her.

The sad image blurred to be replaced by Rachel's smiling face. She was sitting on a barstool, a cigarette between her fingers and in the other hand, she held the long stem of a cocktail glass. The glass contained her favourite drink, a Singapore Sling. She could consume more Singapore Slings than most men. He was sure the night they met she was drunk but she said she wasn't.

After they became a couple she carried on drinking too many Singapore Slings but who was he to criticise her. She only drank too many when he was leaving in the morning and could be away for weeks. She said she needed the courage the alcohol gave her. But she never said anything. She would look at him over the glass and he knew what she was thinking.

The ultimatum never came.

In another dream, he saw them both. He was in between Sammy and Rachel and he knew he had to make a decision. As he looked from one to the other, he saw what each could give him and that they were waiting for his decision.

Pulled in two directions, he had no idea who he wanted the most. Whatever decision he made, he knew he would regret it.

The image left him before he could decide. Anyway, it was too late now.

Chapter Nine

Four days after leaving Kuching, Rachel and the others reached Kampong Punkit.

She thought it rather strange that although they were fed and watered twice a day, and the little food and water they were given was delivered by the same lorries, it was never suggested they could complete their gruelling journey by anything other than on foot. Miraculously only three women and two children were lost *en route*. Via sign language, their captors assured those remaining that the ones who had dropped out would be well cared for. Regardless of what she had previously witnessed, Rachel guessed she was not alone in thinking something ghastly would happen to those who had lost the will to move on.

As each day passed Rachel felt she would have to give up and face whatever fate was in store for her, but somehow she struggled on. When their guards became impatient with the continuing slow progress, her concern for their fate returned but the junior officer with them seemed to understand and made allowances. There were many threats and a lot of shouting, none of which came to anything. Once again the officer seemed – at times – to understand and apologetic about the treatment of her and the others.

At last, and after experiencing extremes that she believed were beyond her ability, the bedraggled group reached what would become *home* for the foreseeable future. The women and children entered through an improvised gate erected between coils of barbed wire. On the other side, Rachel could see a number of wooden huts on low stilts. She felt the little energy she still had, drain from her body.

The guards shouted until they formed a semi-uniform group in front of a lone wooden building that was slightly off to one side from the middle of the main complex.

Standing in the scorching sun and high humidity for nearly thirty minutes before something happened, Rachel wondered if the future was going to be worth living. It was mid-afternoon and the last time they were given a drink and something to eat was that morning.

She was exhausted and on the point of collapsing. Looking round she saw mothers holding their children close to their bodies, trying to stifle their protests. Once again, she thought it incredible that so many had survived the journey from Kuching. Her attention switched away from the others as a Japanese officer appeared on the veranda in front of them. The young officer – he had told them his name was Lieutenant Sato – who was in charge of them since leaving Kuching and looked as tired as the women and children, ceremoniously marched towards the veranda, halted and saluted.

The other officer looked at him before taking in the dishevelled group in front of him. He took a deep breath, hooked his fingers into the belt round his waist, from which hung a decorative sword in a scabbard, and began to speak.

"Women, I am Captain Yamamoto of the Imperial Japanese Army," he said in excellent English. "You are my responsibility from now until my superiors decide that either you or I should leave this place."

He paused to take a breath during which his eyes scanned the entire group. "We are to co-exist and I am sure that if the right conditions prevail our relationship will be not only harmonious but also productive.

"Let me start by making one thing perfectly clear to you all. If one of you misbehaves or does not obey any of my soldiers or me, severe punishment will follow immediately. More seriously, if any one of you is stupid enough to try to escape for each escapee, caught or not, three women and a child will be bayoneted or shot. I assure you I am a man of my word."

Once again, his eyes scanned his charges.

"If you think I am not a man of my word disobey what I have just said."

Chapter Ten

As he finally opened his eyes once the fever had abated, there was initially little understanding of what had happened to him during the preceding week. He had suffered a significant loss of blood: and his injuries were bad, that much he did know. He also remembered crawling into what he believed to be a hiding place, and after a while, he believed it was going to be his final resting place as well.

But even after he was told the full story, he remembered nothing about being carried on an improvised stretcher for nearly a mile by two young Iban warriors: he remembered nothing about being transported for many hours and many miles in a long, narrow, wooden hulled boat: a *prau* in the Malay language.

As the boat sped through the water and moved deeper and deeper into the jungle towards the young warriors' longhouse, he had no idea that they were saving his life. He thought he recalled waking momentarily, seeing the brown legs and feet, hearing the two men talking, but nothing else.

He certainly remembered nothing about the arguments that his arrival at the longhouse generated. As the headman of the over fifty-strong group demanded to know why his two young sons had felt the need to bring this orang puteh to their longhouse, especially when he was so close to death.

But now he had been told the full story and how close he had come to being abandoned to a certain death in the middle of nowhere.

"What did his wife know about the treatment of such injuries?" the headman had said as he looked down at the filthy and blood spattered body at his feet. "A man who is running when injured is normally a bad man, and I do not want bad men here."

The young warriors who had saved Colin's life waited for their father's ranting to cease before they told him what had happened. They knew what they needed to say in front of the entire group which had gathered to witness the scene. Their words were going to affect them all, and not just the orang puteh they had stumbled across as they too made their escape after hiding for nearly three days. They must choose their words carefully because their father's anger was his authority and his authority must not be undermined.

They did not know exactly what was happening but they had seen and heard enough to know that their lives as they knew them were going to change.

Once told what had happened, Colin could not believe the risks the two young warriors had taken to bring him to safety. Nevertheless, he understood that he would not be safe until the headman had listened to what his sons had to say.

The young warriors – whose names were Abas and Babu – had looked across at their mother to see if their timing was right. She gave a slight nod of her head. She did not know what her sons were going to say but she saw in their manner and their eyes that it was something serious. She understood why her husband was so annoyed, but she also understood so much about her sons, things that her husband would never see, never detect.

"Father," Abas, the older of the two sons started by saying. "The respect we have for you and our people is too great for us to do something such as this unless there was just cause."

The young warriors' father lifted his head to look at his elder son. He was obviously proud that such a man had come from his loins: his son was his people's future leader. He was proud of his younger son too: in fact, he could not have wished for two finer young men to be his sons. But maybe their thoughts on this occasion lacked judgement. He was willing to listen although he thought he would not change his mind.

"Then tell us of this cause."

Chapter Eleven

Rachel looked about her, a feeling of total despair overwhelming her.

She was in one of the huts allocated to the women and children. It was nothing more than a wooden floor raised on short stilts with half-wooden walls and a palm-thatched roof. There were no beds or furniture of any sort, and the hut was filthy, full of rubbish and the sides of the hut were open to the elements.

As she looked around, she saw that some women stood with their unblinking eyes trying to take in what they were looking at: others were sobbing, their hands covering their faces. Was now the time to cry? If not she could not think of anything worse that could happen.

Suddenly one woman's voice broke the silence.

"Ladies," this woman said quite forcefully, "whether we like it or not for the foreseeable future this is our home. We can either let these animals beat us into submission or we can stand up to them and demand our rights."

Another woman asked quietly: "And what are our rights?"

"We will find out by trial and error. We will ..."

A Japanese voice rose above the woman's.

"Ow-Si!" this voice shouted as its owner gesticulated towards the area they had been told was their *parade square*. "Ow-Si!"

Rachel watched as Captain Yamamoto surveyed his charges. He was less than five feet six inches tall, he wore glasses and he had a well-trimmed black moustache. His uniform was immaculate and fitted a slightly plump figure like a glove.

"Women," he shouted. "You have seen your living quarters. That building," he said pointing to a smaller hut, "is where you will do your cooking, and that one is for washing."

He paused, appearing not to be happy with what he was going to say next.

"At the top end of the camp you will dig latrines," he said.

A mutter ran through the group of women.

"Silence," Captain Yamamoto shouted. "You will be totally obedient or you will be punished." He paused again. "You will now choose a leader and a deputy to represent you all, and each hut will also choose the same. I want the women you have chosen to represent you to be standing here in twenty minutes."

Rachel was surprised when somebody spoke out from among the women.

"Do we need so many?" the woman asked, and there was defiance in her tone.

Captain Yamamoto fiddled with the hilt of his sword. "You will never speak again unless you are spoken to," he said trying to control his anger. "You will do as you are told. Such insubordination in the future will be punished. Do not test my patience – you will never speak again without permission. You have twenty minutes to carry out my orders."

The women stood in silence in the sweltering heat for a few minutes before anybody spoke. Rachel could feel the sweat all over her body, but it was not only the humidity causing her body to react. The realisation that the state of their living quarters was nothing compared with the regime under which they were going to have to live, hit her like a sledgehammer.

"Ladies," the authoritative and defiant voice said again. "I am Marjory Field. May I suggest we choose the hut representatives first followed by the overall leader and her deputy?" There were no counter suggestions.

Rachel followed Marjory Field back to their allocated hut.

She now knew what hell was really like.

Chapter Twelve

"There has been an attack on Miri, father," Abas said, his eyes growing wild. "It was so sudden, nobody was expecting it. They attacked the oil fields and the airstrip, the town, many people were killed."

"Who, who has attacked Miri, my son?" the headman asked.

"I did not know at first and I have no confirmation of this, but people were saying it is the Japanese."

"The Japanese?" his father repeated quietly, the question rhetorical. "I have heard word of their intentions from other elders. I thought we might be spared."

"What does it mean, father?"

Anak, the headman and Abas and Babu's father, paused for a few seconds as he allowed his eyes to rest on all those who had gathered. Some held his gaze others lowered their heads in deference to his standing.

Ramlah, the headman's wife, who was by his side, was the last he looked at and he noted that her arm was protectively round their daughter's shoulders. Her name was Aslah.

She looked at her father with her big brown eyes and he could see that she did not fully understand. She was aware her brothers were concerned about something but the sight of the blood-soaked orang puteh at their feet seemed to have sapped her concentration.

"It means," her father said, his eyes still moving through the group, "that the authority of the orang puteh having ruled our lands for so long may be brought to an end and replaced by these people who are called Japanese."

"But ..."

Anak held up his hand as his elder son began to speak.

"But," said Anak, "if what has been discussed is true our new rulers are ruthless and we may have dark days ahead of us."

"But, father, the orang puteh have not really affected us, they have allowed us to live –"

"These new rulers will be different," Anak said, interrupting.

"So what should we do?"

"First we must give some attention to this man you have brought here today."

31

"So you think …"

"I think nothing yet my son. I must speak to the other elders. Give this orang puteh whatever is needed to heal his wounds, if they can be healed. He may die. If he does he is to be buried away from our home. If he lives maybe some good will be done before the bad times begin."

"You are wise, my husband," Ramlah told Anak quietly.

"I will need more than wisdom to keep us out of harm's way if what I have been told comes true," he said.

Anak noted that the others looked as solemn as he felt.

He knew little of these new invaders and their customs and traditions. He did not know why they had come to his lands uninvited but they were here and as long as they did not interfere with his daily life so be it. He and his people had survived foreign aggressors before and they would do so again. If this new aggressor did not affect their daily lives, then nothing will have changed.

He would bide his time because he did believe time was on his side.

He only hoped that by helping this orang puteh lying in front of him he wasn't bringing trouble to his longhouse.

Once again time would tell.

Chapter Thirteen

Rachel, Marjory Field and the other women stood in front of Captain Yamamoto's veranda shading their eyes as they waited for him. Spurred on by Marjory's leadership style and example, Rachel had volunteered to be hut leader and women from the other huts had followed suit. All the other women unanimously elected Marjory Field to be their overall leader.

Standing on Marjory's right side in front of the other women as they waited for Yamamoto, Rachel felt both self-important and vulnerable: elected as hut-leader was one thing but when also elected as deputy to the overall leader, extra and unexpected responsibilities were suddenly hers. If illness or – God forbid – anything worse happened to Marjory then Rachel would assume the role. Although Marjory and Rachel were in the same hut, they decided Marjory could not be overall leader and hut leader as well. Her position was similar to that of an Admiral of the Fleet: she was in overall command but did not command the ship in which she sailed.

About a dozen guards stood around the women, their rifles at rest at their feet. The guards looked equally hot and bothered. Rachel was one of the younger women who had volunteered and the vulnerability she felt was because some of the guards were staring at her. She guessed that many of the guards hadn't seen a European woman before other than in pictures, and she wondered if she, along with others, had already been earmarked for special attention. One guard in particular licked his lips when she looked at him – she averted her eyes quickly, a feeling of disgust sweeping through her.

Suddenly the guards lifted their rifles and braced up as their Officer Commanding appeared, once more, on the veranda.

Yamamoto stared at Rachel, Marjory and the other hut leaders..

"Women leaders," he said. "You are the ones who are now responsible to me for what happens in this camp. If there is misbehaviour, the leaders of the hut in question will automatically be punished along with the troublemakers. You," he said his eyes now on Marjory Field, "you have overall responsibility. I will only communicate directly with you, is that understood?"

Marjory Field waited a few seconds before saying, "I understand."

"You will bow before you speak to me. Bow now," Yamamoto commanded.

Again Marjory waited a few seconds before complying.

"I understand," she said lifting her head.

"All women are to bow to Lieutenant Sato and me whenever they see us: they will also bow when one of my guards speaks to them. Do you understand?"

Bowing again Marjory Field said she understood.

"Any woman not complying will be punished."

"Does this apply –"

"Bow!" Captain Yamamoto shrieked at Marjory.

"Does this ruling apply to children as well?" Marjory asked. Rachel could see out of the corner of her eye that Marjory was looking at the dirt at her feet. Her hands were behind her back and her fingers were crossed.

"Yes," Yamamoto told her. "It applies to everyone. Let me remind you. Non-compliance will not be tolerated. I will exact punishment swiftly and I will show no mercy. You will learn and you will learn quickly that I am a man of my word."

Rachel wondered if a man of his word had to keep reminding them all. Perhaps he was less confident than he appeared to be: perhaps such words were for the benefit of the soldiers as well as the women and children.

Did that make him more dangerous?

Chapter Fourteen

The young brown-skinned girl looked down at the pale-faced man who had been in her charge for five days. She knew nothing of his ways. She had never seen blue eyes or blond hair before.

Although he had been lying down for the time she had been with him, she could see that he was tall – a lot taller than any member of her family group. His pale skin appeared unhealthy but the muscles in his arms, chest, abdomen and legs suggested the opposite. Although the hairiness of his arms, chest and legs was something she had not seen before, she was sure it was something she could get used to.

Obeying her father was automatic. Aslah would never question his authority.

Being unmarried, she was the logical choice to nurse this stranger until he either died or got better. Initially she was wary of her task, but as the hours passed, she began to look upon the orang puteh as a challenge. She bathed him, tended his wounds with the medicines and ointments given to her by her mother, covered him with many layers of material when he was sweating and put her body next to his when he was shivering with cold.

She tended to his needs, and called for the Gods to help also.

Every now and then, her mother came to see her, nodding her approval when she saw that the orang puteh was still alive. "You are doing well, my daughter," her mother had said, encouragingly. Her father and brothers came nowhere near her after her patient was moved to the area of the longhouse reserved for people who were sick.

On a few occasions, Aslah was aware that her father was checking on her from a distance but when he realised she had noticed his presence he moved away without a word.

The only time she left her patient during the previous five days was when she needed to eat and tend to her own needs. Her dedication meant she was now looking down at the intense blue-eyes that were trying to discover where they were. She did not understand why this stranger had become so important to her, but there was something about him: she was attracted to him.

Aslah was kneeling by his side: her brightly coloured sarong

35

wrapped around her waist and legs, and she had already noted that the stained blue T-shirt she wore was the colour of his eyes. When her charge was at his worst with fever and he had shivered uncontrollably, she had not hesitated in removing her T-shirt and sarong before lying down next to him to give him her body warmth. It was their way.

Being a few months away from her eighteenth birthday she would ordinarily already be married by now and maybe have children of her own. But because she was the only daughter of the headman, she must wait a little longer so that her family could be sure that their choice of husband was right for her. Although as yet she was officially not spoken for, her father was in discussion with one of the other headmen from a longhouse a few miles away, with a view to her being betrothed to the youngest son of this other leader.

She had not met this man-boy but she accepted that she would do as she was told. It was their way. She could learn to like him.

She suddenly became aware that the blue eyes were looking at her.

"Who are you?" he said, his voice a husky whisper and she didn't understand a word.

Their eyes met and she saw something she didn't expect.

"Where am I?" Once again, his words meant nothing to her.

He looked about him.

Aslah needed to get her brother because he spoke some of this man's language.

Chapter Fifteen

For a few days Rachel was in a state of complete shock.

Their internment followed by the forced move from Kuching to Kampong Punkit had been traumatic enough, but when added to by the worry of what might have happened to Colin and now her incarceration, left her in a state of utter devastation. She saw in the other women's eyes that they too were having great difficulty in coming to terms with their plight – the realisation of what lay before them not so obvious. The younger children and babies had no understanding, the older ones were the same as the adults.

Rachel admitted that Marjory Field, as their leader, was doing her best.

She and Rachel became close quite quickly, and between them they tried to think of ways of lifting spirits but they didn't have the ready answers. Knowing she had to lift her own spirits first was challenge enough for Rachel.

"My husband would know what to do," Marjory told Rachel as they used their fingers to eat the meagre amount of rice and unrecognisable and strictly rationed green vegetable.

"Where will he be?" Rachel asked, aware that for the umpteenth time she was on the point of tears. She had no idea why she had volunteered to be hut leader but maybe she hoped it would give her something else on which to concentrate rather than herself.

"I assume he's interned elsewhere," Marjory said as she looked across the muddy ground towards Captain Yamamoto's headquarters. It had been raining for the last two hours and all the women and children were huddled in their huts.

"What about you, Rachel, do you have anybody?" Marjory asked.

"I'm not married or even engaged," Rachel said. "I came to Sarawak on my own to work for the Far Eastern Banking Corporation but I suppose I do have someone. His name's Colin Freemantle and he's a pilot. I don't know where he is now: he left Kuching a few days ago with his plane to escape the Japanese invasion. He could be anywhere, maybe in Dutch Borneo, I don't know."

Marjory put her hand on Rachel's.

"And he could be safe. Hopefully he would have stood a better chance than the rest of us."

"I suppose so," Rachel said, not convinced by her own words. Rachel tried to imagine Colin's face but it was a blur, although his voice was as clear as if he were standing next to her. She had a photograph that the Japanese hadn't discovered, among her few possessions.

"As long as Sammy was looking after him," Rachel added quietly.

When Marjory didn't ask who Sammy was Rachel smiled sorrowfully. Her opponent for Colin's love was his plane, a plane he called Sammy: it was always Rachel versus Sammy.

Rachel changed the subject and asked Marjory about how they should cope with the guards. "I don't understand," Marjory said. "At first the guards were lenient with us all when we didn't comply with Captain Yamamoto's camp rules, but now the guards have started slapping women for not bowing and taking sticks to the children's legs for the same and other minor offences. What's more the guards find their own actions highly amusing."

Rachel nodded. She had winced when she heard the screams, especially from the children.

Bowing cost nothing but what else was to follow?

It was all so unreal and yet this was no dream.

Rachel saw Marjory Field shudder under the enormity of the responsibility.

Chapter Sixteen

Minutes later, three men entered the area where he lay.

Each man was dressed in a working sarong, beads hung round their necks, they had many body tattoos and their long jet-black hair covered their ears. The eldest man appeared to be in his late forties or early fifties, the younger ones in their twenties.

The men looked down at him and he felt exposed under their gaze. He felt vulnerable lying naked on the floor with only a loose cloth covering him.

"*Sapa nama nuan?*" the eldest man asked.

Screwing up his eyes Colin said, "I am sorry I don't understand."

"*Sapa nama nuan?*" the man repeated.

One of the younger men – the tallest of the three – allowed a brief smile to cross his lips. "My father ask your name," the man said in English.

"My name? You speak English?"

"I speak some English. Your name?" the young man said, still smiling.

"Colin, Colin Freemantle."

The young man repeated the name but it didn't sound the same and he didn't try to pronounce Freemantle.

"*Ari ni penatai nuan, Coy-lyn?*" the older man asked, his eyes unsmiling.

Colin looked at the younger man for a translation.

"My father ask where you from."

"I am from England but I am based in Kuching," Colin told him.

The young man looked confused. "I no understand," he said.

Suddenly Colin felt weak but for whatever reason he realised how important this meeting was. He had no idea where he was or who his interrogators were, but whoever they might be, they must be responsible for his recovery: they, and the girl who had left so quickly after he woke up.

"I was born in England but I work out of Kuching, my work is in Kuching."

The young man nodded and spoke to his father.

"May I know your names?" Colin asked. "May I also know where I am?"

39

The elder man nodded after hearing the translation. "My father name Anak, I Abas and he," the young man said pointing at the man next to him who had said nothing to that point, "is Babu, my brother."

"And the girl who looked after me?" Colin asked.

"Her name Aslah, Aslah my sister," Abas said.

"Thank you. Can I also ask where I am?"

"You half day from Miri. You guest of my father."

Colin smiled as tiredness engulfed him once more. He felt safe, or appeared to be safe for the time being. The three men were still staring at him and he wished he knew what they were thinking. Telling him he was a half day from Miri gave him a rough idea of where he was but it could be in any one of a myriad of directions. As he thought back to his brief period of consciousness when he concluded he was in a boat, and on a river, he presumed that the half day was inland, in the interior of Sarawak. He had only ever seen such places from the air before.

Not having any recollection of how he got there was of little help.

These men did not look threatening. They were inquisitive, but certainly not hostile.

He closed his eyes.

Although he fought against his tiredness, he was not going to win.

He was only aware of a rustle of movement as he drifted back to sleep.

Chapter Seventeen

It was their tenth morning of captivity but it seemed a lot longer.

Rachel had experienced her usual restless, uncomfortable, hot, humid and almost sleepless night. She felt drugged as she made her way to the latrines shading her eyes from the rising sun. She was more intent on her own survival and the survival of others than on what was going on around her.

Doing the best she could with their limited resources wasn't going to be enough so the thought of another day let alone another week, another month or even another year incarcerated in a commandeered primary school with next to no facilities, filled her and all the others with absolute horror.

Captain Yamamoto had told them that they would be moved eventually to somewhere else but he had no idea where to or when. Rachel noticed that the guards spent much of the time enhancing the perimeter fencing, so she assumed that any move would be later rather than sooner. There was little point in improving the security because the women had nowhere to go anyway, and she firmly believed that if any of them did try to escape, Yamamoto would carry out his threat. Seeing one of the women shot, bayoneted or beheaded for trying to escape had been the cause of some pretty nasty nightmares. What if it was someone from her hut, would she suffer the same fate?

But regardless of his threats – and lack of self confidence – underneath Rachel thought Yamamoto seemed a kindly man but she wouldn't want to test his patience. Being put in charge of so many foreign women and their children was probably an insult for a man of his stature – whatever that might be.

"*Sutoppu!*"

Rachel was brought out of her reverie by the shouted command. She stopped as ordered and looked at the shape in front of her. The sun was directly behind whoever it was but she could make out that it was a soldier.

She bowed.

She was suddenly pushed towards the store hut. It was out of view from the rest of the camp. She suppressed any protest, knowing from the experience of others that dissent would result in a good slapping or worse.

She felt the wall of the hut against her back.

It was in the shade and she could now see her abuser.

"*Lagitoru!*" the soldier shouted. Rachel did not understand, but the leering look on the man's face left her in little doubt as to what it meant. She had seen that leer before. It was the guard she had seen staring at her when she and Marjory had stood in front of the other women, waiting for Yamamoto to appear.

Most of the guards looked the same to her and most of them kept their distance, as they appeared to be as unsure of themselves as the women were of them. But this one was slightly taller than the others and he had a prominent scar on his right cheek.

"*Lagitoru!*" the soldier shouted again.

The gesture that followed the command could only mean one thing: he wanted her to strip. He was agitated as he kept on looking from her to either side of the hut, and behind him in the direction of the latrines.

What should she do?

If she screamed, he might overreact, but if she did nothing, God knows what would happen next. She could feel her skin crawling as she imagined him touching her. The sweat was running down her back and between her breasts.

"No," she said, shaking her head. "I won't *lagitoru*."

Chapter Eighteen

This time Aslah did not leave so quickly when she saw his eyes open.

Her brothers had told her that his name was Coy-lyn and he now knew her name was Aslah. She had the urge to lean forward and touch his blond hair: the other girls in the longhouse said it would bring her good luck. They all wanted to know about this stranger but Aslah was reluctant to discuss him with them, she felt their time would come soon enough so for now she would enjoy looking at him.

She knelt by his side and watched as he adjusted to being awake again. Her father had been right: this Coy-lyn had not been ready the first time. He had opened his eyes for a few minutes only to see what would greet him before he went back to sleep to prepare himself for what he must face later.

She looked down at him as she lifted her small hand to her chest. "Aslah," she said a little haltingly.

"I know and thank you, Aslah, for keeping me alive and tending my wounds," Col-lyn said.

Cocking her head to one side Aslah smiled. She heard him use her name but his other words, once again, meant nothing to her. "No, unnerstan," she said, repeating what Abas had told her to say.

"Of course, I am sorry."

Aslah began to get up but the stranger put his hand on hers. Why was she still looking upon him as a stranger? She had done so much for him, now she probably knew more about his body than he did himself.

Only hearing his words and not understanding them, she felt frustrated by her ignorance of his language.

"No, not yet," he said. "You won't understand but I want you to know that I am so grateful for what you did when I was at my worst. My wounds are healing because of you, but most of all I am alive because of you. Thank you."

He squeezed her hand before taking his away. That she understood. A light squeeze of the hand was his way of saying thank you. She could also see in those blue eyes that he was being sincere.

"*Makai, ngirup, tinduk,*" she said smiling again. She deliberately

43

kept her words as simple as possible hoping he would understand, but seeing his questioning expression Aslah showed him what she meant.

Eat, drink and then sleep, she mimed.

Her new friend laughed.

"I am ready for the first two but I have had enough of the last," he said.

Aslah stood up, shaking her head in frustration.

"And Aslah is it possible you could bring me something to wear?"

He had used her name again. She shook her head before cocking it to one side. "No, unnerstan," she said.

Col-lyn touched the hem of her sarong and pointed at himself.

"For me," he said, "can you bring one for me?"

"*Pulai dilu makai, ngirup, tinduk, sarong,*" she said, laughing.

She bent down to pull the loose sheet from his body, thinking he did not need it anymore, but his hand grabbed at the edge of the sheet and he covered himself again. The sheet needed washing, so why was he reacting like that?

She had seen all of him, so what was the fuss?

This man needed a few things explaining to him.

She must go and get her brother.

Chapter Nineteen

"No, I bloody well will not *lagitoru*," Rachel repeated, understanding very well from the leer in his eyes what the soldier's intentions were.

The soldier pointed his bayoneted rifle at her. "*Moro lagitoru!*" he sneered.

"No, I will not," she said between clenched teeth.

Once again she did not know whether to scream, stand her ground, try to run past the soldier: she didn't know what to do. The soldier moved forward grabbing at Rachel's shirt, she automatically pulled backwards and as she did the few remaining buttons ripped from the frayed material.

"*Lagitoru!*" the soldier shouted again, his eyes fixed on her bare breasts.

She did her best to cover herself but as the soldier made another grab for her, she instinctively lashed out with her right foot catching him full force between his legs.

He looked surprised but then the pain hit him.

He let go of Rachel's clothing and grabbed at his bruised genitals while at the same time he made stabbing movements with his rifle, holding it with one hand.

Rachel turned to run but as she did, she ran straight into Sergeant Suratomono.

She immediately withdrew, bowing as she moved away and with her head still bowed she waited. If there was one soldier she really, really feared, it was Sergeant Suratomono. He was one of two sergeants in the camp and both were dangerous. He was a bull of a man compared with the other soldiers and he had a equally bull-like face.

Rachel sank to her knees and bowed her head.

Sergeant Suratomono shouted in Japanese and she did not know whether his words were for her or the soldier. She was just about to speak when she heard the soldier reply through clenched teeth. Regardless of being terrified. she got some satisfaction out of the fact that she had maintained some dignity.

"What's going on here?" Marjory Field asked as she came round the corner of the hut.

45

Rachel looked at her beseechingly but it was obvious Marjory did not need telling what was going on as she took in the scene straight away. She bowed towards Sergeant Suratomono. "I would like to see Captain Yamamoto immediately," she said.

The sergeant looked at her.

"Captain Yamamoto?" she repeated.

Rachel wondered what was going to happen next.

There were a few seconds when nothing happened, the sergeant and Marjory just glared at each other.

Sergeant Suratomono suddenly barked another order and the soldier scurried away, his hand still clutching between his legs. Sergeant Suratomono looked at Marjory Field, his contempt obvious but so was his indecision.

"This woman has been assaulted," Marjory said. "I want to see Captain Yamamoto. This is serious and I must speak to Captain Yamamoto. A soldier of the Imperial Japanese Army has assaulted one of his prisoners and he is not going to like that."

Sergeant Suratomono – Rachel knew he understood some English – nodded, glared at the two women and turned away.

"Are you all right?" Marjory asked, bending down.

"Yes," Rachel said but she felt anything but *all right*.

"Did he ...?"

"No, he didn't," Rachel said.

46

Chapter Twenty

Colin watched as his nurse withdrew from the room and smiled.

He looked around at the decorations hanging from the crossbeams and walls. There were feathers of all colours, bunches of what looked like herbs, dried flowers and grasses. In each corner, dead birds were hanging by their necks and as he twisted his head to look behind him he saw three human skulls, their empty eye sockets staring down at him. The skulls were just a little disconcerting but Aslah and the others had made him feel welcome, so he did not think there was anything to worry about.

Anak, Abas and Babu interrupted his musing as they came slowly back into the room and squatted down as before. Anak's first question, translated by Abas surprised him.

"My father know nothing about Japanese," Abas told Colin. "He ask why they different to other invaders?"

There was no obvious animosity in the question.

Colin was still lying on the rush mat on the floor. His first attempt to stand up after he had eaten the rice and fish Aslah had brought him resulted in a giddiness that made him slump back down again, in exasperation. His shoulder was causing him a little trouble but it appeared only badly bruised. His leg though was a lot more painful but after a lot of sign language between him and Aslah, he understood that it was a bullet wound, but the bullet had passed through his thigh without causing too much damage. The fever went with the shock that had generated most concern.

Now he was on the mend, although not yet strong enough to support his own weight.

Anak, Abas and Babu, their faces placid, were waiting for his answer.

"I understand what your father asks, Abas," Colin said. "But the Japanese have not invaded his country to bring him more than he has already. Things have happened so quickly since Pearl Harbour was bombed."

Anak frowned and Abas asked: "Your words mean nothing, where this Pell Arbor?"

"Hawaii, in the United States of America? You do know the world is at war, don't you?"

47

Abas shrugged before translating for his father who looked intently at Colin. His eyes did not move as he spoke at length. "My father say he know fighting happening far away but he know nothing of Japanese. He say this place we live not part of your war."

Colin lifted himself up as best he could.

"Abas, I don't know what you saw in Miri but the town will be under Japanese control by now. Life here will never be the same, not even for your father and all of you, and certainly not until the invaders are driven from your shores. They are ruthless and cruel people. I don't know how far we are from Miri – you said half a day – but it won't be long before the Japanese come here to your home."

Abas translated for his father, who turned to his younger son and said something Colin did not understand. Babu nodded before leaving. Nothing further passed between them until Babu came back with an earthenware bottle from which he poured a clear liquid into four small dishes.

"My father say some *tuak* help you tell him why you here in our country?" Abas said, handing Colin one of the bowls.

"I would be glad to and also to say thank you," he said. "I'm still alive but only because of all of you."

"We happy you live," Abas said. "Aslah, our sister, also happy."

"I am happy too," Colin said, casting a sideways glance at Anak. "She was a wonderful nurse."

The drink flowed but Colin felt a little uneasy for the first time.

Chapter Twenty-One

Standing at Marjory Field's side, Rachel felt herself shiver.

How could she shiver when the temperature was in the eighties? Being scared was an expectation but she was determined that the others were not going to see just how terrified she was. She was shaking with fear, not because of anything else.

Standing in front of them all next to Marjory, she failed to hide her fears.

She tried to think of something else, anything that would even for a second take her mind off what was happening. Over the top of the hut she could see the grey clouds gathering in the mountains. The rain had abated but the sky was still unsettled, and it was very humid. Although the women and children behind her were wearing little more than rags, she thought they were probably more comfortable in their loose fitting and minimal clothing than the soldiers were in their uniforms.

The soldiers.

She looked at the soldiers – she hoped surreptitiously – who formed the other shorter arm of the 'L' shaped parade. She had no idea there were so many because she had never seen them all together before. In front of the soldiers were Lieutenant Sato and the soldier who had assaulted her. He was facing the front but she was pleased when she saw that he too was shaking.

She glanced back at the veranda. Sergeant Suratomono was standing next to Captain Yamamoto. No doubt he had told the officer a pack of lies about what had actually happened. When Marjory had gone to the headquarters hut, she would have told Yamamoto exactly what she saw.

Who would Yamamoto believe?

He was looking at the women and children on parade and his eyes bored into hers. The shaking became almost uncontrollable as Rachel knew he was about to give his verdict.

"Women," Yamamoto said, "a serious accusation has been made against a member of the Imperial Japanese Army. If this accusation is not upheld its architect will be severely punished. On the other hand, if it is proven, the soldier will be severely punished."

As he spoke Rachel was aware that Lieutenant Sato was

translating to the soldiers. She wondered why if his English was so good he hadn't used it during their journey from Kuching. She must concentrate: she must listen to every word Yamamoto was saying.

"Sergeant Suratomono has told me what he saw," Yamamoto said, "and the leader of the women, Woman Field, has given me her account. It is my decision that the accusation against the soldier of the Imperial Japanese Army is neither proved nor disproved. So with the powers I have vested in me I have also decided that both the accused and the accuser will be punished to act as a deterrent to you all for the future." Yamamoto looked at his second-in-command. "Lieutenant Sato, Corporal Okidisha is to receive twenty lashes for being found alone with a prisoner."

The Lieutenant nodded, bowed and shouted "Hai!"

Yamamoto's eyes once again bored in Rachel's. "The Woman Lefévre is to receive ten lashes and three days solitary confinement for provoking an Imperial Japanese Army soldier."

The women gasped.

"The lashings are to take place in one hour and will be in front of all soldiers, women and children so that everyone will learn a lesson." With a final nod, Yamamoto left the veranda.

Marjory said, "Be brave," as she put her arm round Rachel's shoulders.

Rachel felt the bile build up in her throat before she was violently sick.

Chapter Twenty-Two

"I am a pilot," Colin told his all-male audience, which had grown to about twenty. Abas had explained that the men present were related in one way or another: some were his cousins, some his uncles. The men's eyes were wide in expectation, for some it was the first time they had been in the company of an orang puteh. "I am, or should I say I was, based in Kuching."

Abas looked confused but kept up a running commentary for the sake of his relatives; Colin kept to simple words because he guessed that Abas would not want to lose face in front of so many.

"I used to fly from Kuching to Singapore, to North Borneo, to Brunei, the Philippines and to parts of Dutch Borneo and the Dutch East Indies. In my plane I carried supplies from one country to another, one district to another, and I was paid by the country or district that wanted to use my plane."

Abas translated a question from a man at the back of the audience.

"Carry people?" he asked.

"Sometimes, when there was room I did, yes. I was trying to escape when my plane was shot down, hence my injuries. I crash-landed not far from Miri at the airfield and escaped."

He saw some eyebrows raised and looks exchanged. Another question followed.

"Why Japanese attack Sarawak?" Abas asked.

"They have declared war on the United States of America, on England and her allies. Sarawak and its neighbours have many natural resources, oil and minerals, and it is also under British rule. All are good reasons for the Japanese to come here," Colin explained.

"*You* the reason they come here?" Abas asked as he translated another question from a man in the group. The question shocked Colin. There was no detectable venom in its asking, but the last thing he expected was to feel responsible for what was now happening.

He was a good pilot and used to have a good, reliable plane until Japanese Zero fighters had used him for target practice. He and Sammy, as he affectionately called his plane – an orange and black Dakota or DC3 – had become an efficient unit and since they had

51

teamed up, the work had really begun to roll in. He had enjoyed a reputation that was of little use now because Sammy no longer existed. He would mourn her loss as though she had been alive – for him she really had come to life each time the engines caught and he throttled them up for take-off. The power in those engines was exhilarating but once up in the clouds, Sammy felt as light as a feather, and if it were possible to make love to a combination of metal, oil, aviation fuel and a mass of wires, he did.

"I think the Japanese would have come anyway," he said. "They want to control this area of the world. They need what you have and they will take it. There will feel as though there is nothing left to stop them."

"Japanese come here?" Abas asked, solemnly. "They come here to our home?"

Concerned that he was suddenly a supposed expert on a matter he knew nothing about, Colin said, "I don't know, if you have something the Japanese want, they will come. I think –"

"You? Want you?" asked a hidden voice in English.

All heads and eyes turned to look at the man who had spoken, including Colin's.

"If they find out I am here, then maybe. That is a possibility, but I –"

"Not maybe. They will come," the man said before turning and walking out of the gathering.

Chapter Twenty-Three

As Rachel watched, soldiers hammered two posts into the ground next to Captain Yamamoto's headquarters. They then fastened a crossbar between each post. It was like watching the erection of the scaffold for your own execution. She could feel the noose tightening round her neck.

The parade would reform in about twenty minutes and ... she did not know whether she had the physical and mental strength to cope, but cope she must.

The minutes passed and the parade reformed. Marjory led Rachel once again to the front of the women and children. Rachel stared in total bewilderment as Corporal Okidisha was taken to the lashing posts and had his wrists tied to the crossbar. He was naked from the waist up and the sweat glistened on his back. A stick was placed between his teeth.

"The punishment is twenty lashes," announced Captain Yamamoto. "Commence."

Rachel could not take her eyes off what was in Sergeant Suratomono's right hand. It looked like a short piece of bamboo to which were attached nine strands of rattan rope each three feet in length. She saw Sergeant Suratomono surveying his target. He too was bare from the waist up and his glistening muscular body tensed as he prepared to carry out the sentence.

At first he appeared reluctant to inflict the punishment that Captain Yamamoto had declared as just, but suddenly he lifted his arm and the rattan rope thwacked against Corporal Okidisha's back. Rachel winced and shook as she felt her own skin stinging with the pain.

After five lashes welts were visible on Corporal Okidisha's back, the next five drew the first blood and by the time his punishment was complete his back was raw and bloody. Rachel had wanted to shout at them to stop, but nothing she might say would be of any use. A soldier came forward and threw a bucket of water over the corporal before his hands were untied and led away by two other soldiers.

"Woman Lefévre!" Lieutenant Sato shouted.

Rachel tensed. "Be brave," Marjory said next to her. Rachel closed her eyes and stepped forward. She walked slowly towards the lashing posts. She was wearing a loose well-washed cotton shirt and a torn linen skirt that fell below her knees. In silence, she stopped in front of the crossbar and lifted her wrists so they were resting on it.

She was terrified but she was also determined that she would not let the women down. She would get through this. Her molester had taken his punishment without a sound, and so would she. She drew her hands into tight fists as she tried to stop the shaking.

Two soldiers stepped forward and bound her wrists to the crossbar. One of them tried to put a piece of stick between her teeth but she shook her head as she looked at him defiantly.

She sensed that Sergeant Suratomono had moved closer to her and felt his fingers grip the neck of her shirt just before he ripped it away. The embarrassment of having her breasts on full view to some of the smirking soldiers was nothing when compared with the horrendous anticipation as she waited for the first lash to strike her back. She forced her nails into the palms of her hands, curled her toes into the dirt and tensed her thighs. Get on with it, she wanted to scream, just get on with it and let it be over.

The next few seconds seemed like minutes. She imagined the whip as the sergeant lifted it into the air, poised and ready to lash her back for the first time. The only sound she could hear were some birds squawking in the jungle, otherwise, there was total silence. There would be nearly a hundred pairs of eyes looking at her back and waiting for her skin to split to allow her blood to ooze out from the cuts and flow down her back.

"*Shuushi!*" she heard someone shout.

Chapter Twenty-Four

"You think they will come for me?" Colin said but he knew exactly what Abas meant.

Anak spoke at length accompanied by nods of approval from some of the other men.

"My father say word reach Miri that orang puteh in longhouse and Japanese come."

Colin and Anak exchanged a long look. They did not understand each other's language and unlike the man who had left the group, Colin could not detect any animosity but on this occasion he could see worry. Anak's concern was there in his eyes, the set of his mouth and the way his hands opened and closed. He was justifiably concerned that Colin's continued presence in his longhouse could bring trouble to him and his extended family. None of them knew what they were dealing with but Colin was well aware of the stories that had come out of China during the preceding four years of the Sino-Japanese war.

There were accounts of mass reprisals, whole villages razed to the ground, women of all ages raped and murdered, young girls suffering the same fate and babies bayoneted for sheer amusement. Dead bodies – and some that still hung on to life – burned in open pits.

Accepting that such stories could be exaggerated as they were told and retold in the various watering holes throughout South East Asia, Colin accepted that Anak was right: he was an orang puteh, he was taller by six inches over the tallest of men in Anak's family and he was now an enemy of the Japanese.

Yes, Anak was right but what was the alternative?

He could not survive alone in the jungle and he could not try to escape via a port or airstrip disguised as a local. The only alternative Colin could think of was to give himself up and throw himself on the mercy of the Japanese. What mercy?

He had never worn a uniform – but how could he prove that? – and even if he were believed he would be interned only to experience the depravations that went with such a state. He just prayed that Rachel had escaped from Kuching and was now safe somewhere in India or Ceylon, or even on her way back to England.

As he thought about what he was going to say next he realised that his previous judgments were based on honour and integrity, the way one human being should behave towards another, even in war. Such attributes might exist within the Japanese armed forces but from all reports that is where they stopped. If he gave himself up he would be interrogated, tortured and treated as a spy: he would be shot or beheaded.

The men in front of him had fallen quiet as they watched him ponder his fate. He could see why these men had the reputation for being able to terrify their enemies. They might be small but they were extremely fit, and could be as accurate with a blowpipe and dart as others were with a rifle.

"I will leave," he said. "You have been too kind already. I would be dead if it hadn't been for you, but you are right. If the Japanese were to find out that you were sheltering an Englishman they would take me and punish you."

Abas translated.

The men's eyes were now on Colin as they waited for Anak to respond. He could see what they wanted: they wanted him out of their lives so they could go back to being normal.

Anak spoke after a minute or so. "My father say, Coy-lyn, that you brave and honourable man. You fight wounds and fever and get better. If Gods wanted you die problem not here. You not ready travel, you get more better, he decide what happen later."

"Abas, thank your father for his words. I will abide by whatever his decision might be."

Colin felt so relieved, but he knew his relief might only be temporary.

Chapter Twenty-Five

Rachel chin was on her chest, her eyes were tightly shut as she waited for the first lash across her back. The sweat was glistening all over her skin. Why hadn't she felt the thongs biting into her back?

"*Shuushi!*"

She heard the word again and slowly its meaning permeated its way into her brain. It was Yamamoto's voice and he was telling somebody to stop. She felt the cords rounds her wrists being untied. She turned round slowly. Sergeant Suratomono was standing only feet from her, the whip hanging loosely in his right hand. He was glaring at Captain Yamamoto.

Rachel switched her attention to Marjory and the other women. They were also looking at Yamamoto, some with their mouths open in surprise. She saw Marjory indicating with her eyes and one hand. What was she trying to say? She was nodding – no, she was looking at her bare chest. Marjory's eyes were telling her to cover herself.

Slowly Rachel lifted the torn material and covered her breasts as best she could.

The silence was broken when Yamamoto started to speak. "Women," he shouted. "Let this be a warning to you all. I will not tolerate disobedience and I demand total compliance. Woman Lefévre provoked Corporal Okidisha, a soldier of the Imperial Japanese Army. To show that I govern with understanding and fairness, and to demonstrate the bravery of my soldiers, I allowed the first punishment to proceed." He paused and Rachel was aware he was staring at her. "Woman Lefévre, on this occasion you will not receive the lashes but do not feel that if you come before me again I will be so lenient next time. Provoking my soldiers into acts like this is still a heinous crime and will not go unpunished. You will now be held in solitary confinement for three days to allow you to reflect on your misdeeds." He paused again. "Lieutenant Sato you will dismiss the parade and escort Woman Lefévre to her confinement."

"*Hai,*" Lieutenant Sato replied, bowing lower than he had ever done before. He turned and faced the women and children. "Dismissed!" he shouted, but the women did not move. "Dismissed!" Lieutenant Sato shouted again. This time, the women started to disperse but Marjory Field stepped forward towards

Rachel. One of the guards lifted his rifle and barred her way. Marjory looked and smiled at Rachel. "We will be here for you," she said. Rachel nodded and she tried to conjure up a weak smile. She was led away by Lieutenant Sato, holding the torn material to her chest.

As she and Sato rounded the corner to go behind the hut Captain Yamamoto used as his headquarters, she saw a small slatted wooden shed. It was about five feet, by five feet, by five feet, and had a single barred door. Sato pulled the bar back and Rachel lowered her head and stepped into the gloom. Inside she could see a bucket in one corner and nothing else.

"Food will be brought each evening and morning. Here is some water," Lieutenant Sato said, passing Rachel an Imperial Japanese Army issue water bottle.

"Thank you," Rachel said, trying to sound grateful.

"It could be worse," Lieutenant Sato told her. "A bloody back would have attracted many flies and maybe rats when you were asleep. Captain Yamamoto is a compassionate man, and Corporal Okidisha a brave one."

The slatted door closed.

Rachel slowly sank to her knees.

The shaking returned and the tears came immediately.

Chapter Twenty-Six

The water was cooler than he expected.

As he washed in the river, Abas sat on the bank watching him. After the session with most of the village men folk, Aslah had returned with more food and drink. She had seemed a little bashful but nonetheless attentive.

It was mid-morning and Colin was by the river and downstream from the longhouse. He had needed help in getting there. Washing was a simple task but a luxury compared with what he had been through. The crude soap hardly lathered in the water but it too was an absolute extravagance. His whole body felt invigorated by the sensation. He had not felt so good for a long time.

Having washed his hair twice and coming up for air after rinsing it he looked across at Abas. "I could get used to this," he said, smiling.

"I sorry?" Abas replied, nibbling on a bit of bamboo. His attention had been elsewhere.

"Nothing," Colin told him.

"Coy-lyn, my father not mean what he say," Abas said, looking down at the water.

"Your father had every right to say what he did. I've only known him a matter of days but I believe him to be an honest and forthright man," Colin said.

He began scrubbing his body for the third time but was careful not to touch the healing wound on his thigh. The way in which it had healed was quite remarkable. His shoulder felt a lot better too but it still hurt if his scrubbing became too vigorous.

When Abas said nothing he felt he needed to qualify his opinion of Anak.

"I am an orang puteh," he said. "The English are not in Japan's good books at the moment, and it's unlikely they ever will be."

"I not understand," Abas said, screwing up his face and looking at him..

"No, I'm sorry, it's me. Your English is good Abas, thank God you are able to understand most of what I say and translate for your father."

"My father troubled. He hear what others say and he worry for his

59

family and all the others."

"Under the circumstances that's understandable." Colin moved towards the bank surprised that he wasn't in the slightest bit embarrassed by his nakedness. "Whether I am here or not, the Japanese are now in charge and well, none of us knows what that really means."

Abas leant forward so that he could pull Colin out of the water. Standing naked in front of Abas as he brushed water from his chest, stomach and limbs, he felt it was the most natural thing in the world. A feeling of freedom coursed its way through his body.

"I see what they do in Miri, Coy-lyn, you right, they animals," Abas said.

"They live by their own code, Abas, and if that code is not the same as ours we criticise. In the same way you and I are different. I fly a plane for a living … have you ever been in a plane?"

"No, Coy-lyn, I see plane in sky but never … I often wonder what it like to be so high, nearer to the Gods than the land. I …"

"One day, Abas, I will show you your homeland from thousands of feet up there in the sky. It is the most amazing experience. It's like being a giant bird, the feeling of freedom is wonderful."

"I like that, Coy-lyn. I like that a lot."

"And I would like to show you."

Colin wondered how long it would be before that *one day* happened, how long it would be before he could keep his promise.

Chapter Twenty-Seven

Rachel wanted to cry and cry but she had used up all her tears when she was first put into solitary confinement.

She was huddled into one corner of her hutted cell, her arms folded round her knees, her bare back uncomfortable against the bamboo wall. She had discarded the useless shirt not caring which of the guards looked in on her.

She wanted to do more than cry. She wanted to scream and she wanted to die.

Was it really less than two weeks ago that she had been standing behind the counter in the bank handing out money to frantic customers? Had she really turned down the opportunity to escape from hell because she felt it was her duty to stay at her post?

Then she had not known that hell was just round the corner. Nobody had.

Since then she had been in the company of desperate women who were all experiencing the same shock of war: the explosions, the shootings, the separations, the deaths and equally as hurriedly, the forced internment.

The bank had shut just twenty-four hours before the first Japanese troops had reached Kuching. She had gone to her lodgings, thrown clothes, her passport, and other essentials into a tattered old suitcase before going to the airport with so many others only to see it was out of action. She was told it was being denied to the enemy, but this denial ensured that there would be no escape for anyone – except for Colin, he had escaped and she should have gone with him.

She could hear his tearful pleas, his anger when she said, no.

Now she did not have her suitcase or much of its contents. She had some clothes, underwear, Somerset Maugham's *The Casuarina Tree* and a photograph of her mother and father standing at the end of Southend-on-Sea pier, and one of Colin. Her passport and many other items – scissors, make-up and other toiletries – had disappeared.

This time Colin's face did come to mind. The picture was vivid.

She was looking down at his smiling face, a face that hid so many truths.

He needed a shave.

Her hands were on his chest. She was trying to fight back the tears but there was little she could do as they fell from her cheeks onto his chest. He was watching her, his hands on her hips and his blue eyes trying to send her so many messages.

Was she in love with him?

There was no doubt in her mind. If she didn't love him she would not have put up with what he did. She wanted him with her, not flying all over South East Asia, returning to her only while the other love in his life was serviced, re-fuelled and loaded for her next trip.

How she envied Sammy.

Yes, she was in love with him. It could not be anything else.

That was why she thought she was expecting his baby … their baby.

It hadn't been long enough for her to be sure but there was a change in her, even with the misery she had been through she felt she wasn't alone. Part of him was with her, and it was growing inside her. If she were pregnant: it had not been planned. What would they have said if the war had not come to them? Would he have asked her to marry him … and would she have said, yes? She was being silly, making matters worse for herself by dreaming of what might have been. There would be no marriage, no white wedding.

The thought that she might be pregnant filled her with joy but at the same time she agonised over what had happened … and was going to happen.

This was no place to bring a baby into the world.

Chapter Twenty-Eight

Colin, who was wearing a simple brown sarong, and Abas walked slowly away from the river and back towards the longhouse.

After binding the wound on his leg, Abas adjusted the sling round Colin's shoulder. His injuries had healed well but Aslah had given Abas a lecture before they walked down to the river, she had shown him how to cover the wounds once Coy-lyn had bathed.

Colin stopped when they were a short distance from the longhouse. "Tell me about your home, Abas. What is it called in Iban?" he asked.

"*Rumah panjai*," Abas told him. "It called *Rumah panjai*. It home for over fifty people."

"I have only seen one longhouse from a distance before," Colin said.

"It good, strong house. It on stilts in case river flood and to keep animals out. Pigs, dogs, chickens live under house. Man and woman work there also." Abas pointed upwards. "To front looking over river is place for all, to dry meat, to hang rice and it where visitors sleep. Next open walking place for all to get one end to other, then still open but area outside room for family. Family have own room. Cooking done at back of *rumah panjai* at end of other walkway, keep fly and smell from house."

"And you wash in the river?"

"Wash and toilet, but toilet long way down river."

"The room I am in, does it belong to someone else?"

Colin resumed walking and Abas followed.

"No belong, it for all. It sick room."

"And Aslah is your nurse?"

"No. Aslah learn medicine from mother and her mother sister. My father said she give you medicine."

"And she did well. I have no recollection about you finding ..."

"Sorry, Coy-lyn, word reco ... recol ..."

"Recollection ... it is me who must apologise Abas. Your English really is good but I forget at times that it is not your language. Having no recollection means having no memory. Other than running, being shot and falling unconscious, I do not remember what happened after I escaped from the crash, or you finding me and nor do I remember the journey to your home. I have no idea how far we are from Miri, other than half a day, I think you said."

"We thirty miles from Miri. Yes, a half day travel," Abas said.

"Thirty miles! And where is the nearest long … no, the nearest *rumah panjai* to yours."

Abas smiled.

"It five mile up river and six mile down river. We have close neighbour. We lucky."

"And you found me when you were also escaping from Miri?" Colin asked.

"You close where we left boat. Abas he sees you and we think we save you."

"And you certainly did that," Colin said.

"I glad but my father he worry."

"I can understand why, Abas, but whatever the future holds for me it is because of you and Babu that I have a future. I am so grateful … you will never know how grateful."

Walking to the bottom of the stepped log leading up to the longhouse, Colin started to climb but stopped. "Abas," he said, "this is all like a dream to me. It is something I could not imagine could ever happen."

"It happen, Coy-lyn. It what happen next that matter."

Chapter Twenty-Nine

As her mind played tricks with her Rachel decided that back in England her parents would have heard the news about the fall of Miri and Kuching, or if not the towns, certainly Sarawak. There will have been no word from her to tell them she was safe: in this instance, no news would be bad news because they knew she would have let them know where and how she was.

She could hear her mother now: "We should never have let her go. It's not a good place for a young single woman, and anyway why did she want to go to a hot steamy place like that to work in a bank? There's a war on, she could have found productive work back here rather than gallivanting half way round the world."

She could hear her father's reply: "She's her own woman Elspeth and has been since she became a teenager. She's always known her own mind, by obstructing her we would have made her want to go even more. And don't forget, she's also a survivor."

She smiled as she saw both her parents on the docks at Southampton three years earlier as she sailed aboard the SS Dunera for the Far East. She and lots of others had waved and waved, even when individuals were no longer discernible she had carried on waving ... just in case.

Was it really three years ago?

There was already talk of war on the streets, there was talk even in the depths of Warwickshire as she had packed her suitcases. She had cried and cried, her heart telling her that she was making the biggest mistake of her life but her head advising the opposite – twenty-two, an excellent university degree in accounting under her belt and an opportunity from the Far Eastern Banking Corporation.

How could she have refused? What could be better? Who knows what would be waiting for her?

Unbeknown to her parents she had also taken a broken heart with her. His name was Phillip. He was a dream, he had taken what he wanted from her for three years, and then he had dumped her. She had loved him and he had loved what she was willing to do to demonstrate that love. But if somebody had told her that a little over three years later she would be imprisoned in a tiny bamboo hut, half naked, with nothing more than a bucket and flies and the odd lizard to keep her company, she would have laughed disbelievingly and still she would have left England.

The reality was that is exactly where she was. It was beginning to get dark. And with the darkness came the usual jungle noises but it was different if the noises could be heard when in the company of others in a similar position. There was always security in numbers. God, what had she ever done wrong to deserve this?

She would be there for three days and three nights. She closed her eyes and wished she still had the energy to cry some more.

Suddenly there was movement outside the hut. Above the makeshift but secure door was a three-inch gap that allowed the guards to check on her – their peering eyes were frightening as they looked at her nakedness. But this time a wooden bowl was put through the gap and she took it: it was foul smelling rice and with what looked like grass mixed in it. She took a water bowl but then a piece of clothing dropped onto the mud floor.

She had no idea who her benefactor was.

The cotton shirt was not one of hers but it gave her some encouragement.

She put on the shirt – there were no buttons – and she took the bowl into the corner and started eating.

Chapter Thirty

Colin rested.

The walk to the river and back, and the exertion of washing had taken more out of him than he expected. Abas had told him that he had work to do. Aslah had brought him some more water and yet another bowl of rice and fish, but she too left him alone.

He lay on his mat under the mosquito net, with his head in his hands and thought. He thought of Rachel. Before he left Kuching they had all listened to the radio and he knew what had happened in parts of the Malayan peninsula and the Philippines. The Japanese had moved so quickly after Pearl Harbour, preparations had been made but they were proving to be so inadequate.

Abas had told him that he had heard that fifty poorly armed policemen had defended Miri: it had been captured almost without a shot being fired but it hadn't stopped the cruelty he saw. If rumours were right, Kuching would now also be under Japanese control.

Previously as he and Sammy had flown above the clouds he had often wondered what his real feelings for Rachel were. Finding a single English woman in Kuching had not been easy, not that he had necessarily gone out looking. His needs had been easily and well satisfied when in Singapore, because if you knew where to go, the girls were always more than willing to look after this tall, blond, blue-eyed Englishman. He smiled when he remembered that there were times when the girls squabbled over him – he thought it should be the other way round.

He had to admit though that his attraction to Rachel had been instantaneous, and she had said it had been the same for her. It was as though each was missing a vital piece in an individual jigsaw puzzle and the other possessed it, or perhaps *was* it.

One moment they were apart and without knowing the other existed, the next they were together as though their lives depended on the other's existence.

Was what they felt, love?

They told each other on so many occasions that they were in love, especially during the night before and as he was due to set off on another trip. The look in her eyes and the way his heart seemed to beat harder made saying good-bye yet again so much more difficult.

Colin could picture her now.

Her long shiny blonde hair spread over and in contrast to the whiteness of the pillow. There would always be a smile on her lips but tears in her eyes. The mosquito net would be fluttering slightly under the whirl of the single revolving fan: the dim light of the early morning allowing him to look down at her glowing tanned skin: the slimness of her body, her welcoming breasts that he absolutely adored. The time between leaving her and being with Sammy above the clouds was like a vacuum – once there he would be in Sammy's world and not Rachel's.

Imagining his fingers as they brushed a light line from Rachel's navel up between those breasts he adored to her chin and back again, he sighed. Her smile would broaden and tears would roll down her cheeks as she reached for him.

When they made love, it was as though nobody else existed in the entire world. If somebody had asked him here and now if giving up Sammy for Rachel were an option, he would only have had one answer – yes, it was

Colin moved onto his side as Rachel's image with her large dark brown eyes, small nose, high cheekbones and full lips, faded.

His feelings for her would never fade.

It wasn't a question of loving her because he worshipped her.

Chapter Thirty-One

The sound of her urine hitting the bottom of the metal bucket disgusted her, but at least she must be grateful that she had a bucket. She would be able – would have to – hang on for three days. The thought added to her disgust.

The shirt dropped into her cell earlier made her feel a little better.

She looked out of the slat above the door hoping that she would see some activity but all she could see was the back wall of the hut Captain Yamamoto used as his headquarters. Trying to see through gaps in the other walls was impossible. She had been told it was solitary confinement and that is certainly what it was, and all because she had gone on her own to the latrines and in, Captain Yamamoto's opinion, provoked Corporal Okidisha into assaulting her. How could anybody who looked as she did now provoke any male in that way?

She would know better next time – never go anywhere alone, even to the latrines.

The aftertaste of the horrible rice mixture was in her mouth. Was it really all they were going to have to eat, forever? The water wasn't clean either. God knows what diseases they were going to catch. Should she tell anyone that she thought she was pregnant? Would they give her more food if she did?

The ration store was strictly out of bounds and there was a guard on the door at all times. If given extra food, would it mean that somebody else would go without? Maybe one of the children – she could not take food out of somebody else's mouth, and especially not a child's. It was the children she felt most sorry for, they had done nothing in their young lives to deserve this … but nor had anybody else.

She would keep quiet about the baby. If she were pregnant, it would become obvious after a couple of months anyway.

A couple of months?

The thought of being in this hellhole for another week was bad enough, but months?

She took a mouthful of water from the bottle Lieutenant Sato had given her. The water tasted clean. She would have to ration it. She put the bottle in the corner so that it couldn't be seen from the slat above the door. She was sure Lieutenant Sato should not have given it to her.

She was already learning.

Moving to the opposite side of her cell and away from the bucket, Rachel curled up in the foetal position on the floor. The temperature had dropped a couple of degrees and the humidity had also gone down slightly. It was still hot and sweaty but she would survive.

Only two more nights and she would be back with the others. For the remainder of her isolation she would not make a sound. It would give her time to think, to wish and to dream. What did she wish and dream for the most at that precise moment. Was it Colin? No, sorry Colin, it's not you: not the way she looked and smelt. Was it some proper food? Maybe, but even that was not on the top of her list.

What she would give for a toothbrush and toothpaste, for a shower and some shampoo and to feel clean again. Does that mean she was spoilt? Craving for soap and cleanliness over and above food and water – did that make her peculiar?

She would show the Japanese that she was a strong woman: she would show them that she was stronger than any of their soldiers.

They would never have a reason to punish her again.

She would look them in the eye and say she was their equal … or even their superior.

Chapter Thirty-Two

Even if they were willing to let him stay, what should he do?

It would not be for a week, a month or even six months. He could be looking at a number of years. Although his tan was already a deep brown, with his height, his hair and his eyes he might as well climb the nearest tree and shout: "Here I am, come and get me!"

If he did stay what could he do, how could he help these people?

He could become part of them.

They needed to exist, to farm the land, fish and hunt. The jungle had to be stopped from encroaching on the rumah panjai and its surroundings. The praus and their rudimentary engines needed maintaining – he could definitely do that – and the rumah panjai would require constant maintenance.

And there would be times for rest, for eating and perhaps for a little merriment. He had already established that the Iban – his hosts – were great ones for storytelling, music, dancing and dressing up. They liked bright colours, and their ceremonial dress was something to behold.

Yes, he could become part of them if they would let him.

He was a novelty for now but in time that would wear off. The children would no longer gather around him as they did when he and Abas went down to and returned from the river. Abas shooed them away but they never went far. Others stopped what they were doing and watched as they passed.

Many of the men and women had not seen him other than when Abas and Babu first brought him to the longhouse on the improvised stretcher. They watched, some with suspicion others with bewilderment

They had every right to stare.

It might last for a few weeks but eventually acceptance would follow.

He was like that.

Wherever he went in South East Asia he was accepted: he was like a chameleon, he adapted quickly to his surroundings as long as they were ready and willing for him to adapt. The fact that he piloted a plane, brought them supplies and when appropriate took passengers to wherever they wanted to go, all certainly helped.

It was not the indigenous people he had to worry about, the Japanese were his main concern, not the Iban or any of the other tribes.

Anak was right.

An orang puteh living among the Iban under normal circumstances was out of the ordinary, but now? Word was bound to get out and if it did the Japanese would feel compelled to investigate and come looking for him.

Would he be putting his newfound protectors and hosts at risk? The thought filled him with dread. The stories of the atrocities the Japanese had committed elsewhere were still foremost in his mind. He wondered if he could stay even if Anak and the others wanted him to.

If he stayed, they would be constantly at risk.

If he left, they could return to normal.

Perhaps he had answered his own question.

Perhaps he had little choice but to leave and fend for himself. Where he would go and how he would get there was his problem. He had no right to think he ought to be anybody else's problem.

He should leave.

Chapter Thirty-Three

Although daylight had come and gone through the slat above the door, the sun's glare hit Rachel when she was released. She shaded her eyes, stumbled and had difficulty in following the guard. She could see the heels of his boots and that was all.

Rounding the corner of the headquarters hut, it was all a blur but she could see the women and children lined up on the parade ground. With her eyes still shaded, she walked towards them. Although she felt so weak – weak from lack of food and water, weak from the lack exercise and weak from trying her hardest to be so strong – her legs did not turn to jelly until she saw Marjory Field standing in front of her.

Rachel started falling and nothing she could do would stop her.

She felt Marjory's hands under her arms. "Just a little longer, Rachel, just a couple more minutes and then you can …"

Rachel did her best to stand up and she draped a limp arm round Marjory's shoulders. She could feel the support round her waist so that she would not fall again.

Through her stupor, she heard Captain Yamamoto's voice.

"Women, Woman Lefévre has served her sentence. She served it with dignity and honour, but do not forget that what she has experienced must act as a deterrent to you all. Her sentence was short by comparison with what I will give in the future should there be any further transgression from the rules. I will also not hesitate to allow future lashings to be carried out, and finally you are all aware of the ultimate penalty that will be paid should any of you attempt to escape. I do not relish having any of you shot or bayoneted but I will have obedience." He paused for effect. "Lieutenant Sato, dismiss the parade."

Rachel could not keep her eyes open any longer but as she began to collapse she felt support once again on both sides this time – there was a woman on each side helping her to walk. Through narrowed eyelids she could see it was Elizabeth Stokes and Mary Prentice, two women from her hut. Once back in the hut she literally fell onto her sleeping mat. She could sleep forever.

But once in the shade Elizabeth asked: "Sleep or a shower, which first?"

Rachel managed to open her eyes. "A … a Singapore Sling would be my preference," she told them through cracked lips. "But as that is not on the menu perhaps I would like to clean this filth off me first."

"Drink this," Mary suggested, holding a metal cup to Rachel's lips. "It might not be a Singapore Sling but you can use your imagination."

The same two women went with Rachel to the simple shower that had been rigged in relative privacy behind one of their huts. They helped her undress and then stood with her as she let the lukewarm filthy water dribble over her body. They still had a little soap and for Rachel the magnificence of feeling suds in her hair was better than any Singapore Sling could ever have been.

The shower revived her spirits more than she expected.

Yes, she thought, Yamamoto was right: she did serve her sentence with dignity and honour. He had no right to put her there in the first place because she had done nothing wrong, but at least …

She was the first woman to be punished in that way and Yamamoto did change his mind about the lashes: she wondered why. Yes, she was the first but she certainly wouldn't be the last. It hadn't happened but she could still feel the rattan cutting into her skin and the blood dripping down her back.

She shivered and prayed that nobody ever tried to escape.

Chapter Thirty-Four

As Colin opened his eyes he saw it was already dusk.

He must have slept for a good few hours. His watch was broken and he had no idea what time it was although he guessed it was after six.

He wanted a pee.

Pulling the mosquito net to one side, he rummaged for his sarong. He stood up and began to wrap the sarong round his waist but suddenly he realised he was not alone. Aslah was sitting by the entrance, her back against the bamboo wall, looking at him. He finished wrapping the sarong round his waist and smiled in the gloom.

"You won't understand a word I say, Aslah, but not only are you a first class nurse but you are also a very pretty girl," he said.

He dropped to his haunches a few feet from the young Iban girl, smiled and her face broke into a smile also. As soon as he had spoken he had expected her to leave as she had done before but this time she stayed where she was.

She held his eyes with hers. They were smiling at him and yes, he thought, she really is a pretty young girl. She cocked her head slightly to one side, hesitated, but then said, "*Nama brita nuan?*"

"And I don't understand you," Colin said but added: "*Nuan?* That means *you*, doesn't it? But *nama brita* ... I've no idea." He thought for a moment. It had been a question, so if he asked her the same question maybe he would learn more from her answer. "*Nama brita nuan?*" he said.

Her face broke into an even broader smile showing even white teeth against her dark skin. "*Manah*," she said, "*Aku manah*," she added pointing to herself.

"*Aku? Aku* means *you*, no not you, it means *I. Aku manah*, also," he said, hoping he had understood correctly.

Aslah laughed this time. "*Aku rinduka nuan!*" she said.

"*Aku* is *I* and *nuan* is *you*, so I *something* you, I will have to assume that *rinduka* is something nice. So, *aku rinduka nuan*, Aslah."

"*Manah!*" Aslah said, clapping her small hands together.

"*Manah!*" Colin repeated. "And now I really must go for a pee."

He stood up.

Aslah stood in front of him.

The smile had disappeared but she stayed.

"*Aku* need a pee," he said.

"Nedapee *nuan*," Aslah repeated, hers eyes beginning to dance again. It wasn't really a conversation but it was progress.

He thought for a moment.

She had seen him naked so what difference would it make. He moved the sarong to one side, took hold of himself and made a noise: "psss!"

Aslah covered her mouth with the palm of her hand as she laughed again. She looked down at his hand before lifting her eyes back to his face. "*Tendaka nuan*," she said pulling back the bead curtain.

They left the *bilik* together.

Aslah was still laughing.

As they stepped out onto the *ruai* a group of women who were sitting and weaving some rattan together looked up at them.

Aslah bowed her head and scuttled away.

Chapter Thirty-Five

Regardless of the increase in temperature and humidity, Rachel slept nearly all day.

The shower had been an untainted luxury but when cleansed as best they could and with only a sarong wrapped round her, being able to lie full length on a bed of sorts was utter bliss. She was asleep within seconds of her head touching the makeshift pillow.

At one stage when she awoke, but just for seconds, it was evident that the other women had left her and were doing their best to keep the noise and conversation to an absolute minimum. When she did eventually wake up fully it was approaching dusk and time for the evening meal, although the use of the word meal was a euphemism for the same stale (and now infested) rice and grass look-alike.

Rachel, though, was pleasantly surprised when she saw what appeared to be two or three beans and what unbelievably could pass as fish in her bowl.

"We saved it for you," Mary Prentice told her. "Captain Hitlermoto, or whatever his name is, must have had a pang of conscience because it suddenly appeared for the evening meal yesterday."

Elizabeth Stokes joined them. "I hope you like your fish rare," she commented sitting down on the makeshift bench opposite, "because I doubt if we'll see anything like that again."

They laughed – they really laughed.

"Thank you for helping me when I came out," Rachel told them.

"You'd have done the same for us," Elizabeth said. "If we are going to get through this nightmare that has been bequeathed to us we must do so together."

Marjory Field came into the hut and the other two women began to get up to leave.

"No," Marjory said, "what I have to say is for all to hear. Can the rest of you come over here, please?" she added raising her voice.

When everybody was gathered round Rachel's sleeping mat and the children and babies were as quiet as they ever would be, Marjory said, "Ladies, I have just come back from Captain Yamamoto. I'm afraid our settling in period is over and he is going to put us to work. The work he has planned for us starts tomorrow at seven in the morning and those who leave the camp won't be coming back here until six each evening. This will be for six days a week, but he has agreed that if our work is good enough he will always give us Sunday off."

"Yippee for Hitlermoto," Mary Prentice said, but this time it didn't raise a laugh. "And what exactly is this work?" she asked.

"We are to be divided into two groups: those who are forty and over, and those under forty," Marjory said.

"This sounds rather ominous," said Elizabeth Stokes apprehensively. "For the first time ever, I'm glad I'm over forty."

Again nobody laughed as they wondered what Marjory was going to say next.

Rachel hoped she would have the strength to do anything asked of her, regardless of what it was. While in solitary confinement, a myriad of thoughts had crossed through her mind: some incongruous and others all too sensible. She had no idea how the human body could adapt because she had never experienced any form of deprivation. Her parents lived in a grand house – well it was grand to her – in a well-to-do area of Royal Leamington Spa, and the friends she had left behind were equally fortunate.

Now look at her: rags, filth, lice, rats, malnutrition and an uncertain future. What were they going to have to do to maintain these standards? – work or as Elizabeth Stokes was suggesting, maybe worse.

Chapter Thirty-Six

Two days later Colin felt well and strong enough to move out of the longhouse for the second time.

His earlier trip to the river had been a mistake, it was great at the time but afterwards he had known it was a mistake. Now he wanted a proper wash, he wanted to feel really clean. He had eaten and he was returning to full health so next in line was cleanliness followed by … work. He had to find out how he could help his hosts, albeit for the short term.

None of the men had bothered him again.

No doubt Aslah had reported on his progress.

She continued to be an absolute little marvel.

Each time she brought him his food and water, she gave him another lesson in the Iban language. There were her own chores to attend to but she spent as much time with him as she could. She was patient, laughing when he made a mistake but clapping when he mastered another word, another expression.

In only a couple of days there was no way he learnt enough to speak to Anak on his own – he would still need Abas to translate – but he felt that by using as much of the language as he could he would show willing. Aslah had been so patient with him but seemed as eager as he did for him to learn – he hoped she would not also be as disappointed as him when it came time for him to leave.

As he put on his sarong he was still determined to leave his new friends so as not to endanger them, but he wasn't yet ready to face whatever the alternatives were. He would need at least another week so that he could build up his strength even further.

Maybe the fever had been malaria, he actually had no idea.

Did it take effect that quickly?

He had been up to date with his atradine tablets when he had made his abortive escape in Sammy but he also didn't know how long it took for their effect to wear off. It could have been malaria or just a fever brought on by the sheer shock of being shot and badly injured.

After testing his leg he decided it felt stronger. His shoulder was no longer covered and although a little stiff he once again appreciated how much more serious it could have been. He really was a lucky man.

He moved through onto the *tempuan* which he had learnt from Aslah was the area immediately outside the *bilik* (the room) – not the *ruai* as he originally thought – that although open to general view, was the private domain of the family who occupied the *bilik*. The *ruai* was the pathway that Abas had told him about which ran the whole length of the *rumah panjai*. On the other side of the *ruai* was the *pantai*, and outside the *tanju*, a large veranda that was used to dry rice – *padi*. Running the length of the *rumah panjai* was an attic called the *sadau*, its use was as a general store.

There were no men on the *pantai*, only women and children. Those nearest to him stopped what they were doing and stared at him.

"Good morning," he said in Iban, "I feel much better."

Some mouths fell open as the women looked at each other. Some covered their mouths in surprise while others looked away in embarrassment. Then a couple of the women nearest to him smiled. "Good morning," they said.

Aslah appearing from nowhere moved in front of him and her smile told him she was pleased.

"*Manah!*" she said, her eyes also communicating her thoughts.

"Yes, *manah*," Colin said. It was progress.

Chapter Thirty-Seven

"I, too, thought what you are thinking," Marjory told her audience, "but let me put your minds at ease because that is not what Captain Yamamoto wants from us. He is aware of the meagre rations that he has been provided with to feed not only us but his soldiers as well. He has commandeered some agricultural land from the local kampong and he wishes those of us who are under forty to farm this land. It is not going to be easy but at least it is positive and forward-thinking."

"But it will take ages before anything grows," a voice shouted from the back.

Marjory looked up, perspiration glistening on her face and arms. "This is true Maggie, but better we do something of benefit to us all than the alternative."

Rachel wanted to reach out and hold her friend's hand.

"And what about the over forties?" asked another voice.

Marjory smiled. "We are to become housewives," she said. "We are to remain here, in camp, and keep it as clean as possible, do the laundry, keep chickens – again commandeered from the local village – run a crèche for the children while their mothers are at the farm, and provide the children with whatever schooling we can."

There were a few moments silence before the murmurings started.

"I don't trust him," Mary Prentice said. "This isn't logical. Look at what happened to poor Rachel. He's up to something."

This time Marjory nodded and Rachel was pleased when she looked at her and smiled.

"Your concerns are no doubt mirrored by everyone in this hut as well as me," Marjory said. "The women in the other huts I have spoken to already feel exactly the same. But, Mary, once again think of the alternatives. The –"

"What happened to me," Rachel said interrupting, wanting to support Marjory, "was Yamamoto's way of demonstrating to all of us that he can be ruthless if needs be. Why else did he stop my flogging and yet that Corporal was badly injured? I came out of solitary filthy, tired, hungry and thirsty, that is all. Put yourselves in his position, if he were not born a sadist then being put in charge of us women and children ..."

81

"Are you defending him for what he did to you?" Mary asked disbelievingly. "You had done absolutely nothing wrong and yet you were punished in such an inhuman way, how can you defend what he did to you?"

"No, I'm not defending him but I do believe he is throwing us an olive branch and hoping that we will make our lives easier by making his easier too," Rachel replied.

"Rachel's right, ladies," Marjory said. "We don't really know what we are dealing with but neither does he. Far better we start this way and try to make it work. If the farm proves to be a success we will have better food and with better food hopefully we can ward of a lot of what else could happen to us."

"I hope his lords and masters agree," said another voice at the back.

"That is for him to worry about, not us," Marjory said. "He is in charge here and he has made a decision – in this case a good one."

"And what if we say we won't do it?" Mary asked. "What if we tell him to go to hell? I'm sure some convention or other has said he can't make us work."

"You know saying no would be foolish," Marjory said. "And the alternatives could be a lot worse."

"But they will come," another voice said.

"We must wait and see," Marjory said, glancing at Rachel.

Chapter Thirty-Eight

After bathing, Colin checked his leg.

The wound had closed fully but he knew he would be in trouble if the bandage Aslah had given him was not put on properly. As the adults had called back the children who started after him, Colin thought he was alone. Anak, Abas and Babu and many of the other men were away in the padi that was an hour's walk to the north.

He was beginning to apply the bandage when a small brown hand took it from him. He looked up and shaded his eyes so that he could look at Aslah. She smiled and her touch was like silk.

"Thank you," he said in Iban, "you move with no noise."

"I am a jungle ghost," she told him with another smile as she wrapped the bandage expertly round his leg.

When she had finished she handed him his sarong.

"You how old, Aslah?" Colin asked, picking up the soap he had been given.

"Me? I am seventeen," she said with pride. "How old are you? No, let me guess." They started walking. "I think you are old, I think you are forty!"

"What?"

"You don't understand?" she asked playfully.

"I understand. I thirty not forty," he said.

"You look so much older," she told him. "As old as my father."

"Thank you," he said indignantly.

"I am joking," she said.

Colin stopped and so did Aslah.

They were standing in a small clearing that shielded them from the longhouse.

Colin put his hands on Aslah's bare shoulders. It was really the first time they had touched intimately. Their hands, fingers and arms had brushed on occasions but ... Colin wondered if there was anything more intimate than giving another human being your body heat.

She was wearing a yellow vest rather than the same blue T-shirt she wore so often. It must have been washed a thousand times.

"Aslah, my words still small but ..." he said, hesitating. Some of the words would not come readily to mind. "You save my life and my life is now yours. You not know me. Soon I leave. You always here," he touched his chest. "You always with me, in here."

Aslah looked up at him, her eyes beginning to fill with tears. "Coy-lyn, you are saying you do not want to be with me and that you are going away?"

Shaking his head, Colin once again searched his memory for the right words. "You beautiful girl but so young, you have pick of all young men up and down river. But I leave soon. Maybe three or four days."

"Seventeen is not too young if you are an Iban," she said, a tear falling down her cheek. "And why must you leave, my father has not yet made his decision?"

"But I made mine. I not want put your people and especially you in danger. All time I here you and your people risk Japanese looking for me."

"We will protect you, there is nothing to fear," Aslah said.

"There everything to fear," Colin said. In tears Aslah ran out of the clearing, back towards the river. What had he said? He could not stay … he could not be responsible for placing such wonderful people in danger.

Chapter Thirty-Nine

"Do you think Captain Yamamoto would be able to obtain news of our husbands?" Elizabeth Stokes asked once the women had dispersed.

The question surprised Rachel – it showed naivety and a lack of acceptance but as she would have expected, Marjory was a lot more tactful.

"I doubt it and anyway we must take things slowly," Marjory advised Elizabeth. "I don't want to be over zealous in my understanding of Captain Yamamoto and Lieutenant Sato, but I do believe they don't like what they are doing. They didn't join the Army to be prison warders especially for a group of foreign women who have committed no crimes other than to be in the wrong place at the wrong time."

"We've got nothing to judge either of them by but there are others here who will not support their attitudes," Rachel added. "That Sergeant – Suratomono I think his name is – was more than prepared to use his whip on me, I think he would have got enjoyment out of inflicting pain on any woman. And there will be others. Yamamoto might be in charge but we must watch the others too."

"Wise words," Marjory told the small group of women.

Mary Prentice who had been sitting listening to the others suddenly spoke. "I think we are going about this the wrong way." Rachel looked at her.

"What do you mean?" Marjory asked.

"We've been here such a short time. The Japanese are the aggressors, they are the ones who bombed Pearl Harbour killing thousands, we've all heard about the atrocities they have committed elsewhere. If we just sit back and do nothing other than what we are told where will it all end?"

"What are you suggesting?" Rachel asked this time. After her ordeal, she was wary of upsetting what they had.

"I'm not sure but I don't like to think we are going to *kowtow* to the enemy," Mary said.

"If it ensures our survival," Marjory suggested, "surely it is the right thing to do?"

"Yes it might be but what price do we have to pay for our

survival? We have our pride and dignity to consider, but most of all we have our husbands to think about too. We believe they are all still in Kuching somewhere. We are in a commandeered primary school with some barbed wire thrown about its perimeter. This is probably a holiday camp compared with the conditions under which they will be living."

"But how can we help?" Marjory asked. "We would be of no use to them if we starve, die of dysentery or malaria, or get ourselves shot if we try to escape. And even if we did escape where would we go and what could we do?"

"By doing everything we are told and bowing to the Japanese supposed superiority we are merely solving a problem for them … us," Mary retorted.

"They could have been far more ruthless," Marjory said.

"And none of us has been molested," Rachel added.

"You were," Mary said.

"No, not really."

"He was going to rape you," Mary persisted.

Rachel smiled. "He would have had great difficulty if he'd tried," she said.

"How can you be so blasé?" Mary asked.

"Not blasé," Rachel told her. "If anything like that was going to happen it would have happened by now."

Chapter Forty

Colin almost gave chase.

Aslah was young, she had been responsible for him and she had seen him as no other had ever seen him. She had given him her body warmth when during his fever he had felt so cold: she had removed her sarong and T-shirt to carry out this simple but vital task. He owed her so much but he could give her so little in return.

As he had told her, she would always be in his heart and more likely in his mind too.

She and her people had given him an experience that he would never ever forget but one that he would probably keep to himself to ensure the maintenance of the respect he held for them. He had no idea what awaited him when he left, but if he survived, one day he would return and try to pay back some of their unbelievable hospitality and kindness.

Aslah was the one of sweetest young girls he had ever met. At seventeen, she was a fully-grown woman and well versed in the ways of the Iban. However, there was an innocence he did not wish to take away. If any of her English equivalents were asked to nurse a complete stranger, a foreigner, they would have refused. The thought of climbing naked into bed next to this stranger to give him their body warmth would have filled them with absolute horror and disgust.

But Aslah had not only given him her warmth, she had also cleansed him when his secretions were involuntary: she had held him while he urinated and she had done things for him that were unimaginable in the world he had come from.

There was no one on earth to whom he owed more.

It looked as though she now wanted more, but he could not take any more from her.

There were occasions when he looked upon her as he viewed the other girls in Singapore, but he believed the trust and respect that had developed between them should stay. He also had too much respect for her mother and father, her brothers and all the other Iban who had become his temporary family. It was a long time since he had touched, caressed and kissed Rachel. He had lain awake at night and his memories had played havoc with his feelings. Yes, he was frustrated but it was a small price to pay for what his hosts had given him.

If he had just stolen a simple kiss from Aslah he would have abused the privileges that had been bestowed upon him. He could not think of her like that. No matter how pretty she was, no matter how attractive her body and no matter how in his own world he would have craved for her, she was not in his world. He would be lying if he denied having imagined touching her on the same way he touched Rachel … and the girls in Singapore.

There were so many girls in Singapore who were as attractive and as delicate as Aslah, and with whom he had spent many a pleasurable hour or two, but Aslah – and Rachel – was different. Aslah was worth twenty, no fifty of these other girls. She had the body and the face but … but that is where the similarity stopped.

Colin waited for five minutes but when Aslah didn't reappear he reluctantly headed back to the longhouse. As he climbed onto the veranda and exchanged a few pleasantries with the women sitting there, he noticed that some of them looked beyond him, expecting to see somebody else.

Had they known that Aslah had followed him down to the river? If they had known, what had they expected to happen? Perhaps staying for another four or five days would be a mistake.

Perhaps he ought to leave now.

Chapter Forty-One

Sleep evaded Rachel.

The three days in solitary confinement may have taken its toll but it had changed her. She had got used to trying to sleep in a noisy environment. As she listened now some women were whimpering in their sleep, others snoring: children were restless, babies were crying. Sleeping outside was not an alternative although conditions were only marginally worse than inside the hut.

But Rachel felt she had changed.

Mary Prentice's words were going round and round her head as they added to the thoughts she had while in solitary confinement. She had not shared her feelings with anybody else, not yet, but Mary Prentice's comments, although they had been refuted at the time, suggested Rachel was not alone.

She felt ready to fight.

It wasn't just being locked up that had made her think, that had given her the opportunity. The soldier who had been lashed got what he deserved but the fact that he did it at all suggested little boded well for the future.

The women were not common criminals. The women had done nothing to deserve any form of punishment, let alone imprisonment in atrocious conditions accompanied by verbal and physical abuse.

Mary Prentice was right, it would happen again.

It was bound to happen again, all the ingredients for a disaster were in one place. When it did happen again what were they supposed to do? The lashings witnessed by everyone would not put some of the soldiers off, it might delay what they wanted but they would still commit rape regardless of the outcome. As far as Rachel knew there was no nearby source for their frustrations but there were young women in the camp who had been told to obey orders.

So Marjory and Captain Yamamoto had decided that peaceful coexistence was the best solution, had they? A farm, chickens and a nursery – it all sounded too good to be true and just a little surreal.

It *was* too good to be true.

Would their plans stop the inevitable? If it were inevitable, nothing would stop it. What would happen to their plans when the first woman was raped by a guard, and then the second, the third and fourth?

It was going to happen and everybody knew it but they were not admitting to it.

The pretence that everything was working well would just add to the problem. There was only one way forward: more lashings of women as well as the soldiers? How would peaceful coexistence manage to survive when it started?

It was a waste of time.

All right, the farm might provide them with better food than they had now, the chickens would give eggs and keeping the place as clean as possible was necessary, but nobody could tell her that it would make all the nasty things go away.

Suddenly her deliberations were interrupted by reality.

Had she forgotten?

How could she have forgotten?

There could be a baby growing inside her. If she were pregnant the last thing she should be considering was disobedience. She must conform, do as she was told and get through this hell in one piece.

How could she have forgotten? She was so sorry ... so sorry.

Chapter Forty-Two

The gathering happened sooner than Colin expected.

He sat cross-legged on a mat facing an assembly of almost everyone from the longhouse. Abas had told him that in view of the possible threat brought about by the Japanese occupation a few of the men were now on sentry duty down at the river, and had been for a number of days.

The remaining men and women sat in segregated groups while the children were at the far end of the longhouse being supervised – and kept quiet – by some of the younger teenage girls.

Directly in front of Colin was the governing committee of the longhouse comprising Anak, Abas and Babu, and five other men, all of whom appeared to be in their thirties and forties. There were a couple of men who were much older but Abas had told Colin that Buma, Anak's father and the previous headman, had died two years ago.

Colin had seen most of the men before but some of their names evaded him.

Outside it was raining and earlier there had been a few cracks of thunder. The jungle and the air were sultry. Jungle noises, which by now Colin was accustomed to, were there every now and again. He wondered if the weather and especially the thunder were indicative of what was to come.

Anak spoke. Colin's understanding of the Iban language was much better now but because of the importance of what Anak was saying he asked Abas to translate.

"Coy-lyn we have given your presence with us much consideration," Anak said. "Although I said it would need a few more days to reach a decision and this time would also allow you to become stronger, we have reached this decision a lot earlier so we thought it only right and fair to inform you straight away."

Colin nodded and said, "Thank you." Looking at the solemn faces that were watching him he guessed what their decision was. Although it would be the same decision as the one he had already reached, he in turn felt it only right that he should listen. So, the time had come – it had to come.

"Having you here is a new experience for us all. Although the

91

Japanese now govern our lands, it is early days and as you have seen it has not yet affected the way in which we go about our daily routine. We also accept this does not mean that maybe things will change. You have become part of us quickly. Your willingness to learn our language has demonstrated to us all that you too feel part of this longhouse.

"Aslah has told us that you learn quickly. We have taken into consideration the consequences of you leaving us to fend for yourself. We have already discussed this with you. If you were to stay here we understand that we could be placing ourselves in great danger. That's as may be but after due deliberation and with only a few who do not agree, we have decided that we must offer you our continued hospitality. Coy-lyn, we have decided that you may stay with us for as long as you wish."

"But –" Colin started to say.

Anak held up his hand and spoke again and Abas translated. "My father says that he knows he and all the men in the longhouse can learn much from you. You are aware of the ways of the outside world far more than any of us, so deciding that you can stay is as much for our benefit as it is for your safety. He knows you had decided that you must leave us, if that is still the case, he will respect your decision but you are welcome to stay here for as long as you like."

"I don't know what to say," Colin said.

Chapter Forty-Three

From the day she first realised that what happened in life was not predetermined, Alicia Newton had believed in self-preservation. She was one of the youngest women in the camp, and by whatever means, she was determined to stay one of the most attractive too. It was all part of her plan. When at school she used every trick in the book to obtain and maintain good results, which kept her parents happy, and they in return ensured that she wanted for nothing.

Alicia would admit her parents spoiled her, but she deserved to be treated that way.

She made sure her parents never knew exactly what their pretty and innocent daughter was doing to achieve such grades. She often wondered if the three male teachers for whom she had done a few favours, were aware that they shared experiences of which she was the source. She made them aware, though, who would find out if her grades didn't correspond with her expectations. At university, Alicia found her tactics a little more difficult to apply, but apply them she did although she did discover that if she had believed in herself from the outset, her favours would have proved to be unnecessary. The teachers and lecturers might have been able to influence her home-grown results but once external examiners were involved they could do nothing about how well Alicia did.

The acts of kindness and understanding – as she called them – did make her quickly appreciate the hold she had over boys, the male undergraduates and, once graduated, men in general. She was more than conscious of the fact that her assets were going to get what she wanted and quickly. So for Alicia, self-preservation and the quality of life that could go with it were paramount to her finding a rich husband. It didn't matter what he looked like – well, within reason – because when she wanted to enjoy what a real man might have to offer she could go looking. It would be a bonus though if she could find herself a man who satisfied both desires – and of course, her. She achieved her aim quickly and although Desmond was attractive enough, showered her with gifts and kept her in a lifestyle that was acceptable, when he was at work all day she became bored.

She hoped that by going to Kuching – wherever that was – with Desmond she would find something new, something that would fill her idle time with adventure and perhaps just a little pleasure – well more than just a little. Alicia discovered that the tennis club and dinner parties provided her with both.

The war was not part of Alicia's overall plan. While it was waged in Europe, it was an inconvenience but when it came to Sarawak, Miri and then Kuching it was a downright bore. She should have got out when she had the opportunity but the thought of being cooped up with hundreds of others in a rusty old tin can did not appeal, and anyway she was an English lady of some means and would be treated accordingly by the Japanese, who were an honourable nation and respected their women. So becoming a prisoner, walking to Kampong Punkit and now finding herself incarcerated with lots of other women and their screaming brats was also not part of Alicia Newton's overall plan. She did not intend to suffer the degradation and depravation that the others had already succumbed to. On the surface, she would give the impression that she was like everybody else but in reality that was not going to be the case.

She guessed the soldier had never touched a European woman before and what she had asked for in return was a small price to pay, especially as he had ready access to the ration store. Alicia was now naked and the soldier stood back to look at her. "You like what you see," she said. The soldier, who she had discovered spoke a little English, nodded.

"Hai," he said. "I like."

"Then let's get on with it," Alicia said as she beckoned the soldier closer.

94

Hearing the opposite to what he expected to hear, Colin really did not know how to react.

He had already decided that he would not put his hosts at risk but they had told him it was a risk they were willing to take.

But neither he nor they knew what the risk might be.

Colin lifted his head and studied the expectant faces that were all looking at him. He wondered who had disagreed with the majority decision, who wanted him as far away as possible?

A slight movement at the back of the group of women made him focus in the gloom and he saw Aslah, her eyes intent on his, her lips slightly parted in anticipation. At the front of the group he could see Ramlah, Aslah's mother, as she turned round to see who had his attention and when she saw it was her daughter, her eyes narrowed.

He saw mother and daughter exchange looks that must have meant something to both of them because they smiled, but he had more important things to consider.

What should he do about the offer of a longer stay with the Iban?

He needed more time.

Before speaking he looked at Aslah again and she held his gaze, the corners of her mouth twitched into a smile before she looked away.

"I grateful for decision," he said in Iban. "It not what I think you decide. I not want put you in danger. I better, nurse good." He smiled and a few of the women smiled back at him. For some reason he dare not look at Aslah or her mother this time. "I stay one week, see what happen."

He got Abas's full attention and asked him to translate what he had to say next before continuing in English: "We have a saying in England *let us play things by ear*. In other words we take each day as it comes and if something happens that means I should leave and quickly so be it. Can you translate that for your father and the others?"

Abas stood up and translated.

There was much nodding of heads.

Anak spoke again and Abas translated. "My father say your words give evidence of why their decision right. He welcome you to

95

family but understands if one morning you gone he know why. You a man of honour and he knows his decision will be best for us all."

Colin looked at Anak and bowed his head.

"Thank you," he said again. "I not let you down. I do anything that help you and your people."

Anak nodded before standing up to face the gathering.

He clapped his hands and said something Colin didn't fully understand but Abas was smiling.

How could he not love these people?

"My father say it good reason for celebration, for music and dancing. He order slaughtering of pig, opening many bottles of *tuak*. The night is long. We going to celebrate and for long time."

Just as people began to move away a young man, out of breath and his eyes wide with anticipation ran onto the veranda. He searched the faces until he saw Anak and then he ran forward and bowed his head.

"Japanese come," he said, his breathing heavy with anticipation. "Japanese come up river and they will be here in a short time."

Anak stared at the young man for a few seconds before standing up.

Chapter Forty-Five

Rachel surveyed the piece of land that they were to cultivate.

She could also see many of the locals watching them from the edge of the kampong, which was only a hundred yards away. The 'farm' as it was called, covered an area of about fifty yards by twenty yards: it was stony, rough and full of weeds.

Rachel and the nineteen other women under the age of forty, who had to work on the 'farm', had little protection from the elements. Rachel still wore the shirt from solitary confinement. She still had no idea who her benefactor was. Her skirt was threadbare and torn and the other women were dressed no differently. There was little protection for their heads other than bits of cloth used as *bandanas*.

Rachel noticed that some of the women, and understandably, were looking distinctly unhealthy with dark shadows under their eyes and their faces sallow from the lack of food and sleep.

Four guards had accompanied the women from the camp. As Rachel continued her survey of the area she eyed the guards warily: they were now standing to one side in a group, in the shade of a palm tree smoking and not paying much attention.

"What the hell are we supposed to do with this?" Alicia Newton said at Rachel's shoulder.

"Grow something," Rachel told her. "But before we can plant anything we'll have to dig it over."

"With what, our bare bloody hands?" Alicia said.

Noticing that some of the women had drifted into small groups and others were sitting by the trackside with their heads in their hands, she decided somebody had to take charge and it looked as though it was going to have to be her. She shaded her eyes as she looked towards the kampong and as she did she noticed a man was walking along the track towards her. He was carrying what looked like three or four hoes or rakes.

Other heads turned towards the man as he stopped on the track. He was obviously looking for somebody in charge and as none of the guards showed any sign of doing anything, Rachel went up to him.

He was a little man, no more than five feet three inches tall. As he smiled a greeting she saw he had only a few teeth. His skin was deeply wrinkled but there was a sparkle in his eyes and he looked more Chinese than Malay.

He peered at Rachel and thrust the tools towards her. "For you," he said in English.

Rachel instinctively took the tools from him.

"Thank you," she said, her eyes never leaving the little man.

The man looked towards the Japanese guards, then back at Rachel. "We help if we can," he said solicitously. "We bring food and medicine to camp in the night."

Rachel frowned. "I don't understand."

"We no like Japanese, we want help women and children. We bring things for you, leave them under fence behind huts."

One of the Japanese guards had detached himself from the others and was walking sternly towards Rachel and the man. As he walked the guard unslung his rifle.

"Thank you," Rachel said, enveloped by a sudden feeling of hope.

"It not a lot," the man said, turning away.

"Thank you again," Rachel said.

The guard was close.

Chapter Forty-Six

Hidden by the undergrowth bordering the river downstream from where their praus were moored, Anak and a small group of Iban warriors watched as the Japanese launch made its way slowly upriver against the current.

When the warning had been given Anak had ordered Abas to take Colin out of the longhouse along the walkway to the kitchen, down the back ladder and into the jungle.

Anak was pleased that he had had the foresight to post guards down river. As he watched, the grey launch was still a few hundred yards away. As the sun disappeared below the canopy of trees to the east, he could still see that between its bridge and bow there was what looked like a cannon. Two sailors, who were constantly moving it so that it swept both sides of the river, were operating it.

On the bridge he could see two more sailors, one behind a searchlight the beam from which swept ahead of the launch into the gloom. Either side of the bow were the numbers that he recognised – he mouthed 'Seven Nine Five' to himself. The engines gave a deep throbbing resonance.

Anak glanced towards the praus.

He wished there had been time to pull the boats out of the water but even from where he was, they were not clearly visible – the hurrying darkness would hide them altogether. The early warning of the Japanese approach had been fortuitous.

He had ordered the candles and paraffin lamps put out and everyone was to remain silent. Next to him he felt his son Babu move his position so that cramp did not set in. Anak and the others were armed with their blowpipes, a poisoned dart already in each of the tubes, and their razor sharp parangs hung at their waists.

Anak's attention was drawn back to the launch as its engines changed pitch and it became stationary mid-river in the strong current. It held its position for a short while before he heard a voice quite distinctly above the jungle noises, giving what he assumed were orders. The launch turned sideways. At its stern he saw the flag Coy-lyn had described to him, and drawn in the mud down by the river. He remembered he had called it The Rising Sun. Also towards the stern he noted there was a machine gun manned by another

99

sailor.

He wondered if they were looking for something in particular, or were they venturing upriver from Miri on an intelligence gathering reconnaissance? Were they looking for an orang puteh – his orang puteh?

The engine pitch changed again as more orders were given, the launch gathered pace as it turned and headed back down river and into the darkness.

He watched as the launch disappeared round the corner in the river.

Anak waited a few minutes before making a slight whistling noise and the watchful withdrew as silently as they had been when they first took up their positions. He spoke to the two guards who had first spotted the launch, thanked them for their timely warning and then told them to go back to their positions, they would be relieved shortly.

As he and the others walked back to the longhouse, he wondered whether any of the other longhouses nearer to Miri had been spotted, and if so what had happened. He must always be on his guard and not just because he was protecting an orang puteh.

Anak had never seen any Japanese before and on this first occasion he did not like what he saw.

The young man, who seemed to be in charge, looked arrogant.

Anak didn't like arrogance.

He would deal with it if the Japanese came again.

Chapter Forty-Seven

Exhausted, Rachel sat on the step at the entrance to her hut, a bowl of congealed rice in her hands. Using two fingers she scooped some rice out and screwing up her face, she attempted to chew and swallow it.

It was awful but no different to how it always was.

She saw Marjory Field crossing over the 'parade square' from Captain Yamamoto's headquarters. She sat down next to Rachel.

"You look done in," she said, rubbing Rachel's thigh with the back of her hand.

Despite their age difference and the dissimilarity in backgrounds, Rachel was so pleased the two women had continued to grow closer and closer. She needed to talk and she found herself revealing facts that normally were private. Marjory was equally forthcoming and Rachel assumed it was because of their circumstances.

"It's hard work, Marjory, and some of the women are so weak they can hardly walk to the farm let alone do anything when they get there," she said. "Susan White collapsed today and the guards had to bring her back."

"Yes, I've been to see her. There was nothing to the poor girl at the start so she couldn't afford to lose any more weight."

A guard approached and both women stood up and bowed as he walked by.

It was Corporal Oghadishu, who Rachel believed could be trusted. He had never lifted a finger against the women or shouted at them, and he sometimes played with the children but out of the view from any of the other guards. She had discussed her belief with Marjory and she had agreed.

He acknowledged the two women before moving on.

"That's why I've come from Captain Yamamoto," Marjory continued once they had sat down again. "He tells me his hands are tied and we are getting exactly the same food as his soldiers. But it's not only the food it's also the medicines we need. We already have three cases of dysentery and with all the rats in this place God knows what other diseases we'll catch before long. Once again he said he will ask, but he expects to be told the same: we destroyed so much as part of the denial plan before the Japanese – and using his words –

liberated the indigenous population from our Imperialist rule."

"So we only have ourselves to blame," Rachel said, almost too tired to talk.

She had finished the rice, but regardless of how disgusting it tasted she could have eaten another ten bowls.

"That man you saw down at the farm, have you seen him again? Can he help?" Marjory asked.

"He brings the tools each morning. He said he would help but nothing has appeared yet. Maybe he …"

Rachel stopped as in the gloom of the evening a lorry pulled up at the gate followed by a bit of a commotion.

Captain Yamamoto rushed to the scene and watched as the others watched.

Six nuns in full habit were led into the compound.

Three were obviously European, two possibly Chinese and one could be Malay.

As they walked across the 'parade square', Rachel thought how incongruous their habits seemed. She turned towards Marjory and raised her eyebrows. "It's obvious what they are but why are they here?" she said.

"God alone knows," was all Marjory said.

Chapter Forty-Eight

To Colin it was just another jungle noise but he saw Abas react with a nod, so he guessed it was the all clear.

Abas tapped Colin on the shoulder and smiled before leading him through the blackness towards the longhouse. Once inside they joined the other men Anak had called together, and listened. From where he had been hiding he knew little of what might have happened. In fact he felt hiding had been wrong in the first place but if the Japanese were looking for him it was the logical thing for him to do. He had heard no gunfire or shouting, so he assumed there had not been any contact.

"It was a gun boat," Anak told them. "I think they were just looking. They were noisy and the men were wearing white clothing, perhaps because they have no fear, perhaps because they are stupid. We must find out tomorrow whether the boat stopped at any of the longhouses downriver, and if they did what did they say or do. Before we can decide on the future we must know what we are dealing with. Will the Japanese stay in the towns or do they intend spreading out throughout the jungle? Do they regard us as a threat or will they ignore us? Are they really a danger to us or are we able to live with their presence?"

Anak's eyes turned towards Colin. "Coy-lyn, I know my words may surprise you but you must understand that these Japanese may be no different to the orang puteh who previously assumed supremacy over us. We have not retaliated because your kind has meant us no harm, only compliance with your laws. Your forefathers banned us from headhunting although it was part of our traditions, part of our history, but we complied. It did not physically hurt us, just our pride.

"These Japanese are maybe a better alternative: they are at least from this part of the world and not from its other side. You say that these people have committed atrocities elsewhere but we know how such stories are exaggerated. Here in our lands stories grow from longhouse to longhouse. The size of a fish caught, the meat obtained from a wild pig and the rice harvest from one year to the next. All become exaggerated to make one group feel superior to another. There are also those who tell stories of great victories which do not

103

exist, but when told they put fear into the hearts of their likely enemies.

"We must see for ourselves, Coy-lyn. The decision I must make is whether we wait and see, whether we wait for them to come to us, or whether we go to them and see for ourselves. That is something on which I must ponder and put my thoughts to the council. I think it would be wise if tonight's celebrations were delayed until we know a little more about our future. I hope you understand, Coy-lyn."

"I understand," Colin said in Iban. "I understand *all* you say. I not soldier but I do all I can to help you protect your people and your home, on that I give my word."

"They are now your people too, Coy-lyn," Anak said.

"They are and I owe them so much."

"You owe us no more than we are willing to give," Anak said as he looked around the group, a rare smile appearing on his face. "As I watched the Japanese trying to look so superior on their grand boat, I got a feeling of joy out of knowing that maybe what they were looking for was here with us. In fact I rather wished they would come closer so that I could not only get a better look at this potential enemy, but also so that they were within blowpipe range. It would also have given me joy to see the surprise as their overconfidence was answered with a dart that would carry a poison to their arrogant hearts."

"It sound like you already decided," Colin said.

"No, Coy-lyn, I haven't decided but maybe I am half way there," Anak said, still smiling.

Chapter Forty-Nine

Rachel and the others watched as the nuns walked proudly across the 'parade square' with their heads held high and their eyes taking in all around them as they moved towards the hut to which they had been allocated.

The three guards escorting the nuns appeared to be extremely apprehensive about their task, they were keeping their distance and their rifles were pointing at the ground. Furtive glances at each other only added to their uncertainty.

Rachel could see that Captain Yamamoto was on his veranda, also watching. As the nuns climbed down from the lorry, Rachel was sure she saw him give a slight nod and exchange a few words with one of the nuns before he withdrew. Lieutenant Sato was also on the veranda, which was unusual.

When they were only a few yards away, Marjory excused herself and walked over to the small group.

The lead nun stopped as Marjory approached.

Rachel moved so that she could see and hear the exchange.

"I would like to say welcome," Marjory said, "but under the circumstances perhaps it wouldn't be appropriate. My name is Marjory Field and I am the elected spokeswoman for this camp."

She held out her hand.

The nun smiled, proffering her hand from under the black habit.

"And I am Sister Marie Cuijk," she said, her accent slight but discernible. "We are Sisters from the Order of Mercy."

"I see," Marjory said. "May I ask where you are from?"

"We have been brought here from Sandakan on the east coast of British North Borneo, and we have been told we are to transit here before we are moved further south to Kuching. Evidently camps are being prepared there for us all."

"That's news to me," Marjory replied lightly. "I must let you settle in, but before you do, tell me why you were interned in the first place, surely the Japanese cannot consider any of you to be a threat."

Sister Marie smiled again. "What we do, Mrs Field, is irrelevant. Japan is at war with the countries these Sisters are from. Two from our order, both Austrians, were not interned because the Japanese consider them to be allies."

Marjory stepped to one side.

"Men and their need to fight each other seems to breed incongruities," she said. "I am afraid this is not the Ritz but we get by. I will say welcome after all, and when you are settled I will show you our limited facilities."

"Thank you," Sister Marie said. "May I suggest we leave further introductions until later? The Sisters are tired after a long sea and road journey."

"Of course," Marjory said.

The Sisters from the Order of Mercy moved past Marjory, each sister bowing her head slightly acknowledging her and perhaps her standing.

Rachel wondered whether the arrival of the Sisters was a good or bad omen and her thoughts were echoed when Marjory walked back over to her.

"Most unusual," she said. "But why I say that I don't know, I've got nothing to compare such happenings with."

"Maybe it is a good sign," Rachel said.

"I do hope so," Marjory replied. "I really do hope so."

Chapter Fifty

Colin went down to the river to wash.

His deeply tanned face and body were now as dark as his Iban friends, and the bleached stubble on his face was almost white. He felt fit. Although the scars were still there and he felt the odd twinge every now and then from his shoulder and thigh, he was back to normal health. In fact, he felt fitter than he had ever done before.

The water in the river was brown and moving quite quickly. He guessed the overnight rain up in the hills was now finding its way hurriedly to the coast. It was an overcast morning and as it was also the middle of the monsoon season it would be overcast most of the day, although the weather was always changeable.

As he stood up to his waist in the water he mused over what had happened.

He woke that morning and realised he had completely missed Christmas.

It had been and gone.

He had spent the previous Christmas with Rachel, and for New Year they had joined friends in the Raffles Hotel in Singapore and nearly got thrown out for being a little too raucous.

Where had Rachel been for the start of 1942?

Wherever she was there would have been no cause for celebration.

Putting his sarong on after leaving the water, Colin began to walk back towards the longhouse. Even though he had protested, he had been given his own *bilik*. As a guest he would have been quite happy to sleep on the veranda, but Anak had insisted that he must have his own living space and some privacy.

Anak was waiting for him as he walked through the clearing where he had the misunderstanding with Aslah.

Resting on his haunches and chewing on a bit of bamboo, Anak looked up at him..

"Sit," he said to Colin, who did as was suggested.

He felt slightly apprehensive.

Most of his discussions with Anak, of which there were many as Anak was as fascinated by Colin's way of life as Colin was of his new friends, normally took place on the veranda of the longhouse.

"Abas and two others have gone to Miri," Anak told Colin. "They have gone to see for themselves and for me, what the Japanese are doing there."

"I see," Colin commented but he was a little surprised that he had not been included in the discussion that would have taken place prior to their departure.

"News from other longhouses downriver," Anak said, "is that the Japanese have been only inquisitive. They are saying that the Brooke regime is over and that white supremacy has ended. Asia is for the Asians not for plunderers, murderers and rapists from far off lands. They say they are the friends of all people of Sarawak."

"And what you think, Anak?"

"I think I will wait for Abas to return and tell me what he saw. I will give it more thought before discussing it with you and the others."

"But you must have opinion already. You want send your sons to Miri," Colin said. "You said you want put dart in bodies of Japanese when they here."

Anak smiled.

"Did you not tell us that you have a saying – play it by ear?" he said. "But even when doing that it is possible to plan for the future." Colin nodded. "Well, from what I have seen so far I have learned little but the little I have learned tells me to be cautious."

Chapter Fifty-One

Marjory was not surprised when she saw Sister Marie Cuijk cross the 'parade square' towards Captain Yamamoto's headquarters.

It was approaching eight o'clock in the morning, the farm party had already left and Marjory and the other women who remained were starting the routine of cleaning, tidying and preparing the meagre rations for the midday and evening meals.

Others were already washing, mending and, where necessary, modifying clothing. Marjory had instructed that what had been long skirts were to be shortened, and trousers were to become shorts: the spare material from each garment could be used for any manner of things from towels to protective headgear.

She was annoyed when Captain Yamamoto had ordered that his soldiers' uniforms would be laundered and repaired by the women, but she accepted she had little choice but to comply.

Noting that the guard, who was permanently positioned outside the headquarters, bowed slightly in response to Sister Marie's approach, Marjory wondered what was going on. Sister Marie acknowledged the soldier's deference, not the other way round.

Marjory was surprised further when the nun disappeared into the headquarters whereas she was never allowed to go beyond the veranda. She screwed up her face in confusion, continued sowing the patch onto the boy's shorts, and waited.

Fifteen minutes later Sister Marie came out of the headquarters. She put her hands into the sleeves of her habit and began to make her way to her hut.

Marjory called to her. "Sister?"

Sister Marie stopped and on seeing Marjory she changed direction.

"Good morning, Mrs Field," she said.

Marjory stood up. "Good morning, Sister. Is it possible we could have a word?"

"Of course! Where? Here?"

"It's as good a place as any," Marjory suggested and then said, "If you don't mind my asking, you seem to be on pretty good terms with our captors, why?"

"Shall we sit down, Mrs Field?"

"Of course," Marjory said, indicating the step.

"It's quite simple really, Mrs Field," Sister Marie said once settled. "Captain Yamamoto was injured badly near a place in China called *Changchun*, I think it was in 1938. He was sent to a hospital run partly by nuns, and in particular the nurse who looked after him was Catholic and a Sister from the Order of Mercy. He has never forgotten how she cared for him, although he was the enemy."

"And he now feels obligated to you and the other Sisters?"

"In a way, yes, I suppose he does, but he also feels that incarcerating women and children is so wrong."

Marjory smiled. "That explains an awful lot," she said.

"Yes, he feels that you women are taking vital fighting resources away from where they should be. He and his men should be fighting the allied forces, not playing nursemaid to all of you."

"And now you," Marjory said, feeling a little unsettled by the Sister's choice of words.

"Yes, of course, and now us."

Marjory shrugged. "And there was I thinking he was demonstrating a little altruism towards us."

"He is," Sister Marie said. "But he cannot be too open about it."

Chapter Fifty-Two

"Tell me Anak, why you do this?" Colin asked, still sitting in the clearing with the headman.

It was probably the longest one-to-one conversation he and Anak had managed because normally others were there too.

"Do what, Coy-lyn?" Anak was still squatting in front of Colin, the worry evident in his eyes.

"You cautious but this not your war," Colin said. "You grow rice: the jungle gives meat and vegetables, the river fish. You have wonderful home and people that live here happy with what you give them."

"Are they?" Anak asked lifting his eyes to Colin's. "Are they really happy?"

"But, Anak, before war and when it over there many people who want come live as you live. The peace it offer, not bother by all bad in outside world."

Anak allowed a smile to cross his lips.

Glancing towards the remaining prau moored close by, he said, "Your modern outside world has brought us the engine for that prau; it is so much easier now. It is progress, Coy-lyn. Many Iban no longer live off the land and the river. In Miri there are Iban shopkeepers, Iban policemen, Iban who work in offices, and many other jobs. In my father's time, when he was leader, such happenings were rare, but now in the space of just a few years they are more common.

"That is why Abas speaks your language so well. He will not stay here: although it is our tradition he will not inherit what I may leave for him. Babu is also restless. It is happening everywhere. Like that engine, Coy-lyn, it is progress and there is nothing I can do to stop it. Who will be leader when I go ...?" he shrugged.

"You never leave here, surely? You have long time to live."

"Coy-lyn, nobody knows what is round the next corner in life and my family know where I want to be buried. My spirit is here and it will stay here. But this war that has come to us is also progress. We talk, we hear things about the world outside, and many of us do not want to know about it. But when that world comes to us we have little choice but to take notice."

"I understand but that not tell me why you really allow me stay here. I not question your kindness and judgement but I still worried. That Japanese boat come other day, maybe they just looking but …"

The smile disappeared but Anak maintained eye contact. In his small dark brown bloodshot eyes, Colin could see so much wisdom, so much of times past. The tattoos on Anak's arms, body and legs would only mean one thing to an outsider, but Colin now knew they told a story that went back hundreds of years. There were no history books in the jungle, but each man carried his family history with him – permanently.

"Coy-lyn, I know that in many other longhouses the headman would have said no, they might even have ordered that you should be killed. There are those who live deeper in the jungle who have no contact with any people but their own. If they see a plane fly over they look away because they do not have an explanation, or they are frightened." Anak thought for a moment. "I was annoyed when I saw what my sons had brought to this longhouse, and my instinct was to also say, no. Nevertheless, it was Ramlah and Aslah, as well as Abas and Babu, who persuaded me to help you get better. It is they you must thank, not me."

"But it your word that let me stay after I better," Colin said.

"Yes, because you are also progress."

Colin nodded and smiled his understanding.

Chapter Fifty-Three

Having been sick before she had left for the farm, Rachel thought that the nausea would pass as soon as she got into the fresh air, but if anything she had felt worse.

Although it was an overcast sky, it had not rained but both humidity and temperature were high. Their guards – there were only two of them now – continued to seem disinterested in what their charges did, except when it was time for a water break.

Rachel had sneaked away and was being sick behind a palm tree when she realised she was not alone. When she looked up she saw the little man who brought the tools to them daily.

"You sick?" he asked in almost a whisper.

"In a way," Rachel replied. "I'll be all right in a minute."

"I have medicines," the man said, looking towards the guards. "Food is put by back of huts, under leaves."

"Thank you," Rachel said. "You are kind and you are taking great risks."

She had checked behind the huts after the same man had told her what would happen, but there had not been anything as yet. She must make sure she checked again when she got back this evening.

"And the medicine?"

"For malaria," the man said. "I have here."

He moved his hand under his grimy shirt and produced a couple of white boxes: the labels told Rachel they were atradine and quinine.

"That is kind of you, but don't your own people need these medicines?"

"We have plenty, we hide from Japanese," he said, his eyes dancing.

The man handed the boxes to Rachel, and she quickly looked towards the guards before tucking them under her shirt.

"Thank you so much," Rachel said as she felt another wave of nausea wash over her. She excused herself as she bent down, her stomach contracting involuntarily and hot bile burned the back of her throat.

"You not well," the man said.

"Yes … I am … as well as can be expected," Rachel told him, "it is not …"

"You with baby?" the man asked.

Rachel looked up at him.

"You're wise," she said slowly.

"I no wise," the man told her, "I father many times and grandfather even more times. I see this all the time. How long you got?"

"Another seven months maybe."

"You not in place for baby."

"No, but unless this war is over soon, I may have no choice," she said.

"I unnerstan."

"I only wish I did," Rachel said picturing Colin's smiling face. "I just wish this was no more than a simple nightmare."

"I unnerstan," the man said again. "You strong, you have other women help you, you be ok. I see many baby born to woman not so strong as you and they all right, so you all right."

Rachel wasn't so sure she liked being referred to as strong, but maybe he was referring to her willpower rather than her physical strength.

"I hope to God you are right," she said just before another spasm hit her.

Chapter Fifty-Four

As far as the limited tool supply would allow, Colin stripped the engine.

Anak had accepted Colin's offer to service the outboard motor that had been playing up for some time. That is why Abas had taken the other prau. Although many of the identification marks had long worn off the engine, Colin recognised it as one of the original Seagulls and probably dated back to 1932 or 1933, which made it nearly ten years old. He was amazed it was working at all let alone just coughing and spluttering. It was the long-shafted twin cylinder 10hp version with a water-cooled exhaust: it was the right engine for use on the river but it had not been maintained.

As he cleaned and oiled the various stripped components, he had an audience and every now and again somebody would ask him a question. His use of the Iban language had continued to improve significantly but when asked a technical question about the inner workings of an outboard motor, he became a little tongue-tied.

His misuse of some words made his audience laugh, and he laughed with them.

He had noticed Aslah hovering at the back of the group, but although he caught her eye she always looked away immediately: since the incident in the clearing when she suggested she wanted more than he was willing to give, there continued to be little communication between them.

The situation was very sad.

In a longhouse, it was impossible not to see nearly everybody who lived there two or three times a day. Aslah had also kept to herself and Colin had not gone out of his way to be near her but he had found himself wanting the opposite. He was feeling frustrated but he hoped with time the feelings would ease, and anyway, he should not look upon Aslah as possible relief for his frustration. He respected and owed her too much for that.

He admitted that a closeness was generated while he was sick and regardless of how they both now felt, it was a bond that was not going to be easily broken. But that was as far as it could go. He had convinced himself … he hoped.

As a result he did find himself thinking more and more about

Rachel.

She was always on his mind, but as the days passed and with no news of what was going on beyond the river that formed an information boundary, he wondered. He lay on his sleeping mat at night feeling lonely.

He was unbelievably grateful to his unexpected hosts but he longed to be with Rachel again, smiling when he decided that one day, as well as taking Abas for a ride in a plane, he would also bring Rachel to meet his new family. She would not believe what he wanted to tell her unless she saw it with her own eyes.

Of course, he had been told about the Iban, and all the other tribes that lived in the interior of Sarawak but like so many others, he either disregarded them or he had formed completely the wrong impression. He knew of a few people with whom he had shared the odd beer or two who were going to be re-educated … he wondered if they would believe him.

It was getting dark so Colin reassembled the now clean and well-oiled engine and with many willing hands carried it back down to the river. As he was fixing the engine to the prau he heard another outboard engine, which he assumed was Abas and the others returning, but he realised it was far too soon.

One of the lookouts appeared from his post further down river.

"Boat," he said as he ran past Colin. "Boat, it is not Japanese and it is not Abas. I am not sure who the people are."

Colin wiped his hands as he took cover behind a bush.

Chapter Fifty-Five

"Are you all right?" Mary Prentice asked as Rachel picked up the hoe and half-heartedly stabbed at the ground. She was still feeling awful but she had to put on a brave face because nobody else must know … yet. She wasn't certain herself.

"Yes," Rachel said hurriedly. "My stomach has never settled to the change in diet."

"Diet?" Mary replied. "Is that what it's called?"

Rachel managing a slight smile said, "I've got some atradine and quinine."

"Where? What do you mean?" Mary asked looking towards the guards.

"Under my shirt, the man who brings the tools gave them to me."

"Well that's a start, I suppose." Mary struck a large stone and swore. "Did you get to speak to the nuns?"

"No, not yet. Have you?"

"No, but there are bound to be nurses and maybe teachers among them. Will they be made to work with us?"

"I've no idea and I've no idea why they are here in the first place. I would have thought they ..."

Rachel stopped as her abdomen suddenly contracted and the pain was unbearable. She dropped the hoe and to her knees, clutching at her stomach. She screamed.

"Rachel, what is it?"

Mary knelt down beside her.

"Rachel?" Mary asked again, her arm round Rachel's shoulders. "What's wrong?"

"I …" Rachel tried to speak.

"We've got to get you back to camp." Mary beckoned for some help. "Carry her over to the track," she ordered. "I will go and speak to the guards."

Lying by the trackside Rachel saw Mary approaching the older of the two guards. She stopped and bowed. The guard looked suspicious, peering over Mary's shoulder as he watched Rachel being fussed over by the track.

"Ill," Mary shouted, "she ill."

"You wark!" the guard said, confusion replacing suspicion.

Mary tried Malay. "*Sakit*, she *sakit sakit*."

"*Sakit!*" the guard repeated. "*Sakit!*"

Rachel watched as he lifted his rifle from his shoulder. Pulling the bayonet from the scabbard on his belt he fixed it over the barrel. Pushing Mary to one side, he lowered the rifle as he marched up the track towards her and the other women.

Rachel saw him coming but could do nothing to stop him.

"You wark!" he shouted at the other women. "Wark!"

Reaching Rachel the guard placed the tip of the bayonet against her throat. She closed her eyes as she imagined the blade cutting through her throat and her windpipe. Was she going to die there, by this track in the middle of nowhere?

Another tremor hit her and the pain was unbearable. She wanted to scream but if she moved the bayonet was bound to cut through her skin. Instead, she screwed up her eyes, tensed every muscle in her body and waited, prayed that the spasm would pass.

"You wark," the guard shouted at her.

"And … and you go to hell," Rachel screamed back at him.

"Leave her alone," she heard the other women chorus.

"You wark," the guard shouted again.

"Fuck off," she heard Alicia bellow at him.

Chapter Fifty-Six

There were four of them – two adults and two children.

The boat they were in was moving slowly and the engine sounded distinctly unhealthy, in fact when they were almost opposite the longhouse, the engine died completely.

The current now controlled the boat as it began to drift downstream.

Colin could see the desperation in the adults' eyes, and the elder child, a girl burst into tears. Instinctively, he leapt into the prau and tugged at the engine's starting cord, it caught first time. An Iban called Patchna jumped into the boat with him almost upsetting it, and Colin twisted the throttle.

The prau was alongside the other boat in seconds. The Chinese man looked at Colin in amazement before reacting and throwing a thin rope to Patchna. The woman was sitting in the back of the boat with her arms round the children, their eyes wide open.

Towing the boat back to the bank, Colin secured them both before helping the Chinese group onto dry land.

"Thank you," the man said to Colin, but his eyes stared at the group of Iban warriors who had quickly gathered.

Armed with their blowpipes and parangs, they were quite threatening.

The woman and the children were huddled behind the man. None wore clothing suitable for the jungle and Colin could see they were all very frightened.

Before Colin could speak, the group of Iban men parted and Anak stood in front of them. He looked at the newcomers, his face expressionless.

"Who are you?" he asked in Iban.

The Chinese man looked from Anak to Colin.

"He asked who you are," Colin told him.

"My name is Fung Chan Seng," the man said hesitantly, "and this is my wife Chao Shi Seng, and our children Lim, our son and Chee, our daughter."

Colin translated for Anak and said, "And this is Anak, he is the headman here at Long Lohang. He asks why you are here."

"We didn't know what else to do. We had to escape the Japanese or I would have been imprisoned and probably shot, what would my family have done then? We couldn't go overland to try to escape because the Japanese are everywhere, the same applied to trying to escape by sea. Our only choice was to come up river, I knew that the Japanese hadn't ventured this far."

"Unfortunately, you are wrong, they have been here but only fleetingly," Colin told him.

The man, who was in his early thirties, looked rather incongruous dressed in a dirty white shirt, grey trousers and black leather shoes. He and his family were still frightened. His wife was wearing a summer's dress and yellow sandals.

Colin was about to ask the man to elaborate further when Anak spoke again.

"Ask him why he stopped here?" Anak asked.

"He didn't have any choice," Colin said. "The engine gave up, if we hadn't gone out to them their boat would be drifting back downstream."

"Maybe that would be for the best," Anak said,

Colin looked at him in surprise.

"I don't think you mean that, Anak," he said.

Anak waited a few seconds before he spoke: "No, I don't. We are hospitable people, Coy-lyn. Ask this man and his family to come to the longhouse. We will talk some more and I will decide what to do."

Chapter Fifty-Seven

"You no wark, you no good!" the guard shouted.

The pain was still there but lying on her back looking up at the snarling face, with spittle on his lips, Rachel could see exactly what the guard intended doing. She could feel the boxes of pills against her skin and she prayed that they remained undiscovered. It had to be a miscarriage. The pain was awful but the bayonet that was now hovering between her breasts, was even more terrifying.

"No wark, no good!" the guard shouted again, as he pulled the rifle away in preparation for the thrust that was to follow. His eyes were unblinking as he surveyed his target, which Rachel believed was the middle of her chest.

She was going to find out what it was like to have a bayonet thrust into her body.

The other women's screams were like an echo as Rachel saw what was happening in slow motion. Instinctively as she saw the bayonet being withdrawn and then flashing towards her she rolled to one side, scrambled to her feet, crouched, her hands like claws, as she turned on the man who was hell bent on killing her. Her teeth were together in a snarl, and her eyes narrowed in defiance.

"Come on you little yellow fucking bastard, you want a fight, I'll give you one," she shouted.

The guard, having extracted the bayonet from the ground where Rachel had been lying, looked at her in amazement. It was obvious he did not know what to do. It gave Rachel a few seconds to adjust her footing to get her balance so that she was able to move in whichever direction she wanted.

Out of the corner of her eye she saw that the other younger guard, who was standing a few feet away, also could not believe what he was seeing but he too was holding his rifle in a threatening manner.

"I said come on you filthy coward, you little yellow fucking bastard, if you're going to stick that thing in me get on with it."

Rachel's eyes darted from one guard to the other. She was not sure where the next thrust would come from but remembered hearing somewhere that attack was often the best form of defence.

She opened her mouth hissed liked a striking cobra and took a pace forward.

The older guard looked surprised and stepped back as he lowered the rifle once more, the tip of the bayonet still only a foot from Rachel's body.

She did not budge.

Her hands were still like claws in front of her as she now fixed the Japanese guard with a stare. She was still crouching, her feet apart, her arms outstretched.

Suddenly Rachel grabbed at the barrel of the rifle and tugged as hard as she could. The guard pulled it away but instead of showing anger he started laughing, and as he laughed he began to stab at Rachel, first to one side then the other. The other guard also laughed.

The women stayed silent.

Rachel did not like the fact that the guard was laughing at her, and it only added to her fury. She dodged the thrusts of the bayonet, looking for an opportunity to get to the guard's face, still certain that he was going to kill her. Suddenly the guard's expression changed. He reversed his rife and pushed Rachel away with the butt.

She fell over and the boxes of pills fell on to the ground behind her.

"Wark!" the guard shouted. "You wark! No wark, no good! No good, you dead."

Rachel just looked at him as she scooped up the boxes and put them back under her shirt.

Chapter Fifty-Eight

Sitting on the *tanju* were Colin, Anak and Fung Chan Seng.

Anak had decreed that no one else was necessary until he was ready to discuss his findings with the rest of the council. Fung Chan Seng's wife and the children were at the far end of the longhouse and Colin could see Aslah giving them a drink.

Aslah smiled as she played the hostess: he also saw her furtive glances in his direction.

"Coy-lyn, please ask our new guest to explain why he and his family had to flee the Japanese," Anak instructed.

Colin did as he was asked and in reply Fung Chan Seng said, "My name is a bit of a mouthful for you, Fung is what my wife calls me and she is prefers to be called Chao."

Knowing the Chinese were quite formal when among strangers, Colin bowed slightly in thanks.

"My name is Colin," he said in reply.

"Colin," Fung said with a smile. "Before I answer the headman's question may I congratulate you on your command of the Iban language? It is something I would not have expected."

"And I congratulate you on your English, Fung."

"Thank you, but my understanding of your language was a necessity as so few of Rajah Brooke's staff spoke Mandarin, and by saying that it half explains why we are here."

Fung looked at Anak and bowed slightly but Anak's expression remained impassive.

"The headman appears astute and he obviously trusts you, Colin, therefore I must do the same. As you know the Japanese have been at war with my country for many years. Being resident in Sarawak does not mean that our thoughts and prayers are not with my people after the mayhem and carnage the Japanese have imposed on them.

"I am a civil servant and I worked for Rajah Brooke as the senior Chinese community leader in the 4th Division of Sarawak. That in itself was not a crime, but the Japanese's intelligence is good, courtesy of the many of their countrymen who lived here before the war under cover of running some of the rubber plantations."

Fung looked down at his hands.

"I am partly responsible for organising and sending some of my own countrymen, known as the Mechanics, to China to fight the Japanese. I am also responsible for activating the denial plans in the area that put the airstrip in Miri and oil wells on the coast out of use. In this area, Colin, I am public enemy number one. If I am caught the Japanese will kill me. So I had little choice but to escape and throw myself on the mercy of somebody like this headman."

Colin thought for a moment.

What he had been told generated so many questions, but instead of asking them he slowly, searching for the right words, began to translate but Fung interrupted him.

"My family and I have been in hiding since the Japanese invaded, we were sheltered by many friends as we were passed from one to the other, but I could no longer put their lives at risk and that is why we came upriver."

Nodding, Colin carried on translating.

Anak listened intently and without interrupting. When Colin had finished he expected there to be many questions but there were none.

Anak looked at Fung and they all waited.

Was Anak's silence ominous or had Colin misjudged him once more?

Chapter Fifty-Nine

With her eyes intent on her would-be killer, Rachel managed to push the boxes of pills back under her clothing and inside her pants. The guard was still laughing, but he seemed to have lost interest in thrusting a bayonet between her ribs.

The expression on his face as he looked down at her left her in little doubt that he would have got great enjoyment out of seeing the point pierce her skin, and her blood spurting from her body but fortunately he had second thoughts.

Maybe he had concluded that if he killed a prisoner without his superior's permission, he might find himself in a lot more trouble than he anticipated.

Her mind raced back to the man she had seen killed – murdered – in front of her before they had left Kuching. She had come so close to experiencing what that poor man had endured and she shuddered at the thought.

As Rachel tried to get to her feet, Mary and another woman whose name was Carol, rushed over to her. As the soldier had threatened Rachel all the women had pulled back, their mouths open in shock as the horror of what could happen suddenly hit them.

Now they had regained a little confidence.

"Are you all right?" Carol asked.

"I think so," Rachel told her. "I thought he was going to kill me."

"So did we," Mary said. "If he had ... well he would have had a lot more trouble than he ..." Her voice trailed off as the two women lifted Rachel to her feet.

"Sorry about that," Rachel said, but as she straightened she screamed again as the pain hit her once more and she doubled over, holding her stomach. The pain was so intense it was like bolts of lightning shooting from one side of her abdomen and back again.

"What on earth can it be," Mary asked imploringly.

"I ... I don't know but ... but ..." she screamed again as the pain racked her body.

Mary beckoned one of the other women over to her, and after taking a deep breath she went to the guards, both of whom were looking a little sheepish.

Pointing towards her Rachel heard Mary say: "She *sakit sakit*, she

125

ill."

The guards exchanged looks.

"She wark, no wark no good," the younger guard said but his eyes told her a different story.

"Listen to me you stupid little man," Mary said. "You might be brave enough when you have a rifle in your hands but when I tell Lieutenant Sato and Captain Yamamoto –"

Mary did not get any further before the point of the bayonet broke the skin under her chin.

She held the soldier's gaze.

"*Chui Sato, Sencho Yamamoto*," the guard said slowly.

He would not have understood anything else Mary had said but he recognised his officers' names and Rachel thought it might just work.

Mary smiled as she lifted her head, put her hands on her hips and pushed her chest forward.

"*Hai*," she said, "*Chui Sato* and *Sencho Yamamoto*."

The soldier looked confused but he lowered the rifle, and stood back.

"It's back to Kampong Punkit," Mary told the other women. "We need to use something to carry Rachel on."

"Two of the rakes," Carol said enthusiastically.

"But what can we use between them," Mary asked.

"Our shirts," Carol said. "Come on I want three more shirts," she said as she started to remove hers.

126

"Tell him that the war with his enemies is not our war. By coming here he brings this war to us, and it is a war we do not want," Anak said slowly. "Tell him that he may have removed the risk from his friends but he has now brought that risk to us."

Fung glanced towards his wife and children, the concern on his face expressing the bewilderment he so obviously felt..

"I understand why the headman should say this," he said to Colin after hearing the translation. "But we had nowhere else to go. If the engine on the boat had not stopped, and you had not rescued us, we would not be here." Fung bowed his head. "But whether he likes it or not, the Japanese have invaded his homeland."

"The headman says that the Japanese may be no different to other invaders," Colin said to Fung, translating Anak's reply. "And two of these invaders are in his home at the moment, one from England and the other from China. But there are no Japanese here: they are leaving him and his people alone."

Colin now knew Anak well enough to know that he did not really mean what he was saying: he knew his words used were to test Fung's reasoning.

Fung nodded.

"Again I understand what he is saying, but I have already seen what the Japanese can do. Our people have brought business and prosperity: we live in peace, Colin. The Japanese bring torture, killing, rape – they want this land for their own, its people will be expendable."

"You don't have to convince me," Colin said, "but if I translated what you have just said, the headman would ask where is this torture, killing and rape? He has not seen it, so why should it affect him? The Japanese have been here just the once and that was only fleetingly. There are no reports of anything from the other longhouses either."

"Then I am sorry, Colin, but he is blind to reality. It is only thirty miles away. It will come here and soon," Fung implored.

"As I just told you they have been here already," Colin said. "They came up the river in a gun boat but they didn't see this longhouse."

"They will. They will want the food that the headman and his people can provide, and when they come the women will not be safe. They will be raped and murdered, and the children will suffer a similar fate. I have seen it already. I —"

Anak interrupted, asking Colin to translate.

Colin did so as best he could.

Anak thought for a moment, the others watched as he deliberated.

"If the Japanese come here in peace, if they want to trade, they will be treated as guests. If they come here to steal, if they try to take the women, they will be killed."

Colin translated.

Anak continued: "This man and his family give the Japanese another reason to come here."

"They are no different to me," Colin said.

"No, Coy-lyn, they are different. But I choose the guests I have in my longhouse."

"Of course you do Anak, but this man and his family are no more of a risk to you and all the others than I am."

Anak once again glanced from Colin to Fung and back again.

Fung and Colin exchanged looks, the desperation Fung felt so obvious in his face and the way he was wringing his hands.

"This man and his family may stay one week, then we talk again," Anak said.

Chapter Sixty-One

Feeling totally drained was an expectation but under the circumstances, feeling embarrassed was something she had not anticipated.

Sister Angelique was fussing over her.

She was a midwife.

Rachel felt so vulnerable

She had been carried back from the farm on the makeshift stretcher, the guards letting their lack of direct communication show in their obvious isolation. The one who had almost ended Rachel's life was the more contrite of the two. Every now and again during the walk back he went up to the stretcher and looked down at Rachel, his eyes showing concern, his words unintelligible.

The women took it in turns to carry the stretcher. Two of the women who had given up their shirts were bare-breasted but no-one, including the guards, seemed to take any notice.

After she discovered what had happened, Marjory Field quickly and much to Rachel's surprise and embarrassment, drew the right conclusion before confiding in Sister Marie and asking if any of the sisters were nurses. Sister Marie explained that all Order of Mercy Sisters had training to one level or another in looking after others, but under the circumstances Sister Angelique was the best one to look after Rachel.

After checking her pulse, Sister Angelique gave her a welcome sip of water. The nun had felt all over Rachel's abdomen, her touch light but probing. Eventually she stood back and sighed.

"You are lucky," Sister Angelique said in her indistinguishable accent. "The baby has settled."

"I …" Rachel tried to speak but even the effort of parting her lips seemed too much.

"No, you must rest. With rest we may be able to prevent a repetition of what happened today and save the baby. Sister Marie is thinking of going to see Captain Yamamoto to get you reassigned to those that stay behind in the camp. Hopefully there will be no more work for you in the field."

Rachel could see the stern but sincere face looking down at her. At first she hoped that what she knew was happening would go all the way because a miscarriage would at least remove one of her concerns.

But when it had become so evident that the guard had every intention of thrusting his bayonet into not only her body but that of her unborn child as well, the instinctive need to protect had taken over.

She had been ready to fight, to defend what was hers and Colin's. What was growing in her body was all she had to hang on to and nobody was going to take that child away from her, only an act of God could do that.

If it were true, God had decided on this occasion that this was not the time.

"The next few days are going to be critical," Sister Angelique told her. "There must be no movement. What you have in there," she said pointing at Rachel's stomach, "is no longer yours: the women have been told and they have declared their ownership. It is their baby you are carrying so it is their baby they want you to have."

"But ..." Rachel started to say.

"There are no *buts*, you may have conceived the baby but it is no longer yours," Sister Angelique said, but this time she was smiling.

The tears came immediately to Rachel's eyes as she realised the goodness that was behind the remark.

Chapter Sixty-Two

When Abas and the others did not return within four days, the strain began to show.

Anak became irritable, and Ramlah, his wife, spent many long hours in their *bilik*. Colin witnessed Aslah assuming her mother's duties, going about them quietly, but at every opportunity she would try to catch Colin's eye and the message they sent was that he must do something.

He had stripped, cleaned and rebuilt the outboard motor from Fung's boat – it wasn't perfect but at least it worked – and now it and the remaining prau were out of the water and hidden from view.

Learning how to repair the palm thatch on the roof of the longhouse was for him an expectation; he could now also fish using a short three-pronged spear and combat the leeches that were always waiting whenever he went in the jungle. Identifying the many fungi and other edible plants the jungle had to offer was a challenge but one he had mastered.

Even though he busied himself, he too was worried.

Going to Miri in one of the praus was an option but nothing would come from it. Even going to one of the longhouses further downstream would achieve little: if Abas had stopped there, word would have reached them and they would know. The girl he was courting lived upriver not between them and Miri.

Fung and his wife, Chao, had quickly adapted to longhouse life, and Fung had demonstrated an even speedier ability to pick up the Iban language.

They too were also worried.

As well was watching him, Colin had also seen Aslah watching Chao. She was taller and slimmer than the Iban women, and Colin had to admit, she was also attractive. Her skin colour was pale and she kept herself covered up whenever possible, but when down at the river washing, even her inherent inhibitions disappeared. Colin was slightly surprised when he saw the expression on Aslah's face when she was watching Chao was inquisitive and slightly hostile. On one occasion, she became aware that Colin had seen her reaction and she quickly smiled at him, but her eyes gave him a different message.

Except for the odd nod of recognition, not a word had passed between them since Aslah had felt spurned that day in the clearing. But regardless, and for whatever reason, the silence between them seemed to have generated a stronger bond. Colin accepted that communication by other than words can sometimes send a stronger message than by words alone.

As he walked back to the longhouse after catching a few fish, Anak beckoned Colin to one side. "Coy-lyn, I am deeply concerned for Abas and the other men. They said they would be back within two or three days, it is now four." Anak's eyes looked searchingly into Colin's, his hope for a solution obvious.

"I am also worried," Colin said. "But one more day is all it is, maybe we should wait for a further few days, if they do not return, we decide what we must do," he said.

"If they are dead there is nothing we can do. If the Japanese are as bad as you and Fung tell me, maybe they are captured, and the Japanese do terrible things to them," Anak said.

"The truth is hidden from us," Colin told him. "We should not guess what it is."

"You are wise, Coy-lyn, wise for an orang puteh." Anak allowed a rueful smile to play on his lips. As they stood up Colin heard the distant noise of an outboard engine, battling against the strong river current.

Was it Abas and the others ... or were the Japanese returning?

Chapter Sixty-Three

"We must make Yamamoto understand that if she is moved she will definitely lose the baby," Sister Angelique said as she looked back at the sleeping figure. "Sister Marie agrees and she thinks he might agree."

Marjory Field followed her gaze.

"I know but I'm not so sure that losing the baby wouldn't be a good thing," she said. Rachel's sleeping figure was restless but at least she was not working.

"I understand what you are saying and why you are saying it, Mrs Field, but if we do not preserve life as best we can there is little hope for any of us."

Marjory guided Sister Angelique outside the hut so that they would not disturb the sleeping figure. The sun was beginning to go down and the humidity wasn't too bad. All the other women were going about their respective chores, but it was obvious from the looks they gave Marjory that they were wondering what was happening. Those who had not witnessed Rachel's close encounter with death knew about it. Marjory knew that Sister Angelique's words rang true for most of them – life, including the life of an unborn child, needed preserving, so that there could be a future.

"I understand what you are saying, Sister, but I do wonder if Yamamoto will feel the same," Marjory said. "Even with knowledge of what the Order of Mercy did for him in China."

"I think he might if I were to come with you. Obviously Sister Marie has told you about Captain Yamamoto," she said.

"Yes she did and she also told me he feels incarcerating women and children, is wrong," Marjory said. "Although I have to say his motives on the surface may appear quite different."

"Maybe they do, but he also has a duty to perform," Sister Angelique said.

Surprised by Sister Angelique's choice of words, Marjory frowned. It sounded as though there was a degree of loyalty being shown where it was unexpected..

"And keeping women and children in this hellhole helps Japan's war effort does it?"

"That is not what I am saying."

"Yes, I know and I'm sorry. He might not even be willing to see me," Marjory said. "He normally passes his messages via Sato, but if he does want to speak to me it's usually first thing in the morning. He doesn't let me go beyond the veranda of his hut, unlike Sister Marie."

"If we don't ask –" Sister Angelique started to say.

"I know," Marjory said, "and for Rachel's and the baby's sakes we must make the effort. It might as well be now rather than later, if we wait too long God knows what he will say."

Marjory beckoned to Mary Prentice who happened to be passing.

"Mary, go and sit with Rachel would you please? Sister Angelique and I are going to try to see Yamamoto and get him to agree that Rachel needs rest. Should we check with Sister Marie?" she asked turning back to Sister Angelique.

"I will go and see her now," Sister Angelique said. "But I think she will be happy for just you and me to try to see the Captain." Marjory watched as Sister Angelique went towards her own hut.

"How is she?" Mary asked.

"She came so close to having a miscarriage and –"

"But why didn't she tell anyone?"

"I don't think she was sure herself."

Sister Angelique rejoined them. "Good luck," Mary said as she went into the hut. "I won't hold my breath."

Chapter Sixty-Four

Everybody sat in silence as Abas gathered his thoughts.

Colin smiled to himself – Abas was certainly a chip off the old block: like his father he didn't speak without concentrating fully and giving what he had to say a lot of thought.

Babu sat by his side, his eyes never leaving his brother's.

Like his mother, Colin had not seen Babu a lot since Abas went down river; he had spent most of his time in the padi, staying overnight whenever he could.

Introductions to Fung, Chao and the children took place. They were now sitting with the others, waiting to hear what Abas had to tell them. He looked questioningly at his father when the circumstances of the Chinese family's escape were explained to him, and seemed a little surprised when told that they were being allowed to stay for a week. Colin wanted to tell him a lot more but thought it best to wait.

Now it looked as though Abas was ready to start his story, although Colin thought that might be the wrong word to use. A lot of the Iban's rest periods were spent telling stories but Abas didn't have a story to tell, what he wanted the others to hear was real.

"We hid the prau and our weapons up river from the town and walked in," Abas said. "We didn't see any Japanese on the river, but it was unusually quiet anyway. We walked through the outskirts of Miri, people looked at us with eyes that were scared, but maybe we saw fear in them because that is what we expected.

"There was no sign of the Japanese until we got to the centre, then they were everywhere. Some of the shops were open, there didn't seem to be any damage, and in many ways life seemed quite normal.

"We were not sure what we should do. We didn't really have a plan because we didn't know what we would find. We went to one of the places we always drink at when we go in to Miri for supplies, it was open but few people were there. We sat at one of the tables for ages before old Dong came out from the back to serve us. He did not recognise me at first, but when he did his eyes looked fearful.

"He said, 'You must not stay here, you must leave and go back to your village.'"

135

"'Why,' I asked him, 'I see soldiers but little else. It all seems quite normal.'"

"Dong said, 'What you see is not what is happening. If you stay you will be stopped, you will be questioned, and if you are taken to the *Kempeitei* you will not be seen again.'"

"'Who are the *Kempeitei*?' I asked him. 'They are the secret police,' he said. 'And they are ruthless. They have no respect for human life – they have murdered many and what they do to the women before they are killed is terrible. We are all living in fear that we will be next,' Dong said."

"'I have nothing to hide,' I told him. 'I have come to town to buy some supplies.' But old Dong would not serve us, he ushered us out saying, 'You have been warned. You must leave as soon as you can.'"

Abas paused for a few seconds.

"Father," he said, "I am sorry if I caused you and mother concern but I could not leave when I had nothing to tell you on my return. All I had was what Dong told me, and I have said before that his stories tend to be exaggerated. But what he told me worried me and I had to see for myself. I am sorry for causing you worry."

"You are back," Anak said as he showed an usual amount of emotion. Colin could see tears in Ramlah's eyes. "But what did you see, Abas? Did old Dong exaggerate the truth or should we share his fear?"

Chapter Sixty-Five

Captain Yamamoto was smiling.

His day had been better than most. The pain caused by his war wounds was a constant reminder, both day and night, of what he had experienced. But today, the pain had been not as bad, which meant he could concentrate on some of the paperwork that needed bringing up to date.

Most of the time, he gave Lieutenant Sato his orders to pass onto the guards and to the women. Doing things that way allowed him to stay aloof, to distance himself from the day to day problems this zoo presented.

He did not like appearing in front of either the women or his soldiers because he felt the job he was doing was demeaning. After all, he was a warrior, a soldier, a Samurai, and being put in charge a group of foreign women and children was not his idea of being a brave representative of the Imperial Japanese Army.

Accepting his appointment was only temporary, helped. The women and children would leave eventually and his fate would be once again in the hands of his superiors. Whether they would allow him to fight again was in the lap of the Gods.

From the window in his hut he had watched the women coming back early from the farm. He had also seen that one of the more pretty ones – he knew she was the Lefévre woman – was being carried on a makeshift stretcher. Two of the women carrying the stretcher were bare-breasted but they didn't seem to care.

Lieutenant Sato had already reported to him and told him what had happened, so he wasn't surprised when the Field woman asked to see him. Normally, and particularly at that time of day which was just before the evening parade, he would have refused but on this occasion he decided that he would allow a short audience to take place.

The two women bowed and waited for his permission to speak. Their bedraggled state appalled him but there was nothing he could..

"Yes?" he said.

"Captain Yamamoto," Marjory Field said, "one of the women, the Woman Lefévre, is expecting a baby. She was taken ill at the farm today. We think unless she is allowed to rest she will lose the baby."

Captain Yamamoto eyed Sister Angelique's bowed head and turned his attention back to Marjory Field. They must think him stupid. He knew exactly why the Sister was there – if they thought they could play with his better nature they needed to think again.

"It is of no concern of the Imperial Japanese Army that the Woman Lefévre is expecting a baby. I hope you are not suggesting that the person who impregnated her is one of my soldiers."

"No, no," Marjory Fields," said quickly. "She was pregnant before ... before we arrived here. But unless –"

"Are you suggesting that I should give this woman special attention, especially after she was the one who ... no, she will not be treated any differently."

"Captain Yamamoto," Sister Angelique said. "The child she is carrying knows nothing of this war. It cannot be blamed for anything other than – "

"I will not allow such a situation to undermine my authority," Yamamoto said. He controlled his voice but he could feel the anger building up in him. "You are testing my patience."

"Your authority is not being questioned –" Sister Angelique started to say.

"I have made my decision," he said. "Now go!"

"But Captain Yamamoto –"

Chapter Sixty-Six

The group of men who had gathered to listen to Abas had now dispersed.

It was time for the headman to consider the facts as presented and to decide what he was going to put to his people as options. He would normally have considered alone, but on this occasion he asked Colin, Fung and his elder son, Abas, to stay with him.

"Coy-lyn, Fung," he said, "you have heard what my son has to say. Other than the knowledge each of you has brought, we have had no word from our neighbours. None has asked for help, none has indicated that the Japanese have intruded any more than others in the past." Anak looked from Colin to Fung. "I understand that you both have your prejudices: you, Fung, because of what the Japanese have done in your own country, and you, Coy-lyn, because the Japanese have taken from your countrymen the control of these lands. But I must think of my own people, not only my family and friends that are close by but also those that are spread all over the land that has been ours for many hundreds of years.

"Abas has told us what he saw but he did not witness any of the atrocities you have both mentioned, and the ones old Dong said were happening in Miri. Maybe Abas did not go to the right places to see for himself, but I do not think that is the case. The Japanese are new to our lands so it is understandable that they must impose their authority, as your people did," he said looking at Fung, "and yours also," he added turning his attention back to Colin. "They did exactly the same.

"I expected Abas to return with a far worse story than the one he has described. He hasn't, so I must now ask you what you think but before doing so I have something else to say."

Colin knew better than to interrupt when Anak was stating his case and formulating his intentions, and he was pleased Fung was also refraining. Instead, he nodded his agreement to what had been said already.

"For many generations," Anak continued, "there have been wars between opposing peoples in Borneo. We have fought each other for land, for revenge and for the sheer enjoyment that such violence brought to the minds of men. Now there is relative peace. There are still small disagreements that can lead to bloodshed, even to the taking of heads albeit secretly, but such happenings are becoming less and less. These lands have been controlled by many: the Malays, the Chinese, the British and now the Japanese.

"Many of our people have progressed, if that is what it can be called, with the changes our rulers have brought with them. Some of the Iban are in positions of authority: police, firemen, nurses and government. Others have their shops and others are criminals who prey on those who wish to benefit from the changes.

"For us the changes have only happened if they help us to be better, to make our lives easier but without moving away too much from our traditional way of life. We have engines for our praus, we have cooking oils, generators for light, and guns if we wanted them. We also have what we have always had. We have our pride, our traditions and our superstitions but most of all we are able to live the way we wish to live. The Japanese have not yet intruded into what we hold so sacred, until they do, and after listening to Abas, I see no cause to show aggression towards them."

Anak paused.

"But I am now willing to listen," he said finally. "I am willing to listen to any counter-arguments you may have, and I know that both of you will tell me what you really think rather than what you think I will want to hear. Yes, I will listen and I will give what you have said more thought after which I will decide what must be done … if anything."

Chapter Sixty-Seven

"Silence," Yamamoto said. "I have already told you it is her fault she is the way she is, if she should have special treatment others will suffer. Somebody would have to do her work at the farm and the rest would go with less food if she were to have more. None of these other women should suffer because of her. No, there will be no preferential treatment for her."

Marjory Field started to bow as she prepared to leave, but Sister Angelique put her hand on her arm and stood her ground.

"Captain Yamamoto," Sister Angelique said. "By saying there will be no special treatment for the Woman Lefévre you are showing compassion towards the rest of us. You are saying that we should not suffer because of her condition. But we wish to show compassion towards her and we will suffer if she is not looked after. It is not her baby she is carrying; it is our baby. All the women in this camp own that baby. I hope you can understand that and why."

Yamamoto appeared to hesitate, his obvious annoyance lessened. "There will be no special treatment," he said quietly.

"Captain Yamamoto –"

"I have made my decision and you will not speak again," Yamamoto said, his eyes once again ablaze with fury. "You will not disobey me, or question any of my decisions."

Sister Angelique's grip on Marjory Field's arm tightened. She glared at Yamamoto. "And if –"

"You will not speak –"

"And if the Order of Mercy Sister –?"

"Silence!"

"No, Captain Yamamoto, I will not be silent. If you wish to silence me you will have to do your worst." Sister Angelique waited but when Yamamoto just glared at her, she carried on. "If the Sisters had not shown compassion towards you in China you would not be alive today. They –"

"They had no choice, they were under orders," Yamamoto said.

"They had every choice whether they were under orders or not. Your army was committing atrocities wherever it went –"

"You will stop now before I forget who you –"

"I will not stop. The Sisters who saved your life will have done so

141

even though they knew no mercy was being shown by your army. They could so easily have made you suffer an awful death, like so many Chinese suffered and are still suffering at the hands of your army. But they didn't, they showed you kindness when the opposite could have been done without anyone else knowing. We are all here because of a handful of men: your politicians and the politicians from all the countries involved. The politicians are not fighting, not putting themselves at risk. You are expected to lay down you life for your country –"

"And I will if it is necessary," Yamamoto said.

"I am sure you will but under different circumstances everyone in this camp could live peacefully, side by side and respect each others' differences. All I am asking is for just a little compassion in return for what war has brought to us. Allow the Woman Lefévre to rest. You are assured when she is fit to do so, she will return to the work on the farm."

Yamamoto turned and walked over to the single window that looked out over the 'parade square'. His hands were behind his back, his fingers interlocked.

Sister Angelique and Marjory Field waited.

"I will give her one week," Yamamoto said without turning round. "One week only."

Chapter Sixty-Eight

"I am a pilot," Colin said. "I am not in the army and never have been. I work for myself and I left Kuching to save my plane and my own life. As I left the army were preparing to destroy the airfield so the Japanese could not use it. If I had flown south towards Dutch Borneo I may have escaped, but I didn't know where the Japanese were or how far they had advanced. I had planned to fly to Jesselton for refuelling, then Sandakan and eventually Australia.

"I owe my life to Abas and Babu for bringing me here, and to you Anak, for letting me stay and of course to Aslah for nursing me and to your wife, for watching over your daughter. Other than what Fung and Abas have told us I know little of what is going on. As you say Anak, the war is not here, it is many miles away."

Colin paused to take a sip of *tuak*, a rice wine made by his hosts and the only alcohol that was available.

"As this is not your war, Anak," he continued, "this is not my war either. Abas saw no orang puteh on the streets of Miri and my guess is that they have either been imprisoned or put under house arrest … or worse. I –"

"What you say is true, Colin," Fung said. "The same with some of my people, but please, I am sorry, I interrupted."

"I see," Colin said, "thank you, and interrupt all you like, you have seen more than any of us. Many of my people will have been killed and wounded already fighting against the Germans and their allies and now many will die here in the Far East fighting against the Japanese. I say my people but the only connection I have with them is that they are white, as I am white, and we speak the same language. I was born in England, I went to school in England, I became a man in England but I have no family there. This land is my home now and I have no wish to leave it, ever.

"Fung, you have told us that the Japanese have also invaded the Malayan peninsula and Singapore. My conscience tells me that by saying that this is not my war, I am saying that I do not belong. I do belong. I regard Sarawak as my home and its people, be they Iban, Chinese, Malay or any other, as my people. But I am many miles from Kuching, I have no way of getting there, and even if I did, what would I find when I got there?

143

"Anak, you have your own people to protect, and you have already put them at risk by letting me stay here. In the time I have been with you, you and your people have taught me so much. I have learnt so much about your traditions and your beliefs," Colin said and smiled. "I am no longer white, but I am still tall, I still have blue eyes and yellow hair. If the Japanese bring this war to you, I will fight alongside you, but until then I would like to stay for as long as you let me. The world is at war, but you are still at peace. It is my suggestion that you retain this peace for as long as you are able.

"Yes, I can advise and I can help in areas where I have expertise and where you have taught me new skills. But what I cannot do, Anak, is advise you about your own people. You are assured whatever decision you might take, either now or in the future, I will respect and if it involves fighting I would be honoured to fight by your side.

"At the moment though, I hope it never comes to that. I would not want to see you or your people suffer."

Colin bowed his head and waited.

"Thank you, Coy-lyn. As I have told you before many times, you are wise ... for an orang puteh."

Colin smiled. "Much of my wisdom comes from listening to you, Anak," he said.

"Now you go too far," Anak replied.

Chapter Sixty-Nine

"That was brave of you," Marjory Fields said, as they crossed the compound towards the hut in which Rachel slept.

"It was, wasn't it?" Sister Angelique replied, a slight smile creeping onto her lips. "He is not a bad man, but his superiors are bad. I think self-preservation is top of his list at the moment. He is torn between what he wants to do and what he is expected to do."

She stopped and turned towards Marjory Field.

"We must keep what he said to ourselves. If word were to get to the ears of those who are in charge, he may suffer, and if he suffers we will suffer also, and probably a lot more than we are already."

Marjory returned Sister Angelique's smile.

"I can understand why he relented in the end, but is a week enough?"

Sister Angelique shook her head.

"I don't think so but if after a week Rachel is still not fit for work we must try something else. We may be Captain Yamamoto's prisoners but he still has to maintain face in front of us."

"In front of you and the other Sisters you mean," Marjory said. "I think the rest of us are incidental. He would sooner be rid of everyone of us."

"That's as maybe but ... shall we go and see how Rachel is?"

Marjory followed Sister Angelique into the hut. Rachel was still lying down and she looked as though she might be asleep. Crossing over to her, Sister Angelique bent down and picked up Rachel's wrist.

"Her pulse is strong, so there is hope," she said.

"Will extra food help?" Marjory asked.

"It will but whether she will agree to taking it, I don't know."

"I ... I will do no such thing," Rachel said weakly as she opened her eyes and looked up at the other two women. "The pain is a lot less severe, and I think –"

"You will have a week's rest and then we will see," Marjory told her.

"A week? But ..."

"As I explained to Mrs Field, Captain Yamamoto is not a bad man. When he had you put in solitary confinement he did not know you were expecting a baby, but the fact that he stopped the lashes showed the sort of man he really is."

"I think you are being kind," Marjory said. "We must not take his altruism for granted. You say he will not want to lose face, but that applies to his own kind as well, and I would not like to put him in a position where he has to make a choice."

"Yes, that is what I meant earlier," Sister Angelique said as she lifted Rachel's tattered dress and felt around her stomach and abdomen. "Oh, how I wish I had a stethoscope."

She smiled.

"Now you must rest and let nature and God take their course."

"I … I would have thought for you, Sister, it would be the other way round," Rachel said. "I mean God followed by nature."

"God is nature," Sister Angelique said. "He is all around us all the time, even in this awful place. Now you must rest."

Rachel nodded. "Thank you," she said. "Thank you to you both."

"We did nothing more than what you would have done for us," Marjory told her, but wanting to ask Sister Angelique how God, if he was all around them, could let such things happen.

Chapter Seventy

"In many ways," Fung said speaking next, "my situation is similar to Colin's although China was invaded by the Japanese for the second time, five years ago. What you now know about the atrocities they have committed is not just rumour: there are many I have spoken to who have had first hand experiences. Japanese soldiers are brutal and often inhuman, but such brutality is in their psyche. They regard themselves as superior and many of those they attack as little more than animals, when in fact because of the way they behave they are the ones who are animals.

"The similarities with Colin continue but I was born away from China. My grandparents came to British North Borneo sixty years ago and eventually migrated south until they eventually settled in Kuching, which is where I was born.

"I went to university in Kuala Lumpur and on my return I became a junior Government officer, first in Kuching, then later in Bintulu and now in Miri. I am, or I should now say *was* in charge of the land reform department.

"When the Chinese anti-Japanese movement came to a head overseas in 1937 and we raised money for the China Relief Fund, I was active in this organisation.

"Later in 1939 when the Chinese of Nanyang – which in Cantonese means South East Asia – recruited many young Chinese, mainly mechanics and drivers, to go to China to fight the Japanese, I volunteered to go but by then Chao and I had been married for six years, Chee was four years old and Lim, three. I was annoyed but relieved when told I could not go because of the work I did in the Government.

"We now know that some of the Japanese who lived freely and were welcomed in our community despite what their army was doing in China, were spies. As they worked in the rubber estates and as farmers, they were compiling lists of who was to be classified as hostile after the invasion of Sarawak. Because of my involvement with the China Relief Fund and the volunteers, I was and still am high up on that list.

"I think you will already have concluded that I am in many ways more of a risk for you than Colin. The Japanese know me and they will still be looking for me. Colin, and I don't mean this rudely, is an unknown Englishman who they may or may not bother about. If they hear that I am in a longhouse somewhere up this river, they will come looking, that is for sure.

"As I have already told you, the resistance in Miri was negligible. Once established the Japanese, through informers and their own people we had interned when we knew what was going to happen, the army began to track down those who could not be allowed to stay free. The rest you know. My family and I are still free, and thanks to you, Anak, we have remained undiscovered. But I must tell you that I saw some of the atrocities that Abas did not see. I saw the bodies of men, women and children in the streets of Miri.

"I have no idea what happened to many of my English friends and work associates because we went into hiding so soon after the invasion. We were moved from safe house to safe house, and once we moved only hours before the Japanese raided where we had been staying. The situation was untenable and we had to leave.

"I agree with Colin, Anak. Although my heart tells me the opposite, my head tells me that we must wait. Nothing would be gained and much could be lost if we act hastily. If and when the Japanese come and if I am still here, I will also be at your side to do whatever is necessary to protect your people the way you have offered protection to my family and me.

"But, and once again I agree with Colin, they are your people and only you can decide what is best for them, I have no right to attempt to influence your decision in anyway. I will also respect whatever you decide to do," Fung said finally.

Chapter Seventy-One

The first few days of the week's grace given to Rachel by Captain Yamamoto went by without incident. Sister Angelique continued to fuss over her like a mother hen, and although on numerous occasions she said that she was feeling well enough to go back to work, Rachel was not allowed to move a muscle.

She did admit though, if only to herself, the rest had done her the world of good. Having help to the latrine when she needed to go was a Godsend, and then after three days the shower, where willing hands washed her from head to toe, was ... a luxury.

Although initially she felt highly embarrassed, Rachel did get used to the pampering offered by the other women, who reminded her every time there was a word of protest that they were doing it for *their* baby. She had been helped when she came out of solitary confinement but that was different ... she had been too tired to care who did what to her.

One of the children – a twelve year-old called Jasmine – made Rachel a dried flower (grass) arrangement and put it by her sleeping mat. What did surprise her even more was that a few of the guards, and especially Lieutenant Sato, asked how she was.

She decided that when word got round, it seemed to bring out the human side in everyone, including some of their enemies.

On the fourth day of her rest period Rachel was lying on her mat and beginning to feel really guilty when there was a sudden commotion outside. There was much shouting and she could see there was a lot of scurrying about. She went to the entrance of the hut and looked out.

The guards appeared to be in a bit of a panic as they rushed around, ignoring the women and children. They seemed to be concentrating on reinforcing the perimeter barbed wire fence, filling in holes under the fence that had been created by rats and other unwanted visitors. Rachel wondered what on earth was going on.

She knew the evening parade was not due for a couple of hours, and the farm work party had yet to return. Just as she was going back to her mat, the whistles were blown and a guard rushed into the hut and ordered her outside. Wondering where Marjory and Sister Angelique were, she went outside. As she got the 'parade square', she could see the guards rushing around the camp herding the remaining women and children into its centre, opposite Captain Yamamoto's hut. Marjory and Sister Angelique were already there and they beckoned Rachel towards them.

"Sorry about that," Marjory said, "but they wouldn't let us come to help you."

Yamamoto emerged five minutes later.

"Women," he shouted, taking up his usual hands-in-belt and feet-apart stance. "Tomorrow we are to be honoured with a visit from Rikugan Taisa Masandou Tsuji; he is a Colonel Staff Officer with the Imperial Japanese Army. He is a mighty and powerful man, but I must warn you, he is known as The Wolf, the God of Operations. He is responsible for much of the success our great army, air force and navy have had throughout Asia. For this small command to receive a visit from him is a great, great honour for us all."

He stopped and looked at all the faces before him.

"We have little time to prepare," he continued. "I have sent for the farm work party, and you will spend as long as is necessary cleaning your huts, showers and latrines."

Rachel sighed as did the other women.

"There will be no dissension," Yamamoto shouted. "Colonel Tsuji holds your futures in his hands, remember that."

"And yours Yamamoto," Marjory Field whispered as she stood next to Rachel.

Chapter Seventy-Two

Lying on his sleeping mat under the mosquito net, hands behind his head, and watching a moth doing its best to commit suicide against the paraffin lamp, Colin tried to come to terms with the decisions taken only a matter of a few hours ago. He thought back to every word that had been spoken ... and some that had not.

Like the others, he had drunk too much *tuak* and he knew he would have one hell of a head in the morning. The drink had flowed steadily all evening but after the final gathering, it had flowed even more quickly.

Evidently, his and Fung's words were unexpected but nonetheless they were what Anak wanted to hear. If either of them had recommended that they should adopt a belligerent stance against the Japanese, their ongoing welcome in the longhouse and its accompanying hospitality would have ended the next day.

Anak had reiterated this repeatedly during his address to his people.

He went on to explain that he had no grievance towards the Japanese, they appeared to have no problem with him and so he had no problem with them. Anyway, he had enough worries on a daily basis in running the longhouse, making sure the threshed padi was stored correctly, meeting with other longhouse headmen and all the other duties that went with his position.

He welcomed Fung Chan and Chao Shi to his longhouse on a more permanent standing and he made a particular fuss of their children, Lim and Chee. He said that having them and Coy-lyn as part of their group, although unusual they were welcome. He did not repeat what Fung had said about placing the longhouse at a greater risk than Colin had done.

Anak went on to explain to his people that he wanted them to treat their unexpected guests as one of them. He understood that when the time came they would lose their newfound friends back to their previous lives, but until then they were as one.

Colin had not sensed any dissension this time.

After opening many bottles of *tuak*, four decoratively dressed Iban girls performed an elaborate dance of permanent welcome in front of their long-term guests.

Colin lay and wondered how long long-term would be.

He had almost lost track of time.

The New Year – 1942 – had arrived and was no longer in its infancy.

He thought repeatedly about Rachel and wondered whether he would ever see her again. He thought about his new family, and how much there was still to learn about these fascinating and proud people and about his own future and how long it would be before he could return to his world. Although at this moment he had no wish to return to what he thought was his world. Where he was at this moment was his world – but isn't that how he had always lived since coming to Sarawak?

Then he thought about Aslah.

Once again she had stayed in the background but he sensed that her eyes were on him permanently. When the young girls were performing their welcome dance, he saw Aslah watching him watching the girls. He would admit the dance was sensual and if he were honest, his imaginings did not just rest with his appreciation of their movements. He wondered if Aslah had drawn the same conclusion. As soon as he tried to make eye contact with her, Aslah would either drop her head or look away.

If he was going to be with Anak and his family for a good deal longer he was going to have sort out his relationship with her.

Neither of them could go on like this – not long term.

Chapter Seventy-Three

It was just after dawn.

Everyone was on parade including Rachel. She had automatically left her hut with the others because she did not want to give cause for trouble. Yamamoto would not have let her stay there anyway.

Sister Angelique had protested but without success.

As she waited, Rachel thought.

There was only one thing to think about – the baby. She asked herself constantly whether she was surprised how she had changed. It was not because the guard had threatened to thrust his bayonet into her stomach and her baby, or because she was being pampered, and the way the other women said she was carrying *their* baby. The change was within her – it was a feeling that consumed her every thought. What was growing inside her was why she existed.

Rachel looked up to the sky. It was a wet sultry morning, the humidity was high but the temperature had yet to reach its peak. Lowering her eyes she could see Captain Yamamoto, Lieutenant Sato and Sergeant Suratomono, with a small guard of honour waiting at the open gate.

How much longer were they going to have to wait? At exactly eight o'clock, a convoy of three large black cars pulled up at the gate. Sergeant Suratomono leapt forward to open the rear door of the first car.

A small, bespectacled, clean-shaven man got out. His grey uniform appeared to be pristine. At his throat there was what looked like a George Cross – but it couldn't be – and above his left tunic pocket there were two rows of medals. There was a lot of saluting and bowing, after which Captain Yamamoto led the man – who Rachel guessed was Colonel Tsuji – and his entourage to his headquarters hut. Rachel thought the ceremony was amusing.

After nearly an hour of further waiting the officers reappeared and stood on the veranda at the front of the headquarters hut. Rachel wanted to help when one woman fainted but Marjory stopped her. Two of the younger children started crying and to her surprise, they and their mothers were ordered to return to their huts.

"Women," Captain Yamamoto shouted. "You will listen."

Colonel Tsuji surveyed the women and children, and it was

obvious from his expression that he had nothing but disgust for them. Well, Rachel thought, the feeling is mutual. She and the others had done what they could, even in the face of a cruel enemy, to look their best but they were still emaciated, sick and forlorn.

After clearing his throat Colonel Tsuji started to speak. His voice was high pitched and his English good enough for everybody to understand him. "Women," he said. "You are all the enemies of Japan, and the children here are the spawn of our enemies. You do not deserve to live in such conditions when some of my soldiers are facing honourable deaths at the hands of your cowardly men who bear arms against us. It is within my powers to have you all shot. Your deaths would not be on my conscience because you are what you are. I have discussed your immediate futures with your commander, and although I would prefer to put a bullet in the backs of all your heads – women and children – he has convinced me that you are not worth even that. I will leave now and discuss what will be done with you with higher command. In the meantime I have instructed your commander to be ruthless, and any woman or child who steps out of line will be disposed of immediately."

With his last words hanging in the air, Colonel Tsuji and his entourage left Kampong Punkit and Rachel shivered and clutched at her stomach.

Chapter Seventy-Four

Colin decided that perhaps it was time to reflect.

His experiences to date since he took off from Kuching airport had, to say the least, been amazing, often frightening and thought provoking.

When he was at Sammy's controls he always felt indestructible as the adrenaline rushed through his entire body.

After taking off on that day and as he rose through the clouds he felt as though he was in a different world. The blue sky above, the glimpses of sea or land many thousands of feet below were a reminder of just how surreal the experience of flying could be.

Every now and again he would lower his altitude and identify a coastline, an island or a river estuary, but quite often flying over the jungle was like flying over the sea; it was difficult to identify one area from another.

He used triangulation to check his position but the operators at the airfields were not always accurate enough with their bearings, and therefore quite often he was more dependent on his own visual knowledge rather than a given bearing to follow to a selected airfield. There were few other aircraft in the sky, but when appropriate he sometimes followed another aircraft, the pilot of which seemed to know where he was going.

Then came that never to be forgotten day when he had lost Sammy and almost his life.

After taking off from Kuching he headed north out over the sea, and for a good hour he wondered what all the fuss was about. In retrospect he could not have chosen a worse direction.

He saw them after they must have spotted him.

Three fighter aircraft – which he later identified as the Mitsubishi A6M Zeroes – decided to use him as target practice. He flung Sammy into a steep dive, but as the ground raced towards him he knew he was never going to out manoeuvre the fighters. He was in a lumbering Dakota whereas they were in planes designed for aerial combat.

By looking at the coastline, he could see he wasn't far from Miri, so he dropped to a couple of hundred feet and skimmed the jungle canopy hoping that he would make the airfield there before anything serious happened. Once on the ground, he would have to head for immediate cover because they would certainly manoeuvre so they could strafe him.

The Zeroes continued to play with him for a while, skimming across his nose so close that he could see the pilots clearly, but after a while they seemed to get tired of the game and he guessed they drew verbal lots as to who should administer the *coup de grace*.

He was only one hundred feet off the ground when he felt Sammy's body shudder as the cannon shells penetrated her skin, then her port engine caught fire. He was low but the airfield was close. Maybe he could hang on. The controls were shaking but she was doing her best to stay alive. Suddenly the other engine was also on fire. He glided in over the trees and crash landed on the airfield which much to his horror was already the home for more Japanese aircraft.

Fortunately, the direction in which he crash landed meant he was by the far perimeter. With a crunch and the tearing of metal Sammy came to a grinding halt where she took her final breath, her back was broken. Flames were everywhere and as he scrambled out of the cockpit he hardly had time to say goodbye.

Abas and Babu had saved his life. And now he was living among some of the most incredible people he had ever met. He wondered if his immediate and longer term future was really with them or was it still to be decided.

Chapter Seventy-Five

Much to Rachel's surprise the next four months passed almost without incident.

After Captain Yamamoto's early threats, the arrival of the nuns from the Order of Mercy seemed to bring with them the unexpected. Further surprise came when the food improved slightly – although it never reached above a basic level of subsistence – medicines appeared and the locals quite openly helped the internees in any way they could.

It was not what Rachel or any of the others expected.

The little old man who had brought the rakes and hoes to Rachel on her first trip to the farm, often came into the camp. She saw Sergeant Suratomono scowling at him whenever he was there, but Captain Yamamoto's orders were there for a reason – and for everyone to follow

After discussion between Rachel, Marjory and Sister Marie, the women and children showed respect towards their guards. Rachel was not as eager as the others were but whenever she felt the baby move, she appreciated the wisdom of the decision. Marjory had told her that Alicia Newton's methods of self-preservation were over! Having discovered the truth behind the liaison with the Japanese guard, Marjory Field dealt with the situation swiftly. The guard disappeared from the camp within an hour of it being reported and it was explained to Alicia Newton – in Rachel's presence because she was Alicia's hut leader – what was expected of her but more importantly, what would happen to her if she did not meet with expectations.

A more formal committee was formed, and Rachel and the other hut leaders plus Marjory and Sister Marie met regularly to discuss the way forward. The Order of Mercy nuns took over the education of the children, and caring for those that fell ill. Sister Marie accepted Marjory Field's overall authority, but with this acceptance there was an understanding that Sister Marie had far more influence over Captain Yamamoto, who seemed, now, quite happy to sit out the war in the internment camp.

At the morning and evening parades when head counts were conducted, Rachel thought he often seemed reluctant to tell them how the war was going in Japan's favour, especially when he reported that it wouldn't be long before the Imperial Japanese Forces invaded New Zealand followed by Australia.

Rachel did not believe that would ever happen.

Lieutenant Sato, who had always shown consideration towards the women and children, was more than willing to fall in line with the softness of Captain Yamamoto's new and more acceptable regime. Even Sergeant Suratomono mellowed – a little – and the other soldiers seemed to take their lead from him rather than their two officers.

Rachel's stomach grew, and as it grew the soldiers kept well away from her. The other women continued to fuss over her and Sister Angelique was always there acting like a mother hen. Whether Rachel liked it or not, extra rations nourished her and the baby.

She was told repeatedly that she and her unborn infant were symbols for the future, he or she represented hope.

When Rachel reflected on Colonel Tsuji's visit and his accompanying threats, she decided her fears had been unfounded. If anything the reverse applied – his visit seemed to be the turning point for all of them.

There were even times when she lay down on her sleeping mat at night, and as she tried to get comfortable, she smiled.

Perhaps there was a little light at the end of what used to be a dark tunnel.

Maybe everything would turn out all right in the end.

Chapter Seventy-Six

At first, Colin could only see the cruelty that surrounded the sport of cock fighting, not understanding why such a hospitable people could gain enjoyment out of this blood sport. However, as the weeks and months passed, he began to appreciate why it was such a sport.

All the white cocks fought at certain times of the day and speckled cocks at other times. These traditions went back hundreds of years and passed from generation to generation: evidently, to break such a tradition would bring years of bad luck on the wrongdoers. Abas did admit that he did not fully understand why cockfighting was still the sport it was, following his admission was a shrug and the words 'bad luck is bad luck'.

Adam also learnt about the tradition of diving competitions still used as courts of law to settle disputes. This tradition, surrounded in spiritual beliefs, went back many hundreds of years.

Abas explained.

"If it is not obvious where the fault lies in a dispute, the accused and the appellant dive under water and the one who holds his breath for the longer time is deemed to be innocent."

Colin would admit that as Abas told him about this tradition, he did do it with a smile although he didn't understand what Colin meant by the expression *tongue in cheek*. It was uncomplicated, far from fair, but nonetheless accepted by participants and onlookers. Colin wished that such methods existed in his real world.

When he asked Abas about the fairness of such an activity, Abas had looked at him in contrived amazement. "But Coy-lyn," he said, "surely the Gods are more powerful than any man who might sit in judgement?"

As there were few disputes, and those that did happen were minor, Colin accepted Abas's logic without further question He did hope though that nothing he did ever warranted him having to hold his breath underwater.

Colin and Fung went by prau with Anak and Abas to meet the headmen and their followers in other longhouses. He was not surprised to discover that word had already reached these groups that Anak was host to strangers. Although eyed suspiciously by some, the other headmen they met mirrored Anak's initial welcome.

159

As nothing had occurred that suggested the Japanese were aware of Colin's and Fung's presence, Anak seemed proud to introduce his semi-permanent guests. But Colin's concern was well intentioned – by becoming the talking point in so many other longhouses, the Japanese would definitely be alerted to their presence and come looking. They were assured this would not be the case and as the months passed their concern began to fade also.

Colin was pleased when he and Fung became good friends and they spent many hours talking. He noticed that Chao took longer to settle but she too had now become part of the longhouse, she had even introduced the other women to the many and varied ways in which the Chinese cooked rice! The children adapted more easily, picking up the language, learning the Iban children's games and under the guidance of their mother, continued their schooling. Chao also taught English to many of the Iban children and adults, who in turn took great delight in practising their new skills on Colin.

Almost the only person who remained withdrawn was Aslah. To his regret, there had been no progress in mending their relationship. She went about her daily chores without complaint, but she did not join in with the story telling, the dancing and the general merriment. She was always there, but in the background.

Colin's determination had achieved little, but it was not for the want of trying.

.

Chapter Seventy-Seven

It happened overnight.

Marjory remembered waking up at some stage wondering what all the noise was, but she must have gone back to sleep thinking that she was having a bad dream or even a nightmare. It was Sister Marie who hurried into the hut just after daybreak and roused Marjory to tell her what she believed had happened..

"Mrs Field," Sister Marie said, as she knelt down by Marjory's sleeping mat. "I think I must prepare you for a bit of a shock."

"The war is over," Marjory said, her eyes still feeling full of sleep.

She really liked Sister Marie and had tried to make her relax but without success. She lifted herself up on her elbows and tried to focus. Since the positive changes Yamamoto had introduced to the camp, she found she slept a lot better, sometimes going the whole night without waking up.

"No, I'm afraid it is quite serious." Sister Marie paused as she looked around at the others in the hut. "Captain Yamamoto and Lieutenant Sato have gone, or should I say they have been removed. The *Kempeitei* came during the night to take them away. They have been replaced by a Captain by the name of Oshida and if my informant is correct, he comes with a reputation."

Marjory looked confused but what she heard began to sink in.

"You mean that somebody objected to the way Yamamoto was running this camp and they've replaced him?"

"Yes, Mrs Field, I believe Colonel Tsuji is behind this so that is exactly what I am saying and I don't think it is going to be a change for the better. Tsuji's visit may have been four months ago, and we'd almost forgotten about it, but –"

"But why?" Marjory said, lifting herself off the mat. "Captain Yamamoto, thanks to you and his experiences in China, had as happy a camp as was possible under the circumstances. Tsuji was here for just over two hours. Why on Earth did he want to change anything? We weren't giving any trouble."

"That I don't know, Mrs Field, but I must ask you to warn the ladies that this new man has the reputation of being ruthless."

"Captain Yamamoto tried …"

"I understand and yes, we have been lucky for the past few months but I am afraid for all of us now," Sister Marie said.

"How do you know this, Sister?"

"One of the soldiers converted to Catholicism four years ago and he has been coming to me in secret."

"And he came to you this morning."

"Yes, and he is scared for himself as well as us. He said that Captain Oshida hates all Europeans. He is known for his sadistic nature."

"Thank you, Sister, I must warn the others."

"My Sisters are in the other huts as we speak, telling the others what has happened. I hope you don't mind –

"Of course I don't mind," Marjory told her.

"What ... what's going on?" Rachel asked as she rolled over on her sleeping mat.

"I think the party may have just come to an end," Marjory said.

"What –?" Rachel started to say but a lot of shouting and banging outside the hut cut her off.

Chapter Seventy-Eight

When Abas and Babu, who appeared inseparable, gave Colin the status of elder brother his delight was obvious. It was the highest honour they could pay him. Such an invitation was unprecedented and he knew it would become the foundation for a long-term bond between the three of them.

Over the weeks, they taught him all they knew and were just as keen to learn from him. Abas reminded Colin at least once a week about his promise to take him high up in the sky in a plane: Babu then made sure Colin extended the promise to him.

Sitting close to the muddy slipway they used to launch the still hidden praus, Abas suddenly asked Colin whether he had a wife in the white man's world. The question was justified but why ask it now?

As he cast the line from a makeshift fishing rod, it gave him a few seconds to think about how he should answer the question. He knew both Abas and Babu were going regularly to another longhouse upriver to see prospective wives. They went at night but always returned before daylight the next day.

Watching the float bobbing in the water, he said, "No, not a wife." It was an honest answer to the question.

As he spoke, Rachel's smiling face was there in his mind as it had been so many times every day since he had last seen her. He longed for her: every night. As he lay beneath the mosquito net he imagined her moving it to one side as she joined him. Nearly every morning he would wake early and his longing was so intense it was painful.

"But I do have a girlfriend," he said, "she is, or should I say was in Kuching. Where she is now, I have no idea."

Colin saw Babu nudge his brother, egging him on.

"This girl, will you marry her?" Abas asked, moving his fishing rod slowly so the float was over some bubbles rising from the rocks.

"Maybe one day," Colin said automatically.

He and Rachel had never really discussed marriage but faced with a direct question he realised that perhaps he had always believed that one day they would get married. He often pondered the same question once he and Sammy settled on a course for their next destination.

163

Him a married man, a father?

He had a lot of settling down to do before anything like that happened.

"It is many months since you saw her," Abas said, stealing a glance at Colin. "You must be in need of a woman."

Colin found it difficult not to react to Abas's directness, but he knew he was being goaded, although light-heartedly. Regardless of his longing for Rachel he had coped. He did not want the thoughts to go away, but he had tried to put all his energy into learning what his new family wanted to teach him.

"Our sister wants to lie with you," Abas said suddenly and rather bluntly.

Colin felt his face flush and he hoped the darkness of his skin hid his confusion. What did Abas mean by *our sister wants to lie with you*? Such a statement could have so many nuances. He did not know what to say.

"Before you came, she was being courted by Tanak but she is no longer."

Babu now assumed the initiative.

"But Tanak was not right for her," he said.

At that moment, Colin felt the rod wrenched from his grip as the shadow of a large fish fought against the hook in its mouth.

Chapter Seventy-Nine

Holding her stomach, Rachel could feel her unborn child kicking.

She moved her fingertips all over her abdomen not believing that what she was feeling was a human being. It was one of the most amazing of sensations.

It had been an uncomfortable night.

Sister Angelique, who gave her spare time to Rachel and she in turn was appreciative of the attention, had told her that the baby, who was still two months away from being born, was going to be about six or seven pounds in weight. Rachel had no idea how she could tell that. She would not be scared when the time came, she was too much the centre of attention to let the others down, but she was apprehensive.

Now she stood with the others in the heat and humidity – it was a Sunday so it was their day off – waiting for the new camp commander to appear on the veranda. She had been told that Captain Yamamoto and Lieutenant Sato had gone but she, and many of the others, had not really taken on board the significance of why they had gone although she was warned that whoever the new commander was, he was by reputation, ruthless.

"Are you all right?" Mary Prentice asked next to her.

"Yes," Rachel lied, "I'm just tired and a little uncomfortable. The baby's using my stomach as a football."

"Hopefully we won't be kept waiting much longer," Mary said.

A few minutes later their wait was over.

He was short, plump, his *kepi* seemed about two sizes too big for him and he was wearing the predictable glasses that made his eyes look twice their normal size. The neatly trimmed black moustache merely added to the threatening expression on his face.

He looked the picture of evil.

Hooking his fingers into his belt – a trait that all Japanese officers seemed to adopt – he surveyed the group of women and children standing before him. Except for the odd birdcall from the trees outside the camp, and the flies buzzing round the women's heads, there was complete silence. All eyes, including the guards, were on their new commander.

"Women, my name is Captain Oshida," he shouted. "I have little

165

to say. Captain Yamamoto and Lieutenant Sato have been removed from post and will be dealt with."

Although Captain Oshida's accent was a lot more pronounced than his predecessor's, his English was precise and spoken with authority. Rachel thought that his use of the words *dealt with* was not only ominous for Captain Yamamoto and Lieutenant Sato but also, and more importantly, for them too.

"This is not a holiday camp," Captain Oshida said. "You are all enemies of Japan and the children are the spawn our enemies."

Rachel remembered where she had heard those exact words before.

"Our countries are at war and while this state exists you will be treated as prisoners because that is what you are. As prisoners you have no entitlements other than what I am prepared to give you. I am here because I am recovering from an injury inflicted by the English. My aim is to return to fight for my country as soon as possible, none of you is going to prevent that from happening. If you disobey an order from one of my soldiers or me you will be punished, persistent disobedience will be dealt with severely. There will be no fraternisation between you and my soldiers. Obey me and you may survive to serve Japan after the war, but if you disobey me you will be severely punished."

Rachel wondered why all these little men had to threaten them with severe punishment if disobeyed, were they all lacking in something, somewhere?

Chapter Eighty

Colin had no real idea what day it was but he guessed it was Sunday.

All the days were the same: the Iban rested when they needed a rest, not in accordance with a programme. Away from the river the heat and humidity were stifling, everyone seemed to be in the shade and little work was being done.

As he walked back from the river carrying the fish he had caught, Colin wondered why Abas and Babu had been so open about their sister and her needs. He did not intend to discredit his close relationship with Anak, and although there had been only a few passing words with Aslah's mother, Ramlah, he liked her and she seemed to like him.

On occasions, it was obvious to him that Ramlah made many of the decisions Anak presented to the council. Colin often smiled when he thought of the similarity to the world he had temporarily left behind.

Now, Abas' question had created a predicament. Colin felt he had coped so far so he wanted to carry on coping, but that was before temptation had been put in his way.

Of course, he sometimes thought of Aslah in that way but …

Fung and Chao were given the *bilik* next to his, and there had been times when little was left to his imagination. Initially he was aware that Anak's other guests were sneaking off into to the jungle to be alone, but they became more confident and conscious of the fact that their need for each other was no different to the others in the longhouse. It was an expected and accepted way of life. He also assumed that the jungle presented quite a few hindrances for a couple who wished to have privacy. Leeches did not seem to mind what sort of animal they were attached to and what part of the anatomy was considered a fair target. And while making love, the thought that a cobra might be only a few feet away and preparing to spit its venom, could be quite the opposite to an aphrodisiac.

"You are quiet," Abas observed, walking beside Colin.

Babu had dropped back a few paces.

"I am sorry," Colin said, "but I think this heat is making us all tired and less responsive."

Abas put a hand on Colin's arm and they stopped. He looked up

167

and smiled.

"Coy-lyn, I asked you if you had a woman because Aslah is unhappy. From the time she nursed you back to good health she has wanted to lie with you. She has told our mother that she wants no other. She wants only you. You can see the way she is: she performs her duties but nothing else. She walks about as though she is with the living dead. If she were not young and strong she would be ill by now."

"And your father and mother, what do they think?" Colin asked. His mind was racing and his imagination was conjuring up images of him *lying* with Aslah as Abas put it.

"At first they would not accept how Aslah feels, but now they want to help their daughter be happy again. They are willing to give their daughter, my sister, to you so that she can be happy again."

"So did Anak put you up to this?" Colin asked, his eyes narrowing as he sensed complicity.

Abas smiled. "Yes, Coy-lyn, my father is offering you his only daughter. He will do so officially if he knows you will accept."

"And if I don't?" He wanted to know what *officially* meant but dare not ask.

"Aslah will leave her family and live in another longhouse. She cannot stay here but she does not want you to leave," Abas said.

Chapter Eighty-One

Marjory Field called together the hut leaders and Sister Marie – the council.

She thought that Rachel looked exhausted and decided to suggest afterwards that she relinquish the responsibility of her hut and concentrate on getting through the next couple of months without further mishap. She smiled as she looked at Rachel's tired face: she would also have to remind her that the baby she was carrying belonged to all of them.

"Ladies," Marjory started by saying. "You will have drawn the same conclusion as I have, we are under a new regime and Captain Oshida is going to be different to Captain Yamamoto." She turned to Sister Marie. "Sister, I presume your access to Captain Oshida will not be the same as it was with Captain Yamamoto?"

"No, Mrs Field, regrettably I will have little if any influence over this new man. I have already warned the other sisters that we must expect some changes to our daily routine."

"We must expect everything to change," Marjory said, "and if we are able to retain some of what we already have that will be a bonus."

"We must be totally compliant," Rachel suggested. "If we give no cause for criticism maybe we can keep some of what we have."

"I sincerely hope ..." Marjory faltered as she heard a lot of shouting coming from the entrance to the camp.

She went with the other women to the side of the hut so that she could get a better look at what the fuss was all about.

To her amazement and great concern, the old man who had originally brought the tools to the farm, and had been responsible for organising the medicines and extra food for the camp, was between two guards who were pushing him towards the hut the Japanese used as their headquarters.

The guards forced the man, whose name they had never learned, to his knees, with his hands tied behind his back.

After a few minutes Captain Oshida appeared.

He stood on the veranda looking down at the old man.

Marjory could see that all the women in the other huts had gathered so that they could see what was unfolding. She wondered if this was exactly what Oshida wanted – her stomach churned as she hoped what she thought was going happen, didn't.

The guards had also stopped what they were doing and were watching.

Slowly Captain Oshida stepped from the veranda. He walked across to the small group and motioned for the soldiers to move away.

The little Chinese man was still on his knees his head bowed.

He looked so pathetic: he was small-framed and he was not carrying an ounce of fat. His backbone and ribs were prominent. The soles of his feet and the palms of his hands were shades lighter than the rest of him. Once Captain Yamamoto had allowed the local villagers to help in any way they could, this man had been the stalwart behind many improvements in the camp. Marjory thought he was now going to be punished for being so kind – how many lashes was he going to be able to withstand?

Captain Oshida moved closer to the Chinese man who was now visibly shaking. Almost in one movement, Captain Oshida slowly withdrew his *samurai* sword from its scabbard, the movement made a rasping sound. He raised the sword into the air and the blade swished as he brought it down onto the back of the old man's neck.

There was complete silence.

Chapter Eighty-Two

"*Ngayap* is an Iban tradition, Coy-lyn. It is a way for a man and a woman to discover whether they are ready for marriage," Abas said. "That is where Babu and I go at night sometimes: there are two girls in a longhouse about five miles from here that we are courting."

Still reeling from the speed with which things had happened, Colin was only half listening to Abas. Anak was all smiles when Colin told him that he did find his daughter attractive, his smile broadened even further when Colin went on to say that he was highly honoured to be considered a possible suitor but ... He chose his words carefully because he did not want to offend his benefactor. He thought that if he tried to explain that although he found Aslah attractive and desirable, he did not think taking the relationship any further was to anyone's advantage and especially not Aslah's.

Unfortunately, his words were either wrong or misinterpreted. He saw from Anak's expression that he assumed Colin wanted Aslah as much as she wanted him ... he did but ... He tried to extricate himself from a situation that was quickly becoming set in stone.

"But, Anak, my friend, Aslah must also want this to happen," Colin said.

"Coy-lyn, my daughter wants nothing else. She is the one who thought you would not want her.

With those few words assumptions suddenly became reality.

The atmosphere in the longhouse changed almost instantaneously.

There was a wedding to arrange.

By the time he realised what was happening, Colin was already being swept along at an incredible speed. Eventually it reached the point where he felt he would offend everyone in the longhouse if he did not go through with it.

He would not see Aslah before the big day, which was a surprise. She would go to another longhouse to prepare. There would be no *ngayap* – a word he had heard before but never fully understood its meaning.

"With *ngayap*, you spend many hours travelling to and from the girl's longhouse," Abas told him as they sat together on the riverbank. "It is in the hope that her parents will be asleep when you get there. You spend a long time talking, and the girl must

171

traditionally spurn your advances but if she likes you things move on. Some parents block the entrances to their *bilik* so that boys cannot get in: others, who like the boy and want their daughter to marry, pretend to be asleep so that the boy is not frightened away. There is a lot more to *ngayap* than that, Coy-lyn, but for you some traditions are unnecessary."

Colin and Abas often went down to the river to talk or fish or both. It was cooler and it meant that they could watch out for the Japanese. It also allowed their close relationship to grow.

There had been no further sign of the invaders.

Other prau*s* from distant longhouses called in regularly, going both down and up river. The visitors enjoyed the usual hospitality. There were reports of incidents in Miri and other towns, but generally, life on the river did not change. When men from Anak's longhouse returned from Miri after getting supplies, they too had little to report.

"Word will be sent and there will be a great gathering," Abas said excitedly. "When people hear that an orang puteh is to marry an Iban girl, everyone will want to be here."

Colin nodded. He still was not sure where in the mêlée of his mind he recalled agreeing to marry Aslah.

He thought he had agreed to wanting her, but not to marriage.

What could he do?

Chapter Eighty-Three

There was complete silence that only added to the absolute horror of what she had witnessed.

Some of the women next to her lifted their hands to their mouths and whispered, "Oh, my God!" while others turned away automatically with unbelievable shock. Mothers bent down to reassure their children but not sure what reassurance they could give.

It had happened so quickly.

In less than thirty seconds, Captain Oshida had left the veranda, drawn his *samurai* sword and beheaded the man who had been so kind to her and to all the others. Understanding their needs had cost the little man his life. As Rachel's bump grew bigger, he used to stand with her for a few minutes and regale her with stories of the births of his many children and grand children. He had been so true to his word and he – or somebody else – had left medicine, drugs and some food by the fence up near the women's latrines – mainly because the guards hated going anywhere near there – but as Captain Yamamoto had mellowed the man had openly delivered what he could directly to the women.

Now, the old man's blood was soaking into the ground with his head lying a few feet from his body. Rachel could not take her eyes off the scene. She wanted to turn away and be sick but she became transfixed by what she saw.

Captain Oshida was on his veranda: he looked at the women and children crowding the front of the huts and smiled. "Women," he shouted. "Let that be a lesson to you all. He was an enemy of Japan and that is how I deal with our enemies. His head will be put on a stake as a reminder to you all that I will not tolerate such behaviour."

After a few seconds to let his words have the right effect Captain Oshida turned, snapped out an order in Japanese and then disappeared back into his hut.

Rachel watched as the guards dragged the Chinese man's body away. Her disgust increased as she then watched one guard drive the little man's head onto a stake. After pushing the stake into the ground by the gate, the guard walked away as though he had only pinned a notice on a board. It was an extremely gruesome sight, the man's eyes and mouth were open, and blood still dripped from the neck.

Rachel stared at the severed head, not believing that another human being could be so sadistic as to perform such an act. It was the second murder she had witnessed.

A few of the other women began turning away.

Others began to cry.

Regardless of what she thought, Rachel realised that Captain Oshida's demonstration of his brutality was having the desired effect. The women would not dare defy any order from him or any of his soldiers. They would obey automatically.

Rachel went over to Marjory Field and it was obvious she didn't know what to say.

"At the meeting," she finally said in a whisper, "I was going to suggest that we tested Captain Oshida. I was going to say we shouldn't be openly defiant but the odd minor transgression would see how different he really was to Captain Yamamoto … but now I know what he is like. The man is a monster."

"Marjory, I think –" Rachel started to say.

"I am now so worried," Marjory said. "I am worried for the women and children. I am not sure I want the responsibility anymore."

At that moment, Sister Marie joined them.

"May I speak with you?" Sister Marie asked at Marjory's shoulder.

"Of course," Marjory told her, her voice catching. "But …"

"Don't," Rachel said. "Not yet, there is nobody else."

Chapter Eighty-Four

Swept along with the preparations, Colin was still in a trance when on the evening before he and Aslah were to be married his trusted friend and brother, Abas, took him to their place by the river to tell him what he could expect the following day.

"Tomorrow," Abas said, "is your *ngambi indu*, your wedding day. You have seen the *tuak*, chicken, pork, wild palm cabbage, fish, wild boar and rice being prepared: it will be a grand feast.

"As you have no relatives to invite, my father has asked the headman and his family from the next longhouse – the one where the girls Babu and I are courting live – to represent you. The family will be arriving later this morning to help with the preparations.

"A slight break in tradition means that Aslah will be arriving by prau. As she arrives, there will be others boats with musicians, drums and gongs. Before we converted to Christianity you would not have seen Aslah until after the wedding, can you believe that?"

Abas's enthusiasm was contagious and Colin could not help but smile although his head was in a total spin.

"What happens now?" he asked.

"After Aslah has arrived, you, the headman from the other longhouse and other men will stage a mock battle with us as we will be protecting the bride. It is nothing to worry about, just more tradition. When we see that you have come as friends, you will be asked if you have brought any bad omens with you. We will drink *tuak* and toast the spirits. There will be formal introductions, and much more drinking of *tuak*."

"We will all be very drunk very quickly," Colin suggested.

"Sometimes that is a good omen but you will be kept away, this part is only for those chosen to represent your family," Abas replied smiling. "The visiting procession will go three times round the longhouse and afterwards they will sit on the decorated area of the *ruai*. Then there is much talking, exchanging of stories, much eating and more drinking. The wedding ceremony proper does not take place until dusk.

"You and Aslah, who will have arrived but kept hidden from you to this point, will sit on a large gong called a *Ketawak*. A rooster will be waved above your heads and the marriage ceremony will begin

175

but because you are an orang puteh it will be shorter than our traditions should allow. It has been decided that you and Aslah can sit together during the ceremony, which is a big break in tradition."

"And then?" Colin felt nervous.

"Again, normally you and Aslah would be kept apart for maybe two or three nights so that the bride's modesty is maintained, as would be expected, but for you an exception is being made."

"I rather wish many more exceptions could be made," Colin said but added: "I mean you are all being so kind."

"You have made my sister, your wife to be, very happy, Coylyn."

Colin thought for a moment.

There was no way he could back out now. Half his mind was letting him imagine what would happen later with Aslah, the other half was wondering whether he had made the biggest mistake of his life. "And I am happy that she is happy," he said.

"She will bear you many children," Abas told him.

"That's good," Colin said.

"And I know you will enjoy making those children," Abas said with a glint in his eye. "My sister will be good for you."

Chapter Eighty-Five

"My Sisters are available to anyone," Sister Marie said, "especially the children, after that demonstration of utter barbarism. If he were to be called an animal it would be a gross insult to any other species. He is sub-human and one day he will pay for his atrocities."

Marjory nodded but kept an eye on the movement of the guards. Something else was happening and she had yet to determine what it was.

"We must do nothing to provoke him or it could be one of us next," Marjory said.

"That is what I wish to speak about," Sister Marie said. "I do not think some of the women are going to be able to cope. They are weak anyway through lack of the right food but now with the prospect of things worsening, we have to be especially vigilant and not only of the Japanese."

"What do you suggest?" Marjory asked.

"I wondered whether we have the right mix of women in the huts. For a start my sisters and I are segregated, I think we should be more integrated. We need an even balance of the strong with the weak, the capable with the forlorn."

"Will Oshida allow it? We mustn't make him suspicious," Marjory asked.

"We are so few the roll call is always as a total. We do not parade by huts. If we do it carefully he would be none the wiser," Sister Marie said.

"I'm not so sure."

"Mrs Field, other than evil, we don't know what we are dealing with. I think we must reorganise so that we use our strengths and protect our weaknesses. How would we feel if one of the women were to be decapitated in front of us all, or even, may God preserve us, one of the children."

Such a picture made Marjory screw up her eyes. "He wouldn't," she said.

"That man he killed was not an enemy of Japan or anybody else. His mistake was that he was a good man with a good heart. He was murdered for no other reason than for Oshida to demonstrate his brutality and dominance."

"But to a woman or child? Surely not even he …"

"Do you want to put it to the test, Mrs Field?" Sister Marie asked.

"No of course not."

"Then we must build our own defences."

"I will get the hut leaders together," Marjory said with some relief. She took a deep breath and thought of her earlier misgivings about being able to cope. In Sister Marie, Marjory believed she had at least found the person who would take the responsibility she no longer wanted.

But she would make the change slowly and delicately – she would begin doing as she was told but make it look as though what it was would be her decision. Sister Marie would know what was happening, but nobody else would.

As Marjory crossed the open space between the huts, averting her eyes from Oshida's monstrous symbol of obedience, a lorry pulled up by the front gate and about twenty soldiers jumped from the back.

They were different, their uniforms and their stature were different.

Even in the heat, Marjory felt herself shiver.

She stopped in the middle of the 'parade square' and watched these new soldiers form a line as Sergeant Suratomono approached them.

She realised the gates of hell were opening in front her.

Chapter Eighty-Six

With his head still reeling from the ceremony and the *tuak*, Colin looked down at Aslah's readiness for him. She too had seemed totally mesmerised by the entire ceremony: they had both been picked up in the fast moving current of misunderstandings and enacted what by tradition needed to accompany the confusion.

It was as though they had both gone out into the middle of the river in a prau, thrown themselves out of the boat into the treacherous current and been swept downriver out of control.

But In all other ways the ceremony had been amazing.

The Iban music was bewitching, the food magnificent, the men and women's ceremonial dress wonderful, the dancing expressive, the hospitality enormous: but surpassing all other unbelievably magical sights and happenings was Aslah herself.

As she was brought to him on the central *ruai* he felt his heart stop beating, his legs turned to jelly and if the *tuak* had not already taken affect he would have been thoroughly intoxicated by her sheer beauty. The silkiness of her sarong, the beads, the feathered headdress, and the decoration on her face and limbs, made her look like a goddess. Desire immediately replaced his earlier concern.

Wearing nothing but a coloured sarong, a necklace made of shells and bones, Colin felt naked beside her. As she sat next to him on the large gong, her bare arm touched his and he felt an electric shock run through his entire body. Suddenly it felt as though what was happening was meant to be from the moment he arrived at the longhouse.

She did not look at him.

Her attention was on her father, the witch doctor and the master of ceremonies.

After speeches by Anak and Kedorah, the headman chosen to represent Colin, and more entertainment, they were married.

Ramlah, Aslah's mother, and two other women had escorted Aslah through the guests to Colin's *bilik*. An hour and many more cups of *tuak* later, Colin was told his bride was expecting him and he could go to her. This he did, swaying under the influence of the *tuak*: his obvious drunkenness causing much laughter.

There was a single candle burning on the floor. The light from the

179

candle was behind Aslah, its radiance enhancing the air of mystery and expectation.

She was uncovered and her naked body glowed in the dim light from the candle.

As Colin slipped the sarong from around his waist, his anticipation was evident. He moved the netting to one side and Aslah was looking into his eyes properly for the first time since he had rebuffed her those many months ago.

Her smile was mesmeric.

Now, with the beads, sarong and headdress discarded, she still looked magnificent.

The candlelight flickered against her skin. Her radiant smile was an invitation as she breathed steadily in anticipation. He had seen her naked before, she had held her body against his when he had the fever, he had imagined what they were about to do so many times, but nothing that went before could have told him how he now felt.

He was looking at his wife, but suddenly the most vivid image of Rachel appeared and he closed his eyes as he tried to dissolve the image.

In reality, though, he did not want it to go away.

What had he done?

He should have stopped the ceremony before it started.

Chapter Eighty-Seven

The pain was agonizingly intense and her scream that went with it must have pierced the minds of everyone who heard it.

Rachel had been determined not to make a noise but she had little choice, she had to expel the torture that engulfed her body and mind in the only way she knew. All thoughts of what had happened in the preceding months left her with that single, heart-rending scream.

On numerous occasions, her weakness, tiredness and fear had made her think that she would lose the baby. But Sister Angelique, who was also weak having only recovered from a bout of dysentery a matter of weeks before, continued to be the strength behind Rachel's determination. The previous three months had been terrible. The threats that Captain Oshida made had materialised in the only way they could: pure sadism. It wasn't a hatred for all Europeans, Chinese and Asian women that took up every minute of his time but also it was a loathing of anything that wasn't Japanese. The truck that Marjory had seen three months earlier had contained new guards but they were not Japanese, they were Korean, forced to serve in the Imperial Japanese Army. Rachel always marvelled at how Marjory got the information she passed on to everybody else.

But from what Rachel saw afterwards, Captain Oshida despised the Koreans as much as he did the women and in turn, she witnessed the soldiers taking the treatment they received from him out on the women and children. Sergeant Suratomono, who unwillingly mellowed under Captain Yamamoto's command, came into to his own with Captain Oshida. His sadism was in the same league. However, for some reason he seemed to steer well clear of Rachel. Was it because she was pregnant or did she have some form of misguided respect for her as she had been the first to be punished?

Rachel did witness two further public lashings, both European women from the hut nearest the main gate, and who had upset Oshida in the most minor of ways. One received a lashing because he did not like the way she walked – he thought it was provocative. Seeing Suratomono enjoying drawing blood on a frail woman's back made Rachel want to break out of the group forced to watch the punishment and physically attack the sergeant. It was despicable in her and all the other women's eyes but they knew if they showed the slightest dissension, they would be next. Both women were lucky to survive their punishment.

There was also another execution: this time one of the Koreans who had fallen asleep while on guard. Rachel only heard the shots but evidently the man was executed by firing squad in front of all the soldiers and their prisoners. However, even the execution paled into insignificance when compared with the abuse some of the women began to suffer.

"None of the younger women are safe," Marjory told her one night as she sat by her sleeping mat. "Carol Brown from Hut 2 attempted suicide when she was told to report to Oshida's quarters. Sister Marie found her after she had slashed her wrists. She pleaded with Oshida to spare Carol but to no avail. Surprisingly when Carol returned to her hut after going to Oshida she seemed to have changed.

"The women and children have become zombies, hardly making eye contact with each other let alone their guards. Many are falling ill with beriberi, dysentery and malaria. You are one of the lucky ones, Rachel."

The cry of a newborn baby was therefore a reawakening to the fact that life must go on.

Being born into the horrors of their world was not the baby's fault, but she was a new life and one that offered hope, a hope that they had thought was lost forever.

Chapter Eighty-Eight

With her head against Colin's shoulder Aslah murmured her delight at what she believed to be true. The past few months had been absolute bliss for her. When he first arrived and was so ill, she had seen the differences straight away. The way he looked at her, the way he treated her. His behaviour towards her was as though she was an equal.

From that first day, she remembered as the seeds of an idea implanted themselves in her mind.

When he later rejected her she was devastated. Even now when she had what she wanted she shuddered when she thought back to how close she had come to losing him.

She had to see him every day, watch him as he talked to her father, as he repaired the engines, as he went fishing with her brothers and as he worked in the padi – it had all been so unbearable. When the Chinese family arrived, she had another idea. She saw the way Fung treated Chao: how the children, Lim and Chee, were so much part of the family.

That is what she wanted and that is what she would have.

She would not give up.

It took a while and a lot of cunning, but once she had convinced her mother that it was the orang puteh she wanted, her mother worked on her father, her father on her brothers and all she had to do was mope around in the background looking unhappy.

And it worked.

She did not feel in the slightest bit that she had done anything wrong. If he had not wanted her, all he had to do was say so.

She would admit and thanks to her brothers, he had little time to think about it. Before she knew it she was sitting on the large gong with what she wanted by her side. Now she was so happy, especially because of what she believed was happening to her.

"Coy-lyn," she whispered, running her finger down his chest, "I think I am with child."

She could tell sleep had not taken him.

Dawn was breaking and it would soon be time to begin another day.

She was worried though. He had done everything in his power to

183

make her happy, and she had done the same for him, but she believed that he still had doubts as to whether he had done the right thing. After so many moons had been and gone, his inability to hide his true feelings from her was still evident.

Aslah knew she now provided him with all that he needed: she had made sure her attitude towards their physical relationship changed to that of an orang puteh woman. She learnt quickly that she could enjoy sex as much as he did. She was there for him but now he was also there for her. When she had told the other women about it, they had not believed her.

She cooked for him, washed his clothes, cleaned the fish he caught, kept their *bilik* tidy and clean, repaired the mosquito net, and she was there for him at night … every night. No wonder she felt the way she did. She knew that if he stayed in the jungle for the next ten years he could not want for more. But as she watched him close his eyes at night, she wondered if it would last. Her brother had told her that her Coy-lyn did have a woman in his orang puteh world and she worried that once the war was over … well, maybe not now, not if how she felt was telling her the truth.

"Did you hear me, Coy-lyn?"

"Yes I heard you Aslah and yes, I know," he said.

Aslah took his hand and laid it on her tummy. "And are you happy, my husband?" she asked.

"Yes," he said. "I'm happy."

"We will be a proper family soon," she said.

184

"It's a girl." Sister Angelique said weakly, holding the baby up so that Rachel could see her daughter.

Sister Angelique looked as exhausted as Rachel felt but they both momentarily forgot their despair and smiled as a pair of unfocused blue eyes looked about for what she most wanted, her mother and food.

"I hope to God …"

"Don't," Sister Angelique said. "Let us enjoy this moment as though the rest of the world does not exist. There will be plenty of time to return to reality." She handed Rachel her daughter. "Do you have a name for her?"

"I was so sure it was going to be a boy," Rachel said, the effort making her feel weaker. "May … may I name her after you?"

Sister Angelique smiled. "Of course you may, if you are sure."

"If it weren't for you neither she nor I would be here."

"There would have been others to help," Sister Angelique suggested doing her best to clean up. "It's a pity we cannot let your husband know that he has a daughter."

Rachel hadn't told Sister Angelique that she was not married.

"His name is Colin," Rachel said, "and he will know."

"Then perhaps we should now pray to God that you can be a family again one day."

"I have already," Rachel said. "And we will be."

"Can we come in?" Marjory asked at the entrance to the hut with Sister Marie at her shoulder.

"Of course," Rachel and Sister Angelique said in chorus.

"Please say hello to another Angelique," Rachel said weakly, holding her daughter up for the others to see.

"How marvellous," Marjory said. "The others are waiting to see."

"Not yet," Sister Angelique suggested. "She is weak and she could do with having a good rest."

"Of course," Marjory said.

Suddenly there was a commotion outside and Captain Oshida closely followed by Sergeant Suratomono barged their way into the hut.

The women, even Rachel who could only lift her head, bowed.

They kept their eyes on the floor so that they could not offend.

"A baby!" Captain Oshida shouted in mock glee.

"Yes sir," Sister Angelique said without lifting her head. "Mrs Lefévre has had a daughter."

Captain Oshida moved further into the hut and looked down at Rachel and her baby.

"You keep the baby quiet," he said menacingly. "If you do not it will have a short life, do you understand?"

"I understand, sir," Rachel said, back in the real world.

Oshida smiled again and left, but at the door Sergeant Suratomono stopped and drew one finger across his throat.

"Baby here, no good," he said. "Better dead."

Rachel felt the tears come to her eyes straight away.

Sister Angelique leant over her and took the baby from her arms. "Sleep," she said. "Ignore what those animals say."

"How can I?" Rachel said, her whole body shaking.

Chapter Ninety

Going to Miri for supplies, and to sell their own products continued but less frequently.

It was evident from the beginning that essentials were going to be in short supply. Anak's longhouse could be self-sufficient especially if they returned to some of their old ways. He was aware via other headmen and Iban who had settled in the town, that everything they used to buy was still available but at a cost.

Drugs were obtainable to combat malaria and to get these drugs the Iban still living upriver needed money. To get the money needed before the war to buy drugs, petrol and oil for the praus, paraffin for the lamps, mosquito nets and many other items, the women made among other things decorative hats, necklaces and earrings that they sold in local markets. However, since the Japanese invaded the markets for such non-essentials had disappeared and there really were no alternatives. Anak knew he had to sell rice, vegetables, fish and meat, but to do this he would have to cut back on what his own people consumed.

Therefore as the months passed the essentials became harder and harder to obtain. There was a black market but as with all black markets all over the world, commodities considered essential cost a lot more.

Anak was not happy with the way things were going and he was becoming increasingly worried. He chose to share his concerns with Colin and Fung.

They knew about the outside world so they must have a solution.

"The Japanese will be taking everything they need," Fung said reluctantly. "That is why this area was so important to them. They need the oil and other natural resources. They take the food, the medicines and everything else that we need for day-to-day living. The people in Miri and all over Sarawak will be surviving on what is left."

"But it is not theirs to take," Anak said rather innocently.

"Did your ancestors not take after a great victory?" Colin asked. "Taking what is not yours is often what war is all about. Where I come from they are called the profits or spoils of war."

"So what must I do? You and my people will suffer if we cannot

187

get what we need, what we have become dependent on."

"The obvious answer is to take back some of what has been stolen from you," Fung volunteered. "The black market thrives on what it can steal. If they can do it so can ordinary people. It is –"

"But," Colin said interrupting, his concern obvious. "There would always be a risk, a high risk. If the Japanese catch the thieves they will be severely punished, if not killed."

"Is that not a risk we have to take?" Anak asked. "The word from the other longhouses is that my people are becoming increasingly hostile, they do not like what is happening. I think we –"

A young Iban rushed onto the *ruai* and looked around until he spotted Anak.

He hurried over, out of breath.

"They come," he said. "They come again."

Colin, Fung and Anak exchanged looks.

A well-laid plan was put immediately into operation. Anak went to alert his people and Colin and Fung ran quickly to their *biliks* to collect a few essentials.

Because of what they had just been talking about, Anak thought it too much of a coincidence: this time the Japanese would not stay in the middle of the river, this time they had come to take and Anak was ready to stop them.

"Abas," he shouted, "we have visitors, get the men together."

Chapter Ninety-One

Everyone in the camp carried with them evidence of the brutality of Captain Oshida and his guards. Even the children had scars that came from being whipped by a thin piece of bamboo, a simple but effective device for causing immediate pain.

Others had grotesque bruises caused by rifle butts, kicks and punches.

Marjory Field despaired at what she saw because there was nothing she could do about it. Such physical injuries had to be endured on top of malnutrition, the diseases that went with subsistence living, flies and rats and the heat and humidity.

It had become a living hell.

She was aware of those who would have the mental scars, those that had been *selected* by Captain Oshida to provide entertainment for him. None of the women ever spoke about what happened when it was their turn, and none of the others who were lucky enough to escape his attentions – including Marjory who thanked God – ever asked those who were not so fortunate.

"He must be a masochist as well as a sadist," Marjory said to Sister Marie. "Even the younger women are skin and bones."

As she watched her people – that's how she regarded them now having decided not to shun her responsibilities – move around the camp she saw that most of the women and children were sick in one way or another, but some were worse than others.

She had dealt with Alicia Newton, the young woman who had flourished so well under the Captain Yamamoto regime, but she was now one of the sickest. She was one of the first to be summoned by Captain Oshida and she had been one of the first to fall ill with leptospirosis. One of the nuns told her that It was a disease that could be passed to humans when they came in contact with the urine from infected rats, and the camp at Kampong Punkit was now infested.

The women did all they could to kill the rats but even so, most survived.

Alicia Newton was ill, and Marjory believed that she could die from the disease. Regardless of the conditions under which they all lived, if Alicia did die she would be their first death and Marjory felt that she would be to blame.

The nuns had been magnificent but especially Sisters Angelique and Christa, the fully trained nurses. They worked day and night, only using the limited medical supplies when necessary. And of course Sister Marie was always there to give Marjory her fullest support and offer alternative suggestions.

Since the loss of the old man from the kampong, they relied on what they had previously hidden and the few pills and potions that Captain Oshida allowed to be passed to them. On a couple of occasions, and to Marjory's absolute amazement, Oshida had also allowed the distribution of some Red Cross parcels that had arrived weeks, even months, earlier. Marjory had known better than to ask for them. She insisted the children's schooling should continue, as should the work on the farm, but under Captain Oshida completion of the tasks was in the hope that some would survive, some would be alive to tell of the atrocities committed by him and his cohorts.

Sister Marie interrupted Marjory's reverie.

"Mrs Field, come quickly, it's Alicia Newton, I think she close to dying."

The despair Marjory immediately felt was indescribable.

She was about to lose one and now there would be more to follow.

As she stood over Alicia's sleeping mat, with Sister Marie saying a prayer next to her, she saw Alicia take her final breath.

Chapter Ninety-Two

Although Colin and Fung's family were only a matter of fifty yards away from the longhouse, Colin couldn't hear or see anything that might be going on down by the river They were well hidden and the pre-positioned water and food would keep them going for a couple of days if necessary.

Lim and Chee were nestled against their mother's shoulders and they looked terrified, their eyes like saucers as they tried to take in what was happening.

Fung put his hand on his wife's arm and squeezed.

Chao tried to smile in return but her state of mind was equally obvious. Colin thought she and the children had done so well since their enforced separation from normal life. Chao's English and Mandarin classes had grown as she had accepted some more children from other longhouses. There were adults too who wanted to learn something of the other languages. Word got round and her services were now well sought after.

However, this popularity worried him. Nothing could be done about word spreading, it was inevitable, but if it reached the wrong ears, Anak and his longhouse could find themselves in deep trouble. Colin had raised the subject on numerous occasions but had bowed to Anak's belief that after so long the Japanese were no longer interested in coming that far upriver.

Well, he wished now he had persevered.

As if reading their minds, Chao whispered her question: "Do you think it is because of me and my lessons?"

"It could be anything, any one of us," Fung told her. "We have all been to other longhouses."

"I have been out and repaired engines, generators, helped in the padi with Fung," Colin said. "Unless we joined in we would have gone mad, we had to do something, and anyway, we owed it to Anak."

"But why are they here? It has been so long since they were last here. Anak thought they never would come again."

Colin could not answer Chao's question. The Japanese would be well established in Miri and the other coastal towns, and maybe – hopefully – they were just being a little more adventurous. It could be because of Anak's guests but then again it could be …

"We know they have been to other longhouses nearer to Miri," Colin said. "All they seem to be doing is telling the Iban to become more self-sufficient and not to expect anything from them."

"And from my people," Fung added. "They want to suppress the influence of the Chinese."

"That's as maybe," Colin said, "but they haven't – as far as we know – brought trouble to the longhouses. They are probably just being a little more exploratory, they are spreading their direct area of influence. There is nothing to say we have ever been at the longhouse, Anak and the others won't let us down."

"I hope you are right," Chao said.

"When the Japanese leave, Anak and the others will wait to see if they go up or back down river. If they go downriver it will only be another hour or so before we can return, if they go upriver we will have to wait until they are seen coming back. We are safe here."

"Now the Japanese have come this far, we will not be safe anywhere," Chao said, hugging her children to her.

"Have faith," Fung said.

Chapter Ninety-Three

Whether it was because of little Angelique, Rachel had no idea but after she had recovered from the trauma of giving birth, especially in such horrific conditions, she expected to be summoned by Captain Oshida as so many of the younger women had already been summoned.

The summons had not come.

Rachel was so pleased she was no longer the leader of her hut.

She had, on Marjory's advice, asked to be relieved of her duties because of little Angelique. Marjory Field took the opportunity to suggest that there was a complete change round so that others could assume some responsibility rather than being dependent on the same people all the time. Because of Oshida, Rachel was not surprised when told that volunteers were not so forthcoming although eventually others succumbed to persuasion and took on the responsibility.

She started work on the farm again two weeks after giving birth because she felt so guilty about the way the other women pampered her. She was also amazed when Oshida had not ordered her back a lot earlier. On returning from the farm exhausted from another day's hard work, she went to Sister Angelique to collect her daughter.

Little Angelique was always a boost for Rachel's morale: she was living up to her name. She really was a little angel.

Of course she cried at times but only when she wanted feeding. As soon as she latched onto Rachel's breast, silence and contentment ensued. The lack of milk and its quality worried Rachel. Her breasts were wasting away and their usefulness was becoming less and less. She reluctantly allowed some extra rations to come her way and when on the farm she stole and ate whatever she could.

She tried to supplement little Angelique's diet with whatever she could lay her hands on, she would mash it down and add water.

Angelique seemed to thrive on a mixture of her mother's limited milk and the extras she was given. As Rachel looked down into her baby's eyes, she could see Colin. She knew that identifying likenesses in babies that young was more out of need than what she saw, but her little bundle was half Colin and she wanted to see a resemblance in Angelique.

Her eyes were big and blue, and her wispy hair was blonde.

That was all Rachel needed.

"Come on trouble," she said, "you must be starving."

Sister Angelique looked at the adoring mother.

"She is so good," she said. "Thank God she will never remember where she was born."

Rachel looked up. "You are presupposing that one day we will be free," she said forlornly.

"We must all pray and have hope," Sister Angelique commented. "We have no contact with the outside world so we have no way of knowing for sure, but I cannot believe that one day we will not be free to live our lives in peace."

"But will what's in store for … what if Japan wins the war?"

"We have heard whispers that the tide is turning and they are being defeated more and more," Sister Angelique said solicitously.

"If that is true," Rachel said, "and if we get through this, whatever else may be in store for us has to be better. I just pray this baby's father is safe."

"I'm sure he is," Sister Angelique said with a weak smile.

"Yes, and so am I."

Chapter Ninety-Four

Abas noted that the Lieutenant from the Imperial Japanese Navy and his father were of a similar height but the similarities stopped there. Whereas his father was in his sarong, wore a bead necklace and with the tattoos on his arms, legs and body prominent, the Lieutenant was wearing a mud-spattered but otherwise pristine white naval uniform, a pistol was holstered over his right hip and a curved samurai sword hung in its scabbard on the other side. He was small, young – probably in his late twenties – and he had a formal peaked hat on his head.

Abas thought the officer looked ridiculous.

His father stood proudly in front of this intruder, his blowpipe in his right hand and a parang at his hip. Abas tightened the grip on his blowpipe. The sharpness of the parang at his side would slice the man's head off with one blow, if necessary, and what a prize, he thought. If use of the parang were not suitable, the poison on the tip of the dart that was already placed in his blowpipe would guarantee a unpleasant death.

He could see that the Japanese officer was looking at his father and the others with disgust and utter disdain. Even early on Col-lyn and Chao had never treated his father as anything but an equal. No doubt this officer disliked having to associate with people he would consider to be natives, and he would regard how they lived as primitive.

Unlike the officer, Abas could see that his father was not letting his feelings show.

Abas moved forward slightly so he was at his father's shoulder. Babu took up post on the other side. Behind them were another six Iban warriors and hidden in the undergrowth but well within blowpipe distance, a further dozen men waited for Anak's sign to kill.

The Japanese Lieutenant looked straight at Abas who deliberately stared at him and tried not to blink. There was a slight movement of the officer's hand which suggested he might be reaching for his pistol but he seemed to change his mind. Looking over the officer's shoulder, Abas could see the sailors had their rifles at the ready and were waiting for a command. A couple of them were looking up towards the longhouse where the women were gathered. He could see in their eyes that they were trying to seek out the ones they would want. He hoped he was wrong but during a trip to Miri he had been told that the Japanese officers imported their women from Japan but the soldiers were reliant on local girls – Chinese, Malay and any others they took a fancy to.

"You speak English?" the officer suddenly said.

Abas knew his father would understand what the officer had said, in return for their guest's willingness to learn their language, his father had attended the classes run by Chao. He had difficulty with some of the pronunciations but he tried whenever he was in the mood.

Although his father understood, he just glared at the officer so Abas thought he ought to assume the role of interpreter: "I speak English so may I ask what we can do for you?" Abas said.

The Lieutenant seemed momentarily startled.

"You speak English?" he said, his disbelief apparent.

"Yes, I do and is there a reason why I shouldn't."

"No, no reason," the officer said, still flustered.

"Unless you speak Iban, I suggest we converse in English and I will translate for my father, the headman of this longhouse," Abas said, inwardly smiling.

"Yes, yes of course," the Japanese officer said, now looking more confused than flustered.

Chapter Ninety-Five

Rachel would not have called it complacency but she would admit that, and almost certainly because of little Angelique, she was in denial.

The summons came within thirty-six hours of her believing that she had escaped.

Arriving back from the farm, once again exhausted, she pampered her daughter as she carried her back to her hut.

It had been a particularly debilitating day.

The heat and the humidity when combined with the digging, weeding, and hoeing for hours on end, would have sapped the strength from the strongest.

Three women had collapsed and even the kicking and threats they received from the guards did not force them back to work. It was only the intervention of Sister Barbara, who accompanied them on their daily trek to and from the farm, which stopped the guards from beating the women to death.

Regardless of Sister Marie's wise belief that Captain Oshida and his regime regarded her and her sisters as no different to the other women whom he and they openly despised, some of the guards remained in awe of the women who represented a religion they did not understand.

Even when Carol Osborne – the new hut leader – told Rachel that Captain Oshida had said that she had to report to his quarters later that evening, Rachel heard everything but did not seem to react.

"You do realise what this means?" Carol Osborne asked her.

"I have no idea," Rachel responded. "None of the others have ever said."

"It's obvious isn't it?"

"Is it? Have you ever been?"

"No," Carol said, "but, surely, it can be for only one thing."

Rachel lifted little Angelique to her breast. Of course she knew what was going to happen. She was not stupid. How such a man who obviously hated anything or anybody who was not Japanese could bring himself to touch let alone rape – because that is what it would be – an English woman was beyond her. It would be rape because she would not want it to be happening, but she did not intend to try to fight him because she had Angelique to think about. She would lie still and pray it would be over as quickly as possible. She had little choice.

"Don't you find it rather strange," Carol said breaking into Rachel's thoughts, "that they have all come back sworn to silence? Surely one would have broken whatever promise they made to that animal, but none has."

"What are you saying?" Rachel asked.

"Well, we all assume it's for his sexual gratification, but nobody has ever said."

"I don't know what it's for but no doubt I am going to find out shortly," Rachel said.

"You seem calm about it all," Carol Osborne said.

"What's the point in being otherwise?" Rachel asked switching little Angelique to her other breast, her nipples were sore and there was so little milk. "Look at me and look at the others. You can see every bone in my body and my breasts are half the size they used to be, how this little mite gets anything from them is a wonder. How could any man find what I've got alluring?"

"But he's, using your own words, an animal. Perhaps –"

"And animals can be tamed," Rachel said, dismissively.

"And you are the one to do it are you?" Carol said, smirking.

Chapter Ninety-Six

"You speak English," the Lieutenant asked again, regaining his composure, as his surprise became suspicion.

At the other longhouses the officer visited, Abas thought, he would have used his authority without explanation ... and taken what he wanted. Abas knew of a couple of others who spoke English as well as he did, but there were not that many. Knowing that he was dealing with a warrior who spoke English – and probably better than he did – the officer would consider it an unnecessary intrusion, and possibly his authority was being questioned.

"I do," Abas repeated his earlier words. "May I ask again and on behalf of my father, who is the headman of this longhouse, what we can do for you?"

The Lieutenant took a deep breath.

"I search this place," the officer said.

"Why?" Abas asked before he translated for his father.

"You not question officer of Imperial Japanese Navy."

The sailors behind the officer tensed and Abas saw their fingers move to the triggers on their rifles.

"By standing where you are," Abas told the officer, "you are a guest of my father but only if he wishes you to be. You are not in control here, my father is."

The officer said something that Abas did not understand but then he added in English: "You not question what I say."

Abas stepped forward, his blowpipe across his chest.

"If my father lifts his left hand you and your sailors will be dead in less than a minute. I need only use one word and he will do exactly that."

The officer looked about him, his confidence suddenly sapped.

"You ... you not threaten me," he said uncertainly.

"I am not threatening you," Abas told him. "You have come here uninvited but you will be treated as a guest if you behave appropriately. However, if you come as an enemy you will be regarded as such."

Abas felt pleased, the English lessons he had with Colin and Chao were really proving to be of great use.

He was very aware that the officer felt embarrassed so he must be careful because embarrassment and the subsequent loss of face could lead to trouble. He must not be too cocky.

The officer spoke in Japanese and this time the sailors put the rifle butts to their shoulders.

"You not speak to me –"

Abas smiled.

"For your own safety please order your sailors to lower their weapons," he said slowly. "You will tell me why you are here so that I can inform my father, or you will turn now, get back on your boat and leave us in peace."

"I officer in Imperial Japanese Navy and you do as I order."

"That is not the way we do things round here," Abas said. "I have tried to explain that you are the guest."

The officer reached for the pistol at his hip but before his hand had touched the holster there was a parang at his throat.

"I repeat, tell your sailors to lower their weapons and then maybe we can talk," Abas said.

Chapter Ninety-Seven

Handing little Angelique to Marjory, Rachel touched the tip of her daughter's nose with her finger. "She's going to have her father's nose," she said, taking a deep breath.

Marjory looked at her. "I don't know what to say."

"There is nothing to say," Rachel said. "There is absolutely nothing I can do about it, so as I suggested to Carol Osborne, I must think of Angelique and do whatever he wants me to do. It's as simple as that."

It was just after seven o'clock, it was almost dark but she could feel all eyes on her: the other women and the guards were watching.

They all knew where she was going and why.

Rachel wondered if any of the women not chosen were asking themselves why. Did any of them think it was an affront? There were one or two, Rachel thought, who might fit the bill. She allowed a smile to cross her lips.

At the veranda, she bowed and waited as the guard standing by the door, tapped on it and entered. A minute or so later, he reappeared, beckoning Rachel to go inside the building.

With her head lowered onto her chest, she crossed the threshold.

She waited just inside the door as the guard closed it from the outside. The room was small, well lit and smelt clean. It was the first clean smell she had experienced for many months. The women did their best to keep their huts and themselves as clean as possible, but they knew they were fighting a losing battle.

Her head remained lowered, and with her hands clasped in front of her, she waited.

After a few seconds of silence, she looked up as she believed she was still alone. There was a desk, chair, wireless, and a bookcase, and on the walls were maps and a couple of oblong prints of butterflies. On the desk, besides the expected official looking paper work, were a phone and two photographs: one of a pretty women in a kimono, her hair piled on top of her head and held in place by a couple of ornamental sticks. The other photograph was of two children, both smiling, the boy younger than the girl, neither yet ten years old.

It looked so normal.

"My wife and children," Captain Oshida said behind her.

Rachel bowed her head and froze.

She sensed the Japanese officer moving closer to her.

"They live in Nagasaki."

His voice was softer than she had ever heard it before, almost conversational.

"Niki, my wife is a teacher at the school my children, Oshi and Taka, go to. She teaches English," he laughed as he spoke. "Ironic isn't it?"

Putting his hand on her shoulder, Captain Oshida turned Rachel round so that she was facing him.

"How is your baby?" he asked.

Rachel lifted her head.

His question was a complete shock but it sounded genuine.

"She ... she is as well as can be expected, thank you," she said.

"Good, good," Captain Oshida said smiling. "The conditions are not good, I understand."

Putting the backs of his fingers against Rachel's cheek, he stroked her face.

Rachel flinched.

"I suppose you want to know why you are here," Captain Oshida said.

Although her head was still bowed, she nodded.

Chapter Ninety-Eight

The look in the young Lieutenant's eyes told Abas that he knew bullets would not stop him from slicing his throat open.

"Bajen sus armas!" the officer croaked.

The sailors reluctantly lowered their rifles.

"That is better," Abas said taking the parang away from the officer's throat. "I think we understand each other."

"You not …"

"Perhaps I am wrong," Abas said slowly raising the parang again. "You are not in the position to threaten us. You are on our land, so you are guests, I must therefore ask you behave accordingly."

"What does he want?" Anak asked in Iban.

"Don't know yet, father," Abas replied. "As you can see he would sooner shoot us than talk."

"Let him try," Anak replied. "He and his followers would be dead before they could point their rifles at us."

"I think he is beginning to understand that, father."

Abas hadn't taken his eyes from the Lieutenant.

"My father asks what you are doing here."

"The … the Imperial Japanese Armed Forces control all Borneo, the white oppressors all gone, dead, or captured. We now in charge. Chinese also no good, they bad men. Here," the Lieutenant looked over Abas's shoulder towards the longhouse, "you hide bad men here. We want."

Abas didn't allow his expression to give away his feelings.

He had guessed right, and he knew his father would have understood enough of what the Japanese officer said.

Shaking his head Abas said, "There is nobody in this longhouse but the Iban people who live here."

"You lie," the Lieutenant said, unwisely but allowing some of his courage to return.

Visibly tightening his grip on the parang Abas said, "To call an Iban a liar is an insult. There is nobody in that longhouse but Iban. I suggest you withdraw your remark."

"I want see," the Lieutenant said.

The sweat on the officer's forehead was visible and Abas guessed it wasn't just because of the humidity. The Lieutenant's eyes were darting from Abas to Anak and back again. He also looked towards the longhouse and at the undergrowth around him.

Abas turned to his father and translated. Anak nodded.

"My father will invite you and one sailor to his house, the others must return to the boat."

The Lieutenant thought for a moment before issuing his orders.

One of the sailors, who was wearing Corporal's stripes, was quickly silenced when he began to protest.

The Lieutenant and the Corporal followed Anak, Abas and Babu towards the longhouse, the other sailors returned to their boat.

Abas congratulated himself for the way things had gone … so far. He had the upper hand but he must be cautious. By ordering the other sailors back to their boat, they would have access to the machine guns and would be harder targets for the blowpipes.

Chapter Ninety-Nine

"You have lovely pale skin," Captain Oshida said as he surveyed Rachel.

She was naked: her ragged dress at her feet.

The numbness overcame her the moment she undressed.

She let her arms hang by her sides. There was little point in trying to be modest. Nobody had ever looked at her body this way before. No, that was a lie. When she went skinny-dipping the men she was with had stared at her and Colin often stood back so that he could look at her body, but she did not mind that because she wanted him to admire her ... and she supposed she wanted the other men to approve of her as well.

Staring defiantly at one of the prints on the wall, she tried to imagine that she was far away in some distant land. In fact, if she discounted skinny-dipping, she had only been naked in front of two men before: one decided that after their time at university together, she had served her purpose and the other ... she had no idea where he was.

"In that room," Captain Oshida said indicating the door behind him, "is a tub containing warm water, there is soap and a towel. You will wash yourself."

After closing her eyes momentarily, Rachel went through the door into the other room.

The window was open, the beaded curtains moved in the breeze, and also from the fan that whirred above her head.

A single light bulb in the far corner, over by the bed, lit the room.

Walking slowly over to the tub, Rachel stepped into the water and sat down. It was an exquisite sensation. The water was warm and smelt of soap.

She knew that Captain Oshida was standing by the door watching her, and she knew what was going to happen, but just for a few minutes, she was determined to enjoy the feeling.

As she reached for the bar of soap, she thought of little Angelique and Colin.

The smell of the soap was wonderful.

Cupping her hands, she scooped water over her head and began rubbing the soap into her hair and scalp.

"You feel good?" Captain Oshida asked as he sat on the bed watching her rub the soap all over her body.

"Yes," Rachel said instinctively, "I feel good."

She stopped, realising what she had said and why. Closing her eyes against the sting of the soap she turned to face Captain Oshida.

"Why are you doing this? Why when you have us beaten for doing nothing are you treating me as though –?"

"Because," he said, cutting off her words, "in here," he tapped his chest, "I am not the beast you all think I am. I am a considerate man. I do not like what I have to do but it must be done to maintain discipline."

"Captain Yamamoto treated us with respect and didn't use us the way you are going to use me."

Rachel carried on washing her hair.

"I think you have misunderstood me," Captain Oshida said. "I am not able to do to you what you are thinking. I am here in this camp because of an injury, the injury means I am no longer a complete man. I could not do such a thing to you even if I wanted to."

"So … so why am I here?" Rachel asked.

"To do exactly as you are doing," he said.

Chapter One Hundred

Sitting on the *ruai*, the Lieutenant looked uncomfortable.

He was eyeing the others with great suspicion, his head turning every now and again to look towards the river. He was obviously uncertain as to what he should do or say next.

Perhaps he was wishing he had withdrawn to the boat rather than lose face in front of his men.

After showing the officer every room in the longhouse, he was taken out to the kitchens and to where they did their washing.

The way the officer had looked disgusted at everything he saw amused Abas. He caught his father's attention every now and again and raised his eyebrows. Abas was pleased to see the women carried on with their work, only looking up momentarily before they returned to what they were doing.

Once the tour was complete, Anak led them back to the *ruai*. He clapped his hands and two young women brought bottles of *tuak* to them. Abas smiled again when the officer turned up his nose at the taste of the alcohol. No doubt he was used to *saki,* Abas thought. Also made from rice, when Abas had tried *saki* during one of his trips to Miri before the war, he had found it smoother but it did not have the kick *tuak* had.

"You have seen the longhouse and our people," Abas said. "We are many miles upriver; it is not likely that the men you are looking for would come here."

The Lieutenant drained the cup and appeared relieved when he wasn't offered any more.

"I see what you show me," he said. "It late to go further up the river." He began to get up. "You understand the punishment for hiding our enemies."

Abas translated for his father and smiled before he gave Anak's reply.

"My father said that when the orang puteh came here they never threatened him, it is a pity for you that you feel the need." Anak stood up and Abas and the others stood with him. The Iban women, including Aslah, were at the other end of the *ruai*, but now all were watching what was happening.

The Lieutenant readjusted his belt before putting his hat back on.

"Tell your father Imperial Japanese Navy offer no threat, we men of honour. I ask if he understood punishment."

"The Iban are a proud people," Abas said without referring to his father. "You give pain to one of us you give pain to all. There are many Iban in Sarawak so it would be wise if you were to remember that."

The Lieutenant looked at Abas unable to disguise the hate and disgust he felt. "In same way we not threaten, we not like threats. I think we meet again," he said.

"I look forward to it," Abas said, a broad smile on his face.

He could have said a lot more but he did not want to irritate the Japanese officer too much: they did have an orang puteh and a Chinese family to protect. He wished Colin could have witnessed everything that had happened, he would be so proud of him. There would be plenty of time to sit round, drink *tuak* and regale a minute-by-minute account of what had happened. Perhaps he would have to add a few things to make the story really worth telling.

The Lieutenant bowed slightly and when nothing happened in return he carefully found his way back down the ramp and to ground level. The Corporal followed him.

"We haven't seen the last of them," Anak said as he watched the officer and corporal return to their boat.

"I think he will be planning my death," Abas said, smiling, "as I am planning his."

Chapter One Hundred and One

Rachel went from being audacious to feeling embarrassed in a split second.

Because of the degradation they had suffered at the hands of the Japanese and now the Korean guards, she would not have believed she could feel human again but in such exceptional circumstances.

The sadistic and ruthless Captain Oshida had just confided in her: he had explained his injuries and why he was treating everybody so brutally.

Until now that is. Rachel did not know whether she understood or not, but confusion was a price she was willing to pay for the luxury of a warm bath and exquisite soap.

Those that had escaped Oshida's attentions to that point were obviously curious as to what had happened but none of the summoned women had ever said anything in response. It had been noticed that for days afterwards they seemed to be in their own world although eventually they came out of it, but still they said nothing. Now Rachel understood.

"I do not hate any woman," Captain Oshida said. "I am doing what I can but even with what is brought back from the farm, other rations and medicines have been reduced so that there is now barely enough for any of us. The war is not going as planned and all supplies are being diverted." Reaching for the towel, he said, "I mean neither you nor any of the other women or children any harm but I am being watched too. There are two soldiers in this camp who are not what they appear to be, that is why Captain Yamamoto and Lieutenant Sato were removed. I have my wife and two children to think about, so I must survive this war and this is my way of letting you know."

Standing up in the tub, the towel held in front of her Rachel looked at Captain Oshida.

"This is absolutely surreal, you do realise that."

"I know it must seem peculiar. You will need some water to rinse your hair. I will go and get you some," he said.

"No, wait," Rachel said. "I need to understand what has just happened." She stepped out of the bath, the towel wrapped round her body. "You beheaded a man who has shown us great kindness. You had a guard shot in front of us. You have had two women lashed, and other women, even a nun put into isolation for no reason at all, and yet here I am having just had a bath in your quarters, whereas I was expecting to be brutalised and raped."

Bowing his head slightly Captain Oshida sat down again.

"What I need to do out there is abhorrent to me. It disgusts me as much as it does you and the other women. This is for my conscience and me as much as it is for you. I am being watched as well, so I must be seen to be doing as you describe to protect you all."

"I don't begin to understand, but I now know what you are really like, nothing you do out there will … I don't know, I really don't know."

"You will promise to say nothing. The other woman must think you have been raped, in this way the soldiers who are watching me will think the same. Also I must ask you to accept that what I do is necessary for all our futures and you will pray to your God that it is soon all over."

"And that is all you want from me?"

"That is all. If it is necessary for me to punish you for any reason you will know why. But I promise, no harm will come to your baby."

"And … and I promise you Captain Oshida that although I don't understand I will say nothing."

Oshida smiled.

"Thank you, he said.

Hearing the all-clear whistle Colin and the others emerged from their hiding place.

Abas waited for them on the track.

They were tired, thirsty and hungry.

The children, who were now old enough to understand what was happening, had been good.

Abas smiled as the group emerged from the jungle.

"The Japanese have gone," he said, "and down-river, but I think they will be back."

"Was it us they were looking for?" Colin asked as they started to walk back towards the longhouse.

"Yes," Abas told them.

"Then they will be back," Fung said, looking at his wife.

They walked on in silence, but Colin realised that their complacency had been short-lived. What had happened had brought immediate danger to not only them but to Anak and his people.

Now there was Aslah and their unborn baby for him to consider.

Back at the longhouse, Anak called an immediate council meeting.

As had become usual he sat with his sons on either side of him, and Colin and Fung on either side of them. Sombre looking faces had replaced the usual gaiety and laughter as the men waited for Anak to open the discussion.

There had been no time for him to tell Colin and Fung what he was going to say, so they, having had a drink and something to eat, were as apprehensive as the rest.

"It is not Coy-lyn and Fung that brought the Japanese here today, the Japanese would have come anyway. Before I was willing to live and let live but now I have seen how they are with my own eyes and I do not like what I see. I saw on their faces the disgust with which they looked at us, and they were just waiting for an opportunity to start trouble. They would not have lived to tell what had happened but their deaths would have brought more. The sailors looked at our women with disgust and that was a great insult.

"This is not something we can do alone: I must speak with the grand council. I know of other occasions when the Japanese have been to longhouses, I know what some of the other headmen think, but now I can see that what a few of them have said is right. The invaders cannot be trusted, they are here to take and they bring nothing that will be good for us.

"We are a proud people but we are also tolerant. We have lived under the rule of many invaders but most have left us alone. We have had some of our traditions outlawed because they do not conform to what is expected. Our history tells others that we were violent, that we hunted for the heads of our enemies. This was true and I am going to recommend to the grand council that it becomes true again."

Most of the men nodded in agreement.

Colin looked at Fung and raised his eyebrows in surprise.

Was he really surprised? The Japanese were responsible for killing many of his native countrymen, the English, and now they will have done the same within his adopted country to the Sarawakians, regardless of their religion, creed or culture.

He was not a man of violence, in fact he did everything he could to avoid violence, but like Anak he had his limits. Although he had no idea what might have happened to Rachel, she could be safe but then again maybe she was suffering as so many others were suffering.

Fighting was alien to him but now he was willing to learn.

Chapter One Hundred and Three

Returning to her hut, Rachel felt as though she was in some sort of trance.

As she entered the hut the other women looked at her but did not ask the obvious. Other women had returned with washed hair and clean bodies, and the assumption was that Captain Oshida did not want to touch the women's bodies if they remained filthy.

It might be their turn next and they would prefer not to know.

Rachel crossed to Marjory Field and took little Angelique into her arms.

"You poor thing," Marjory whispered.

Rachel looked at her. "It is over," she said, knowing that for some reason she could not break her promise to Captain Oshida. It had been a surreal experience and one she found played a part in restoring her faith in human nature ... to some extent. Oshida was doing what needed to be done to protect him and his family, she had been willing to do the same to look after little Angelique and both of their futures ... both? She should be including Colin as well.

She had no idea whether the other women's treatment was the same as hers, but under the circumstances, if what he had said were true, that must be the case. No wonder they had kept quiet ... it was not just a promise to Oshida, it was a pledge, a belief that by saying nothing they would survive.

Little Angelique wanted feeding so Rachel took her across the hut to her sleeping mat and sat down. She bowed her head so that she did not make eye contact with any of the other women. What had happened was personal. The other women would be wondering what Oshida had made her do, the answer was nothing. Nobody would believe her even if she told them the truth. She was also scared that she would give something away that perhaps she should not – something that might add further danger for them all. It was a bizarre feeling but she was determined to remain silent. The other women who had not been summoned would have to think the worst and believe that Rachel was traumatised by her experience, but, as with the others, it would be something from which she would recover.

The ones that knew the truth were those who had experienced the truth.

Watching little Angelique feed as best she could was an absolute delight. Everything about their situation was unnatural, what had just happened was unnatural and their futures were unknown. However, having her baby suckling against her breast, her big blue eyes staring up at her mother, was a moment of normality.

When Angelique had taken the little milk that Rachel could provide naturally, she screwed up her face as she tried to spit out the watered-down rice mixture that Rachel fed her.

There was nothing else for her to eat.

"One day," Marjory said sitting down by Rachel, "that little girl will have some proper food and will be able to live in a proper house. Fortunately for her she will remember nothing of this, and when you tell her she will think you are exaggerating."

Rachel smiled. "She has given me a reason to go on. God forgive me for the thoughts I often had while I was carrying her, I still frighten myself when I think of what I sometimes contemplated. But now she is everything. We are going to survive this ordeal and, you are right, she is going to have a normal life. Her father does not know she exists, but I know that one day we will be a family. I don't know where he is but I do know he is alive. He will also survive. We will find each other after the war."

Rachel felt the tears welling up in her eyes.

She prayed that what she had just said would, one day, come true.

Chapter One Hundred and Four

"If he comes back to tell us that the Iban are going to start attacking the Japanese, I'm going to have to get out of here," Fung said. "Regardless of what I said before, I have my family to think of and anyway, I'm not a soldier. I've never handled a weapon in my life."

Colin and Fung were sitting in a clearing about fifty yards from the river. The clouds were scudding overhead but there was a momentary break in the incessant rain that had fallen all night and most of the morning.

They had watched Anak leave by prau with Abas and Babu.

"I don't know," Colin said light-heartedly, "you're a dab hand with the blowpipe. But I know what you mean. These men are trained jungle fighters: it's a skill that is passed from generation to generation." He thought for a moment. "With Aslah here, and expecting a baby, I don't have any choice. My place is with her and therefore with Anak and the rest."

"You'll stand out a mile," Fung told him. "You'll last less than a day."

"Only if I am seen," Colin answered with a wry smile.

"I believe you are serious," Fung said.

"I am," Colin told him.

"Do you mind if I ask you a personal question, Colin?" Fung asked. Colin nodded his agreement. "Aslah?" Fung said. "Do you love her?"

"That is personal, but," Colin said, holding up his hand, "it's a question I have asked myself. I am not sure what loving someone really means. She's a good wife, she looks after me – I'm alive today because of her – she's intelligent, pretty and understanding of my orang puteh ways. But do I love her? I am trying to be a realist. When I leave here, do I take her with me? I will have a son or daughter by then, so would I be able to leave them behind? Perhaps the right question to ask is, would they want to go?"

"But that doesn't tell me, or you, whether you love her. You have mentioned the name Rachel a few times, when you leave here will – ?"

"I don't know, Fung. The last time I saw her was as I took off from Kuching just before the Japanese came. I don't know if she got

215

away before the invasion, I tried to persuade her but she wouldn't go. She has no idea whether I am alive or dead."

"Did you love Rachel?" Fung asked now slightly embarrassed.

"Yes," Colin said without hesitation. "I did and I do. I had decided to ask her to marry me, I was going pop the question on Christmas day last year but the bloody Japanese got in the way."

"And when you leave here, will you try to find her?"

"If I survive, yes, I will. I will go to Kuching or wherever to try to find her," Colin said. "I will need to know that she is all right."

"And then what of Aslah and your child?"

"That's another question I have asked myself many times, Fung."

"And the answer?"

"I really don't know."

"But surely, Aslah and your unborn child are your family now?"

"My answer should be of course they are, but … but could I keep Aslah happy if I know I could leave and find out if Rachel is well? I really don't know."

"You will break her heart," Fung said.

"Mine is already broken," Colin replied.

Chapter One Hundred and Five

When the shouting woke her, Rachel was having a vivid dream about bathing in a luxurious bath with candles burning, a Singapore Sling in her hand with six others lined up on the edge of the bath. She was annoyed because just before she woke up a naked Colin was about to join her in the soapy water.

It was still dark.

"What's going on?" a voice asked from somewhere in the gloom.

Little Angelique disturbed and Rachel held her closer.

Something had happened or was happening. Even with all the awful experiences they'd had in the last ten months, they had never been woken in the middle of the night like this. Rachel tried to see through the gloom for an explanation.

Suddenly two guards appeared at the opening to their hut.

"Out! Out!" they shouted as they banged on the supports with their rifle butts. "Out!" they shouted again.

Rachel quickly tied her makeshift sarong around her waist before moving out of the hut with the others. She was in the middle of the group, little Angelique in the crook of her arm, her head lolling against her mother's shoulder.

Standing in the middle of the 'parade square' the women waited expectantly. There was enough illumination from the perimeter lights to see each other but none spoke because speaking while on parade was against orders.

Angelique had gone back to sleep.

Captain Oshida appeared on the veranda of his headquarters, the light was behind him so he was difficult to see. As was usual he surveyed the women, narrowing his eyes a little in the murkiness.

It was beginning to rain.

"Women," he shouted. "The war is not going for Japan as we expected. We will ultimately be victorious but for now the Imperial Japanese Army need all the soldiers to fight and that includes the guards here and of course me.

"This does not concern me because as I have told you from the start I do not regard being the overseer of women as being the proper way to serve my country. This small camp will close and you will be moved to Batu Lintang camp in Kuching. There are already many

217

more in this camp. The women and children have their own compound and it is to this place you will be taken."

Captain Oshida fell silent for a few seconds before he turned away as though he had finished speaking, but he stopped and thought for moment before facing the women again.

"This place you are going to is not good. You have been lucky that for the last ten months you have been here in Kampong Punkit camp. I have demonstrated the need to be strict, all I have done was necessary in the name of the Imperial Japanese Empire. Some of the things I have done you did not approve of but there are those among you who have seen a different side to me. I wish you no harm but I am afraid for you and for what you must now endure."

There was an audible gasp from the gathered women.

Captain Oshida's final words were unexpected … except by those who had visited his quarters. For them, his words added credence to what he had told them.

Nevertheless, knowing a different side to him, Rachel thought, was not going to change what he had described.

"They have taken all their guns and ammunition," Anak said. "They are left with only their blowpipes with which to hunt. The Japanese have demanded that half of their rice is gathered and sent to Miri to feed the soldiers. If they do not obey they say that everyone will suffer. We will all suffer because we will not have enough to feed ourselves."

"So what did the others say you should do about it?" Colin asked, knowing the answer already.

"They said we must fight but not in the way that soldiers fight," Anak said. "We must be careful what we do and where we do it and it will be slow. We are unable to defeat them in numbers, they have the weapons and they will not come into the jungle where we would be at our best. It has been decided that small groups of maybe only three or four at a time will go to Miri to discover what can be done. If we are able to disrupt or even destroy without being caught they will not know the cause." Anak smiled almost as though he relished the thought of some action ... perhaps he did.

Colin did not want to quash Anak's enthusiasm, nor that of Abas and Babu, who were looking equally excited by the prospect of some action, but he felt the need to introduce a modicum of thought and planning into their passion for battle.

He did not want to remind them of the warnings he gave from the start ... he needed to be positive. But now that they had decided to fight he had to advise caution. As far as he knew, the whole of South East Asia was now under Japanese control and that would have been against the might of the USA, regardless of their losses at Pearl Harbour.

By comparison, dealing with the Iban would be a drop in the ocean. Yes, he must advise caution but at the same time he must not suppress their enthusiasm.

"You are brave men," he said, giving a sideways look at Fung. "The Japanese soldiers have incurred a formidable enemy in the Iban. But I must ask who is going to co-ordinate what is done? Who is going to issue orders? How will you know when other longhouses have sent men into Miri?"

Abas nudged his father, who nodded.

"We are not as backward as you imply," Abas said jokingly. "Each longhouse that is within a few hours of Miri will take part, and each longhouse will be given a period in which to operate. We will have regular council meetings so that we can use the intelligence gathered to plan what must be done next."

Colin returned Abas's smile.

"I am no soldier," he said, "but that sounds a good way forward and I am sorry if I implied that you didn't know what you would be doing. But there are a few other areas that should be considered."

"And they are, Coy-lyn?" Abas asked.

"Reprisals and informants," Colin told him. "The Japanese will not investigate why something has happened before they punish those who could be responsible. It will be of no matter to them whether those they kill were guilty or not. And they will not stop at the men: the women, Ramlah, Aslah, the others and the children could all suffer."

"Our women are as brave as the men," Babu said proudly. "And one Iban will not inform on another. It is not our way."

"Babu is right," Anak said, "It is not our way."

"Of course," Colin said.

He hoped he and they were right.

Chapter One Hundred and Seven

As the women and children approached the gates of the Batu Lintang camp, their hearts were in their mouths.

Their move from Kampong Punkit to Batu Lintang was by lorry so at least this time they had not had to walk. Rachel was as grateful as the others but now she was just as fearful. She was looking at a purpose built prison camp. Painted in various shades of grey and black, it looked ugly. There was no jungle to act as a backdrop to give some colour and sounds.

After dismounting from the lorries, the nuns from the Order of Mercy were segregated before being led away in the opposite direction. Rachel had no idea why. She and the others did not have the opportunity to say goodbye although Rachel was able to catch Sister Angelique's eye so that a knowing look and smile could pass between them. She did not think she would ever meet anybody like Sister Angelique ever again. She was a true Christian.

Little Angelique was fortunately oblivious to what was going on.

Rifle wielding guards pushed the women and children roughly into a group by the front gate. There was a barbed wire fence stretching to both left and right and at intervals there were watchtowers with searchlights and machine-guns prominent in them all. The guards in the towers, whose faces were mere blurs, watched as these new inmates looked up at the sky for encouragement.

A Japanese officer, who looked a good deal older than Yamamoto and Oshida, stood on a box in front of the group and looked down at the apprehensive, tear-streaked faces.

"Woemen and chillren," he said in heavily accented English. "This Batu Lintang internment camp and I, Majoh Suga. This vely big camp but lules easy to unnestan. You do as toll, you bow to guads, you no escape. You obey lules, I happy, if I happy, you happy. Unnestan?"

Just the sound of his voice sent a shiver down Rachel's spine. The women's faces around her were filthy from the journey, their bedraggled clothes were soaked with sweat and most of them could have squatted down and fallen asleep on the spot. Some were shivering, a sure sign that malaria was beginning to take a hold, and others had fouled their clothing, unable to contain the dysentery from which they were suffering. And yet, Rachel thought, all this bloody little man standing on a box in front of them was interested in was his bloody rules. She was becoming sick and tired to death of inadequate little men ordering them about.

"Unnestan!" Major Suga shouted at the women. "You bow and say, we unnestan!"

There was a murmur of, "We understand," from the dishevelled group. Rachel held Angelique in front her as she bowed. One woman, her name was Shirley Bartholomew who Rachel knew was behind her, shouted, "I unnestan!" as loud as she could. She was known for her disrespectful humour but as none of the recipients ever realised she was being disrespectful she always got away with it.

"Right, you go in sigh now."

Major Suga climbed down from his box and stood to one side as the women and children walked forlornly through the gates. As Rachel passed him, she saw him look at Angelique and nod. With slumped shoulders and suspicion written all over their faces, it was obvious Rachel was not alone in wishing she could go back to Kampong Punkit.

"What sort of hell camp is this?" Marjory Field asked Rachel.

"We are about to find out," Rachel told her solemnly.

Chapter One Hundred and Eight

The tears were streaming down Aslah's face.

"Your father said the Iban women were as brave as the men," Colin said as he tried to take hold of Aslah's hand, but she snatched it away.

"We are brave but we are not stupid. You would be committing suicide," she said.

"I will be in no more danger than I am here," Colin implored. "You are my people now, I am one of you. So I must do what the men do."

"Are all orang putehs so brainless?" Aslah almost shouted. "The Iban men have black hair, brown eyes and skin, they are short, they have tattoos and they can survive in the jungle for weeks, even months. All you have in common is that your skin is brown. You will not only put yourself in terrible danger but those with you too, and they are my brothers not my dim-witted husband."

"Try to understand how I feel," Colin said.

"Understand how you feel? I know exactly how you feel but …" Aslah shook her head. "And what about our child growing here?" she asked, her hand on her stomach. "This child is going to find life hard enough but without a father to teach him it will be so much harder."

Aslah did at least let Colin put his hand on hers.

"And if the Japanese are still here when our child is growing up? What then?" Colin asked.

"We will manage." He smiled.

"What are you laughing at? This is not funny," Aslah scolded.

"You have learnt so many orang puteh ways, you even argue like a white woman," he said.

Aslah wiped her eyes. "You have taught me these things, and when we can I want you to show me how the white women live as well. You won't be able to do that if you are dead."

"Are you saying that you would leave this longhouse if you could?" he asked, hoping his apprehension was not obvious.

"I have talked with my mother, and she spoke to my father. When they gave our marriage their blessing they knew that you might take me away," Aslah said.

"But only if you want to go."

"My place is by your side."

"And you would give all of this up for me?"

"Yes," Aslah said without hesitation. "The Iban understand the word *love*, but you have taught me stronger love than I could imagine."

"And it is strong enough for you to leave here?"

"Yes, of course. I did not think I could ever feel about somebody else the way I feel about you, except my family that is."

"But you know nothing of the outside world," Colin said.

"Then you must teach me and show me."

"There is a lot to learn."

"And you don't think I am able to do this? I already speak your language better than you do and you have taught me so much already, so …"

Colin nodded. "I will enjoy teaching you." He took a deep breath.

"Good," Aslah said. "Now stop changing the subject, we were discussing how stupid you are."

"Yes, dear."

"And don't call me a deer," Aslah said, smiling through her tears.

Chapter One Hundred and Nine

The women and children from Kampong Punkit were going to go into the same hut.

The huts were much larger than the ones at the old school in Kampong Punkit. Rachel looked at some of the women who had been in the camp for months and she quickly realised this was not hell, it was worse. Emaciated was not a word she could use to describe the Batu Lintang women and children, they were walking skeletons. Their skin was like thin parchment and it sagged from their arms, legs and faces. Seeing the women like that was bad enough but to see young children who were now shrunken human beings was a sight that sickened her

Rachel and the other *Punkit* women – as they were called – were sitting on the floor of an almost empty hut as they listened to the first white man they had seen since their initial incarceration, over eleven months ago. He was tall, with thinning grey hair and a large nose. He wore a black loincloth, self-made sandals and an old uniform shirt. His skin had a grey-brown sheen to it making him appear maybe twenty years older than he was. He looked as though he did not have enough strength in his body to stand up, let alone speak.

"Ladies," he said in a surprisingly deep voice. "My name is Lionel Hodges, and before the war I was the padre with the Kuching army garrison. I am now the nominated padre for Batu Lintang camp and the only man, other than the guards, who is allowed into your compound. There are other priests and ministers incarcerated in the camp but I am the only one allowed near you."

When Rachel saw a smile cross his lips it was almost as though this man was thinking of making a joke about his access to the women, but no doubt looking at the forlorn faces in front of him put him off.

"I have come to terms long ago with the skeletons I see walking round the men's compound: the sores, the bruises and quite often the broken bones. I am not going to make light of what it's like here because I have already given the last rites to so many and accompanied them on their final journey to Boot Hill, the Batu Lintang Camp cemetery." He paused to take a breath. "But I will never get used to seeing women and children in the same state. I am pleased to say that at the moment you all look relatively healthy by comparison. God knows where you have been but you must thank Him for putting you there. But now you are here … and I'm sorry. You can see for yourselves what it's like. I hope most of you will survive, but I am afraid some of you might not. In saying that I am trying to give you the will to live, the determination to prove me wrong." He paused again as he surveyed the pitiful faces in front of him. "Ladies, and of course children, it would be polite to say welcome but I am sure you will understand if I dispense with the formalities." Rachel realised the priest was looking straight at her. "How old is your baby?" he asked.

"Two months," Rachel said.

He nodded, and Rachel thought he wanted to ask her more about Angelique but instead he looked at the whole group again. "I will give you a description of what you can expect from Batu Lintang Camp in a minute but before anything else, and not knowing where you have come from or what you have already been through, I must tell you that the guards are mainly Korean and there are also a few Formosans. They are little more than wild beasts. Do as you are told, bow, do as you are told again and you may get away with only verbal abuse. I pray for you but unfortunately, here we need more than prayers."

"Here we go again," Rachel muttered to Marjory Fields.

"But I have a feeling this is going to be a lot worse," Marjory said.

"So do I," Rachel replied.

Chapter One Hundred and Ten

Sitting on the *ruai* outside the Fung family room, Colin assumed that Anak and the others knew what their discussion was about, so they also knew it was best if they did not interrupt.

Fung and Chao sat side by side as did Colin and Aslah.

In many ways, Colin thought, Chao had taken far better than her husband to the Iban way of life. Maybe it was because of the children, but although her features were so different, her skin shades lighter, and her manner more sophisticated in the western sense, she was now one of the Iban women. She spoke their language, understood and followed their customs and had used her own skills to the benefit of her new family. He was pleased as he watched the Iban women treating her as one of them.

"I am still concerned that little good will come from what is proposed," Fung said, opening the discussion.

Colin had asked them to speak in Iban for Aslah's sake because although her English was by now quite good – although she did think it was a lot better than it was – the inferences and nuances would be lost on her if the other three had spoken in English. Aslah pointed out that the same would apply if they were to use her language but he had insisted.

"That is because," Chao said in answer to her husband's comment, "you are thinking of the children and me. When we came upriver, we had no idea what or who we would meet. We followed you because the alternative wasn't an option.

"We have been accepted at some risk by what I can only describe as the most amazing people I have ever met." She smiled at Aslah. "They did not have to take us in but they did. If it is Anak's decision and that of the other headmen that the time has come for us, not them but us, to fight then so be it. The risks they have already taken for us must be answered with the risks we are now willing to take for them."

Colin saw Aslah lower her head slightly.

"I," Aslah said quietly, "have already told my husband how I feel. What you have said, Chao, is admirable but it overlooks one basic issue." She lifted her head and looked straight at Chao. "Our husbands, who will be in the most danger, are not Iban. They cannot

227

be as my brothers are, they only have to be seen but once and we will be widows.

"Their bravery will be answered with torture and death. Neither of them are soldiers, their skills are better placed here than with my brothers. My father is of the same opinion but he cannot say it to their faces because they are men. I must speak for him. I would not be allowed to say the same if our men were Iban."

Aslah lowered her head again and Colin guessed the others were waiting for him to say something.

"I could not," he said slowly, "and cannot see Abas, Babu and the other men risking their lives while I service the engines on the *praus* again and again. I understand the risk but it is a risk I have to take. It is my war now as much as it is theirs. The Japanese will have killed many of my countrymen, so I can longer sit back and use what I look like as an excuse."

"But I have to agree with Aslah, Colin," Chao said. "Because of the way you look, the risks are enormous for both you and Fung."

"But no more so than – as we have said many times – the risks Anak was willing to take for us."

"They are different," Aslah said.

"But even so, I for one must take them," Colin told her.

"Then you are still stupid," Aslah said in English.

"You will have many questions but they could come later if that's what you want," Father Lionel Hodges said, his eyes once again surveying the upturned, expectant and worried faces. "I do feel that as I stand before you representing a Christian faith I am letting you down but I am not willing to raise your hopes. I will of course pray for you, but even prayers will have little consequence for some.

"Ladies and children, I really must prepare you for the most awful conditions in which we live. When I saw you at first I wondered where you may have been since the war came to us but now I have been able to look into your eyes I can see the fear. You may have been better nourished wherever you were but other than that, there is little difference.

"Batu Lintang is the largest internment camp in Borneo. We estimate, although we cannot be sure, that there are well over four thousand of us here in total."

Rachel gasped along with all the other women around her.

"The perimeter fence measures nearly five miles round and within the wire there are nine distinct compounds, each separated from the others by paths which are patrolled by the soldiers to stop any communication between compounds and of course to stop escape attempts. You saw the towers at the entrance, they are on the inside as well, manned by soldiers with searchlights and machine guns."

Lionel Hodges closed his eyes and had to steady himself against one of the uprights.

"I am sorry but the nausea hits me every now and again. It has been happening for quite a while though and when compared with so many others it is a minor burden to carry. Maybe now would be the right time for you to ask any questions."

"Father, these compounds, who is in them?" Marjory Field asked.

Opening his eyes, Lionel Hodges took a deep breath.

"There are the military compounds," he said slowly. "Australian, Dutch, Indian, Indonesian, and the British but it is only with the British that the officers and other ranks, for some reason, have separate compounds. Then there are other compounds for European male civilian internees, Dutch male civilian internees and finally you, the women and children. You will meet the other women shortly, but your coming here increases the number of women and children to over two hundred."

"There were some nuns with us but they have been taken away somewhere. Do you know where they will have gone?" Marjory asked.

"Nuns?" Lionel Hodges sounded genuinely surprised. "I'm afraid I don't know. There are a few clergymen here but no nuns as yet, so, no I'm sorry, I don't know. I will try to find out for you but I can't make any promises ... maybe they have been taken to a smaller but segregated compound."

Rachel asked a question that had been on her lips from the start. "Father, is it possible you could find out if our husbands and other friends are here?"

"Yes, of course. Give me their names and I will see what I can do, but I must warn you, we have already had many deaths, and although it is mainly soldiers who have died the news I bring you might not be what you want to hear."

"Not knowing one way or the other is further torment for us all," Marjory Field said.

"I understand and I will do what I can," Lionel Hodges said. "Any more questions?" he then asked. "Not now maybe, but there will be time ... we all have time. Now, I appreciate there might be non-Christians among you, and even those that are Christians might well have had your faith sorely tested by what has happened. But I am here for all of you in whatever capacity you might want, but I hope you will all join me now in a short prayer ... it may just help a little."

There was no escaping the most obvious of truths – he was the only European in sight. It was inevitable but because he had been the only orang puteh among so many Iban and for such a long time, and although more recently and repeatedly he was reminded he was different – now he could see for himself as reality hit him between his blue eyes.

He, Abas and Babu had managed to use drainage ditches, the jungle and buildings to get as far as they had unseen, but now peering from the relative security of the undergrowth towards the Miri to Bintulu road, it was evident, even to Colin and his stubbornness, that he could go no further.

"And both of you could have reached this point without having to hide," he said, his eyes following the Japanese military lorry that was moving slowly down the road.

It was the first time he had seen any of the enemy and yet what he saw looked so commonplace. There were no other vehicles on the road, but there were pedestrians shuffling along, some of the men had sacks hanging from the bamboo poles across their shoulders. There were others on bikes.

The people he could see about fifty yards away looked demoralised.

"We could," Abas told Colin, "but you had to find out for yourself."

"And I have put you in danger," Colin said.

"We are all in danger all the time, Coy-lyn," Abas said as he pointed towards some buildings at the junction with Jalan Cahaya. "That is where some of the soldiers live. They control movement on the main road from there. It has been suggested at one of the meetings my father has attended, that it ought to be one of our first targets. It is close to the jungle. Also this road is used by officers to and from where they are living."

"What is going to be used? We have no rifles," Colin pointed out.

"Explosives have already been stolen, that is all we will need," Babu said enthusiastically.

"Having the explosives is one thing," Colin said not wishing to dampen Babu's eagerness, "but getting them to the building and setting them off is another."

"That is why we agreed for you to come," Abas said. "You know about electrical wires. Could we put the explosive in the building or under the road and set it off from here?"

Colin hesitated.

"I am not an expert on such matters but in addition to the explosives we would need detonators to set off the explosive, safety fuse or a way of generating a current to an electric detonator. Have these been stolen too?"

"I do not know but you are saying that with these things it would be possible?" Abas asked.

"Yes, it would be possible." Colin hoped he was right.

"Good, now you stay here Coy-lyn, Babu and I are going to get a better look at the buildings."

The three men – brothers – clasped hands momentarily before Abas and Babu backtracked into the jungle and disappeared.

Colin turned his attention back to the buildings and the road but as he did he had a feeling that although brave, the Iban were not going to succeed unless they had the right level of leadership and knowledge. And where the hell were they going to get that from because he could provide neither? They seemed to think that just because he was an orang puteh he knew about such things.

He did not.

Chapter One Hundred and Thirteen

Even in her most vivid of nightmares, Rachel could never have imagined the squalor in which they were going to have to live. There had been an obvious smell in the compound but as they got closer to their hut, the smell became a stench. It was nauseating and there could only be one source.

"There is nothing we can do about it," their guide said. She was a woman called Caroline who could have been in her early forties. "It's the toilets, if that's what they can be called, the lack of drainage, unwashed bodies and despair. It's the hopelessness that smells more than anything else."

The hut, although much larger, was similar to the ones in Kampong Punkit: bamboo walls with a palm-thatched roof, a rough floor and little else.

As Marjory and Rachel with little Angelique in her arms, stood at the top of the steps and surveyed the scene before them they understood what Caroline had meant by the all-pervading hopelessness. Women and children were sprawled on the floor on makeshift beds, their sunken eyes lifeless, their bodies emaciated and their souls departed. It was the most awful sight to behold and Rachel's first feeling was one of guilt.

She had no idea why they were sent to Kampong Punkit before Batu Lintang – maybe it wasn't ready for them – and now she had no idea why the conditions there had been so much better. Should she regard Yamamoto and Oshida in even better lights?

A woman walked unsteadily towards them, her eyes suspicious.

"So you've arrived," the woman said.

Before the war, Rachel thought, this woman would have had a pretty face and a attractive figure, but her face was now so lined her age was almost indeterminable. The skin on her arms and legs was loose, her nails dirty and broken, her hair a matted mess and the rags she wore extenuated her skeletal body underneath.

"Welcome to your worst nightmare," the woman added.

Rachel immediately recalled her thoughts of only minutes ago.

"Are we to be in here with you?" Marjory asked.

"This is all there is. There is hardly enough room for those that are already here but we either make space for you or you all sleep outside."

The woman proffered a hand.

"But I am forgetting my manners," she said. "We might be in hell but we can still maintain a little decorum. My name is Grace, Grace Manders, and I am the nominated, elected, whatever you want to call it, leader of this hut."

"Marjory Field," Marjory replied taking the skeletal hand in hers, "and this is Rachel Lefévre and little Angelique."

Rachel nodded but did not smile a greeting: she thought it would be inappropriate.

She just looked at the other woman in abject horror.

Grace Manders glanced at all the others behind Marjory and Rachel.

"How we are going to fit you all in I have no idea, but fit you in we must. We've cleared an area at the far end of the hut which will have to do." She stood to one side. "Welcome to hell but even in hell you are entitled to make yourselves as comfortable as possible."

"We have brought little with us, just the bundles you can see," Rachel said.

"Furniture removals not available?" Grace asked, attempting to smile.

"No," Rachel said, "the three piece suites and double beds will follow on later. The bath tubs might take a little longer though."

Chapter One Hundred and Fourteen

Lying in the undergrowth, Colin continued to watch the activity in front of him.

There were constant comings and goings from the buildings that Abas had pointed out to him, which led him to conclude that they were more than just a control point for the main road to Bintulu.

The feeling of foreboding had not gone away but whether it was because he had never looked on something with a view to destroying it before, he did not know.

Coils of barbed wire were round the perimeter of the camp and all the well-guarded buildings. To the rear of the buildings, Colin could see a compound that was being used to park vehicles – cars and lorries.

A leech dropped from the leaves above him onto the back of Colin's hand and he watched in fascination as its mouth immediately latched onto his skin. He could feel nothing due to whatever existed in the leech's saliva that not only dampened the pain of the sucking but also stopped the blood from clotting. It began to gorge itself, its slimy black body starting to bloat.

Colin hunkered down further into the undergrowth, lit one of the Iban cigarettes and holding the glowing tip against the leech, he waited. It squirmed, shrivelled and fell off his hand.

He smiled as he sucked at the spot of blood the leech had left and wished he could have a day's freedom for every time he'd disposed of leeches in that way. He also wished it could be just as easy to get rid of other irritations in life. Suddenly, his attention switched away from his hand as he heard orders barked by a Japanese soldier over by the buildings.

He looked back through the gap in the undergrowth and saw that a large shiny black car had pulled up. Six Japanese soldiers had formed a line, their rifles by their sides, their heads tilted backwards as the rear door of the car was opened and what could only have been an officer climbed out. Much to Colin's surprise, a woman followed the man out of the car. In contrast to the officer's drab grey uniform, she was wearing a white, pink and blue kimono. Standing dutifully behind the officer as he inspected the honour guard, the woman looked around her and at one point she looked towards the exact spot where Colin was hiding.

Even from where he was observing, Colin could see that her face was translucently white, her lips a bright red and she was young in comparison with the officer. He smiled: he guessed she was a *Geisha*, shipped over from Japan to entertain the officer corps of the Imperial Japanese Army.

He wondered what was going through the woman's mind as she took in her surroundings. Did she view everything she saw, including the officer, with disgust or did she regard her presence as being her duty?

The visiting officer was small, bespectacled, clean-shaven, quite young looking and had two rows of medals above his jacket pocket, and another medal hanging from his throat. As he disappeared with his escort and two other soldiers inside the building, Colin watched as the six members of the guard dispersed back to their posts.

The young woman looked a little lost when she was left on her own but a soldier – maybe a young officer – went up to her, bowed, and guided her away into another building.

After the guards re-opened the road, the locals began moving again and Colin saw Abas and Babu moving with them.

They blended in beautifully and although they knew exactly where he was hiding, they did not look in his direction as they passed him.

"It's awful," Rachel said as much to herself as anybody else.

Her mind was in an absolute turmoil, her thoughts trying to see a way for little Angelique to survive the utter misery to which they had now been introduced. The baby appeared physically strong enough and although conditions at Kampong Punkit had been bad, from what she had seen so far in Batu Lintang, the whole situation was inhuman.

By comparison, Kampong Punkit really had been a holiday camp.

She felt the tears well up in her eyes as she arranged and then re-arranged her few possessions. Little Angelique was lying on the mat in front of her, her big blue eyes looking up adoringly at her mother. It was almost as though Angelique knew what was happening and that she was trying to tell her mother not to worry.

"It is, my dear, but it's all we've got now," Marjory said forlornly next to her. Her sleeping mat was only inches from Rachel's. "I think Lionel Hodges will be accompanying me up to Boot Hill before long."

She sounded tired: she looked tired.

Rachel was worried, Marjory used to be such a strong-willed woman but now she seemed to have lost her strength of character and not just her physical strength. Although she had given the priest her husband's name and age, Rachel knew that Marjory already feared the worst. She had often said that her husband was not a physically strong man but with a smile, she always added that he put on a brave face when adversity entered his life. She had already told Rachel that if he had been in Batu Lintang from the outset then he would not have lasted for more than a few months. "From what I've seen," she said, "if he is dead he will be better off where he is. I will miss him but I love him enough not to want him to go through the hell with which we are now faced."

"Don't you think," Rachel said, wanting to cheer her friend up, "we ought to remember what Oshida said, Japan is losing the war so it won't be long before we are out of here."

"I'm sorry, Rachel, but –"

Marjory stopped as Grace Manders shuffled over to them.

"I'm sorry but I heard what you are both talking about. This hellhole is all we have got," she said, repeating Marjory's words. "And some of us are determined to survive. It cannot last forever and the body is a lot stronger than we give it credit for. We must survive so that we can bring these animals to justice when it's all over."

"The body might be strong," Marjory said, "but what about the mind. The mind gives in long before the body is ready."

Picking up little Angelique, Rachel said, "Marjory, this is not the person we all admired at Kampong Punkit. Where is the fight you had in you there? Grace is right, we must fight, we must find the strength and we must not let them beat us."

"I did not want to be admired," Marjory told her. "At Kampong Punkit we could see a way forward, we had what we needed to survive, even under Oshida's command, but here we have nothing."

"We have our spirits and we have our dignity, Marjory," Grace said quietly. "I have buried six women and two children since we arrived here. Their spirits were broken long before their bodies or their minds. They lost the will to live. We cannot let the Japanese kill us all. For the sake of little Angelique here if nobody else, we must survive."

Marjory looked at the baby in Rachel's arms. "That little mite seems to have one hell of a responsibility heaped on her young shoulders."

"She seems to revel in it," Rachel said with a smile.

Chapter One Hundred and Sixteen

Sitting on the *ruai* eating a bowl of fish and rice, the adrenalin was still rushing through Colin's bloodstream.

The return journey had been as uneventful as the outward trip – almost. As they rounded a bend in the river about ten miles away, a speeding Japanese launch coming downriver with the current took them by surprise. It was smaller than the one they had seen previously, but its size meant it could move more quickly.

Colin was sitting with his back to the bow when suddenly Abas yelled: "Down! Get down!" Colin instinctively threw himself into the bottom of the prau, and Babu covered him with an old tarpaulin they sometimes used as protection from the sun.

Abas deliberately steered the prau towards the bank hoping that the crew of the launch would think he was heading for a longhouse that was another few hundred yards upriver.

The sweat was pouring from Colin as he heard the Japanese launch's twin-outboard engines throttled back, but he also heard Abas and Babu shouting Iban greetings. There were a few seconds when nothing happened but unexpectedly the pitch of the launch's engines rose again and he guessed the Japanese were continuing on their way.

"I have to admit that was close," Abas said sitting next to him on the *ruai*.

"It was my fault," Colin told those close enough to hear. "I thought we would be safe once we left Miri, I was stupid and we could have paid dearly."

"We learn and when we learn we do not repeat," Babu chipped in, his comment attracting a few raised eyebrows.

Colin, Abas and Anak exchanged looks also.

Anak had commented before that his second son had grown up quickly since the Japanese had been to the longhouse. He was now proving to be quite profound as well as brave.

Aslah took Colin's empty bowl and gave him another cup of *tuak*.

"You must not go again," she said quietly next to him, "your son is kicking well and as I have told you so many times I would like him one day to meet his father."

Colin patted her knee reassuringly.

He had already drunk too much *tuak* but he knew he was in for a long night. They must now tell Anak what they had seen and what their plan was, he would discuss the detail with other headmen and only then would they be given the go ahead. Accepting the incident with the Japanese launch was a silly mistake, Colin breathed a sigh of relief. It was a mistake but as Babu said, it was not for repetition.

"We must all learn not to take unnecessary risks," Anak said. "It was probably the Japanese you saw who had already been here and they took away some of our food reserves."

"And you let them?" Abas asked.

Surprised by his son's question Anak frowned, and Colin understood why. It was the first time he had heard Abas suggest that something his father had done, or in this case not done, could have been in error.

"With you, Babu and Coy-lyn away," Anak said slowly, "I had little choice. The Japanese only took what I was willing to give. It meant they left satisfied."

"I'm sorry, father," Abas said. "I did not mean to –"

"No, you were right to think maybe I should have acted differently."

"There will soon not be enough food for any of us," Abas said.

"Then we take back what has been stolen from us," Anak replied.

From their compound and every morning, the women watched the men going to work.

Rachel stayed in the background with Angelique. She knew there was not a hope in hell of her spotting Colin but she also did not want her daughter to see too much, the men really were as bad as Lionel Hodges had described.

Nevertheless, even from further away the men's embarrassment was obvious, as were their skeletal bodies and sunken eyes. There were a few furtive waves as husbands and wives acknowledged each other, but under the ever-watchful eyes of the brutal Korean guards – who looked for every reason to beat and humiliate the men – none of the women let on that they recognised any of their men.

By seeing each other, Rachel thought, at least some knew that their loved ones were still alive. Keeping the children away from this morning ritual was difficult but necessary: the shame shown by their fathers would have been too much for them to understand, but for Rachel the temptation was too much, she had to see. Maybe she was just hoping that one day …

As the last man passed out of the camp, Rachel saw Lionel Hodges crossing over from the men's compound. As he had told them before, he was the only male prisoner allowed relative freedom of movement about the camp, a strange but acceptable benefit.

The guard on the gate to the women's compound glared at the priest as he entered.

Grace Manders spoke to the priest and led him towards the *Punkit* hut. Rachel and those who had gone to the fence on the off chance they would catch a glimpse of their husbands, without knowing whether they were there or not, followed the priest.

"I am not allowed to write anything down," Lionel Hodges said solicitously, but with a wry smile he produced a tightly folded piece of paper from his loincloth. "Ladies, I was given twenty-five names and my investigations have accounted for all but four of the men being sought. There is no easy way of doing this so I am going to start with the names of the men who I was unable to trace, followed by those who have died." He stopped and surveyed all the faces that were watching him in anticipation, good or bad. "The ones I couldn't find are," he read the names and watched as four of the women covered their faces and started crying. "Those that have passed on, and may God have mercy on their souls, are," again he read the names but this time he paused between each name so that he could seek out the woman who had just discovered she was a widow.

With each name Rachel also looked round until she found the same woman. She would go to her and console her afterwards. Earlier discussions suggested that many of them had felt the same as Marjory – their husbands would be better off if they were dead.

The worst of his job done, Lionel Hodges smiled before giving the names of the men who were still alive. He explained that all were obviously in a poor state of health, some were worse than others, but at least they were still alive and fighting.

Hearing their husband's names gave some of the women renewed hope, for others it appeared as though their worries and responsibilities were added to.

"… Simon Walsh, Graham Boddington and finally, Peter Field."

Rachel put her hand on Marjory's arm and squeezed.

"He's stronger than you gave him credit for," Rachel said.

"I'm not sure what I should thank God for: he will be in a pathetic state," Marjory said.

"We are all in the same state now, but as we say all the time, being alive gives us hope."

"For what?" Marjory asked. "A quick death?"

Chapter One Hundred and Eighteen

Anak and Abas had left this morning to speak with the other elders.

The plans were bold and could lead to more problems than they had already encountered. Most of the supplies taken by the Japanese were either easy to replace or recovered by other means. Colin was worried that if they over-committed themselves, the outcome could be worse than they envisaged.

There was a twinkle in Anak's eye when he had explained his intentions.

"There are so many other matters to consider so the loss of a few bags of rice is one thing, the killing of Japanese soldiers is another," he said.

Colin and Fung were down by the river.

Colin was yet again stripping and cleaning the second outboard motor. The little fuel they had left was behind the longhouse and hidden in the jungle: when Anak and Abas had set off that morning, they had used paddles.

"I am worried by what is being suggested," Fung said as he watched Colin at work. "I have seen what the Japanese are capable of, many would suffer in retaliation if their own were to be attacked."

Colin wiped his oily hands on a bit of cloth.

"The alternative is becoming unacceptable to the Iban," he said. "If the Japanese had left them alone they may have been willing to sit and wait, to bide their time. But taking their supplies is humiliating, and you don't humiliate the Iban. Your own people in China have put up a tremendous resistance, so why not here?"

"But at what cost, Colin? In China whole villages have been wiped out, women raped and murdered, children bayoneted in front of their parents, men beheaded in public and all for no reason. We are dealing with barbarism, and here these sub-humans have the upper hand."

"So you are suggesting that the Iban should do nothing, is that it? If there is no resistance the Japanese will have achieved their aim. They have no right to this land: they have no right to any land outside Japan. They are International criminals and they should not go unpunished."

Fung weighed up what Colin had said.

"It sounds as though you are as much for action as the Iban. If Anak returns having agreed with the others that armed resistance should begin, will you be part of it?"

"You know my answer because I may have little choice, Fung. They know nothing about explosives, not that I know much more, but without my help they would kill themselves before doing any damage to the Japanese."

"And what about Aslah and the baby?"

"You mean what about you, Chao, Lim and Chee. Do we really need to go round this buoy again?"

Fung's expression changed but Colin knew he was right: Fung would put his family first.

"Yes, I mean my family, I am frightened for them."

"I am scared for all of us, Fung, but we must do something."

"I hope you are right," Fung said.

"We really have little choice. If we do nothing, one day they will come here and take more than a few bags of rice. You want to protect Chao and the children, what if the Japanese did to them what is happening in China?"

"I would kill them myself before the Japanese got anywhere near them," Fung said. "Chao and I have already agreed that's what would be done."

Chapter One Hundred and Nineteen

"At least we had something to occupy our minds before," Rachel said as she sat at the opening to their hut. "We had the farm, we had the camp to keep as clean as possible, we had the lessons for the children, we were organised and we had a future."

She looked over her shoulder as Angelique disturbed on the mat in the corner. She was amazed as to how strong her baby's constitution was. One of the other women had tried to suggest that because she had been born into deprivation and squalor she had learned to survive, to adapt to the conditions.

"Here we just sit around," she said to no one in particular, "and do nothing. No wonder the mind goes before the body, there's nothing to keep it occupied."

"There are the lessons," Barbara suggested. "You could learn Dutch, Spanish, French, German, even Japanese!"

"I know, but I've tried and I find it so difficult to concentrate, and anyway babysitters aren't always available," she said, smiling ironically.

Rachel liked Barbara Trowbridge. She was of a similar age, single and seemed to have a bit of fire about her. She often laughed when explaining that internment had meant she had lost the three stones she had wanted to lose for a long time.

"Do you think of Colin? You did say his name was Colin, didn't you?" Rachel nodded. "Do you think of him often?" Barbara asked.

"All the time, I think of him constantly. With that bundle of fun over there, I can't not think of him, if you see what I mean. I look at her and wonder if she'll ever see her father, and if her father will ever see the daughter he doesn't know he's got."

"He didn't know you were pregnant?" Barbara asked.

"I didn't know I was pregnant until it became obvious. No, if Colin's alive, knowing he's got a daughter might just give him what he needs to carry on." Rachel slapped at a mosquito that had landed on her leg. "Damn things!"

"Why do you say that? You make it sound as though you know where he is."

Rachel shook her head. "No, I haven't the faintest idea where he is. The last I saw of him was when he waved to me before he and

245

Sammy flew into the rising sun." She paused. "He's out there somewhere: I know he is. Do I think about him? All the time. I think about him before I go to sleep, when I wake up, in my dreams and then all day long. I think about nobody else. He gives me strength. I just want to have back what we had before, but this time we would be a family. If the bloody Japanese hadn't got in the way, he was going to ask me to marry him and I would have said yes straightaway."

"If you remain positive it will happen one day, Rachel. You will have your husband and Angelique will have her father."

Rachel closed her eyes. "They are all I have to keep me going."

"Then carry on thinking of nothing else," Barbara said.

"I don't know whether you're the same, Barbara, but sometimes I look to the future and it scares me."

"What do you mean?"

"Well ... we will have been away from society for so long. People will look at us in the streets and have no idea what we have been through, and if asked, when we try to explain who is going to believe us?"

"Just by saying that you are being positive, Rachel. You believe there is a future, that is your strength and one day it will mean you and Colin will be together."

Chapter One Hundred and Twenty

As the sun rose over the jungle canopy, Colin's eyes scanned the scrub for any telltale sign of the wire they had laid a few hours earlier. In the culvert, over one hundred yards away from them, were fifty pounds of high explosive, with a single electric detonator embedded in it.

Colin had no idea whether it was adequate for what they intended, but the decision had been made and Anak and the others had immediately looked towards him for the knowledge and leadership – something he'd denied having just days ago – needed to start the resistance movement.

Blowing up one or maybe two Japanese military vehicles was hopefully the signal that their enemy's complacency would come home to haunt them.

Babu had pleaded with his father to let him go but Anak had not relented. He would risk one son but not both. In fact he decreed that his boys would not go beyond the longhouse together again until the war was over.

"One of you is a future headman," he said. "If both of you were lost who would lead our people?"

Abas therefore lay beside Colin.

Another young warrior called Mabilu had been chosen to accompany them: he lay on Colin's other side. No one had slept the previous night.

Laying the explosive charge and the wire had taken many hours. The Japanese did not patrol the road that often but general traffic was frequent and had needed avoiding at all costs.

Daylight brought increased activity on the road.

The local Chinese and Malays scurried along, some on bikes, their heads bowed. The Japanese guards in front of the house, where Colin had seen the officer and his concubine, stretched as the rising sun reminded them that they were tired after being on duty for many hours.

It was a normal morning, but at the right moment the peace was going to be shattered.

It would be the start of the fight back.

That moment did not come until mid-morning.

Japanese military vehicles passed over the culvert but at the same time there were too many locals in the vicinity. Abas did not agree that they must avoid civilian casualties at all costs, there were going to be casualties in the future, so they must start the way they meant to continue.

On this occasion he bowed to Colin's insistence.

"I accept that civilian casualties are inevitable but if we kill so many the first time we attack the Japanese we will lose the support of the people who live in the town," Colin explained.

At just before ten o'clock the road was clear except for a single Japanese lorry, which appeared to have mechanical trouble. The engine was coughing and spluttering as it moved slowly along the road. The lorry stopped before the culvert, its driver and co-driver got out and lifted up the bonnet to inspect the engine.

Eight soldiers in the back of the vehicle also got out to relieve themselves and have a cigarette. Twenty minutes later they all got back on board as the lorry's engine started again and it inched forward.

The lorry was moving slowly as it crossed over the culvert.

Colin pressed the button.

The silence was shattered with the most horrendous explosion.

"I don't believe you," Marjory Field said weakly. As with all the others she was suffering from malnutrition and dehydration, but from the moment she had arrived at Batu Lintang the will to go on seemed to leave her.

Once Marjory found out that her husband, Peter, was in the same camp and alive, Rachel hoped it would reduce her early concern, but the reverse happened. Regardless of how the women she had once considered her responsibility cajoled her and attempted to lift her spirits, she seemed inexorably to be slipping away.

"It's true," Rachel asserted, as she knelt by Marjory's bed space. "Barbara told me."

"And she was told by whom?" Marjory asked. "It's malicious gossip spread by someone with a sick sense of humour."

"So why are you the only one who doesn't believe it?" Rachel said, feeling her patience wearing a little thin but knowing that she must not let Marjory detect it.

"Because I seem to be the only one who knows how the Japanese think, that's why. Why would they allow something like this to happen when at the same time they are doing all they can to kill the men in one way or another?" Marjory tried to swallow. "I'm surprised after what we have been through that you are taken in by such insensitivity."

"Why would I be?" Rachel said smiling. "It means nothing to me. My man is God knows where, if he's anywhere. If you want to wallow in self-pity, Marjory, that is your decision. I thought the opportunity to see, talk to and even hold your husband again might just be the tonic you needed to pull you out of whatever you are in."

"You have no right to talk to me like that," Marjory spat at Rachel. "I'm not in anything."

"I have every right, Marjory. You were everybody's strength when we were in Kampong Punkit. You kept us all going. You maintained our spirits. You fought on our behalf. Now look at you. You've given up. You are doing exactly what you told us we mustn't do. The priest told Barbara that married couples are to be allowed to meet. Lionel Hodges is waiting for confirmation from the Commandant and once he has that he will ask for an official announcement so that doubters like you can be convinced."

Marjory turned her head away.

"Peter is alive: you have seen him," Rachel said.

"I … I know, but I am not sure I want to talk to him. I am not sure I could cope with the emotions that such a meeting would cause. And anyway, what are the Japanese really up to?"

"Marjory, I can see no other reason for allowing married couples to meet other than a moment of understanding. We know from our experiences in Kampong Punkit that behind the façade that Yamamoto and Oshida hid behind, there were two men who didn't want to be doing what they had been ordered to do. Maybe Suga is the same."

"I doubt it but if this is true where will we meet?" Marjory asked, her expression changing slightly.

"I don't know any of the details."

"But …"

"There should be no *buts*, Marjory. It is a flicker of hope. It suggests that humanity is not dead. Who knows what might come next, perhaps this is just a start."

"But the start of what?" Marjory asked.

"Marjory, will you stop it and try to be the woman you once were?"

"There's no hope of that," Marjory said.

There was no cheering, no nervous laughter, no gratuitous backslapping: Colin surveyed the scene that he had just created, with his mouth open.

It was horrific.

There were the screams of those that lay injured, some with limbs missing. There were others, perhaps the lucky ones, who lay motionless in the road. There were pieces of what used to be human beings scattered indiscriminately.

The devastation was complete: vehicle and its occupants torn apart.

The culvert under the road was now a deep hole, the area around it strewn with burning and smouldering debris.

Movement dragged Colin's eye away from the gruesome scene and he saw soldiers, their rifles held across their bodies, running towards the remnants of what used to be life. Two of the soldiers ran to the side of the road, lifted their rifles and started firing indiscriminately towards the jungle.

Colin and the other two dipped their heads down as one bullet whizzed through the foliage above them, a little too close for comfort.

"We must leave," Colin said unable to take his eyes from the carnage.

He had never witnessed such a scene before.

The injured and dead were his enemies but they were still human beings and he had been the cause of the butchery in front of them.

More soldiers were coming out of the buildings, some carrying stretchers: others had now formed a cordon around the scene as best they could. There was much shouting, and running back and forth, as though they did not know what to do.

What appeared to be a couple of light machine guns had joined the haphazard firing into the jungle, most of which was now aimed well away from where Colin, Abas and Mabilu were lying.

"We must ..." Colin started to say again, but he stopped when he heard the commanding voice of one of the soldiers, maybe an officer.

The firing suddenly stopped.

Colin watched as a couple of orderlies ran past the officer with one of the victims on a stretcher. The officer gave an order and a group of soldiers ran up the road that led towards the town. The officer moved to the edge of the road. With his hands on his hips, he looked defiantly towards the jungle, knowing that if the perpetrators of the scene behind him were still there, he was a target.

In less than two minutes the soldiers returned and they had a young man and woman with them. The officer, without taking his eyes from the jungle, gave further orders. The two young captives fell to their knees in front of him. Slowly the officer withdrew his pistol from its holster on his hip.

He cocked the weapon.

As he surveyed the jungle in front of him, he smiled.

Walking behind the young man, he lowered the pistol and pointed the barrel at back of young man's head.

There was a crack and the pistol jumped in the officer's hand.

Through his binoculars, Colin saw the young man's face explode into a red mush.

The man's body slumped forward into the dirt. The officer moved to the woman, and lowered his pistol. Colin could not stop himself from focussing on the woman's face. Her eyes were squeezed shut but even from that distance, he could see the tears streaming down her face. She was so young.

Her whole body was shaking with fear.

There was another crack.

Marjory Field was both nervous and apprehensive.

She searched the men in front of her for her husband's face. Men and women were hugging each other, tears streaming down their faces. A few children pulled at their mothers' and their fathers' hands and fingers, wanting to be part of this unexpected reunion.

Then she saw him, and he saw her.

He looked so small, so weak, so ... how she remembered him.

He had never been strong, not physically powerful.

However, his mind was his strength, his intellect allowed him to appear six feet tall when others felt small. She had married him for his mind, and it had worked. Marjory wasn't a physical woman: she accepted in their earlier years that they both had their needs but as physical desire waned she was not disappointed because it was replaced by a total meeting of their minds.

They never discussed what had been, only what could be.

She knew others did not understand but she did not care what others thought. Their lack of understanding proved that they moved on a lower intellectual plain.

He stood before her, his head bowed, his hair wispy and the greyness of his stubble an unexpected but understandable addition to his previously impeccable turnout.

Marjory reached for his hand.

"Hello, Peter," she said, unable to stop the tears welling up in her eyes.

Looking up at her, Peter screwed up his eyes slightly. "Hello Marjory, I thought we would never meet again."

He took off his cracked glasses and began cleaning them. Marjory knew that it was just a mannerism. He always cleaned his glasses when he was nervous, which was not often.

"I've never seen you in a sarong before," she said, allowing a smile to find its way onto her lips.

"This," Peter replied, looking down, "it's my Sunday best. I pressed it especially for you."

"Is it bad?"

"Not as bad as it is for those who were in uniform. The guards take every opportunity to beat the soldiers. With us it is more random and not as severe. And you? How is it with you?"

"I have only been here a short while." Marjory paused. "We were sent to a place called Kampong Punkit at first, a long walk to the north of Kuching. When we were there we had no word of what we'd left behind. I thought you wouldn't have the physical strength to survive conditions in a place like this. So it is so good to see you, Peter. I was so sure that you wouldn't be able to withstand the deprivation."

It was Peter's turn to smile and shrug. "When the body is weak, it is time for the mind to take over," he said.

"Somebody in our hut said that as well but at the time I thought she was talking a load of baloney. Seeing you, I know that it is true."

"My mind lives on," Peter said.

"Then I must make sure mine does the same," Marjory said.

"You seem to be as strong as ever," Peter said.

Marjory allowed a wistful smile to cross her lips. "In Kampong Punkit I volunteered to speak on behalf of the other women: that kept me going."

"And here?" Peter asked.

"Here?" Marjory said. "Here I feel lost."

"You must find yourself, Marjory, because we will get out … eventually."

"You are quiet, Coy-lyn, what is the matter?" Abas asked.

Colin understood why Abas needed to ask the question. None of them had spoken since withdrawing to the river. He had paddled in silence, and in deep thought. He was reliving the horror of the scene on the road and the aftermath of the devastation.

He tried to disguise his feelings because of the need to stay alert: a Japanese patrol boat would mean disaster, and failure after their first attack would not augur well for the future.

Colin knew he wasn't alone.

He had seen the way Abas had reacted although in many ways he was more experienced in such matters. Initially it was the bodies of the soldiers they had killed, after which it was the screams of the injured, but seeing two young Malays dragged from their home and then summarily executed was too much.

The expression on the young girl's face just before she died would stay with him forever.

Because the explosives had caused so much carnage, the officer felt the need to retaliate. If they had left well alone, there was no justification.

What would have been lost?

What was the gain?

Maybe the two youngsters had been husband and wife, brother and sister, boyfriend and girlfriend, but regardless of what they were, they were now dead, their bodies retrieved by relatives and buried. Two young lives ended and all because of a few stolen chickens, rice and a loss of pride.

Who would be the locals blame – the Japanese?

Colin did not think so.

The officer may have pulled the trigger but he would not have done it if … Colin dug the paddle into the water, he did not want to answer Abas but he knew he had to.

"Are we able to justify what we saw?" he asked. "When the innocent suffer because we feel a need to strike at those that steal from us, I have to question our motives. Are a few chickens and some bags of rice the same as two young lives? They were executed, Abas, they were put to death because of us. They were the start, how many more will suffer because of us?"

Abas stopped paddling, instead he steered the prau towards the river's edge.

There was no further exchange until the boat was moored out of sight, shielded by the mangrove.

"In every war the first victims are the innocent," he said. "In our history many have died when they wished no part in the violence. If you had a daughter and she was violated you would seek revenge. Our lands are being violated and we must therefore seek our revenge.

"I, too, was sickened by the murder of two innocents but what does it tell us about our enemy? It tells me that he is a coward: it tells me that if he has to resort to such weakness he can be defeated. If he had the strength such setbacks would have been expected and dealt with in a fearless manner.

"The execution of two blameless people tells me that he is worried, scared, and the frightened make mistakes, and mistakes can be used by us. The innocents died for a cause, it is that cause we must develop with strength and not run from at the first unacceptable occurrence. The loss of two lives could save many."

All Colin could do was nod in acknowledgement of Abas's wise words, because they were wise words.

But they didn't make what happened any more acceptable … for him.

"And how was he?" Rachel asked when Marjory returned to the hut.

Other women whose husbands were in the men's compound had also returned and Rachel had noted a mixture of feelings. Some appeared elated by the experience, others quiet and some obviously distraught..

Marjory took a sip of water from the wooden bowl lying next to her small area of personal space. Lying down with her back to Rachel, she either hadn't heard the question or had chosen to ignore it.

Rachel put Angelique onto the mat before leaning across and touching Marjory's shoulder.

"Leave me," Marjory said, "please leave me."

"But ... but, I thought you would have wanted to talk about Peter, about what you saw," Rachel said.

Marjory turned her head and didn't try to hide the tears in her eyes.

"It was awful," she said, sniffing. "Not only seeing him and the others and the way they are, but also hearing about the dreadful state everybody is in." Marjory rolled onto her back. "Information seems to flow far more easily between the other compounds, probably because they talk when they work at the docks and the airfield. They shouldn't be made to do that because it is helping the Japanese war effort, but since when do the Japanese worry about such things."

"Was Peter in a bad way?"

"He was ... thin. He was never a big man but now he is so small, he's like the others, he is a walking skeleton."

"As we all are."

"Yes, but the men are treated so badly compared to us. Many have died, from not only dysentery, beriberi, malaria and malnutrition but also from the beatings they receive. One man was beaten to death for not bowing low enough to one of the guards." Marjory wiped the tears away from her eyes. "Seeing Peter and the others made me wonder if any of us will ever get out of this hellhole."

"You must try not to talk like that, Marjory. We have got to survive."

"That is easy to say: you are young, you have Angelique and for all you know Colin is out there somewhere waiting for the war to be over so that you can be together again."

"Yes, I have all those things but you have too. Peter is still alive and one day you will be together. They will allow husbands and wives to see each other again."

Marjory allowed a sardonic smile to cross her lips. "I am not sure I want to see Peter like that again."

"How can you say that?"

"Quite easily, Rachel … it is how I feel."

"Then I pity you," Rachel said.

"Don't pity me, Rachel. I have to come to terms with what I saw. Peter told me that although his body is broken his mind lives on. I know I must try to do the same but it will take time. Maybe there is a future, maybe one day when something goes wrong I will look back on this nightmare and realise everything else is so insignificant. But getting me to believe that day will come is going to take time."

"That is something we have all got – time," Rachel said.

"Yes, and none of us knows how long – we've got nothing to guide us. Will it be a month, a year, two years – how can we try to be strong when we don't know how long that strength must last?"

Chapter One Hundred and Twenty-Six

Colin sat cross-legged on the *ruai*, his head bowed.

Everything happened on the *ruai* and so many of his memories will have originated from where he was now sitting. It was the source of everything.

Now it was the source of an admission.

"I have no wish to dishonour the Iban in general or my new family in particular," he said, "but seeing that young man and woman executed because of what we had done, it was too much. My conscience will not let me be the cause of unnecessary death."

"Father," Abas said, "I have told Coy-lyn that to save many lives we must sacrifice a few. It is sad that such things must happen but for the good of us all it is a price that must be paid."

Anak looked from his elder son to Colin. "Coy-lyn, you have proven your bravery, none of us doubt you and so you could never dishonour us, but Abas is right: to save many we must sacrifice the few. The Iban are not frightened of death, it is not so long ago that a man demonstrated his bravery by presenting the head of another to his betrothed. It is a tradition that is still in our blood but for different reasons.

"Nobody takes from the Iban without our permission. If we allow the Japanese to take what they want without a fight we are abusing all that we stand for and more importantly, we are insulting our ancestors. It has been agreed by the council that we will fight: so that is what we must do. Whether this is your fight, Coy-lyn, is for you to decide. We shed tears for the innocent who will die in the process but far better they die with honour than the Iban die in disgrace."

Colin thought for a moment, his eyes catching Aslah's as she sat at the back of the group, her tummy large with their child. Her expression told him that, regardless of what she had said before, her loyalty for her own father and to her husband, the father of her unborn baby, was now pulling her apart.

Colin could also see Fung and Chao, neither wanting any part of the violence and therefore grateful that they were not in the same position. Did they understand what he was trying to say?

"I bow to your wisdom, Anak. I also respect the words Abas has used, but I would now be a hindrance to what has to be done. A split

259

second's hesitation could determine the difference between the success or failure of an operation and with failure would come the destruction of what we would be fighting for.

"I accept that in this war many more innocent people will die so that the majority can survive but I cannot accept the responsibility for the carnage this would bring. I had no idea that I would react and feel the way I do. I have never needed to give a value to human life before."

Colin was aware that everyone was looking at him, their expressions mixed.

"I will train our people in handling explosives and I will do whatever else I can to help. If the Japanese come here I will fight to the death alongside any one of you to protect our people, but I cannot repeat what I saw today."

Everyone remained quiet, waiting for Anak to speak.

"Coy-lyn, as you respect me I respect you. You are from a different culture but I don't think that is the cause of your concern – your concern is from the heart and none of us can control how we feel. You are man enough to admit how you feel – so many men aren't able to do that. But your help in the fight against the Japanese is welcome in whatever capacity."

"Thank you," Colin said as he looked at Aslah.

Sarawak, Borneo June 1963

Chapter One Hundred and Twenty-Seven

"This is quite amazing," Marjory Field said over the noise of the aircraft's engines going into reverse. "I do believe in coincidences but this one is quite remarkable. How is your mother? We seem to have lost touch over the years and well …"

"She's well, thank you," Angelique replied, relaxing now that the aircraft had landed and was taxiing towards the terminal building. She could not remember her mother mentioning anybody called Marjory Field.

"And you, you're quite a lovely looking girl." Marjory Field poked her husband again. "This is Angelique Lefévre, dear. Her mother and I were in Kampong Punkit together when this young lady was born." For Angelique's benefit, she added: "Not all there dear and deaf."

Peter Field leaned forward and smiled. "Nice to meet you," he said.

"And you too," Angelique acknowledged.

"What brings you back to Kuching?" Marjory Field asked.

"I'm hopefully meeting my brother."

"Your brother? You mean …"

"No, Mrs Field, he is not strictly my brother, he's my half-brother." Angelique didn't feel the need to offer any further explanation but Marjory looked confused.

"Your half-brother?" she said.

"Yes," Angelique replied. "It's a long story and the reason I am here is to bring its parts together."

"Oh, I see, or I think I see. Well, I hope if you are staying in Kuching we will have the opportunity to meet again, Angelique. There is so much to catch up on. I am so sorry your mother and I lost touch."

"I am staying in Kuching for just tonight, Mrs Field, and tomorrow I am flying to Brunei and later I am going to Miri. What happens after that is a little undecided at the moment. But if we don't see each other I will remember you to my mother."

"Well we are staying at the Ramada and we'll be here for four weeks, so if the opportunity arises it would be lovely if we could meet up again."

"Yes, of course." Angelique was just a little relieved to know that she wasn't staying in the Ramada. She was being unfair but her visit was personal and she would prefer it to stay that way.

"It's just so wonderful to see that out of the hell we endured, blossomed such a lovely – no, beautiful – young woman. You belonged to all of us, you know," Marjory said.

"Yes, my mother told me how you all pulled us through. I think – "

"Captain Strong and the crew of this Malayan Airways flight from Singapore would like to welcome you to Kuching *International Airport. Please do not unfasten your seatbelts until the aircraft is stationary. We would like to thank you for flying with us today and we hope you enjoyed the flight, and also that you enjoy your stay in* Kuching, *the capital city of the state of Sarawak."*

The plane came to a halt and the seatbelts clicked as the passengers became eager to be away from the metal coffin they had shared for the previous two hours. The Fields got up and other than nods and smiles there was no further exchange.

Marjory Field did give Angelique a concerned look as they waved goodbye.

Angelique's apprehension about the meeting she was about to have caused her to stay in her seat and wait until all the other passengers had disembarked.

Sarawak, Borneo December 1944
Colin's continuing story

Chapter One Hundred and Twenty-Eight

Much to Colin's and of course Aslah's delight Dani was born without mishap.

As a newly born baby, the colour of his skin was more Iban but his hair was fair and his eyes blue. As soon as she was able, which meant within only a few hours of the birth, Aslah took their son to show the other women who marvelled at his colouring.

His name, Dani, was the subject of lengthier discussion. Aslah wanted a name that was a combination of Iban and English, so she asked Colin to give her as many names as he could think of. When he reached *Daniel*, she stopped him.

"Dani," she said, "his name will be Dani."

"But *Dani* in Iban means *wake up*?" Colin said.

"Exactly," Aslah replied smiling. "He has been asleep inside me for nine months but he is now awake."

Colin was pleased when Ramlah and the other women approved of Aslah's choice.

In the six months between Dani's birth and now, Colin watched as the others went down river to wage their limited war against the Japanese. Seeing them go played havoc with his conscience. When the war parties returned they regaled him of their successes but deliberately did not mention any collateral damage or deaths that might have occurred. He knew why they were hiding such facts from him but it did not help.

Then tragedy struck as they all knew it would one day. In fact, tragedy hit them twice within the space of one week.

During a raid on Miri, a well-laid ambush awaited Abas, Babu and three other Iban warriors. Three of the raiding party did not return to the longhouse. Anak and his family mourned both deaths, but as Babu was one of the two warriors lost their grief was unprecedented. Abas thought that the third warrior lost was now in the hands of the Japanese.

"Miku and I managed to escape with only slight wounds as you can see," Abas told them, "but … but Babu and the others didn't

263

stand a chance." Overcome with grief Abas then said, "Why did we let him go, father? We had agreed that he and I would never go on the same raid. I was responsible for him, and now he is dead."

Anak took a deep breath. Colin could see that inside every sinew of Anak's body was tied in knots with the pain of his loss, but outwardly, he had to be the leader, the man with a heart of stone. He may have lost a son but the fight must go on. "The risks were there, Abas, we all knew what they were. Babu was old enough to understand. His passing will help give us freedom and he will be remembered for his bravery. I know I went back on my decision not to let you both go together, but circumstances had changed and I had to change with them." Abas bowed his head.

"He was by my side when he was hit, we were running, I didn't have time to stop, I left him."

"Your recent words, my son: we must lose a few to save many. If you had not run I might be mourning the loss of both of my sons."

"At the moment I might feel better if you were," Abas said.

"You are alive to fight another day," Anak told him.

Abas nodded slowly. "And fight I will," he said.

"And so will I," Colin said. "Anak you have lost a son. I have lost a brother, and I will replace that brother." He looked towards Aslah and she was nodding, she understood.

Chapter One Hundred and Twenty-Nine

Only a matter of days later, tragedy struck again.

The first that Colin and the others knew that they were under attack was when machine gun bullets swept through the longhouse, splintering wood, shattering cooking pots and biting into flesh.

It was two hours before dawn and Colin was asleep so it took him vital seconds to realise what was happening. With the awareness came immediate action and he and others began to execute a well-rehearsed plan. However, like so many excellent rehearsals, when the unforeseen is introduced, the most detailed of plans can go wrong. He ushered Aslah with Dani in her arms down the back steps, gave her a quick kiss and melted into the darkness.

The screaming started almost immediately.

Discussion as to what to do in the event of Japanese attack had taken place as soon as the Iban decided to take the war to the Japanese. Sending a launch upriver was an obvious counter-tactic for the Japanese. The discussion had developed into the plan Colin was now about to put into operation.

As he and Aslah had moved swiftly from their *bilik* to the back of the longhouse where there was some protection, he saw that there were already dead and injured but he had no time to stop. The Iban guards must have been asleep because they gave no warning until it was too late.

Arriving at the *rendezvous* seconds after leaving Aslah, Colin saw that Abas and four other warriors, armed with their blowpipes and parangs, were already there.

"Telaku, the one who was captured, must have been tortured," Abas whispered. "He will have told them."

"Now is not the time to blame Telaku," Colin said. He peered through the foliage. The launch was mid-river, its searchlight bright as the machineguns continued to strafe the longhouse and its surrounds. The gunners would not have a full view of the longhouse so the firing was indiscriminate, but as the strafing continued the bullets would cut down much of the protective foliage and their target would be more visible.

In the backwash of light from the searchlight Colin could see a Japanese officer standing on the launch's small bridge, his teeth showing white as he smiled and took in the devastation his gunners were causing. Colin believed the officer would stop the firing shortly and come closer to the bank.

"Leave the blowpipes," Colin said, "We will take them out there."

Slipping into the water upriver from the launch Colin, Abas and the other warriors used the current and swam unnoticed towards their target. The blade of the razor sharp parang between Colin's teeth was facing outwards. He could hear the bullets whizzing over his head and he prayed that all the others had managed to withdraw to the relative safety of the jungle.

Going round the far side of the launch, he waited until the others joined him before they climbed silently up and over its side. The sailors were so intent on what they were doing they were unaware that they were not alone until they felt the parang blades against their throats. There was no hesitation from any of the Iban warriors and Colin followed their example. The sailor whose throat he cut fell silently to the deck.

The machine guns stopped firing.

Colin turned towards the bridge in time to see Abas and the officer squaring up to each other. The look on the officer's face told him that he had underestimated his enemy and he would pay for the mistake with his life. As the officer reached for the pistol at his waist, Abas drew back his arm and with one movement decapitated him.

"For my brother, for Babu, and you are the savage." Abas said.

Chapter One Hundred and Thirty

The scene that greeted Colin and Abas was one of death and destruction.

Dawn was rising and the light now filtering through the jungle brought home to them the sheer devastation caused. There were bodies on the *ruai*: they were the ones who had not been quick enough to get away. When Colin saw the body of a baby no older than Dani lying next to his dead mother, he rushed over but the baby had died alongside his mother. He was looking at Sumba, a woman a little older than Aslah. There was a lot of blood. Her staring eyes were asking why she had annoyed the Gods so much, because only the Gods could reap such misery on the innocent. Colin reached for a discarded sarong and covered the mother and baby as best he could.

"Coy-lyn, Coy-lyn," Abas called from the rear of the longhouse. "Come quickly."

In the light now filtering through the jungle canopy, Aslah, the sweat pouring from her face and body, looked up at her husband and smiled.

"You are safe," she said softly, pain evident in her eyes.

Colin knelt down beside her and picked up her hand. "Where are you hurting," he asked looking from Aslah to her mother.

Ramlah was holding a cloth against Aslah's hip.

"She has a wound in the shoulder and here, her hip. Her shoulder is not too bad but I think the bullet here may have shattered the bone."

Lifting the pad from her shoulder, Colin could see the entry wound, he felt gently round the back of her shoulder and was pleased when he could also feel where the bullet had exited: it was all bloody but as Ramlah suggested, not too bad. Aslah's hip wound was a different matter and far more serious.

From his own experiences, he knew that the Iban had all the herbal remedies they needed to help repair straightforward gunshot wounds. Aslah would go into shock and no doubt she would also have a fever, but they were the least of his worries. Broken bones were hard enough to reset in the jungle but a shattered hipbone would require hospital treatment and where were they going to get that?

267

Dani, thank God, was unharmed.

At that moment, Anak came over and stood by Colin's side. He looked down at his daughter. In the growing light, everyone could read his thoughts. He had lost one son and now it was possible he could lose his only daughter, and Colin his wife.

After a few seconds, he looked up and said, "We must move, we must move today."

Unknown to Colin until a few days earlier, about a mile further upriver and on higher ground, there was another but far more basic longhouse. This longhouse had remained unoccupied for many years. Anak's father and others built it as an alternative place to live should the ground around their current longhouse become flooded or if the longhouse were to be destroyed by fire.

After helping to bury the fifteen fatalities suffered during the Japanese attack, those that remained moved to the new longhouse. Colin helped carry Aslah on a makeshift stretcher, her face screwing up in pain every time there was a jolt. There were others with injuries but none as bad as Aslah. It took them over an hour to reach their destination. The longhouse was small but adequate for the survivors of the attack.

Her mother and two other women immediately took Aslah to a *bilik* at the far end of the narrow *ruai*.

"We must reconsider what the future holds for us," Anak said at Colin's shoulder.

Chapter One Hundred Thirty-One

After the short fight, the current took the unmanned Japanese launch downriver and it became wedged in some mangrove a short distance away. Once established in the new longhouse, Colin, Abas and four others had re-boarded the launch, and fortunately with his technical knowledge, he was able after much manoeuvring, to disentangle it and move it back upriver before hiding it up a small tributary. They buried the Japanese crew deep in the jungle. Colin and the others stripped the launch of anything that was useful.

Colin was surprised another launch had not come upriver to investigate the disappearance, but fortunately, and for whatever reason, nothing happened.

On this day, a week after the attack, he was on his way back from the hidden launch and about half a mile from the new longhouse when he became aware that the jungle was silent. The track was narrow but well worn because jungle animals as well as humans used it. It took a while for Colin to realise what had changed, he stopped and listened but there was nothing. Silence could only mean one thing. He moved forward cautiously, trying to see beyond the jungle on either side of him. Something was not right.

The shape that suddenly appeared in front of him, its face blackened and with the whiteness of its teeth and eyes standing out in contrast, made him go rigid with fright.

"Hello, cobber," the shape said. "Whata you doin' here?" Colin had frozen in mid-step and was speechless, his mouth locked open in surprise. "What's a white man doing out here, mate?" the apparition said in a whisper.

As the man spoke, three others appeared behind him. All were carrying machine pistols and although they were different shapes and sizes they all looked equally menacing. The barrels of their guns were pointing at Colin.

"I ... I am sorry, who the hell are you?" he asked.

The leader smiled, his teeth too white against his camouflaged skin.

"At least you speak English! I think perhaps you should answer our questions first don't you, mate? We seem to have the upper hand."

The leader indicated that they should step off the narrow track. The other three soldiers moved further along the track before they too stepped off it, becoming immediately invisible.

"My name is Colin Freemantle," Colin said, "and you're the first white man I have seen in over three years. I have been living with the Iban since the war started."

The other man raised his eyebrows. "We meet at last," he said reaching forward to shake hands. "I heard about you from the *Kelabit* further up river. You've got a bit of reputation, mate."

"And you?"

"Don Williams, Major, Z Special Unit, I'm from Australia, as if you hadn't already guessed."

It was Colin's turn to smile. "I had. What is a Z Special Unit?"

"I'm sure you will understand if I don't tell you much," Major Don Williams said. "But we and quite a few others are here to pave the way for the liberation of Sarawak. We are here to train the locals and prepare the ground to make things go a little more smoothly."

He paused as he heard some rustling in the undergrowth away to his left, but relaxed as a face appeared. "All clear down to the river, boss," the face said.

"Thanks, Tom," Don Williams said. "Meet the infamous white man of Borneo."

The face nodded and disappeared.

"Man of not many words, is our Tom," Don Williams commented.

Colin shook his head in disbelief.

"This is so unbelievable but so welcome," he said.

"Are we far from your longhouse?" Don Williams asked.

"About half a mile," Colin told him. "We've only just moved, we had a bit of trouble with the Japanese, but that's another story. Is there any chance you've got any drugs and medicines with you, we have injured but nothing to treat them with."

"Better than that, mate," Don Williams said. "Charlie is the next best thing to a doctor, although he reckons he is a doctor. He'll be able to help."

"Thank God for that," Colin said.

Anak and the others were understandably wary when thirty minutes later Colin led the small group of Allied soldiers into the camp. Carrying their heavy rucksacks, the soldiers were also bristling with weapons and ammunition. They looked fearsome. Some of Anak's warriors reached for their blowpipes, others felt for their parangs.

"Wait here," Colin told Don Williams and the others. He went forward to Anak. "They are friends," he told him. "They are here to help us and they are here to prepare for an Allied invasion that will free Sarawak."

Colin waited. After the attack, Anak, like all the others, was devastated. His worst fears could never have imagined that his earlier decision to take the war to the Japanese would result in the deaths of so many of his own people. He had ordered an immediate cessation of any further attacks by his men until he had reorganised and come to terms with what had happened.

Anak now eyed the group of soldiers with suspicion.

After a while, he said slowly: "If the war had not come to us then I would send them away but our war is also their war and any help they can provide will be welcome."

"They have a doctor and medicines," Colin said eagerly, thinking of Aslah.

As expected, shock set in soon after she was injured, followed by a fever but it only lasted a couple of days. Earlier this morning as he sat by Aslah holding her hand before he left for the hidden launch, she reminded him of the first time they had met.

"Did you not wonder who was lying naked next to you to keep

you warm?" she asked, and there was a wicked glint in her eye.

"I had a fever and knew little of what was happening," Colin replied.

"That is not what a girl wants to hear." Aslah smiled but winced as the pain from her shattered hip shot through her body. "Your ... your fever lasted a long time, I think I must be stronger than you."

"You are, you are a lot stronger and much braver."

"Again not what a girl wants to hear."

She was losing weight rapidly and it was obvious that unless she received professional help she might even die let alone never walk again.

The arrival of the soldiers was therefore a Godsend.

Others would need their help too, but Aslah was the most urgent case.

"They can sleep in the ..."

"They will not need accommodation, Anak. They would prefer to stay close by but in the jungle."

Anak looked confused. "But they are orang puteh, the jungle is not their home."

"These men are different, Anak," Colin said. "These men are highly trained, they move silently through the jungle like our warriors, they are trained to kill in many ways, but they are here for us."

"Then they are welcome. Take me to meet them, Coy-lyn," Anak said.

Waiting for Captain Charlie O'Malley to come out of the *bilik* they shared was, to that point, the most awful moment of his life. Initially Aslah had been reluctant to allow a complete stranger to look at her wounds, but after some persuasion she agreed. Colin feared the worst.

"So," Major Don Williams said to break the tension, "tell me about this Nip boat you've got."

Colin and Fung proceeded to tell him everything from the moment the strafing started. The other two members of Don William's team were out with Abas. They were checking on the positions allocated to the Iban warrior that would give early warning of a Japanese approach. Either the enemy could come by river or land, the latter though was unlikely.

The new longhouse was smaller and more basic than their previous home, it was also further from the river and well concealed.

"Unless the Japanese search every inch of the riverbank and the many hidden lagoons they won't find it," Colin told him.

"And the bodies of the sailors?" Don Williams asked.

"Buried deep in the jungle," Fung told him.

"Good. You said the attack was just over a week ago?" Colin nodded. "And you haven't heard nor seen any Nips since?"

"No, neither have we been out on raids."

"The Nips are well aware that they are losing the war and won't necessarily risk another boat and crew by coming this far up river again. Their reprisals will have been on those closer to Miri."

Colin nodded, guessing that would have been the case, although he preferred not to think about it. The sailor whose throat he had cut was the first time he had ever killed another man in that way and he had re-lived the experience repeatedly. As the parang's blade had sliced through the Japanese sailor's throat, Colin had said a silent prayer but he also pictured the young couple who been executed by the Japanese officer.

"We may be able to make use of the Nip boat. You removed the guns and ammunition, what about the fuel?"

"Enough to keep us going for a long time. What about you? You came from upriver. How did you …?"

273

Don Williams smiled. "Parachuted in up in the hills, less hazardous and we knew there were no Nips in the area. Some of the locals up there aren't too friendly, are they?"

"Some of them will have never seen a white man before and –" Colin's attention moved to the rattan curtain on his *bilik* as Captain Charlie O'Malley came out. He was drying his hands. They all looked at him.

Capt O'Malley nodded his head as he said, "Her shoulder wound is healing well, the bullet went straight through and missed everything, lucky girl." Because of the Australians' accents Colin immediately translated for Anak who was sitting with their group and Ramlah was just behind him. "The wound to her hip," O'Malley continued, "is not infected but the bone damage is quite severe. Without opening her up and having a look there's no way of knowing how much will knit together. She's a brave girl and she knows the truth. She wants to see you Colin."

Moving across the narrow *ruai* to the *bilik* Colin finished translating for Anak and Ramlah before entering the room. Peering down at his wife, Colin thought how beautiful she looked. "*Aku runduka nuan*," he said

"And I love you too," Aslah replied in sleepy English.

Colin knelt down by her slim body and picked up her hand.

"Try to get some sleep," Colin urged.

"I cannot sleep until we have made the decision. If he cuts me I may become infected and die but if he doesn't then I may never walk again."

"There is no guarantee that you will walk again even if –"

"I … I know but I am not sure I want to live if I am to become dependent on others," Aslah said as she clutched at Colin's hand. "I think I have answered my own question."

"I think you have."

"Then tell him."

Six hours later Captain Charlie O'Malley had done what he could and had given Aslah something to make her sleep.

"I repeat myself but she's one hell of a brave girl." O'Malley said.

"Thanks," Colin said. "And what is your verdict?"

Charlie O'Malley shook his head.

"I never like to predict but I think the hipbone will heal. She may walk in a month or so, but until then she is going to need a lot of care and more importantly, understanding."

"She will have both," Colin said. "I must go and tell Anak and Ramlah. I –"

"How come you're married to a native," Charlie O'Malley asked. In his early thirties, O'Malley's rugged outward appearance suggested that few would guess he was a doctor. He had already told Colin he was married with three young children all living back in Sydney. "I only ask," he continued quickly, "because my wife is pure Aborigine and did we come in for some stick."

Colin smiled. "I have been here for well over three years. Anak and his family are my family. The colour of Aslah's skin and the fact that she is Iban are irrelevant. She is my wife and the mother of our son, that's all that matters. If it wasn't for these people I wouldn't be alive today."

"Didn't mean to offend by asking, mate," Charlie said.

"No offence taken," Colin said. "Aslah means more to me than life itself and that is why she will get all the care and understanding I am capable of giving. She will walk again. If you hadn't come along it wouldn't have been an option, but now it is."

"I've done what I can," Charlie said gathering his equipment. "The war will be over soon and you will able to get her into a hospital if necessary. All I will say is, and again I hope you don't mind me describing her in this way, she's one hell of a pretty girl. I could only give a ring anaesthetic around her hip, so she was talking while I was operating. She wants out mate, when the war's over she wants away from the jungle. I hope I'm not letting out too many secrets."

"No, no," Colin said. "She's said the same to me, and well ..."

"She said you are a pilot."

"Yes, well I was, lost my bird the day the Japanese invaded."

"Well when peace comes I suggest you get another plane and fly into the sunset with that gorgeous wife of yours."

"Yes, that's what I'll do," Colin said, wishing it was his only option. "Without telling me too many secrets, when will it all be over?"

"I reckon by Christmas."

"That long?"

"I said Christmas, I didn't say which year," O'Malley added with a apologetic smile.

"This one I hope," Colin said.

Chapter One Hundred and Thirty-Five

In the three months after Don Williams and Colin met on the jungle track, they and the local Iban warriors created havoc among the Japanese occupying forces. Colin admitted that the Australian Special Forces brought with them the leadership and knowledge he believed he and the others lacked from the start of hostilities.

The captured launch and its machine guns were a bonus. After extremely concentrated training in the use of explosives, ambush techniques and the use of many types of weapons, Abas and his warriors became an even more formidable force.

Colin's fluency in the Iban language was put to good use but when the various teams were ready, he, and this time with Aslah's blessing, decided to join them in their various exploits. On some forays, they remained covert and gained intelligence on Japanese troop dispositions in the Miri area. Don William's Z Special Unit after receiving this intelligence passed it on to the main force. Colin had no idea where the main force was based, all Don William's told him was that the operation they were part of was called Operation Python.

On other occasions, the now well-trained Iban warriors actively attacked the Japanese. Casualties occurred on both sides but the indigenous forces became so good that some believed the attrition rates were at least ten to one in their favour.

Miraculously there were no further casualties among Anak's immediate family but at times the combined indigenous attacking force amounted to three hundred and fifty warriors, and casualties were inevitable. Colin, too, escaped injury, although known for his daring exploits, his bravery, and now leadership and knowledge – two qualities he believed he did not have.

While he fought, Aslah slowly, and with much help and encouragement, progressed in the space of three months to being able to walk.

She could not go far, and when she did walk it was with a limp, but she was able move about on her own. One night when Colin returned from an attack on Miri airfield, Ramlah, with Dani on her hip, caught his eye and said, "My daughter, your wife, is ready for you."

Colin did not understand what she meant but once in their *bilik* the meaning of her words became obvious. Aslah was lying naked on their sleeping mat, her hands were behind her head and there was a broad smile on her entire face.

"Thank you for being so patient," she said. "If you are gentle with me I need you as much as you must need me."

Don Williams was able to give updated reports on what was going on in the area. "The Japanese forces in the Miri area are in disarray," he told Colin, "not only because of our localised ground attacks but also because of the constant bombings by Allied aircraft. But the great news is the Australian 9ᵗʰ Division have landed on *Labuan* Island, they are moving on Brunei and then they will come south towards Sarawak. Not long now, mate."

Except for small pockets of resistance, news of the Japanese unconditional surrender and peace came to Anak's longhouse and the many other longhouses along the river in August 1945. Don Williams and his team melted away in much the same way as they appeared in the first place, but they left behind enough drugs, medicines and supplies to last the longhouse for many, many months to come. Colin was sad to see them go.

That night, he, Anak, Abas and Fung and all the other men got very drunk on *tuak*.

As the war ended, so did a chapter in Colin's life.

Turning the page was not going to be easy, but turn it he must.

Sarawak, Borneo – Liberation of Batu Lintang Camp
Rachel

Chapter One Hundred and Thirty-Six

Via Lionel Hodges, the women got to hear about 'The Old Lady' which was the secret radio in the British other ranks' camp built from the necessary components that had been stolen or purloined while working out of the camp at Batu Lintang. "They face certain death if this radio is found," Grace Manders told Marjory and Rachel. "But if the rumours are right the tide has really turned dramatically against the Japanese in all areas of the Pacific."

It was late 1944 when further good news reached their ears. The American navy was conducting effective operations off North Borneo. But it wasn't for a further three months – in March the following year – that progress became visual when Rachel to her amazement saw fifteen aircraft, with Australian Air Force markings, flying over Batu Lintang camp. The guards looked up appearing disinterested by the fact that their days as captors were numbered. Later Rachel and the other women heard the crump of bombs detonating when a single bomber started attacking Japanese positions in Kuching itself. "As far as we can work out," Lionel Hodges told them during one of his visits, "they have also been bombing raids on Miri, Manggar and Sepinggang airfields and the oil storage tanks near Lutong. It won't be long, ladies so keep thinking positively."

The bombing raids continued, even on the oil and petrol stored near the Batu Lintang camp, and air activity remained intense but although further reports suggested Allied landings had taken place elsewhere on the island of Borneo, the elation generated by the first sightings of 'friendly' aircraft waned as the days became weeks and the weeks, months. Rachel looked up one day and saw three Allied aircraft that were so low she could also see the pilots and gunners, but she couldn't even summon up the energy to look for long, let alone wave. The reports were still coming in but nothing seemed to be happening close by.

Rachel smiled as Marjory returned from meeting an ever-resilient Peter. She had a bounce in her step that Rachel had not seen since the better times in Kampong Punkit. "It's over," Marjory said looking at the others. "The war is over. Something called an atomic bomb was dropped on Hiroshima on 6th August and another on Nagasaki on 9th August and yesterday, 15th August, Japan announced its official and unconditional surrender."

"What we are free?" somebody shouted from the back.

"Shortly," Marjory said. "It appears that we know before our captors ..."

"Ex-captors," the voice shouted again.

"Ex-captors," Marjory agreed. "The men have been celebrating but the guards think it's because it's an official camp holiday, it's the third anniversary of the opening of this hell hole."

Once again the women's high spirits were lowered when the Japanese remained in control until 11th September. "They know though," Marjory said. "The men haven't gone out on their usual work parties and I saw one man failing to bow to a guard and he wasn't beaten." Later the hut that was referred to as a hospital was given mosquito nets for the first time and suddenly significant amounts of medicine appeared from nowhere.

On 16th August pamphlets headed *JAPAN HAS SURRENDERED* were dropped over the camp and more were dropped on 20th August. Rachel picked one up and read: "*I know that you will realise that on account of your location, it will be difficult to get aid to you immediately, but you can rest assured that we will do everything within our power to release and care for you as soon as possible.*"

Signed: Maj-Gen Eastwick GOC 9th Division.

280

Chapter One Hundred and Thirty-Seven

The summons came on 24th August and the women and all the other prisoners and internees gathered at the main parade ground.

Suga, who was now a Lieutenant Colonel, stood on his box in front of them. The guards were at ease but the inmates had nowhere else to go. Suga, in his pristine uniform, puffed out his chest as he let his eyes move over the crowd in front of him. He knew that any one of them would gladly shoot, stab or throttle him to death if they had the strength.

His accent was still strong but his English somewhat better.

"People," he shouted. "Nine days ago after two of the most inhuman acts known to civilised nations, The Imperial Japanese Forces had no choice but to surrender their arms. To this end, I am no longer the commander of all prisoners-of-war and internees on the Island of Borneo and you are free to go as you please. However, for your own safety, I do suggest you stay in the camps so that when your soldiers arrive you can be processed as quickly and efficiently as possible.

"In the meantime, as you have already witnessed I have ordered the release of more food and medicines to you. This food and medicine was being rationed for your benefit so that you never went without in the future, but now there is little point in continuing with this altruistic motive. I trust when your soldiers do arrive you will tell them that you have been treated well and with understanding. Thank you."

Suga's last statement initially caused little reaction but when the soldiers realised they were free to express themselves, there were cries of 'murderer', 'animal' and 'may you rot in hell.'

The men surged forward to try to get at Suga but their commanders held them back with, "Not now lads, your time will come."

The men who refrained from tearing Suga, his officers and the guards that were still there, limb from limb, had heard that just before Japan's surrender Suga intended having all prisoners and internees executed rather than allowing them to go free.

These rumours were confirmed when papers were found in Suga's quarters after the liberation of the camp ordering the executions to take place on 17th and 18th August.

It was assumed that the orders were never carried out due to the unconditional surrender on 15th August. What the men and women didn't know was that as Suga spoke there were revised orders sitting in the administration office in Batu Lintang camp that authorised the executions for 15th September 1945.

The orders were indisputable.

They read:

Executions will take place as listed:

Group 1 – Women and children to be given poisoned rice.
Group 2 – Priests are to be shot and burned in the camp
Group 3 – POWs to be shot and burned in the jungle.
Group 4 – The sick to be bayoneted and the whole camp burned.

The man, who expected to be shown clemency and consideration when the camp was eventually liberated, signed these orders.

Chapter One Hundred and Thirty-Eight

As she lay in bed on the first night after being repatriated to England, and to the security of her old bedroom in the family home, Rachel looked up into the greyness and cried. She was reliving every moment of her incarceration and she wasn't reacting in the way she expected.

Batu Lintang Camp was liberated on 11th September 1945. Over two thousand men, women and children were only four days away from being brutally murdered by a beaten Army, but as Rachel shuddered at the memory of being told about the execution order she could not dispel the longing to be back.

She could see the images of the suffering against the ceiling. What was it? Was it the feeling she had of total belonging and complete dependence on each other? Being back in the real world was an anti-climax – why? Was it the shared suffering, the utter deprivation, the humiliation countered by the feeling of achievement having survived another day? From that first day when she looked around Kampong Punkit, it had been hell so why did she now feel so desolate, so isolated and so lonely?

Her body was free but her mind was still a captive of the most oppressive regime.

In the end she witnessed the Japanese offering no resistance as the Australian troops occupied Batu Lintang Camp, and at a formal parade on the main square Major General Eastwick – the General Officer Commanding of the Australian 9th Division – accepted Lieutenant Colonel Suga's sword. As the General was about to speak to the ex-PoWs and ex-Internees, Rachel saw three skeletal soldiers push their way forward through the massed crowd to the front.

"Hold on," one of them shouted looking at Suga. "We have something to show you." The men proudly held up *The Old Lady*. "Well what do you think of about that, Suga?" they chorused.

Rachel was close enough to see the look in Suga's eyes. If he had still been wearing his sword, she wasn't in any doubt as to what he would have done with it. He was totally humiliated, and so he should be, she thought. She learnt later that Suga committed suicide five days after being taken to the Australian headquarters on Labuan Island off the North coast of Brunei.

283

Swept along by the urgency to remove the women from the disgusting conditions of Batu Lintang, Rachel boarded a Douglas DC3 Dakota with other mothers and children, the first people to be moved from the camp to Labuan Island. The irony of the type of aircraft she was to fly in struck her. The image of Colin flying off that day nearly four years ago was crystal clear, and that is when the tears really started. For most of the previous two days, the women had been in a state of suspense, but now realisation that they were really free was accepted by some but for others they were living in a parallel world. Marjory Field, Rachel's closest friend and confidant throughout their internment, was to be flown out on a separate aircraft with her husband Peter, who was extremely frail but still as defiant as ever.

"Where will you go?" Marjory asked as they said their goodbyes.

"My parents initially," Rachel told her, "but then … who knows?"

"Will you look for Colin?"

"Where do I start?" Rachel asked. "He could be anywhere."

"Your heart," Marjory suggested, "start with your heart, that is where he has always been and that is how you will find him."

"I will take your advice, Marjory and start with my heart."

Sarawak, Borneo September 1945
Colin's discovery

Chapter One Hundred and Thirty-Nine

"Name?"

"Colin, Colin Freemantle." Colin watched as the Australian soldier slowly wrote his name on a form. "Wouldn't it be quicker if –?"

"Nationality?"

"English," Colin said, letting his frustration show.

The soldier looked up. "You're English?" he asked.

"I am. You look surprised."

"Passport? Identity card?" the soldier said, his forehead showing his confusion at being faced with what for him was a unique situation.

"No, no passport and no identity card," Colin told him. "I have no form of identification whatsoever. I have been living –"

"Why'ya here?" the Australian soldier asked, cutting him off.

"Why am I here? I am here because Miri and I presume the rest of Sarawak, has been liberated. As I have been trying to tell you, I have been living with the Iban for the last four years and for the last three months I have been working with your special forces – they were called Z Specials – in preparation for the invasion ..."

"Z Specials?" the soldier repeated, his confusion still evident.

"Yes, Z Specials. Have you heard of SEMUT?" – the soldier shook his head – "SEMUT," Colin told him, "was the code word for the Z Special Forces the Australians – you – sent here before the invasion. I would have thought you would have known about them."

"And you were fighting with ..."

"Yes, me ... I was fighting with your special forces. As I've been trying to tell you, I was living with the Iban when your lot made contact and –"

"But ..." the Australian soldier said interrupting again.

Colin was getting a little frustrated; he wished he could complete a sentence without interruption. "But what?" he asked.

"Well, if what you say is true ..."

"I can assure you every word is true," Colin told him. "But I have

285

no identification to prove who I am, where I am from or anything else about me. I can give you the names of the people I fought alongside but I would understand if –"

The soldier's confusion finally got the better of him. "I need to get an officer," he said hurriedly.

"Yes, I think that would be a good idea," Colin said as he gave the soldier a wry smile.

Collecting the incomplete form the soldier left the veranda on which Colin was being questioned. Sitting back Colin shook his head. He supposed he should have expected nothing else. He leant back in the chair and closed his eyes.

If somebody had come to him with his story he might have taken quite a lot of convincing too. But it wasn't as if what he had been doing and who with was relevant. He was there to discover one piece of information, and after getting it he could return to *his* people.

His escapades of the last few months whirled round in his mind and he could not believe that he had come out of them all unscathed. He shook his head in disbelief.

Perhaps it shouldn't surprise him that he was now being treated with such caution.

Chapter One Hundred and Forty

Remembering some of the detail from the fifty-five missions he went on was not difficult for Colin, but there was one operation – if he were to be asked – that took primacy in his memory over all the others because to a great extent it compensated for an earlier experience. Another reason why it was uppermost in his mind was because what they achieved was not what they had set out to do.

Early on after their training was completed, he operated as part of a four to ten man group, one of whom was a member of the Australian Special Forces. On this occasion Colin, Abas, Don Williams and Keling – a young Iban warrior who was particularly adept at handling explosives – set out to destroy as many aircraft as possible at the Miri airstrip. Their aim went to the wall because on the way to the airfield they came across a situation that needed to take precedence.

The group were skirting round the town of Miri and heading for the airstrip when Japanese voices wafted through the jungle. As they were a good mile into the jungle from the town, Colin thought they had come across a Japanese patrol so he and the others waited for it to pass, but the voices stayed where they were. Crawling closer to the source of the disturbance, what he saw changed the aim of that particular mission but not immediately.

In a small clearing in the jungle covering about half an acre, were half a dozen Japanese soldiers sitting down, chatting and smoking. Lying next to them were shovels and picks. They seemed to be waiting for something.

Don Williams ordered a withdrawal. Once withdrawn, he was telling them it would be best to bypass the group when other noises caught their attention. Creeping back to their original observation point Colin saw another group of Japanese soldiers entering the clearing, and they were guarding a group of ten locals – from their clothing and skin colour he could tell that two of the group were Chinese, three were Malay and the other five were Iban. Abas nudged Colin and said he recognised two of the Iban: they were from a longhouse about ten miles upriver from Miri.

All the Iban were men, but there were two women among the others, one Chinese and the other Malay. The captives appeared to be in their twenties or thirties. With their hands tied behind their backs, they shuffled along. There was a noose round each of their necks, which linked them to the person in front and behind. Each captive was blindfolded and barefooted, and their clothing was ripped and bloodied. The six soldiers put out their cigarettes and stood up. The guards pushed and shoved their captives towards the end of the clearing where – for the first time – Colin noticed a trench. It was about twenty feet long, four feet wide but he could not see its depth. It was suddenly obvious what was going to happen.

The Japanese soldiers detached the two women from the group, and then lined up the men with their backs to the trench before forcing them to kneel. Other soldiers tied the two women to Casuarina trees and removed their blindfolds. Colin was close enough to see the women's bloody noses and mouths, and their badly bruised faces, legs and arms.

Their staring eyes now took in the horror of what they saw was going to happen to the men.

Colin was pleased to see Don Williams move his Thomson sub-machinegun into the ready position before motioning for the others to do the same with their weapons. As well as the rucksacks carrying the explosives – which they had taken off their backs – the Iban warriors also carried their blowpipes and parangs.

Colin had a sub-machine gun and a parang.

Raising his hand Don Williams indicated that they should wait.

Colin felt a rush of adrenalin as he always did before going into action.

Chapter One Hundred and Forty-One

Two soldiers went forward and cut the rope between the two men in the middle of the group before removing the blindfolds from all the men. They joined and lined up with the six other soldiers facing the four captive men on the left.

Two other soldiers stood to one side. One of them was obviously a junior officer – there was a Samurai sword in a scabbard hanging from his belt – and the other, who was older than the rest, a non-commissioned officer. The officer withdrew the sword from its scabbard and said something to the NCO. Colin and the others watched as the NCO went across to the women, untied the Chinese woman from the tree and dragged her to a spot about ten feet from the captive men.

The NCO forced her to her knees facing the kneeling men. Taking a knife from his belt the NCO then put the blade between the material of her bloodied and ripped blouse and her neck, and sliced it all the way down her back. The blouse fell away. He grabbed her hair and forcing her head back, he tore the blouse completely away from her body. Standing back he nodded to the officer who stepped forward and to one side of the woman. Her face was in profile but as Colin watched she seemed to take a deep breath, straightened her body as far as she could and thrust out her chest in defiance of what she knew was going to happen to her.

Don Williams raised his weapon again before indicating the officer and the NCO to Abas and Keling, and the other soldiers to Colin, who nodded his readiness.

The officer moved the Chinese woman's black hair away from her neck before forcing her head down. She had a long slender neck and the officer smiled as he placed the blade of the sword against her pale skin. Holding the ornate handle with two hands, he raised the sword slowly above his head, his eyes never leaving the intended cutting point on the terrified woman's neck.

The dart from Abas's blowpipe penetrated the officer's right cheek with such force the point could be seen protruding from the other side of his face. The Ipoh tree poison used on the dart would begin to take effect only seconds later. The sword fell from the officer's hands and his fingers grabbed at his face as he tried to pull

289

the dart from his cheek. The NCO suffered a similar fate from Keling's blowpipe, the dart piercing the soldier's chest through his shirt. He looked down and seemed surprised when he saw a narrow wooden stick with feathers on the end sticking out of his chest. At the same time the eight soldiers in the firing squad didn't even have time to lift their rifles to their shoulders before the bullets from two Thompson sub-machine guns ripped into their bodies.

The noise was initially deafening but silence followed within seconds. The captives were all looking around wondering what had happened: the Chinese woman was still kneeling with her head bowed.

Emerging from their hiding place the group must have looked fearsome with their blackened faces and bodies. Colin went to the Chinese woman first and untied her hands. Don Williams went over to the Malay woman. Meanwhile Abas and Keling, with the parangs in their hands, dealt with the officer and the NCO first: they were still alive but paralysed; the poison would take at least twenty minutes to kill them. A razor sharp parang blade across their throats was a lot quicker. The two Iban warriors then made sure none of the Japanese soldiers who may have survived being shot, lived a moment longer.

Colin and the others put the dead Japanese soldiers into the trench intended for the now free men and women. As they led the group from the clearing, Colin watched their surprised but grateful faces. The Chinese woman stopped, looked at him and then took a few paces forward. She kissed him on the cheek and said, "Thank you."

Colin smiled. The deaths of the young Malay couple whom he saw summarily executed on his first mission had their revenge.

Returning to the present Colin realised that he had been waiting for the officer for what seemed like an eternity. The waiting had pitched him into reverie but his memories were different to the ones he had since he decided to try to regain his identity. It wasn't just the outside world that was a like a magnet, it was not knowing.

What had drawn him to Miri was the answer to the same question he had asked himself God knows how many times over the years. He had no idea if he was going to be given an answer but if he did not try he would not be able to rest. Although the reason for being there was obvious, he needed to get his head round his conscience before he admitted it was the only reason. If he told himself there was no other reason he would need to admit the same to Aslah ... and he had.

"I expected this to happen," Aslah said when he told her that he needed to go to Miri to make contact with the Allied forces.

It was late September 1945 and six weeks since peace had come to Anak and his longhouse. After a lot of work on the original longhouse, they were a matter of weeks away from returning to it. The damage was immense and it brought back the devastation caused that night, including the significant loss of life. Aslah's progress continued and now she only had a slight limp although Colin had seen her wincing every now and again when her toe stubbed a tree root, or one of the steps up to the *ruai*.

"You may have expected it to happen but do you understand why I need to go? I'll only be away for a few days," Colin said.

"The time you are away is irrelevant, Coy-lyn. Do I understand? You are an orang puteh who has brought tremendous happiness into my life I didn't know could exist. We have loved, we have fought, but that little warrior in the corner over there is evidence of my happiness, maybe our happiness. A blue-eyed Iban warrior: such a creature did not exist until you and I made one." Aslah reached for Colin's hand. "But you are not Iban, regardless of what you mean to all of us and especially me, you are from a land many thousands of miles away. It is a land you have not seen for a long time. A land shattered by war, and therefore a land to which you must return but hopefully for just a short while. Of course I understand."

"I have not said anything about going anywhere other than Miri," Colin told her.

"Miri is but a stepping-stone, my husband, my Coy-lyn. All I ask is that one day you return to Dani and me. If you do not find there what you are looking for you will have to look somewhere else, and then ..." The tears welled up in Aslah's eyes as she spoke.

"I ..." Colin had never mentioned Rachel to Aslah, but her brothers, Fung and Chao all knew of her existence. If they knew, Aslah would know, so why couldn't he be honest with her and explain the reason why he must go to Miri?

"Please ... please say nothing more. Tomorrow you will go to Miri, tonight you are mine," Aslah said.

Colin gripped Aslah's hands a little tighter and stared at her tear-filled eyes. "You know the real reason I must go, don't you?"

Her head dropped. "Yes, Coy-lyn, yes I do and I understand."

"Once I find out if she is alive and safe, I will come back to you."

"I pray she is safe," Aslah said. "If you return I will be happy."

He had turned the page with Aslah but what he read was not in the same language. He would return but maybe not in just few days. He had to find out and whatever he discovered would determine what he did next.

The bespectacled officer was middle-aged with thinning hair and a prominent scar on his left cheek. He eyed the incomplete form the soldier gave him before he sat down opposite Colin.

"Not a lot of information here," he said disinterestedly. "So why don't we go back to the beginning? Your name is Colin Freemantle, let's start from there."

The officer, a captain, stared at Colin over his glasses.

Having spent so many years wearing so little, the fatigue trousers Don Williams had given him seemed strange and the army shirt an unnecessary addition. But Colin accepted that a European walking through Miri wearing little more than a sarong and maybe carrying a blowpipe, would generate unwanted interest.

Fung, who had travelled to Miri with him, had secreted away his clothing when he first arrived at the longhouse but now it looked freshly laundered. Colin was amazed because in the jungle clothing normally lasted only a short time.

Colin and Fung had called at a Chinese barbers before reporting to the nearest Australian army unit. Their crude haircuts were commented on but in less than fifteen minutes each, their appearance resembled what might be expected by those they were due to meet.

Separated straight away after reporting, Colin had no idea where Fung was now.

He told his story again but in more detail this time, and the officer's interest seemed to grow with each word.

"Well," the officer said as Colin explained that among other things, he was there because he needed to arrange for supplies to be sent to the longhouse, "that is some story. But so that there are no misunderstandings can I just confirm that you are and never have been in the British Forces?"

Colin shook his head. "I am not a deserter if that is what you are trying to establish."

"I didn't mean to suggest that you were but I just needed to clarify a thing or two," the officer said.

"Of course, you did. Do you have a name? You know mine, it might help if I knew yours," Colin suggested.

"Phil, Phil Sanders," the officer said looking slightly

embarrassed.

"Okay, Phil," Colin said. "I am here after spending nearly four years living in the jungle." He had not mentioned Aslah or Dani: he felt such detail would complicate matters unnecessarily. "I have no wish to return to England or anywhere else, but as well as arranging for some supplies, I do want to try to find out if somebody I knew before the war either escaped before the Japanese invaded or has since been repatriated."

"Whoever it is, I'm afraid they are more likely to be dead," Captain Phil Sanders told him. "If they didn't get out before the invasion, that is. Those camps were bloody awful and death was sometimes considered to be the better option."

Colin shrugged. "I have no idea, but is there a way of finding out? I have a name and a description."

"Was he a soldier?" Phil Sanders asked.

"She was a civilian."

"She!" Phil Sanders eyebrows shot up. "Well, that could make a difference. Any surviving civilian internees were processed through Labuan Island before being shipped home."

"So can you help me?" Colin asked.

Phil Sanders smiled. "I think so, yes."

"So what do we have to do?" Colin asked enthusiastically.

After Phil Sanders had checked with his superior officer, Colin received the necessary paperwork to allow him to go to Labuan. Before leaving courtesy of an Australian Air Force aircraft from a repaired Miri airstrip, he managed to locate Fung.

"Did you get a grilling?" Colin asked him as they walked in the compound outside the local army headquarters.

"There were a lot of Chinese collaborators in this area, I am still not sure they believe what I have told them," Fung said as he watched half a dozen Japanese soldiers being marched towards the local police station. "It's strange," he went on, "the officialdom, the suspicion and many other things I'd forgotten about made me rather wish I was back at the longhouse."

He smiled and waited for Colin's reaction.

"I've got a couple of hours before I need to be at the airstrip, I'll see what I can do. Didn't you mention Don Williams and the others?"

"Yes, I did, although reluctantly," Fung said. "That is why I am out here, they are doing some checking."

"I'll still come in with you," Colin said.

He looked towards the road as a couple of military vehicles went by generating dust and noise, the gears grating.

"Further along that road," Colin said, "is where we blew up the Japanese truck and that young Malay couple were executed. I will never forget the look on their young faces before their murders. Even through binoculars it was easy to see the complete lack of understanding on the young girl's face. War is barbaric and the people who perpetrate it are savages. We have had the honour of living among people who value life and its simplicities, who the so-called civilised world call savages." Colin held up his hand. "All right, I know that a short while ago they were head-hunters and some of their current activities could be considered as cruel, but they are genuine and honest people who do not take before they have given. Yes, Fung, the longhouse and its people feel like home. But you will go back, collect Chao and the children, say your goodbyes and it won't be long before you are back in an office wearing a shirt and tie."

Fung shrugged, as he allowed an ironic smile to cross his lips. "I do not relish the idea and I know Chao is equally confused by what she wants. But you have two good reasons to spend the rest of your life there."

"That's the irony," Colin said shaking his head. "Aslah wants out, she wants to see what the world beyond the longhouse has to offer, but most of all she wants a proper education for Dani."

"I see," Fung said.

"So do I but before I can make any decision I have to clear up a few matters. Come on let's go and see if we can find your cynics." Colin wanted to move on. Fung's penetrating questions needed answers and at that moment, he did not have any.

Side by side, they went back into the headquarters.

Colin once again wondered whether he ought to give up on what was, to all intents and purposes, a wild goose chase. However, he knew if he did not follow through with his investigations he would always be asking what he would have found if he did not go to Labuan.

He had to know.

So perhaps there was only one way of finding out.

Chapter One Hundred and Forty-Five

"Look, I'm sorry if by saying this I'm being difficult, but I have no wish to be repatriated to anywhere. Sarawak is my home. I have a wife and son to go back to, so I am merely here to try to trace somebody." Colin said as he lifted his hands to his forehead in an attempt to hide his exasperation.

Fed up with dealing with minor officials who seemed hell bent on protecting anybody in a superior position, he wanted to move on. Having told his story for the third time, he thought the least he could expect was getting an answer to a simple question.

"But this desk deals with repatriation," the soldier said.

"Exactly, and that is why I am here, but not for me. I don't want to be repatriated to anywhere. But the person I want to locate will hopefully have passed through here and may well be back in England by now. I just want to know that she is safe."

The whirring fans were beginning to irritate Colin as well. He shook his head when he realised he could not remember the last time officialdom had irritated him. He had been scared witless on any number of occasions but never irritated. He, like Fung, was longing to get back to the longhouse.

The young soldier, who, Colin had to admit, was trying to do his best, looked about him. "We've seen thousands of people," he told Colin. "They've come here from Jesselton, Sandakan, here on Labuan and from Batu Lintang in Kuching. The –"

"That's the one, Kuching, Batu Lintang did you say?"

Colin felt that he was at last getting somewhere. It had to be the right one, he thought. The trouble was if they did not have a record of her it could mean one of two things: either she got out early or … no, he did not want to go there but he had to accept that Rachel could be dead. Nevertheless, the speed with which the Japanese advanced would have meant the authorities did not have time to organise any further …

"Yes, Batu Lintang," the soldier said. "Mixed soldier prisoners-of-war, priests, civilian men and women, and children internees. Like all the others, it was an awful place by all accounts. Over two thousand came out but more than double that number died or were killed, the same thing really."

"And do you have a list of those who came out?" Colin asked, aware that the urgency in his voice was obvious.

"No, not here, but if … *she* you said. If the lady you're looking for came through here there will be a record."

"And who can I see who may have access to these records?" Colin asked.

"Me," the soldier said with a smile.

Colin closed his eyes. "Okay, if I give you a name can you check for me?"

The soldier nodded enthusiastically. "Certainly can, mate."

"Right, her name is Rachel Lefévre, she'll be twenty nine now, five feet six, long blonde hair, slim –"

"Everyone we saw from these camps was slim, mate. Emaciated would be a better word. Just need the name." He got up. "It'll take a while to sift through the records."

"I'll wait."

The soldier was back in less than fifteen minutes. He was carrying a piece of paper and had a smile on his face. "Good news, mate. She passed through here on September 16th and sailed for England a week later. She was in a large group of women and children. Says here she and her young daughter weren't –"

"Daughter, did you say she has a daughter?"

The soldier looked at Colin. "Yes, I said she had a daughter. Well, she told us the little girl was her daughter and we had no reason to doubt her. Why would we?" He checked the piece of paper again. "Her name is Angelique," he said.

"How old is she?"

The soldier looked down. "Let me … let me see, yes, her date of birth was 30th September 1942 and she was born in a place called Kampong Punkit. Says here it was a temporary holding camp for female internees and children in the Kuching area. Erm … and some nuns were there as well. They were all held there until Batu Lintang was extended or built, not sure which."

The thoughts that were whirling round in Colin's mind did not make sense but one *fact* emerged from the cauldron: if Rachel had known she was pregnant before they parted, she would have told him. Maybe she did not know. He shook his head – no, that was unfair, he should not be thinking such thoughts: they had both survived the war and were safe in England, that is what mattered.

"Thank you," he said slowly. "You won't get into trouble for telling me that, will you?"

"I bloody hope not," the soldier said. "There'll be thousands of people looking for loved ones, friends," he smiled, "and even enemies. You are my first case but I bet there will be one hell of a lot more."

"Are you able to tell me whether she said where she was going to live in England?" Colin asked.

"Erm … well I'm not sure –"

"Was it Leamington Spa?"

"Yes," the soldier said smiling. "It was Leamington Spa," – although he pronounced it Leemington – "Beauchamp Avenue to be precise, No 24."

"Thanks."

"Is there anything else, mate?"

The soldier was looking towards his sergeant who was indicating that he was spending too long with whoever it was.

"No, and thanks … yes, yes, there is something else. If I were to want to be repatriated, would that be a problem?"

The soldier smiled again. "No, mate, it might take a while, ships are at a premium at the moment, but we'd get you home."

"Thanks again, you've been most helpful. What's your name?"

"Ben, mate, my name's Ben Griffiths, Lance Corporal Ben Griffiths to be precise."

"Ben," Colin said standing and shaking the young soldier's hand. "I came here in the hope that I would find out if somebody who was close to me had survived the war. Thank God she did, but I wasn't expecting to hear about the little girl. That came as a bit of a shock as you probably saw."

"Hope it wasn't too much of a shock," Ben said, smiling yet again. "But finding out you're a father when you didn't know can come as a bit of a surprise."

"Surprise? What you have told me was more of a reality check," Colin said. "It may just have changed the futures of three other people as well."

As he turned to walk away from the desk, Colin wondered what he was going to do.

He could not believe he had a daughter … but he also had a wife and son.

Surely, he didn't have to make a choice.

Before discovering he had a daughter he didn't have a choice. Rachel had survived the war and that is all he wanted to hear … his place was back with Aslah and Dani … but now?

Leamington Spa, England
Rachel's misgivings

Chapter One Hundred and Forty-Seven

Seeing Angelique sitting at the kitchen table with a boiled egg and some toast in front of her was the miracle Rachel knew would happen one day, and now it had come true. Something as simple as the bemusement on Angelique's face as she looked at the egg, her spoon poised, was testament to everything having been worthwhile: the pain, the agony of watching others die: the threat of mass killings: the degradation, and the embarrassment generated by the humility shown by those who found them.

Rachel believed she would never forget the look of abject horror on the faces of the Australian soldiers when they arrived at Batu Lintang. They could not believe their eyes. As she and the other mothers and children stood in line for their flight to Labuan Island, one of the soldiers told her that when he first saw them he had not known whether to cry, scream or turn away.

The egg and toast were miracles in their own right: the table, the chair, the metal spoon, the china plate and the location were all dreams come true. They had to be careful what they ate, even with rationing and its restrictions the food was rich by comparison with what they had become so used to, but one egg would not do any harm. Rachel had received appropriate advice from the authorities, as had so many others. Glancing towards her mother, she could see the look of incredulity on her face too.

"I can't believe it," her mother said, tears appearing in her eyes for the umpteenth time. "I never thought I'd see you again but to see you and your little girl, my granddaughter, whom I knew nothing about, it's just too much. It's …"

"Don't cry, Mum, or you'll have us all blubbering," Rachel said.

"They are tears of happiness, Rachel. I can't take my eyes off Angelique."

"And we can't believe we are here," Rachel said.

Her mind went back to the previous night. Lying in the warmth and security of her own bed, she wanted to be back in Sarawak, the longing to return overwhelmed her. She definitely did not want to be where she now was, but how could she explain that feeling to anyone when she could not explain it to herself?

She smiled as she saw Angelique screwing up here eyes with her first ever taste of the yoke of an egg. "Do I like this, Mummy?" she asked.

"I don't know, darling, you've never tasted an egg before so you tell me whether you like it."

"I think I do," Angelique said as she picked up the toast.

"Good," her mother said.

"I prefer the chocolate the soldiers gave us at the camp," Angelique said as she dipped her spoon back into the egg.

"Of course you do, I think it was the most fantastic taste ever," her mother said.

"Was it really bad, my dear?" Rachel's mother asked. "We only ever knew what we read in the papers or heard on the wireless. We never gave up hope that you were alive, but now you are here and with my granddaughter, well …"

"Mum, I will tell you all you want to know when I am ready."

Rachel knew she was being cruel, but what could she do? If Angelique had returned from a war after Rachel had convinced herself her daughter was dead, she too would want to know everything that had happened. How she had managed to survive. Her mother had lost her husband, regained an only daughter, and a granddaughter she had not known existed.

"Mummy," Angelique said that evening as Rachel was giving her a bath before bed, "I don't like it here."

"Of course you do," Rachel told her. "You don't want to go back to that smelly old camp do you?"

But Rachel knew that her daughter was sharing her own dilemma.

Since their return to post-war England, Rachel had done nothing but think about how she found herself longing to be back in the squalid environment that had become so much part of her life. Her experiences in Kampong Punkit and Batu Lintang, even the loss of some of her friends and their children, could and would not mask her longing.

She found herself despising her own people. They too had been through the hell that war brings. She did not have any idea of the suffering that had gone on, the continuous bombing, the losses of thousands of civilians, the heroism of many and the cowardice of some.

Still she loathed them, but why? Loathing them was perhaps a bit strong and the wrong way to describe her feelings: she did not want to be with them, or be part of their lives. She did not want to go out, or enjoy the colours brought on by the change in seasons – autumn had meant nothing to her for so many years, so why should it mean something to her now?

Rachel found herself despising her own mother and she could not even mourn the loss of her father – he had died in a traffic accident in 1943. She and her father had been particularly close and she knew she should have felt grief-stricken but she had seen so much death, she just hoped her father did not suffer.

She knew there had to be something wrong with her. She had paid the physical and mental price brought about by total deprivation for almost four years. Maybe one day she would learn to respect, even enjoy, what her return to England really meant.

Nevertheless, for now she could not do any of those things.

She fully understood what little Angelique was saying to her, because she too wanted to wake up each morning and be back in the hot and smelly confines of Kampong Punkit or Batu Lintang.

Understanding this longing was both alien to her and yet, not surprising.

Was it because she had been part of a group of people who were fighting for their survival? There had been no weapons with which to fight: all they could rely on was their mental strength.

She and the other had survived against all odds.

So why did she long to go back?

From the moment they boarded the DC3 Dakota in Kuching to fly to Labuan Island, the Headquarters of the Australian 9th Division, Rachel and Angelique had grown even closer … if that were possible. Messages passed between them that nobody else could detect. They had an undetectable means of communication. They had a secret language: their eyes, a touch and the slightest movement of the head, all replacing the need for words.

Was this what she dreaded losing?

As Angelique grew up and memories began to fade, would she also forget how close their relationship had been? Not yet four years old but she had experienced the unbelievable, the indescribable. Her behaviour and speech were more akin to a five year-old.

Would she ever forget?

Surely, it would be impossible to forget, but until the memories perhaps faded, it was something they both wanted to hang onto. No mother and daughter could ever have a closer relationship.

A relationship borne out of such squalor and degradation.

The doctor draped the stethoscope round his neck. "All right Mrs Lefévre, you can get dressed now," he said, returning behind his desk. "Quite remarkable, quite amazing," he muttered as he sat down.

After buttoning up her blouse, Rachel sat opposite the doctor and lifted Angelique onto her knee. "*Miss* Lefévre, doctor," she said and waited for a reaction.

The doctor looked up from his notes. "Mrs or Miss," he said, "it's still quite remarkable."

The doctor appeared to be old school, and Rachel guessed that the war had brought too many young pregnant and unmarried women into his surgery and she assumed he would not have approved, albeit Angelique was now over three years old.

"Up until eight weeks ago you and your daughter were the prisoners of the Japanese," he said, "and had been for nearly four years. Looking at you both I cannot believe it. You both need to put on some weight, you especially *Mrs* Lefévre, but otherwise you are both unbelievably healthy." He coughed and shuffled his papers. "May … may I ask if your cycle has started again yet?"

"No, doctor," Rachel replied, smiling. "As I told you the first time we met, my periods stopped two years ago."

"I see, I see. Diet, that's what will have caused it, diet. Once your body gets used to proper food again it will return to normal. If they don't start again we'll …" His voice trailed off.

He made a note.

"In that sense I hope they don't," Rachel said, wishing she had kept her thoughts to herself.

"What? Oh, yes, I see, I see," he blustered. "It will, it will." He looked at Rachel over his glasses. "Diet, yes, you are using the advice sheet you were given? After what you have both been through, too much too quickly could do you more harm than good."

"Yes, doctor, we are being careful," Rachel told him.

"Good, good. Now, it's all very well me examining you and forming an opinion but nobody knows their bodies better than the people who live in them. So, is everything else all right? No aches, pains, headaches, rashes, sensitivities, anything at all?"

"No, not really, I feel tired on occasions and I was told that would be the case." Rachel stroked Angelique's hair. "And my daughter is fine too."

"Remarkable, quite remarkable," the doctor said again.

"Doctor …" Rachel hesitated, "I…I am fine physically but I am finding it difficult to settle, so is Angelique, aren't you darling?"

"Yes, Mummy, I am." They were the first words Angelique had spoken; she had just watched the doctor's every move, with her eyes wide open.

"Quite normal," the doctor said dismissively, "that's quite normal."

Rachel wanted to ask him how he knew it was quite normal but instead she said, "We have been through absolute and unimaginable hell, why would I want anything other than what we have been returned to. I have this longing –"

"Quite normal, quite normal," the doctor said again but it was now obvious he did not have the faintest idea what he was talking about. How could he if he had never experienced hell himself.

"I see, quite normal," Rachel said, lowering her head.

"What about your husband, sorry Angelique's father, is there any news?"

"No news, doctor, but perhaps that is good news."

Angelique looked up at her mother and her eyes were full of questions.

Chapter One Hundred and Fifty

Watching her mother as she fussed over the evening meal, Rachel once again hated herself for thinking such terrible thoughts.

Her mother had lost her husband, Rachel's father, and as far as her mother knew, she had lost her daughter as well. All right, she had many friends locally who had rallied round after the accident, and were still there whether they were wanted or not. There were the bridge evenings that Rachel remembered from her childhood and when she spent a short while at home after university. The innocence of childhood led her to think that such activities were boring, but after having had her eyes opened at university, she often wondered if there was something more sinister, or even scandalous about the twice-weekly get-togethers … to play bridge.

Why were these thoughts now coming back to her?

In an effort to rid herself of such feelings, she switched her thoughts to the doctor. Doctor Desmond Waterman: his name alone conjured up images of the late 19th Century but his attitude maybe moved it to an even earlier period. This thing he had about having to be married to have a child – silly old fool. There would be many an English rose who was now a mother courtesy of home-grown servicemen, the United States Armed Forces, the Polish or even, in a few cases, the German and Italian prisoners of war.

She was a *Miss* regardless of what Doctor Desmond bloody Waterman thought and to some extent regardless of what her mother thought too. From the outset, neither Marjory Field nor any of the nuns, had ever even hinted at any form of disapproval, and she supposed none of the other women had either.

She had never seen them whispering about her.

If anything – and she had thought this so often – little Angelique had been a tonic for them, she had been what they all needed: a new life, the next generation.

What about little Angelique's father?

Colin?

Oh God, why did there have to be a bloody war?

Angelique had not asked yet, but she would. She had seen it in her eyes in the doctor's surgery. As soon as she started school, she would ask. There would be so many others of her age at school who were also fatherless. That was silly because she did not know that Angelique was fatherless … not yet. Maybe she never would. If she and Colin were married – as Doctor Waterman desired – maybe the authorities would notify her one way or the other, but there was nobody to connect her with Colin Freemantle, pilot, entrepreneur, self-employed and single.

He could be living in the next street and unless they bumped into each other, they would never know. Rachel was sure she had told him where her parents lived in England, but maybe that would not be enough.

What was she to do? She longed to be back in hell: was that any way for somebody who was supposedly sane to think? Had her incarceration turned her mind as well her body. They had all agreed that the body went before the mind, but her body was now recovering so what about her mind?

She missed the constant contact with others who understood, others who were suffering the way she was suffering, but others who were also able to latch onto the slightest hope and know that such little things meant that there could be a future.

Where there was hope there was a future.

Not knowing what her future held for her was giving her a big problem.

Having her worries dismissed was also hard to live with.

What could anyone who had never experienced somewhere like Batu Lintang know about it? There would be theories, and people who tried to impose their superior *knowledge* on others, but what did they really know?

Rachel's longing did not change and she found herself spending more and more time alone in her room with Angelique who played like any other little three-year old girl. She was also full of questions, but Angelique's questions were different, or so Rachel thought.

"The doctor didn't believe us, Mummy. Why?" Angelique asked.

"It's something new, darling. They haven't come across this sort of thing before. They can only imagine what we have been through: how we lived, what we ate, the filth we lived in, the lice in our hair and on our bodies and the mental shame of it all."

Rachel was mending a tear in a skirt, she could have thrown it away but that was no longer her way, it would never be her way again. "If they don't understand they don't believe," she said and she was sure she was right.

"I didn't like him, he was old," Angelique said, innocently.

"Being old is a reason to love darling, not to dislike." Rachel flinched as she pricked her finger with the needle.

"Yes, I know, I love Grandma and she's old. I watched the doctor and I saw the way he was looking at you. He … I don't know, I just didn't like him."

Rachel thought it best if she changed the subject. She had not liked Dr Waterman from the moment they had met, and when he had been examining her, his fingers had touched her at times in an unprofessional and inappropriate way. All right, the stethoscope needed placing over her heart, but his fingers did not have to touch her breast at the same time.

"Darling," Rachel said, finishing off her repair, "What would you say if I were to suggest that we go back?" She was talking to her daughter as though she was years older. Angelique's vocabulary, sentence construction and more importantly, understanding, were well beyond her years.

"Go back, Mummy? What to the camp?"

309

"No, no, I didn't mean to that horrible camp, silly, but to Kuching, the town itself where mummy lived before the war? The people living there will be getting their lives back together again after the war and they will need help." As she folded the skirt she watched Angelique carefully. She had no idea whether they would be allowed to return, but as well as speaking Malay fluently, she had relented and learned to speak Dutch, and above all she knew and understood the people.

"What about Grandma? Would she go with us?" Angelique asked.

"No, darling, Grandma would stay here. We would go for only a year or two, until you are old enough to start school." She thought it might be for longer, a lot longer.

Angelique put down the building brick she had been holding. "I would like that, Mummy," she said.

"Are you sure?"

"Yes. When can we go?"

"It will take a few months I think, but shall we start planning today?"

"Yes, it will be something to look forward to, won't it, Mummy?"

"Of course it will, darling."

Both of their faces broke into smiles as they hugged.

Sarawak, Borneo
Colin's Conscience

Chapter One Hundred and Fifty-Two

Sitting down by the riverbank watching the water rush by, Colin searched it for inspiration.

Aslah's eyes had asked more questions than her spoken words allowed. Anak and Ramlah had watched him closely and Abas had kept his distance. Therefore, Colin was well aware of the feelings of those closest to him but because of their respect and traditions, leaving him alone was their choice. The only one who knew of his real plight was Fung. On the way back to the longhouse from Miri, Fung had explained that he, Chao and the children would be returning to Miri soon and maybe later they would move down to Kuching. They would leave the longhouse as soon as they could because it was pointless delaying their departure, which was going to be difficult enough as it was.

Fung knew Colin had a battle on his hands and he must face facts … and reality.

Colin thought back to Fung's inquisition.

"And you? Did you find out anything about her?" Fung asked as they travelled back up the river.

Colin smiled. "You are as astute as ever, Fung." He paused. "Yes, I did and thanks for waiting for me until I returned from Labuan." Fung smiled. "She was … was in Batu Lintang camp in Kuching for most of the time," Colin said hesitantly. "It was a living hell by all accounts but nothing should surprise me anymore. But she is safe now and she has been back in England for weeks."

"I was told of the misery they all suffered, but at least some of them survived," Fung said. "They could so easily have all been slaughtered." Fung paused. "But there is more, there is something you're not telling me."

It was a full minute before Colin spoke. "She has a daughter who was born in September 1942, while she was in captivity. The girl's name is Angelique and as she's a little over three years old – well, I can only draw one conclusion."

"I see," Fung said. "I can see what you saying."

"Yes, Fung, she would have been conceived just before the

311

invasion," Colin said.

"And?"

"Yes again, I must be her father ... Rachel wouldn't have ... well, let's not go there."

It was Fung's turn to stay silent but he then asked: "What are you going to do?"

"At the moment I haven't the faintest idea. I cannot leave Aslah and Dani whom I love deeply, and yet I have a daughter whose mother I was in love with."

"The love you had for, what is her name again?"

"Rachel."

"The love you had for Rachel was not enough to stop you from marrying Aslah." When Colin only shook his head, Fung continued. "Your world is with Rachel and your daughter, your life is here with Aslah and Dani. It's a situation, Colin, for which I cannot provide a solution. Whichever way you turn your conscience will tear you apart. All I can suggest is that you tell Aslah, everything, she is no fool. She knows that you had a European lady-friend before you came into the jungle and she will have guessed why you went to Miri. By being honest, my friend, you may get help with your problem from an unexpected source."

"She did know but you think Aslah will ...?"

"Yes, Colin, she really is no fool. She will fight for you but in the end she will do whatever is needed for your happiness."

"And can happiness be divided down the middle?" Colin asked.

They were sitting opposite each other, cross-legged, Aslah's hands in his. Her eyes were full of tears and her cheeks were wet from the tears that had already escaped.

"You ... you must go," she said slowly. "When Fung and Chao leave you must leave with them. The world is returning to normal, this longhouse must do the same."

She lifted her hand to wipe a tear away from her cheek.

Colin bowed his head as he listened to her.

"Look ... look at me, Coy-lyn, I want you to see that I mean what I am saying. I am not just saying this because it is what I think you want to hear."

Colin looked up.

Her face was as pretty as ever, her skin smooth and shiny. The tears in her eyes were breaking his heart. He told her everything and she listened without interrupting. When he mentioned Angelique, she closed her eyes and lowered her head. It was the turning point. If it had just been Rachel he believed Aslah would have fought for him the way Fung suggested, and she may well have won, but hearing that he had a daughter who was born before Dani changed her straight away. She appeared defeated by her own conscience.

Sitting cross-legged was the most comfortable position for her. Her hip was much better, the pink scars that formed a cross on her hip a constant reminder that she had been so close to death. She had never told Colin that while he had been away she had already concluded that it would have been better if she were dead. The bullet that shattered her hip should have passed through her heart instead.

When he mentioned he had a daughter, she told him exactly that.

She truly did wish she were dead.

Of course, she had known why he really went to Miri and she told him she knew from his face and the way he had been since his return, what he had discovered.

"Dani is young, he is Iban and his place is with me in the longhouse," she said. "I hope one day to introduce him to your world but that can wait. Coy-lyn, from the moment you arrived here and I nursed you back to good health, you broke into my heart. You have stayed there ever since and you will stay there forever. You have your funny ways, not Iban ways, but I have learnt to love those too." She held his fingers a little tighter. "Do not worry about my father and mother. My mother also knows why you went to Miri because I told her, so my father will know now. When we first lay together my mother warned me that when the war was over you would want to leave, you would want to go and see what the war had done to the world you had left behind but I hoped when you left you would take me with you and show me your world."

"You ..."

"No, Coy-lyn, I must say all I have to say now because when I have finished there will be nothing more to say. You are feeling bad, I am feeling bad and Dani does not know what is happening. When you leave, I will not expect to see you again but I do want to stay married to you. I understand that an Iban marriage is not binding in your world. What you do with that knowledge is your decision. I love you Coy-lyn but I love you enough to let you go."

"And I love you too Aslah but I –"

"No, Coy-lyn, there is no more to say. You must not make promises that you might not be able to keep. I am giving you your freedom because I too have a conscience. Yes, we are married but my mother and father, my brothers and I were not fair with you. You are now free from the trap we set for you." Aslah bowed her head as her tears dripped onto her sarong.

"I never felt trapped," Colin said.

Chapter One Hundred and Fifty-Four

There are no secrets in an Iban longhouse.

Fung, Chao, Lim and Chee had reluctantly said their farewells and were waiting in the prau with Abas. Colin and Aslah were standing midway between the longhouse and the river: Anak, Ramlah and all the others were either on the *ruai* or at the bottom of the log steps. The jungle and the river provided the only noise.

Colin guessed that few of those watching would fully understand why he was leaving and what would be confusing them even more was why Aslah, her father and mother, were letting him go. The tears suggested that none of those directly involved really wanted any of this to happen. Tears were not something the Iban shed lightly, so they would understand what was happening in the hearts of their long term guests who were about to leave.

"Having an audience isn't what we needed," Colin said holding Aslah's hands in front of him.

The tears were streaming down her face. "What … what did you expect?" Aslah said. "You … you must go now."

"I –"

"Coy-lyn, go. Please, go. If you don't go now I …" She bit her lip and closed her eyes. "Please … please go," she whispered.

Two minutes later Colin watched as the longhouse and Aslah, with Dani on her good hip, disappeared from view round the bend in the river. In the prau's stern Abas was concentrating on the river ahead, the outboard motor under his control. He never made eye contact with Colin; in fact, he had not spoken to Colin since the news had reached him that he was leaving.

Any number of times, when Colin changed his mind Aslah over-ruled him. He had made his decision when he was down by the river with Fung, and unless he stood by that decision, he would forever regret not leaving.

When he had told Aslah the truth, he had marvelled at her attitude, so on any number of occasions while they talked his original decision became more tenuous. Now he could no longer see her it was like having his heart wrenched from his body. The guilt had overwhelmed him from the start, but now he was incomplete. The love he felt supplanted the guilt. Their meeting had resulted from the most extraordinary of circumstances: their parting was no different to so many other relationships that had ended along with the war … but why was he thinking like that? Their relationship was not over, he would be back – he was sure of that.

In Miri, Abas bade his farewells to Fung, Chao and their children with them all promising that they would visit each other regularly. Fung had already promised Abas that when he was ready there would always be work for him in Miri or Kuching. Colin barred the way back to the prau, this left Abas with little choice but to stop in front of him.

"I know that the love you have for your sister puts murder in your heart, Abas," Colin said. "We have been friends and brothers for many years, we have fought alongside each other and we have saved each other's lives so we owe more to each other than this."

Abas lifted his head and looked at Colin. "Coy-lyn, when you came to us I gained another brother. You have taught me so much. I now only have you and you are leaving. I love my sister but I know why you must go, it is my love for you that puts murder in my heart."

"I promised you I'd take you up in the sky, remember?" Colin said.

Abas smiled weakly. "One day, Coy-lyn, one day you will come back to us and …"

The two men hugged.

England and Sarawak, Borneo
Rachel's, Colin's and Aslah's continuing stories

Chapter One Hundred and Fifty-Five

"It will not be possible, Miss Lefévre. Our rules now strictly forbid women on their own being given positions abroad, and as you have a young child that only adds to the impossibility." As he spoke, the bank official looked at Rachel over his horn-rimmed glasses.

His recently cut black hair and trimmed moustache reminded Rachel of someone.

She was in a war-shattered Birmingham and the official was from The Far Eastern Banking Corporation, the same bank she worked for in Kuching before the war. She had assumed that going back would not present a problem but she was wrong.

"But," she said, "there weren't the same restrictions before the war, as you know I was in Kuching, and I now speak some Dutch as well as fluent Malay. I would have thought I was an ideal person to help the people of Sarawak and in particular, Kuching."

The official's expression did not change. "It is not possible," he said.

"Tell me why four years of war in the Far East have changed the bank's policy. Why was I eligible before the war but I am not now." Rachel paused. "It's my daughter Angelique isn't it?" Rachel clasped her hands tightly on her lap to stop herself from thumping the desk that stood between her and officialdom.

"As I have already explained Miss Lefévre, the bank's policy has been changed and I am merely ensuring this policy is implemented. The war created a different set of circumstances." The official looked at his watch again.

"I am sorry if I am keeping you, Mr Pennington, but you haven't told me the reasoning behind this change in policy, in fact other than repeat what I was told on the telephone you have told me nothing. It is unlikely the Japanese are going to wage another war for a long time, so if anything it is safer in Sarawak now than it has ever been. So what has really caused this change in policy?" she demanded. The official just looked at her. "All right, tell me Mr Pennington, if I were a man who had been incarcerated for nearly four years by the Japanese: if I were a man who had been physically assaulted, starved, humiliated, deprived of life's essentials: if I were a man who was made to strip naked in front of his captor, would you say the same?" Rachel, who was now close to tears carried on: "If I were a man who had the pre-war experience, spoke Malay fluently and Dutch, would The Far Eastern Banking Corporation being saying there had been a change in policy."

There was a hint of a smile on the official's lips. "No, Miss Lefévre, it wouldn't. You'd be required to have a medical but there would be no restrictions on your employment with us."

Rachel contained her fury and her tears. "And if I were a man with a young child?"

"That situation is unlikely to exist is it, Miss Lefévre? Now I must –"

Standing up Rachel slammed her hands on the desk. "You pompous excuse for a human being," she shouted at him. "Where were you during the war?" she demanded.

"I was in a restricted profession, so I wasn't called up," he said haughtily.

"That," Mr Pennington, "is rather obvious."

"How dare you, I have a good mind –"

"A good mind to do what, Mr Pennington? Do you want to tell me to strip off so that you can leer at my body, so you can see I am feminine and therefore not deserving the same treatment as a man? I suffered as the men suffered for nearly four years. Why should that have changed your bloody bank's policy?"

With her final comment hanging in the air, Rachel stormed out of the office.

Colin was both delighted and saddened when Lance Corporal Ben Griffiths was true to his word. If any obstacles, delays or refusals occurred, he may have had little choice but to return to Aslah and Dani.

However, within a week of returning to Miri and Labuan Island, he was on an aircraft bound for Singapore where he boarded the *SS Monte Rosa* heading for Southampton. The journey would take three to four weeks so he was going to have many daylight hours and sleepless nights to think about his decision.

Once on board the ship he had a feeling of foreboding.

As he rested his arms on the railings on the upper aft deck and stared at Singapore's receding skyline, it was almost as though part of him no longer existed.

His mind went back to what Chao had said to him.

Chao, who previously had kept her opinion much to herself, took the opportunity before Colin left Miri to tell him exactly what she thought of his behaviour.

"I watched you closely after your return to the longhouse from Miri and I have to say that I did not like what I saw. Although I have not told you before, I have always admired you. I admired the way you became as one with the Iban, I admired your bravery, and I respected the way you reacted to the murder of the young Malay couple after you returned from that first mission. But from the outset I was always apprehensive about your marriage to Aslah. She is a beautiful girl in every respect, and any man white, black, yellow or brown would have wanted her physically, but you chose marriage. By marrying Aslah you made a commitment. At the time it was an honourable decision but now I think it was the wrong one."

"Chao, all you are saying is true but we cannot wind the clock back," Colin said.

"That is also true. You have not seen this woman who is drawing you away from your wife and son for nearly four years and her internment will have been a traumatic experience for her, let alone having to bring up a child while in captivity. She will have changed. The fact that she had a daughter while she was a prisoner and they both survived the war was incredible, but I am confused why the discovery that they are alive should be the reason for you to leave Aslah and Dani."

"It is not a decision I took lightly," Colin told her. "The guilt I feel has engulfed me but Aslah would not let my guilt be the reason for me to stay, if I did I would be unhappy and I would blame her."

"And what about her happiness?" Chao almost shouted at him. "That young girl did everything she could to make you happy and you have now thrown all that back in her face."

"I know, Chao. You have every right to be critical and angry but it is too late now. I couldn't go back even if I wanted to, not before I have been to England and spoken to Rachel and met my daughter. Afterwards, I will have another decision to take."

"Tell me Colin," Chao said. "If you had discovered that Rachel had died during the war and there was no daughter, would you now be preparing to spend the rest of your life with Aslah? She had so many plans for you both and for Dani. And they were plans that would have allowed you to return to your own world."

Colin bowed his head.

"You are asking me whether I am using Rachel as an excuse to leave Aslah, Dani and the Iban."

"Yes, that is what I am asking."

"I don't know," Colin said. "I really don't know."

"Mum, I need to find somewhere to live," Rachel said.

The interview with Mr Pennington had taken the wind out of her sails so she needed time on her own to decide what she must now do. Her plans were in turmoil.

"But darling," her mother said, "this is a big house, you and Angelique can have all the privacy you want. Why do you need to find somewhere else? You both still have to get completely well."

"We are completely well, Mum, the doctor said so."

Rachel had not told her mother why she had gone to Birmingham the previous day. She had decided not to break the news until everything was in place and she would not be changing her mind. She was so convinced she would be telling her mother she was going to return to Sarawak.

Because of the disgusting treatment she received from her former employers, Rachel felt the need to move out even more. She wanted to be on her own with Angelique while she decided what their future was to be. The previous night she had a dream about Colin: his smiling, tanned face was looking down at her from the middle of a white cloud. He was beckoning her, telling her to come home.

Since leaving Kuching she had tried to push him to the back of her mind, it had been easier than she thought because during the journey and once back in England there was nothing – other than their daughter – she could associate him with. Although the journey home had been long and boring, and she had time to reflect, she found that her reflections were more recent than the last time she saw him.

She had to get used – for a while anyway – to being in England. "I'm twenty-nine, I have had four years of my life stolen from me, I need to catch up, I need to get used to being on my own," she told her mother.

"You won't be on your own darling, you'll have Angelique."

Rachel knew her mother would have seen a big change in her. She had always been stubborn, even as a little girl – or so her mother said – and she had gone against her mother's wishes when she went to Kuching in the first place. Now her mother needed to cope with a different person who was equally obstinate. Rachel had lost her spark, she rarely had reason to smile – except when she and Angelique were playing – she hardly spoke, she did not want to meet anybody and she did not care what other people might think.

She knew she was abrupt with her mother and often to the point of rudeness. She regretted every situation when she saw the hurt in her mother's eyes but she was still her mother's daughter and the love she had for her would mean she would do anything to help – even let her daughter go for a second time.

"Being on my own is with Angelique, she is part of me," Rachel said.

"Is there anything I can help you with, darling. I know you have been through hell, but you are home now and ..."

"Mum," Rachel said standing up, her chair scraping on the kitchen floor, "you don't know what I have been through." Angelique looked startled as her mother raised her voice. "And the need to be on my own is my way of coping with everything. I need to start a new life, I need to move on, if I don't I think I will go mad. I need a job and I need something to occupy my time."

"But where will you go, darling?"

"Away from here," Rachel said, regretting her choice of words straight away. "I'm sorry, Mum, but I've got to do this in my own way."

Chapter One Hundred and Fifty-Eight

He kept himself to himself for the entire journey.

He shared a cabin with two young officers who were going home on a spot of leave. They were nice enough blokes but Colin found their high spirits and constant chatter about the war, excruciatingly annoying. They asked him where he had been and what had he done during the war. It was nothing more than ice breaking as far as conversation was concerned, but Colin did not want to go there.

"Batu Lintang camp," Colin said for a reason he couldn't quite put his finger on, "and as far as what I did: rot." He had no idea why he lied straight away. He was proud of where he had been and what he had done, but the one thing he did not want to do was talk about it.

"You were a prisoner?" the young Coldstream Guards officer asked.

"No, I was a bloody camp guard," Colin spat at him. He thought they might ask why he looked so healthy if he had been a guest of the Japanese, instead the two officers exchanged looks, shrugged and left Colin to his own devices.

They appeared happy to ignore him after that and he was happy to be ignored. The officers spent most of their time mixing with the other soldiers on board, he spent most of his time tucked away in a secluded spot by the aft funnel, reading and thinking. He found it difficult to concentrate and although he managed to obtain a copy of George Orwell's *Animal Farm*, he found his mind wandering.

He asked the purser whether he could have a bunk on his own but it was impossible due to the numbers that had been crammed on board, so he continued his seclusion by the rear funnel.

The last conversation he had with Chao was still preying on his mind, as were Aslah's and Dani's faces. Anak and Ramlah had said little, there was no need; their expressions had said it all. Abas was the same, and no doubt Babu was looking down from the Gods disapprovingly.

How could he expect anyone else to understand when he did not really understand himself? Perhaps Chao was right: he was using Rachel as an excuse to do what he really wanted to do. If he had heard that somebody else had done what he was doing, he would have called them all the names under the sun. Was he really *that* bastard?

Refuelling at Colombo, in Ceylon, Aden, at the southern end of the Red Sea, and Port Said at the northern end of the Suez Canal gave him temporary respite as there was something to look at other than vast expanses of water. The flying fish that kept pace with the ship for a while seemed to lighten his heart a little, but only temporarily.

The Suez Canal was like a collage of the devastation of war: piles of scrap metal that used to be military vehicles: vehicles with human occupants when destroyed. Bulldozed into heaps of what used to be, they were epitaphs to human wanton destruction. Colin felt it was a good demonstration of the stupidity and futility of war. He could make out German, Italian and British insignia, all together in their scrap metal grave. There were the real graveyards, some looking temporary, the bodies they contained maybe also waiting for repatriation.

The Mediterranean brought more vast expanses of water and its accompanying isolation of thought, but Gibraltar became the final turn, the final corner. As he saw Lagos and Faro in the distance and the ship turned north for the last leg of their journey, he found his apprehensiveness increase.

England was now not far away.

As he looked he had no idea what might await him when he got there.

Having to queue and be processed along with hundreds of servicemen – and some women – was a complication that Colin could have well done without. He had no means of identification, his passport burned along with Sammy. He didn't have 'dog tags' – the identification discs worn round their necks by servicemen and women on active service – all he had was what he was able to tell his questioners and a piece of paper given to him by the Australians on Labuan Island.

Having got him this far, it appeared this piece of paper was not enough to get him into his country of birth.

"I am sorry if this is becoming a little cumbersome, Mr Freemantle, but you must appreciate that this is an ideal time for undesirables to attempt to sneak into the country," the officer said.

The young officer, in front of whom Colin now found himself, looked too young to be in uniform but he appeared competent, and certainly patient enough.

"I understand," Colin told him, "but I really can't tell you any more than I have already. It is seven years since I was last in England, I have no brothers or sisters and my parents died in 1920. It was their deaths that really forced me into going abroad in the first place."

"Aunts, uncles? Surely you have some relatives in England," the officer asked.

Colin shook his head. "My mother's sister brought me up but she is also now dead. There was another sister on my mother's side and my father had two brothers, but there was little enough contact before I left the country and there certainly hasn't been any since. I couldn't even tell you where they live."

"May I ask why you are returning to England after so long abroad?" the officer asked. "I appreciate the war is over but I would have thought after so long you would have wanted to stay where you were." The officer studied the form he had been filling out. "In Sarawak, that is."

Nodding, Colin looked down at his hands. He knew where Rachel might be and she could confirm his identity but she didn't even know he was alive. There was literally nobody who could vouch for him, confirm who he was or even verify his presence with the Iban for four years. As had been explained to him, the bit of paper the Australians had given him was worthless – all they were doing was processing people out of a war zone. What happened to them after that was none of their business or responsibility.

Colin took a deep breath. "This is the fourth, no the fifth interrogation I have been through: Miri and Labuan with the Australians, Singapore with British and on the ship. I have been allowed to get this far, am I to be stopped from entering my country of birth at the final hurdle?"

The officer smiled. "No, Mr Freemantle and I don't regard this as an interrogation, merely a safety valve." He looked at the form again. "You say you lived in Oakham before going overseas."

"Yes, that's right," Colin said.

"What is the name of the pub nearest to the railway station?"

"The Grainstore," Colin said without hesitation. "I used to go there and hopefully I will again before too long."

Shrugging and with the smile still on his lips the officer picked up the form. "So did I when I was detached to Cottesmore. That'll do," he said. "Come with me and we'll get you some identification papers."

"Is that it?" Colin asked.

"Knowing the Grainstore got you into England, Mr Freemantle."

Listening to the noises of the night had never meant so much to her, but now that he was no longer there, Aslah heard them for him. She could see him now as the light from the moon shone onto his glistening body; his eyes wide open as he tried to put a source to every sound. If he was uncertain, he would say a name and she would correct him if necessary.

Sometimes they would argue but only lightly, they had never really argued. She had always known when it was time for her to back down, except when he was being stupid.

She had counted the number of moons that had passed since he had left: it had reached thirty-five. "Thirty five," she whispered in English. "There have been thirty five days and now thirty five nights."

She was so pleased that she had made him teach her English because when she spoke the language she felt she was nearer to him. She and Abas often spoke in English so that they could learn from each other.

However, Abas was preparing to leave.

He had his father's and mother's blessing because they wanted the best for him and he wouldn't achieve that by staying in the longhouse. Since losing Babu and with Coy-lyn no longer there, Abas had become even more restless. Her father was wise enough to know that the days of the longhouse were numbered and the future for his people was in the modern world. Some may stay but she knew he believed that within a few generations, the longhouse would be no more.

Aslah turned over under the mosquito net so that she could see Dani sleeping beside her. How she longed for her husband. She could picture every detail of his face, every detail of his body. She knew that his heart had ached as he climbed into the prau to leave. Abas had told her what he had said to her Coy-lyn, and she loved her brother and her husband more because of it.

How she longed to lie in his arms again.

The tears were there every night. She wept silently, not wanting her father and mother to fret over her. She did not regret her decision to let him go, he had to go, she would not have stopped him. But not regretting her decision and the hollow feeling she had felt since he left meant that deep inside she wished that one day he would return. Dani was not old enough to understand, although one day he would ask who and where his father was.

What would she say?

She knew that some of the Iban men wanted to approach her, but they also knew that she was not interested. Maybe one day, if he did not return, she would go with another man, but that day was many more moons away. She fell in love with her orang puteh the first time she saw him and she would love him forever, of that there was no doubt. She had no desire for another man to touch her. If another man touched her, her Coy-lyn would not be the last one to have done so. Her dreams were enough to keep her going … until he returned.

Dani disturbed but only for a few seconds.

He was a lovely little boy, growing bigger every day, his eyes a constant reminder of her Coy-lyn.

He had brought so much happiness into her life.

Aslah closed her eyes as the noises of the night subsumed her.

She did not bother to wipe away the tears.

They flowed over her cheeks as they did every night. While she cried he would always be part of her: if she stopped crying she would be worried because it would mean he no longer meant so much to her, so she would never stop crying and missing him.

"Well, Miss Lefévre," said Mr Prendaghast, the manager of Lloyds Bank in the High Street in Market Harborough, "you certainly have all the qualifications you may need to be considered for an appointment with us. May I ask why you left your previous appointment with, let me see, yes, The Far Eastern Banking Corporation?"

Wanting to tell him that it was a damn fool question as all branches and offices of The Far Eastern Banking Corporation had either been in Japan or overrun by the invading Imperial Japanese Army, Rachel chose politeness as an alternative. "I was in Kuching in Sarawak when the Japanese invaded Mr Prendaghast, I have –"

"Kuching in Sarawak? Excuse me for my ignorance, Miss Lefévre but where is Sarawak?"

"Borneo, Mr Prendaghast. It abuts British North Borneo which sandwiches Brunei between it and Sarawak in the south west and to the east of the island there is Dutch Borneo."

It was obvious to Rachel that what she had said meant nothing. Another uninformed bank official, she thought.

What was the point?

"And you are living where, Miss Lefévre?"

At least this official recognised that she was not married.

"I am renting a small house in the town," she told him. "But let me be perfectly honest, I do not intend staying in the area, I hope to move abroad within twelve months and therefore I regard this appointment as an expedient."

"Thank you for being honest, Miss Lefévre," Mr Prendaghast said.

His *uniform* was almost identical to that worn by Pennington with whom she had had the unfortunate meeting two weeks earlier. In fact, to look at, the two could be brothers, Rachel thought.

"Do you know Market Harborough?" Mr Prendaghast asked.

"Not too well at the moment, but we've only been here a matter of days."

"*We've?*" Mr Prendaghast repeated, noticing the slip.

The similarity in Prendaghast's appearance to Yamamoto and Oshida had not passed Rachel by. She lifted her hand to her mouth to

329

cover a mischievous smile.

"I have a three-year old daughter, Mr Prendaghast. Her father is unfortunately still missing."

Mr Prendaghast steepled his fingertips and smiled. "I am sorry to hear that, *Miss* Lefévre. War is terrible and painful. I fully understand why you regard this appointment as temporary and regardless I am pleased to be able to offer it to you. May I ask when you can start?"

Noting the emphasis he had placed on *Miss* this time, Rachel sighed but accepted that it was going to happen repeatedly. At least this was progress and if employed the chances of her returning to Sarawak might improve. Maybe Lloyds Bank would expand into the Far East in time.

"It can be as soon as I have arranged for somebody to care for my daughter, Mr Prendaghast. Shall we say Monday of next week?"

"Monday next week it is," said Mr Prendaghast with enthusiasm.

"I look forward to working with you, Mr Prendaghast."

"And I with you, Miss Lefévre, such a pretty name."

Rachel smiled and wondered what he was really thinking.

On the journey from Southampton to London there was little to suggest that Britain had just emerged from another world war. In some of the towns the train passed through there were collapsed buildings, but the people on the platforms were acting as though it was a normal Tuesday afternoon.

For Colin it was far from normal.

He left England over seven years ago and seeing his country of birth again was a surreal experience. As he looked at the scurrying people in the streets, the way they were dressed, the number of vehicles on the roads, the smoke from the chimneys and the lack of leaves on the trees, his mind took him back to his home for the last four years.

There was no similarity between the two. Now, he knew where he wanted to be. There was little point in denying the truth ... he wished he had stayed in Sarawak.

Chao had been right.

His apprehension had not gone away.

Unsurprisingly, London presented a different picture.

The aftermath of the German bombing raids and subsequent destruction could be seen everywhere. As he picked his way from Paddington station to his bank at the top of Oxford Street, he marvelled at the way the clearance of rubble and preparation for rebuilding was so advanced. His bank appeared to have come through unscathed, although sandbags still formed its entrance, and the windows remained taped.

He asked to see a manager.

"Yes, Mr Freemantle," the formally dressed man in his mid-forties said as he ushered Colin into a back office. "What can I do for you?"

"I wish to withdraw a considerable amount of money from my account with you," Colin told him, sitting down at the desk. "In fact I wish to close the account."

The man flipped over the pages of the ledger he had brought in with him.

"It's Mr Colin Freemantle, isn't it?" Colin nodded. "May I ask if you have a middle name?"

331

"Anthony," Colin told him.

The man, who had not given Colin his name, peered more closely at the page in front of him. "This account is all deposits from the Far East and no withdrawals," he said without looking up, "but there have been no further deposits since, let me see, September 1941."

He looked up, his expression inquisitive.

"Yes, I have been indisposed since then until now," Colin told him.

"Indisposed?" An understanding smile suddenly appeared on the man's face. "Ah, I see, you were a prisoner of war."

"Something like that," Colin said.

"And how much do you wish to withdraw, Mr Freemantle."

"All of it," Colin told him. "I wish to close the account."

"But there is over five thousand pounds in this account."

"I hoped there would be."

"And you want to withdraw all of it?"

"Yes, does that present a problem?"

"But ... well, yes, I mean no. I'll go and get the necessary paperwork."

Colin watched the man scurry from his office. His decision to empty the account was indicative of the way he felt. He still regretted his decision and he was demonstrating the need to cut all ties with his country of birth ... but first he would find Rachel and meet his daughter.

The three weeks she had spent on her own had helped, but not as much as she had hoped. She did not like leaving Angelique with a stranger during the day, but the girl's references had been good and she seemed a responsible young thing, but her age, just eighteen, did worry Rachel.

The girl's name was Amy and she lived in Market Harborough with her parents.

Market Harborough was not too far from Leamington Spa, maybe forty miles, and she would try to get to see her mother at least once a month.

She would go by bus and train.

Angelique had been good during the move but she did talk about her grandmother a lot, so Rachel felt she owed it to her daughter to allow the relationship to develop. Rachel though, continued to feel detached. Her attitude worried her, as did her constant longing for escape, but as she told herself from the beginning, she would bide her time and see. She needed to get out of England and back to Sarawak. She had not given her earlier plans enough thought but going back remained her ultimate aim.

On her third day in the bank, which was in the High Street next to the old Grammar School in Market Harborough, she had almost fallen off her chair as she looked up to attend to the next customer.

He was tall, had blond hair, blue eyes and a lovely smile. His skin was tanned and when he smiled he had even, white teeth.

"Good morning," he said, "you're new."

"Yes," Rachel said, feeling a little flustered.

The man was the image of Colin Freemantle: a little broader and taller maybe, but facially the likeness was uncanny. Of course she was flustered. Having moved Colin to the back of her mind as best she could, it was just a little scary that something like this should happen.

"Yes ... yes, this is only my third day," Rachel said.

"May I say, in that case, you are a pleasant addition to this somewhat drab scenery?"

He produced a chequebook.

Glancing furtively at the woman at the next till, Rachel felt her face flush. She could not remember when she had last blushed although, now, it was a pleasant feeling.

Without making eye contact with the man as she asked: "How much would you like, sir?"

"Twenty pounds, two fives and ten ones please," he replied, obviously amused by Rachel's reaction.

Counting out the money Rachel glanced at the cheque the man had pushed towards her. From his signature she saw his name was Richard, Richard Brasher.

She handed him the money.

"Thank you," he said. "You have the advantage in that you know my name but I don't know yours."

"Rachel Lefévre, Miss Lefévre," she told him without hesitation.

"Well, *Miss* Lefévre, it was a pleasure meeting you and I feel that we may meet again."

"Not when he finds out about your kid," the woman next to Rachel said as she watched Richard Brasher leave the bank.

Rachel thought her comment was a little unkind … but probably true.

Chapter One Hundred and Sixty-Four

When members of the Red Cross met him at Leamington Spa station, it took some persuasion before the volunteer nurses accepted that he was capable of walking, talking and thinking on his own. However, as Colin looked around the platform he thought some of the soldiers would be grateful that these smiling and willing female faces were there to greet them.

He did accept a cup of tea and a sandwich, he also noticed that a few of the nurses were looking at him and nudging each other. He had bought a new suit, shirt and tie, all of which made him feel extremely overdressed and uncomfortable, and obviously unlike the soldiers in their uniforms.

The soldiers also looked tired and gaunt.

He had never been to Leamington Spa before and had to ask a number of people the way to Beauchamp Avenue.

Rather like his train journey from Southampton to London, he had expected to see more bomb damage. He had heard (or read) that the damage to Coventry and Birmingham was bad, but there was little destruction to see in Leamington Spa.

It was nearly three months after VJ day and he guessed the town was slowly returning to normal, as normal as rationing allowed it to be.

As he got closer to where he hoped Rachel would be, the realisation of how near he might be to her, and his daughter, hit him.

He stopped outside the Grand Hotel on the Parade and went inside where he hoped to get a cup of coffee or tea. As he approached the hotel he realised he had no idea what he was going to say when he saw Rachel. He had not thought things through enough.

What could he say?

What do two people who have survived a war say to each other after so long?

He needed time to think.

He sipped on the tea as he looked out of the window at the people walking up and down the Parade.

Was he looking for inspiration?

Her internment was a fact. She will have suffered the most horrendous of conditions that was also a fact. With her daughter she

335

had survived, they were both facts. What else were going to be facts?

She had left *Labuan* Island more than a month before him so she had now been back in England for six weeks or even longer. What was there to worry about? There should not be anybody else, there hadn't been time.

Did only a man think like that?

Why under the circumstances did he think there might be somebody else? She was with his – their – daughter, so the last thing she would be thinking about would be looking for was another man.

So all he had to do was ... was what? She had said she loved him, she'd had their daughter and he loved her: surely such a scene was being repeated all over the world as soldiers – and civilians – returned from the war.

He took a deep breath, finished his tea and walked to the top of the Parade where he turned right followed by a left onto the Kenilworth Road. Two minutes later, he was at the crossroads with Beauchamp Avenue, and after a further two minutes, he was standing at the garden gate for No 24. He had travelled half way round the world to be where he was.

Why did he feel as though he had wasted his journey?

He had expected to be apprehensive, but why now was he so worried?

Elspeth Lefévre peered round the curtain to see who was at the door.

Since her husband died, she had always been cautious, even during the war there were some funny people out on the streets. Others were ready to take advantage of somebody who lived in a big house on their own. Perhaps she ought to think about selling it and moving to somewhere smaller, but that could wait for a while, not a lot of people were buying houses so soon after the end of the war.

He looked decent enough.

He was tall, probably in his early thirties, his face was … well rugged in a handsome sort of way. His clothes looked new and his shoes clean. Perhaps he was a policeman.

Why would the police …?

She saw him ring the bell again before looking towards the window from which she had been scrutinising him. She let the net curtain drop and went to the front door.

The smile was engaging and he was a lot more handsome face to face. In fact he could quite easily pass as an American film star. Why did she think American rather than English? – what an incongruous thought.

"Yes?" Elspeth asked, she hoped not too haughtily.

"Mrs Lefévre?" the man enquired his nervousness rather obvious.

"Yes, I am Mrs Lefévre. How can I help you?" she said.

"I am sorry to bother you but I am trying to locate Rachel, Miss Rachel Lefévre," the man said, "and I understand that she may be living at this address."

"Do you now? Rachel *is* my daughter. May I ask who you are and why you are trying to locate her?"

Elspeth wanted to invite the young man into her house but she needed to know a little more first. She could see that he was uneasy, she liked that, but she must not make him feel too anxious. He was obviously a man of the world, something about him suggested there was depth to him and she liked that as well.

"Yes, of course, that was rude of me, I am sorry," he said. "My name is Colin Freemantle and before the war your daughter and I were close friends."

"I see," Elspeth said, as she looked even closer at the young man.

"Yes, I see. You had better come in."

She stood back so that Colin could enter.

"Through there," she added when he hesitated by the living room door.

"Give me your coat," Elspeth suggested, "and would you like some refreshment."

"No, no thank you, I have done nothing but drink tea since I arrived in Leamington Spa."

Colin handed her his overcoat.

"If you are sure," Elspeth said as she put the coat over the back of the settee.

"This is kind of you, Mrs Lefévre," Colin said sitting down. "I hope my calling on you is not an inconvenience."

"No, not at all. Now tell me how you know my daughter."

Colin smiled.

"It's a long story so where do I start?" he asked.

"Try the beginning," Elspeth Lefévre said.

Colin nodded. "Yes, that would be a good idea."

"And I am listening," Elspeth said.

Rachel was watching the clock.

Although the bank had closed to the public, she could not leave before five thirty. She knew she would not be in the job for long: it was boring, repetitive and the people who worked there were like stuffed shirts.

Life in Kuching where work was just part of her entire day was what she longer for – the people wanted to be there and their association carried on into the evenings and weekends. They socialised, laughed and had fun. She accepted that had been before the war, so maybe when rebuilding a country, a city or a town such things had to wait until recovery was complete. Then again, the war was over so if anything spirits would be higher and they would need a release valve.

She smiled as she thought about some of the things she and her colleagues used to enjoy. Her mother and father would have disowned her had they known. She remembered the wonderful and secluded beaches a long way downriver from Kuching. The river journeys had been a thrill in their own right because the currents meant they had to be extremely careful. Rachel wondered if Mildred Bryant, sitting next to her doing her knitting, had ever been skinny-dipping. She doubted whether she had ever let her husband see her completely naked let alone men to whom she was not married. Stripping off for the first time had been quite intimidating and embarrassing: she watched the men who for obvious reasons never seemed to have any such inhibitions. The other two girls also stripped off. Rachel followed shortly afterwards and when she lowered her body into the water her shyness disappeared with the marvellous sensation – a feeling of complete freedom. Yes, the men in the party had looked at her, as they looked at the others, but they had never tried anything on with her. Then she met Colin and the need for exhibitionism, if that is what it was, seemed to disappear – she wondered why.

Rachel suddenly recalled Mildred's words after that handsome stranger had been into the bank to cash a cheque, and suggested he and Rachel could quite easily meet again.

"Not when he finds out about your kid."

She and Mildred Bryant had said little since, which was difficult because they spent most of the day sitting next to each other.

How had Mildred known about Angelique?

It could only have come from one source – Mr Prendaghast, the manager: he was the only one who knew, well the only one who should have known.

Mildred was right though.

Anyway, she was twenty-nine and most women were married with a family by then. When any man who might show an interest in her found out about Angelique, regardless of what a delectable little girl she was, she would not see them for dust.

It was not fair to blame Angelique, although blame was not the right word. They had both been through hell's camp together and had come out the other side with a bond that most mothers really want. No, Angelique must always come first. If men were so immature that they were unable to cope that was their failing, not hers.

What about all the widowed young mothers from the war: were they destined for a life of abstinence, without the love of a man?

The big hand on the clock clicked onto the half hour so Rachel collected her things and stood up.

"Good night, Mildred," she said.

"Good night, Rachel," Mildred replied.

No, this was not the life for her: in Kuching, they would all be trooping down to Club after work for a Singapore Sling or three.

Approaching her father with some trepidation and with Dani on her hip, Aslah stopped when she was a few feet away. Anak had just eaten and he always liked time after his meal to sit and consider what the day had brought and what the next day might bring.

Since the Japanese had lost the war, Aslah noticed that her father's wariness was more evident. He did not share his thoughts the way he used to, not as readily anyway. The others still admired, respected and in some cases, revered him ... but the war had aged him and made him more cautious.

Losing Babu, his younger son, had aged him even more.

Seeing his daughter's husband leave with her blessing had confused him, but he had not interfered. Maybe he resented her for not fighting to keep Coy-lyn by her side.

"Father," Aslah said to his bowed head. "I need your advice and guidance."

Slowly he lifted his head.

She saw the tiredness in his eyes but his smile told her that she was still like a beautiful angel to him. Angel was a word Coy-lyn had taught him and he had called her that ever since, but only when they were alone, never in front of anybody else. She also knew he adored the blue-eyed, fair-haired child she had given to him as his first grandchild.

"Yes, Angel," Anak said, "that is why I am here."

The smile disappeared and she saw him sigh. If he was as perceptive as ever he would know why she was there but he would want confirmation of his belief.

Dropping to her knees in front of her father Aslah moved Dani so that he was sitting on her lap. The young child looked straight at his grandfather and he stared back at his grandson with a smile on his lips, and in his eyes.

"Father, when Abas leaves I would like to leave with him," Aslah said, knowing there was little point in evading her reason for wanting to speak to him. Closing her eyes, she wondered whether the words she had used had been the right ones. How else could she have said it?

Her father was silent for a few seconds.

341

"Before your husband left, Angel, I had expected that one day soon you would leave with him for a new life in a new world." He paused as her mother came onto the *ruai* and sat a few feet behind her husband.

She looked at Aslah but not even a hint of a smile appeared on her face. That worried Aslah.

"Babu is with the Gods," her father said. "Abas is leaving and now you have decided that you must also leave. What you say does not come as a total surprise. The war brought much badness, but it also made people aware that there is a greater, but not necessarily a better world out there. Down river there is a new life, and a life to which you have every right to experience. Your mother and I will miss you as we miss Babu and as we will miss Abas, but we must and cannot stand in the way of progress."

"And Coy-lyn, father, do you miss my husband?"

Her father thought again for a moment or two.

"Angel," he said, "the war brought together two cultures that would not normally have met. The little warrior on your knee is the product of such a meeting. Whether you are here or somewhere else one day he will become a leader of this longhouse. I miss Coy-lyn for you but you must do what is best for your son."

"But do *you* miss *him*, father? Do you miss Coy-lyn?"

"Without him we would have survived, but he brought wisdom to this longhouse. Yes, my daughter I do miss him, but I do not agree with what he has done to you."

The journey from Leamington Spa to Market Harborough was slow as it was arduous.

After he finished telling Rachel's mother about how he and Rachel had met and then parted, he expected some of his concerns to lessen, but the opposite applied.

She had listened so he could not take that away from her. Every now and again, and after apologising, she asked him to elaborate on a couple of things he said.

He did not mention Aslah and Dani. Mrs Elspeth Lefévre living at No 24 Beauchamp Avenue, Leamington Spa, Warwickshire, England, would not have understood how an Englishman, especially one who had an intimate relationship with her daughter, had fathered a son with a native who lived in a wooden house on stilts in the middle of the jungle on the other side of the world.

The added concern did not come about because of anything malicious. Elspeth Lefévre told him the truth, or the truth as she saw it.

"Thank you for being honest with me, Mr Freemantle." Elspeth Lefévre said. "I very much appreciate how difficult it may have been for you. You obviously care for my daughter but you did say that you did not know as you flew away from Kuching that my daughter was expecting a baby, a baby that you assume now is yours."

"I –"

"No, please, you have said what you came here to say and now I must reply."

Elspeth Lefévre picked up the china cup and took a sip of tea, her eyes never leaving his. Colin thought he could see bitterness and blame: she would have every right to be bitter if she knew the whole truth.

"My daughter spent nearly four years, and using her own word, in hell, Mr Freemantle. During this period, she not only went through a traumatic pregnancy but it was in the most testing and trying of circumstances. The child she gave birth to is a delightful little girl who survived, with her mother, the horrors of war. I had lost my husband in an avoidable accident and I thought I had lost my daughter too. When she appeared on my doorstep, as you did this afternoon, I was both delighted and overwhelmed.

"But Mr Freemantle, you need to be aware that the daughter who left her father and me so many years ago is not the daughter who returned. She has become a selfish and distant woman who could not even acknowledge the loss of her father. I fully appreciate that someone does not live through hell for so many years without changing as a person.

"You knew her before the war so the woman you will remember is not the woman who has recently moved out of this house and taken her daughter, my granddaughter, with her. God knows why when I could and wanted to help her so much, she chose to leave, but she did. I think it would be best if you –"

"If you are going to say what I think –"

"Mr Freemantle please, this is hard enough as it is. I am sorry to have to tell you that my daughter did not mention you. She did not tell me who the father of my granddaughter was."

"I thought that might be the case," Colin said.

"I have no wish to know the circumstances under which my granddaughter was conceived, but I would have thought … no, that is none of my business. What's done is done, but I am only willing to go so far in assisting you in finding her. I hope you understand. Whether she wishes to meet you must be at her bidding not mine."

"Yes, Mrs Lefévre, I understand," Colin said.

Chapter One Hundred and Sixty-Nine

Sitting at the end of the zinc bath opposite her mother, her hair covered in soapsuds, Angelique screwed up her face to keep the soap out of her eyes.

Amy had left as soon as Rachel had arrived home explaining that she was meeting her navigator boyfriend from RAF Bosworth, which was just up the road from Market Harborough. Amy also told Rachel that Angelique had been unusually quiet all day. She thought she might be coming down with a cold or something.

Rachel therefore decided that a bath, which Angelique loved, would allow her to decide whether Amy was right or not. Normally Rachel had a stand up wash in the morning because it took ages to get sufficient hot water to have a bath. Each time she shared a bath with Angelique her mind went back to the time with Oshida – did that really happen?

Watching Angelique, the flames from the fire flickering on her hair and face, Rachel realised for the first time since arriving home she was happy. The job was awful – she would have to investigate the other banks to see if their working environments were any better, although she doubted that would be the case – but she and Angelique were eating well now and both had put on weight.

And her first period since Angelique was born had descended on her ten days ago. She did not know whether to be thrilled or unhappy because it meant that normality really was catching up with her, and she did not want that.

The weather was awful too, it had been a wet, cold autumnal week, and most mornings she had scuttled to work in the gloom and come home in darkness. How she longed for the heat and humidity.

The soft music from the wireless on the mantelpiece was a novelty and she had it on all the time. As she listened she marvelled at how the soldiers in Batu Lintang had managed to get the parts for 'The Old Lady' and 'Ginnie', the hand generator, both of which provided the source of so much news and right under the noses of the Japanese.

So why did she feel so much better?

Was it because she and Angelique were now by themselves? The previous weekend they had wrapped up well and walked the streets of Market Harborough until they knew every corner, every crossroads and every house – or so Rachel believed.

The old pushchair Rachel had bought came into its own for the last mile when at last Angelique gave in to her weary legs. They exchanged pleasantries with many of the locals, and Rachel did feel a little disappointed when she did not bump into the man who had gone into the bank, although she knew the chances of seeing him were remote. If they had met he would certainly have found out about Angelique, then Mildred would have been proved right or wrong.

"Mummy," Angelique said, opening her eyes slightly to look at Rachel. "Amy asked me a question today."

"That makes a change young lady, what with all your questions."

The water was getting cool so Rachel wiped the suds from her hands and reached for the towel that was warming on the chair in front of the fire.

She thought she knew what was coming and she was right.

"She asked when my daddy was coming home."

Rachel closed her eyes.

Having anticipated the question for so long, she did not know what to say.

Should she lie?

What was there to lie about?

She knew who Angelique's father was but she had no idea if he was alive, and if so, where he could be.

Chapter One Hundred and Seventy

She did not tell me who the father of my granddaughter was – Elspeth Lefévre's words ran round and round in his head.

Why would she?

Why would Rachel have told her mother who Angelique's father was? Rachel had not known whether he was alive or dead – maybe her mother could have asked, but then again maybe she did not want to know.

Colin was only half-aware of the train stopping at Marton, Birdingbury and Dunchurch en route for Rugby Central, the first major stop.

The train jolted and puffed its way along the track. Glancing out of the filthy window, he hoped to see something that might lift his spirits but there was nothing really to see as dusk had passed into darkness.

He shared the compartment with a couple of soldiers to his right, a pretty girl in a floral dress and beige overcoat opposite him and an elderly couple – the old man had been fast asleep since getting on the train – were sitting next to the girl. Colin was amused when everybody seemed to avoid eye contact – eye contact had been so important when living with the Iban.

The soldiers, though, were annoying the girl and the elderly woman with their comments and leers.

"Come on love, we're only bein' friendly. We ain't seen ankles like them since afore the war!" The soldiers laughed and the girl looked most uncomfortable as she tried to hide her legs under her coat

"That'll do no good, love," the soldier further away said, "we got imaginations, ain't we Fred?"

"Yeah, and what I is imagining ain't her ankles."

The soldiers' laughter was suggestive.

Colin looked at the girl and smiled. Turning to the soldiers, he said, "All right, you've had your bit of fun. You're making the young lady feel most uncomfortable."

The soldier nearer to Colin turned in his seat. "And you 'ad better keep yer nose art, mate."

"Yeah," the other uttered.

Colin smiled. "And if you don't stop annoying the young lady I'll have you put off the train at the next stop."

"Yeah? You an' whose army. Fuck off!" the soldier said confidently.

Standing up Colin looked down at the two soldiers. "Do not let the fact that I am not in uniform mislead you into thinking that either of you scare me one iota. If you do not apologise to the young lady now and leave this compartment I will call the guard."

The soldier next to Colin stood up and in the confined space attempted to throw a punch. Before he knew what had happened he was on the floor, his arm twisted behind him.

He screamed in pain.

Colin looked at the other soldier. "Don't even think about it," he said. "One further twist and your friend's arm will be broken."

The soldier thought better of it and said, "Come on Fred, let's leave the bastard, we'll see to him later." He pulled the compartment door open and Colin let go of the soldier on the floor who scowled at Colin but they both collected their kitbags and left the compartment.

"Thank you," the girl said before looking down at her hands.

"It was the least I could do," Colin said.

"They were annoying me," the girl said.

"Well done, young man," the elderly woman said. "They deserved what they got.

"It's all over now," Colin told them.

Her few belongings were in an old battered suitcase held together by some rattan rope.

She put the case into the prau before turning to face her mother and father. Her mother was holding Dani whose eyes were wide open, wondering what was happening. Grouped behind Anak and his wife were the remaining occupants of the longhouse.

"It is time, father," Abas said as he moved to stand beside his sister.

Aslah and her brother had been to Miri on two previous occasions to find somewhere to live, and to visit Fung and Chao. They needed to plan. During their second visit, Fung showed them a short advertisement in the Miri Times:

WORKERS WANTED

After the liberation of North Borneo, Brunei and Sarawak from the Japanese invaders, the correct administration of all states needs reinstating. Regretfully and due to Raja Brookes' ill health, he will not personally be returning to Sarawak. To this end Sarawak and British North Borneo have become Crown Colonies and will be administered by local officers. After the devastation caused by the Japanese occupation and the subsequent fighting during the lead up to and then the liberation, there is much work to be done in reconstruction in every respect. We are looking for people to help with the reconstruction. If you would like to be considered for employment with this worthwhile team, please call into the Miri Administrative Offices.

"There are jobs waiting for both of you," Fung had told Aslah and Abas. "Because you speak English, Iban and some Mandarin, you will be great assets to the administration."

Therefore, Aslah and her brother were now preparing to leave the longhouse to start a new life in Miri. As he was not accustomed to showing affection in front of his people, her father was a little taken aback when first his son and then his daughter embraced him as they said their goodbyes.

When Aslah saw her father's embarrassment, she smiled: "It was something that Coy-lyn taught us, father. It shows we love you."

"He was different," her father said, "he was an orang puteh." But she could see he was pleased.

"We will visit regularly, mother," Aslah told her mother. "Your grandson will want to see his grandparents as often as possible."

The tears were streaming down her mother's cheeks.

Aslah understood why.

Before the war things had been different and all three of her children would not have thought about leaving and going down river to Miri, other than to collect supplies and maybe for the boys to get a little drunk. The war had changed so much and it was change she knew she had to accept. However, seeing her remaining son and only daughter climbing into the prau would not make her acceptance of change any easier.

"It is for the best," her father said looking at her mother.

"Is it?" her mother asked, sorrowfully.

"They are the next generation of Iban and they must meet progress face to face. Losing them in this way is progress."

"If you say so," her mother said.

Chapter One Hundred and Seventy-Two

Wrapped in a warm towel and with a milky drink cupped in her hands, Angelique waited for her mother to speak. It would be obvious even to a little girl that her question had caused her mother some pain, but Rachel had promised she would answer. She just needed to find the right words.

"Your daddy was a marvellous man, Angelique. He was tall, handsome and, he had blond hair and the bluest of eyes. It is from him that you get the shape and colour of your eyes."

Rachel had put on a dressing gown: the room was warm, but she still felt herself shiver. Angelique had finally asked the question she had been dreading, she should have been ready for it. She was not sure what more she could say although she did appreciate that whatever she did say would have an impact on the rest of their lives.

"He was a pilot. At the start of the war, when the Japanese invaded Sarawak he wanted to save his plane from falling into their hands, he begged me to go with him but I refused. I thought the people in Kuching needed me."

"What about me, Mummy, didn't daddy want to save me too?"

"You were still in mummy's tummy, darling, you weren't born until months later."

Rachel took the mug from Angelique as her mind raced to find more to say. In using the past tense she had to a great extent already committed herself.

"Daddy was killed … no, no, that's not right, I don't know that he was killed." She took a deep breath. "I have not spoken to your daddy for four years, I don't know whether he survived the war, I don't know where he is."

"Did you love him, Mummy?"

Rachel smiled, that question was easy. "I loved him with all my heart, darling. And you, young lady, are living proof of that love."

She tickled her daughter's toes.

Angelique giggled. "And if he is not dead, do you still love him?" she asked.

"Questions, all these questions, but yes, if he is alive I still love him, and even if he is not, I still love him. He was a wonderful, caring man, and he would have been so pleased to know that he had a daughter like you."

"You think he is dead, don't you Mummy?"

Rachel thought for a few seconds. "Throughout the time we were prisoners of the Japanese two things kept me going: one was you, you gave many others and me something to live for. And there was the love I had for your daddy. I believed he was alive for all the years we were in the camp, and in here," Rachel tapped over her heart, "in here I believe he is still alive. I don't know where he is but I believe he is still alive."

"Then I will believe that too, Mummy."

Tears came to Rachel's eyes.

"You are so grown up for your age," Rachel said. "Nobody would believe you are not yet four."

"Is that a good thing, Mummy?"

"It is … yes, it is a good thing. It means we can be friends as well as mother and daughter."

"I like that," Angelique said.

"Yes and so do I. I'm sure your father will think the same."

"I really want to meet him, Mummy."

"In that case one day we must find him."

With a clanking of metal on metal and the hissing of escaping steam, the train slowed as it pulled into Rugby Central station. It finally stopped with a shudder and another great hissing of steam almost as though it was exhaling after great exertion.

The elderly couple stood up to leave but struggled with their cases from the rack.

Colin lifted the cases down for them.

"Thank you young man," the woman said. "That was a brave thing you did earlier. I think our soldiers are marvellous but in every barrel there are rotten apples."

The woman smiled and then preceded her husband out of the compartment.

"Don't mind him," she added turning round and indicating her husband, "he's as deaf as a post."

Opening the sliding vent above the window to let in some fresh air, Colin asked the still seated girl: "Are you going far?"

The girl looked up.

"Getting off at Lubenham," she told him, her face slightly flushed.

"Which side of Market Harborough is that?"

Before the girl could answer the loud speaker on the platform spluttered into life. A man coughed a couple of times and said in a slow, deliberate voice:

"*Passengers at Platform One for Clifton Mill, Lilbourne, Yelvertoft and Stanford Park, Welford and Kilworth, Theddingworth, Lubenham and Market Harborough are advised that due to an hobstruction being found on the line between Theddingworth and Lubenham, the train will be delayed leaving Rugby Central by approximately thirty minutes. This delay is regretted but passengers may alight to take refreshments if they so wish. There will be a five minute warning before the train is due to depart for its next stop, which is Clifton Mill.*"

"That tells me where Lubenham is," Colin said, smiling. "Do you think these announcers go on special courses to learn how to speak in a monotone?"

"I don't know," the girl replied, her expression suggesting she did not understand what he was saying.

Seeing others descending from the train, Colin said, "Would you like a cup of tea? We may as well do as the man suggested and *alight to take some refreshments*."

"That would be nice," the girl replied picking up her bag.

"My name is Colin Freemantle," Colin told her as he stood back so that she could step down from the carriage, but he had to make a grab for her arm as she stumbled.

"Oh, thanks, that was embarrassing," she said. Doing up her coat she added, "And my name is Julia Danbury."

They shook hands and smiled.

They were not the only ones who had decided to take advantage of the delay. As he stood in the queue and looked about him, Colin shook his head as he realised how quickly he had fallen back into another way of life. There had been so much time to think since flying out of Labuan and the conclusions his thoughts had given him were sometimes disingenuous and sometimes far too close to the truth.

The doubts had always been there.

The picture of Aslah with Dani on her hip was like a photograph in his mind. Who was it who said, there are times when you only miss something when you no longer have it: life should not be taken for granted … ever. It was probably something he had read, but the words were or so true.

This most certainly was not what he wanted.

Chapter One Hundred and Seventy-Four

Aslah looked warily about her.

It had been exciting searching for somewhere to live. She was so used to being in the longhouse – even the one they moved to after the Japanese raid – she never really contemplated living anywhere else. Had she always thought her dreams of leaving the jungle with Coy-lyn were no more than that ... dreams?

There was a lot of damage in Miri and some buildings were now just piles of timber and bricks, the remnants smouldering from fires started by gas leaks and bombing by the Allies. But she and Abas found a two bedroom flat down a side street called *Jalan Dato Simpson*. The flat had a living space, a kitchen, and inside toilet and one large and one small bedroom. Two things had amazed Aslah, the first was the fact that the bedrooms had real doors; the second was that the living space and the larger bedroom had big ceiling fans. Abas took her to the kitchen and turning on the tap he showed her some more magic: the tap whirred, clanked and coughed, but suddenly a dribble of water came from its spout.

"It will get better," Abas told her, "there are a lot of repairs to be done." He went into the living area. "I do not think the fan will work but maybe ..." He flipped the switch and to Aslah's amazement, the fan started turning.

Now they were there, with her rattan-fastened case on the floor just inside the door, Aslah looked about her and a feeling of utter isolation seemed to engulf her. Dani, as always, was on her good hip and he seemed to sense his mother's concern as he started crying.

Aslah automatically began to bounce him on her hip: "Sshhh," she said, "Sshhh."

Her eyes moved round the living space: it was dark, it seemed so much smaller than before, it seemed so enclosed, it ... Abas threw open the shutters and light flooded into the room. He flipped the switch for the fan again and it started to turn. It was pouring with rain outside but the floor was perfectly dry.

Perhaps it was not as bad as she first thought.

Even Dani stopped crying as he too looked around, taking everything in.

"You and Dani must have the big room," Abas said in Iban.

355

He picked up his sister's case.

"We must speak in English," Aslah told him absentmindedly. "We must practice our English that is why we have been given work."

"You are right," Abas agreed, switching to English. "There are things we need and we will get them with the money Fung gave us."

Aslah was still standing by the front door.

Abas put the case down and crossing to his sister, he said, "You are not happy, Aslah. What is it? Do you not like this place?"

Aslah looked at her brother.

She did not want to say anything because it would only make her feel worse but Abas had asked her so she must tell him the truth. "I miss him, Abas. I miss my husband. I lay awake at nights when he was still here imagining living somewhere like this with him. I am here but he is not."

"You must not give up hope," Abas told her.

"Hope went downriver with him on the day he left," Aslah said.

"I went downriver with him," Abas said, "but I came back."

"But he will never come back."

"Yes, he will. He promised to take me up in his plane so that I, like the Gods, could look down on my homeland."

The tea was weak but at least it was hot and sweet.

As Colin sipped the insipid looking liquid, he thought back to how quickly he had got used to not having many of the luxuries of life before the war. They were not luxuries then: they were expectations. No coffee, no tea, no Players cigarettes, no chocolate and the list was endless.

"Are you still here?" Julia asked, the mug of tea cupped in her hands.

"Sorry," Colin apologised, "I was miles away."

Julia thought for a moment or two, she had appeared more confident since they had sat down. Colin wondered if it was because there were a lot of people about.

"What were you in, or maybe you still are. Was it the army, navy or air force? Perhaps I shouldn't be asking."

For some reason Colin did not want to lie to Julia, but by telling her the truth it would generate more questions. "I wasn't in anything," he said, "not in the strictest sense of the word."

"But on the train, those soldiers, you …"

"I may not have been in the armed forces, Julia, but I did fight, in my case against the Japanese."

"I guessed you did something like that. You were ever so brave doing what you did."

"Those soldiers were annoying not only you but the elderly couple as well. They were rude and suggestive."

"They were a bit, weren't they?"

"We all thought so," Colin said.

"It was still good of you –"

Julia was about to say something else when she looked behind Colin. He saw her expression change, hearing the reason why a second later. He knew who it was going to be before the soldier spoke.

"Decided to 'ave 'er for yerself, did ya? Thought you'd have her later when nobody was looking, did ya?"

Colin did not turn his head. "Just go away," he said slowly.

"Wha' an' leave you to 'ave wha' me an' my mate saw first," the voice said. "We'll giv 'er wha' she needs. She looks as though she

357

could do wiv a good –"

This time Colin did rise, cutting off what the soldier was going to say.

He moved his chair back, stood up slowly and faced the soldier. The people at the tables around them had fallen silent, not understanding what was happening. Colin was a good few inches taller than the soldier, who was the one whose arm he had twisted behind his back. He did not want another scene but he had little choice. If he ignored the soldier, he would not let up.

"We don't want any trouble," Colin told him. "Please just leave us alone."

"*We* an' *us* is it? 'Ad it already 'ave you? In yer mind, I bet. Were she good, was she up to your hoity-toity standards? Did she go like a rabbit?"

The soldier suddenly made a grab for Julia's bag that was on the table.

He turned and pushed his way through the tables towards the exit.

Without hesitating, Colin followed the soldier, surprised at what he had just witnessed.

Why try to steal a bag in the middle of a crowded canteen?

The moment Colin stepped through the door he found out why.

He sensed immediately that he had made an awful mistake.

The soldier had been goading him deliberately and he had fallen for it.

Chapter One Hundred and Seventy-Six

Her eyes shot open.

What was it?

Something must have woken her. Had she heard something?

Was it Angelique?

Slowly Rachel leant forward and listened. She could have heard a pin drop. She looked at the clock on the mantelpiece. Just after seven o'clock. She must have fallen asleep in the chair. The fire needed some more coal on it: the room was quite chilly.

So why was she perspiring?

Rachel sat still for a couple of minutes, she felt slightly dizzy as well. She hoped she wasn't coming down with something, that's the last thing she needed. It didn't help being told that once somebody had suffered with malaria it could return at any time without notice.

Had she actually had malaria? There were so many tropical diseases commonplace in Batu Lintang and with no doctor to advise you, you were just ill and you were going to get better or you would die. Nothing could have been simpler.

She had been lucky because she had not really suffered, not like some of the others. Some of the others gave up at the slightest sign of illness. Diseases had a free run of their bodies because they were convinced whatever they had was fatal and they did not have the strength to fight whatever it might be.

She really had been so lucky in so many ways.

After checking on Angelique, Rachel went into the kitchen to make herself a cup of tea.

Something had woken her.

She took the tea back into the living room, poked at the embers in the fire and put on some more coal – she would have to try to get another bag. Settling down in the chair she remembered what she had been thinking about before falling asleep.

It was not *what* it was *who*.

Who else?

Colin.

This time her thoughts were brought on by Angelique's searching questions about her father. So nothing had changed. For all the time she had spent in Kampong Punkit and Batu Lintang Camp, she had

359

never given up hope. She had known he was alive, and she had known that they would meet again, after the war, somewhere, but she had no idea when. As sure as she had been then, she was also sure that if anything ever happened to him she would know.

As there was nobody to make the connection, she could not be told officially if he were dead ... or missing.

Slowly Rachel put the cup onto the saucer.

"Oh my God!" she said in a whisper. "It's Colin. Something has happened to him."

No, she was being stupid.

Throughout her captivity, she had needed the belief to keep her going. That is what she had told Angelique. She remembered Marjory Field telling her repeatedly: "You hang on to what you believe in, my dear. It'll give you the strength you'll need to get you through this misery."

"And you Marjory, what will get you through it all?"

"The need to see these animals punished, my dear. The day Suga and his cronies are hung for crimes against humanity I will die a happier woman." But she always added. "But hopefully not on *the* day. Years later will do!"

Rachel smiled. No, she was being stupid.

Chapter One Hundred and Seventy-Seven

Aslah woke.

It was four o'clock in the morning and it was humid to the point of being claustrophobic. The shutter was open, the window mesh stopping the bugs from getting in. The fan was on, the mosquito net moved with each turn of its blades. Dani was sleeping next to her, lying on his back as he always did. A little light filtered in from outside and she could see his face even in the murk of the room.

She had not appreciated just how well the air circulated in the longhouse. There were no doors to act as barriers. In the longhouse, the air flowed through every gap it could find. Would she ever get used to not being there? She had to get used to it. There was no going back now.

She reached for the small towel she kept by the bed and dabbed at her face. If she had her way she would be sleeping on the veranda and on a mat, but Abas had insisted they do things the western way.

Was she happy to stay in Miri?

She was not sure.

Being here brought her closer to Coy-lyn, to his way of life, but he was supposed to be with her, so without him by her side ... no, she did not want to be here. She had to think of Dani though, he deserved to see both ways of life before he made a decision as to which he wanted.

Abas talked about going south to Kuching, maybe she would go with him. But that was even further away. She must not become – how did Coy-lyn describe it to her? – a chain ... that was it, a chain round Abas's neck. He had not said that in the same context because when he was teaching her English they could not see into the future. It had been before the Japanese attack.

If Abas wanted to go to Kuching, perhaps she should let him go on his own. But there was still Dani to consider. She was Iban, female, young, had a child and really knew nothing – other than what Coy-lyn had told her – about the world beyond the longhouse and a little bit of Miri. She thought about the towns and cities Coy-lyn had described to her as they lay on their sleeping mat in the longhouse. At her insistence, he went into a lot of detail and explained everything to her because her imagination did not stretch that far.

Even when he told her about London, the size of the buildings, she could not believe it. There was the big time-piece he had called Big Ben – the name she had secretly wanted to call Dani – that was taller than the tallest tree in the jungle.

It was unbelievable.

Why have a timepiece like that when the daylight, the sun, the shadows, the jungle animals: they all told you what time it was?

Maybe Miri was the stepping-stone, like the stones upriver from the longhouse that they needed to cross to get to the padi. Maybe there would be many stepping-stones for her to cross but not trip up on. Maybe there was a future in this new world for her and Dani.

Aslah moved into the foetal position, her fingers resting against Dani's face.

She felt a little happier.

Coy-lyn had always said – what words had he used again? Coy-lyn and his words! – 'Every dark cloud has a silver lining' – that was it.

The dark cloud she had felt was hanging over her already had a silver lining.

Maybe this was the start of a new adventure.

Maybe an adventure would, one day, bring her Coy-lyn back.

A police constable approached Julia Danbury.

Having watched Colin Freemantle being placed on a stretcher and carried to the ambulance, her eyes were like saucers as she tried to come to terms with what had happened.

She had not seen the actual attack. By the time she got to the door of the café it was all over … well almost. A group of men and women were restraining the two soldiers while shouting for two police constables who were at the other end of the platform. Seeing her new friend lying on the concrete concourse with his face turned towards her and his eyes closed, was enough to tell her something horrific had happened.

Tears were streaming down Julia's face as the police constable returned her handbag.

"Miss," he said, "I understand that you were with the gentleman who was attacked."

"Not … not with," she told the police officer. "We … we were both on the train that was delayed and he asked me if I wanted a cup of tea, that's all. Is he going to be all right?"

"Don't know, Miss, one of the witnesses said he was hit with a metal bar one of those soldiers was holding," the police constable said as he wet the end of his pencil and wrote something in his notebook. "Is there anything you can tell me that may help with our investigation?"

Julia looked about her. The soldiers were being led away by some other police constables, but one of the soldiers looked back and glared at her. She felt a shiver run down her spine. The crowd was beginning to disperse, it was cold, and she wanted to go home.

"In … investigation?" she repeated. "There was an incident on the train, so I think the soldiers just wanted to get their own back."

"An incident you say, Miss. Would you mind telling me what this incident was?"

"Can we go into the café? It's cold out here."

"Of course, Miss."

Having told the police constable what she knew, given her name and address and reluctantly agreeing to repeat her account in court if necessary, she sighed in relief. Before leaving, the police constable said that somebody would be in touch with her to take a formal statement.

Julia did not know what she should do but eventually she decided to sit and wait for the announcement to say the train was leaving. Everything had happened so quickly, she did not have the faintest idea what the time was. She had not seen the soldier hitting Colin on the head so she was far from being a reliable witness. All she could repeat was what she had already told the police constable. There must have been others on the platform who saw what happened, so she assumed they had been interviewed, after all they were actual witnesses, unlike her.

The announcement came.

Julia gathered her things together and proceeded out of the café to the waiting train. As she was about to board, she stopped.

She could not just leave him. He had been hurt because of her.

Julia turned and walked away from the train, along the platform and out of the station.

She didn't know where the hospital was but she had a tongue in her head, so she could ask. Was she doing the right thing? He had helped her so perhaps she really ought to help him.

Anyway, he was awfully nice looking. He would be grateful that she had followed him to the hospital and who knows what would happen then. That is how some people who are destined to be good friends – or more – meet, isn't it?

On a train.

En route to the hospital Julia went into a telephone box and called the police house in Lubenham village. By doing that, it eased her conscience a little. Her mother and father would be worried, but as PC Derek Priestland was a friend of the family, she was sure they would understand. He would go round and see them.

"Tell them I met a friend on the train and I'm staying in Rugby tonight," she said.

"Is that the truth?" Derek asked, but his voice suggested he was being light-hearted.

"Nearly," Julia told him.

PC Derek Priestland was nearer Julia's age than her parents but he had become friends with the family not just Julia. She knew he had a crush on her but a wife and two children suggested his thoughts ought to be elsewhere. And it wasn't only his thoughts: she had caught him looking down the front of her blouse when she bent over to pick up a book that had fallen on the floor. He had been ever so embarrassed when he realised she had seen him, but that didn't stop him looking again when she deliberately bent forward this time … and for a little longer. She liked the way men found her attractive. She had the assets so she could really exploit them in the future.

"All right, but you take care," he said.

"I will," she told him.

After asking a couple of people, she found the hospital without any problems. The austere looking matron who was behind the desk in the reception area talking to two nurses was a different proposition.

Julia waited by the desk until the matron had finished.

"Yes, can I help you?" the younger of the two nurses asked.

"You have just admitted a man called Colin Freemantle, I was wondering if you could tell me how he is?"

"Are you a relative?" the nurse asked.

"No, I'm, erm, a close friend. We were on the train together. It was delayed at Rugby station where he was attacked."

"And your name?" the nurse asked officiously.

Julia wanted to ask what her name had to do with it but she thought it best to respond politely. "Julia Danbury, my name is Julia

Danbury and Mr Freemantle and I are close friends. We were travelling together."

"You were with him when he was attacked?" the nurse asked.

"Yes, I was delayed coming here because the police wanted to interview me."

"I see," the nurse said. "Mr Freemantle has been put into a sideward, Miss Danbury. He is unconscious, the doctor is with him now, but I am sure that you may sit with him once the doctor is finished."

Twenty minutes later Julia was doing exactly that.

Colin Freemantle was a complete stranger, so getting permission to sit with him was a surprise … but after all, she did feel responsible.

He was lying perfectly still and his were eyes closed.

They had taken off his shirt and bandaged his head. The dim lighting made him look quite mysterious.

Julia smiled.

He had a lovely brown chest.

"I'm pleased I bumped into you, Mr Freemantle," she said.

Chapter One Hundred and Eighty

After an hour, Julia began to wonder what good she could do.

Other than a slight tic at the corner of his mouth, Colin had not moved. He looked incredibly handsome lying there, the bandage round his head making him look quite mysterious.

Well he was a bit of a mystery. He had not been in any of the forces, but had handled himself as though he was an expert in unarmed combat. Perhaps *he* was in the police. Perhaps he was one of those special police officers who must not let people like Julia know what they do or where they go.

As she mused Julia held and stroked the back of Colin's hand.

Like his chest, his skin was brown. She wondered if either his mother or father had been foreign, well from the Far East or somewhere. It could only be one of them otherwise he would not have blue eyes or blond hair.

Greg would be leaving soon. The other night he told her he was due to go back to the States in a couple of weeks. She did not love Greg, but he was funny and caring.

Her parents would have a pink fit if they knew she had to let him do it to her. Well, she had to start with someone, all her friends had, so why not her? But she didn't love him. He gave her presents, silk stockings and chocolates, and there was the food that she was able to take home. Her mother and father asked where the sugar, eggs and some meat every now and again, came from but seemed to accept her answer when she told them the truth, well most of the truth. She would never tell them that they had done it together.

Her mother might have guessed though because she did take her to one side to say: 'Be careful', 'Don't bring disgrace on the family' and 'You are all right, dear, aren't you? You do know how to …'

Julia did know how to take precautions, and had been and was being careful. Well, she always made sure Greg was careful. He hated wearing one of those 'Johnnies' but she hated the cap even more – she only tried it once and it was far too messy.

After the first time she really began to enjoy it. She did feel a little shamefaced because she really did not love him. It was a lovely feeling – all tingly and special – when he was doing it to her she felt so powerful, so in control.

The control she seemed to have over men would be her future.

Anyway, to be truthful she was not sure that *he* loved *her*, regardless of what he said. She was his English rose, he said. He liked her long dark brown hair, her pug nose, her big brown eyes and her cupid lips – cupid lips? They were no different to anybody else's. She felt herself blush as she thought of the words he had used to describe the rest of her. She wondered what Derek Priestland would be like if he got his hands on her breasts, rather than just looking at them that is. Maybe one day she might find out. It would be fun to see how he reacted when his dreams came true. His wife need never know.

Greg was ever so gentle with her, and if she wasn't in the mood and said no, he had never forced himself on her. Not that she said no often. Had she ever really said no and meant it? He said he adored everything about her but he said he absolutely loved her English rose accent and the mole that rested half way up the inside of her right thigh. Anyway, he was leaving her to go home to the States. She had never asked him whether he had a wife and kids like Derek Priestland. She knew that their relationship would not last – the memories would because he had been the first man she had ever gone all the way with – so what was the point in complicating what they already had?

Julia wondered if the man lying in the bed in front of her was married.

She smiled as she imagined him touching her, doing it with her.

He seemed quite special.

Aslah opened her eyes.

It was still raining. The noise the rain made on the roof was not the same as hearing it fall in the jungle. The rain gave the jungle its life: it was like the blood running through its veins. It needed the rain to survive.

There was a tap on the door.

"Are you awake, Aslah?"

The door opened and Abas walked into the room. She knew he could see her and Dani through the mosquito net. The single sheet had slipped but she did not attempt to cover herself. There had been no time and place for modesty in the longhouse. Perhaps she would have to learn. It was something Coy-lyn had told her about life in the western world, people were far shyer about their bodies. In the world outside there would be many different things to discover. But for them things were still as they used to be, her brother would have been surprised if she had pulled the sheet over her body.

"Is it time?" Aslah asked, swinging her legs from the bed.

That was something else she would have to get used to. She had spent some of the night worrying that she was going to fall onto the floor and anyway the bed was too soft ... but Dani seemed quite happy with the new sleeping arrangements.

"There is some rice prepared. We must go to Fung's house to leave Dani before we meet Fung at Government House and start work," Abas said as he opened the single shutter.

Light flooded into the room.

Aslah padded naked past her brother to go to the toilet but she stopped at the door and turned round. She watched Abas look down at Dani and saw the love in his eyes. Like her, she guessed every time he smiled at Dani he was also smiling at Coy-lyn – he would be missing his remaining brother.

An hour later Aslah gave Dani to Chao.

"Do not look so sad, Aslah. He will be perfectly safe with me," Chao said, smiling. "Next to you and your mother, I probably know him the best."

"I understand and appreciate what you are doing," Aslah replied seriously, "but it is the first time ever that he will not be on my hip

369

or next to me. He has become part of me, he is part of me."

"And he will still be part of you when you are at work, and he will be here when you have finished. What you are doing today Aslah is starting the first day of a new life. You are young and you are clever. Fung knows that you will not be here for long. You will want more. So go to him now and start this first day." Chao lifted Dani towards the ceiling. "This little man and I are going to have some fun."

Aslah watched as Dani's face lit up as he gurgled with laughter.

She dismissed the slight feeling of resentment straight away.

"This is kind of you," she repeated.

"No it's not. I will enjoy it. Now go!"

Aslah turned to leave. The tears were back.

"You mustn't cry, my sister," Abas said. "We are both still mourning the loss of our brother, and Coy-lyn is going to come back. We must make sure we are ready for him and we can show him the progress we have made."

Aslah stopped and stood in front of her brother. "I thank you for trying to make me believe that Coy-lyn is coming back … but …"

She was unable to finish what she wanted to say.

"Miss Danbury, how well do you know Mr Freemantle?" the police sergeant asked.

He had already told her that he had come to the hospital to see whether Mr Freemantle was ready to give a statement, but when told he certainly was not, he decided to take one from Julia instead.

"Well ..." Julia started to say. She had no idea whether to keep up the pretence of being good friends. Colin Freemantle would quickly deny the association and there would only be one outcome if she told the truth. It was all quite exciting and she had begun to feel quite important. The nurses who had come in and out of the ward to fuss over Colin had been respectful towards her, and the doctor had told her that her *young man* should be conscious within a few hours.

She liked that.

Her young man – they had that wrong because he was a good deal older but it didn't matter, not when he looked the way he did.

"Well ..." Julia said again, "not long but well enough, if you see what I mean."

The sergeant looked puzzled.

"No, I am afraid I don't see what you mean," he said. "His papers suggest that he only returned to England a couple of days ago and that previously he hadn't been in the country since 1938, that's seven years ago. Excuse the impertinence, Miss, but you don't look old enough to have known him that long. May I ask how old you are?"

Julia's mind was racing.

"Nineteen," she said. "I'm nineteen and when I say not long, I mean ... well ... not long. But as I told the constable who questioned me at the railway station, when somebody does what he did you feel close to them quite quickly."

Shaking his head the sergeant said, "Miss Danbury, I know that Mr Freemantle helped you on the train – defended your honour so to speak – and you both went for a cup of tea because the train was delayed, but are you able to tell me anything more than that? Anything about him you think I ought to know?"

"Erm, no, I suppose not," Julia replied sheepishly.

The sergeant closed his notebook.

"Then why are you here?" he said, his exasperation rather

obvious.

That was easy. "Because I feel responsible for what happened, if it hadn't been for me Mr Freemantle wouldn't be in hospital. Those soldiers were disgusting and they … well, they were looking at me and…" She would never admit she got some pleasure out of their leering eyes and suggestive remarks, but when Colin Freemantle defended her that was even better. He was her knight in shining armour; she just hoped he would whisk her away on his charger to live happily ever after.

"All right, I will leave you to come to terms with that responsibility," the sergeant said. "If you think of anything else please pay a visit to the station," he added as he went to the door of the ward.

"Yes, I will."

The sergeant left the ward.

Julia picked up Colin's hand again.

"That was close," she said. If only she had been able to tell the police sergeant a lot more than she had. Nevertheless, he had let her stay – it was not his decision whether she could or couldn't, but he might have said something to one of the nurses.

"So, Mr Freemantle, you've got me for a little longer."

Chapter One Hundred and Eighty-Three

Looking at his two new workers, Fung smiled.

He had explained to his superiors what his plans were and they had readily agreed. It was part of the post-harmonization process, they had said. He wondered what they had meant by that. He just regarded it as taking advantage of the opportunity to give two bright young people a fresh start after they had played such a significant part in his life for so long.

Abas was looking confident, even cocky, but Aslah appeared apprehensive. There was no eye contact and she seemed more interested in the floor than her surroundings.

They were in Fung's large office in the Miri administrative headquarters, which miraculously remained undamaged, although the Japanese had used it, also as a headquarters. The simply decorated office had a large ornate fan slowly turning above them.

Outside, the morning rain had temporarily stopped but the clouds were grey and threatening.

"I'm going to speak in English," Fung told them, "because that is obviously the language of the administration but eventually I will be making use of you being Iban but not straight away. First, we must get you settled in. Aslah," he said, hoping she would look at him.

Her head remained bowed.

"Aslah, I am going to put you with a pleasant lady who will show you what we do here. She is the wife of a junior manager who has only recently arrived in Sarawak and she is working as part of a team that will help restore normality to the country, especially though, to the interior."

He was talking to Aslah's bowed head, but when Fung looked at Abas, he shrugged and smiled. Fung stepped closer and putting his finger under Aslah's chin, he lifted her head.

Her eyes were full of tears.

"What is it, Aslah?" he asked. "Do you not like what I am saying?"

"No, no, it is not that, Fung. You … you and Chao are being so kind, but it is everything else. I can't …"

Fung smiled sympathetically.

"What you are doing is brave," he said. "It is bringing a lot of change into your life and quickly. That is why to begin with we must take things slowly. You will be missing Dani already. This is all strange for you," he added looking round the office. "The people you will meet will all be strangers, as you will be a stranger to them. For some you will be the first Iban they have met."

Aslah tried to smile.

"The lady you will be working with is called Norah. She is waiting outside to meet you. Would you be happy if I invited her in?"

Aslah nodded slowly.

Going to the door, Fung ushered in a young woman who was of a similar age to Aslah.

In contrast, her skin was porcelain white and her hair a light brown. She was wearing a floral dress and tan sandals. Her legs and arms were also white. Her lips were bright red and her finger and toenails were the same colour.

As Fung watched the two women taking in each other's detail, he saw the expression on Aslah's face change. She was looking at the other woman's eyes and suddenly her hand shot up to cover her mouth.

Norah's eyes were exactly the same colour as her Coy-lyn's.

Chapter One Hundred and Eighty-Four

She had fallen asleep in the chair with Colin's hand still in hers.

It was the slight movement as he slid his fingers from hers that woke her. She had forgotten where she was, but then she saw his blue eyes smiling at her.

"God!" she exclaimed, "you're awake."

"It appears so, but awake with one hell of a headache."

"The doctor said your skull isn't fractured," she told him.

"It feels as though it's more than fractured. But what …?"

"Do you want me to get somebody?"

"In a minute … what are you doing here?" he asked. "I remember chasing after that soldier who had stolen your bag but then the lights went out."

Colin screwed up his face and he appeared to be in pain as he tried to move.

Wanting to reach over and touch him, Julia said, "The other one was waiting outside. He hit you with some sort of iron bar. They were caught and the police took them away."

"And what time is it, or should I ask what day and time?"

Julia looked at her watch. "It's one o'clock on Wednesday morning, you've been out for nearly seven hours."

"You've been here for that long? Why?"

She thought his question was a little hurtful. It must be obvious why she was there. "I … I felt responsible, after all it was me …" she said.

Her skin tingled as Colin reached for her hand.

"That's kind of you, but I am back in the land of the living with no more than a headache to show for it, so you can go … no, that's silly of me. How are you going to get home at one o'clock in the morning?"

Julia shrugged.

A nurse entered the ward.

"Ah, Mr Freemantle, you are back with us."

Still holding Julia's hand, Colin said, "It appears that way."

"I'll go and get the doctor, but don't get any ideas about leaving, Mr Freemantle. I doubt whether the doctor will let you go for at least another day or so. You had a nasty crack on the head and you will need to be kept under observation."

"So what are we going to do with you?" Colin asked Julia after the nurse had left. "I've had seven hours sleep but you haven't. You must be tired … it really was good of you to sit with me like this."

"Oh, I'm all right. The police said that you've only just come back to England, after seven years was it? If you feel up to it, why not tell me what you have been doing for all that time?" Julia covered her mouth with her fingers. "Oh, but perhaps you can't. Perhaps you've been doing things that you can't talk about."

"In a manner of speaking you're right, Julia, but …"

"So you can't tell me?"

"Well, I suppose I could tell you where I've been and who I have been with," Colin said. "It could be a long story but I'll give you the short version." He smiled and she liked that.

"And you won't get into trouble? I mean if –"

"No, I won't get in to trouble, but you could find it boring."

"I doubt that, Colin." There, she had used his name for the first time. She felt as though she knew him well now. She had never spent so long with one man before.

The nurse went into the ward every thirty minutes to take his pulse and blood pressure. She recorded her findings on a chart at the bottom of the bed and left, normally without saying a word.

Colin wondered what Julia had told the nurses that allowed her to stay on the ward. Hospitals, or so he thought, usually had strict visiting hours and they certainly were not during the early hours of the morning.

Telling Julia where he had been for the last seven years, Colin was surprised when she sat and listened so quietly. He did not say much about the war but he did relate some of the more amusing incidents that occurred to him when he and Sammy were still a viable team. She had said she liked the name Sammy and she was so sorry that he had lost her. He did not mention Rachel or Aslah – she had no need to know and that would have been getting too personal.

Julia laughed at some things he said but she suddenly appeared to lose interest as she became more and more tired. Her eyelids began to droop and eventually she fell asleep.

She looked so young and innocent.

One of the nurses might be able to tell him when the first trains left Rugby station, because he would suggest – quite firmly – that Julia ought to leave in good time to catch the one she wanted. He wondered where she worked, or where she needed to go. She had mentioned the village of Lubenham.

His head still throbbed but in many ways he was pleased what happened had caused a delay. He had been racing towards Market Harborough in the same way he had gone to Leamington Spa, not knowing what he was going to do or say.

Perhaps he needed time to think things through a little carefully.

Rachel's mother said that Rachel had not been able to settle and that is why she needed to be on her own.

Why Market Harborough?

He remembered his aunt mentioning the name of the town but he knew nothing else about it.

Julia moved a little in the chair.

She was pretty but she was also very young, maybe twenty. For most of her teenage years, she had lived through a world war, a war that had brought bombing, fire, death and destruction to the civilian population: to people's front rooms, to people's kitchens and their gardens. He wondered how the Julia had coped. Maybe where she lived escaped any destruction, but the radio and the papers would have brought the war to Julia's isolated world.

The war will have changed so many people's lives ... permanently.

"Are you awake?" Julia asked sleepily.

"Yes, wide awake," Colin replied. "What time is it now?"

Julia held her arm up so that she could see her watch in the dim light.

"Nearly four."

"You'll be able to get a train in a couple of hours. Were you on your way home from work when we met?"

"No, I've had a couple of days off. I'd been visiting friends in Warwick. I'm not due into work until Thursday," she told him.

"And where is work?"

"In a shop in Market Harborough. That's where you're going isn't it?"

"Yes."

"Do you live there?"

"No, just visiting ... I think."

The clock on the town hall struck four o'clock.

It was a windy and wet night. Rachel lay with her hands behind her head watching the reflections from the street lamps dancing on the ceiling above her.

Since moving to Market Harborough, there had been time to think, analyse her thoughts and think again. No doubt others would tell her that her thoughts were irrational. She was where she should be, she was where her daughter could have a proper upbringing, receive a good education, find a husband, have a family, and then carry on with life's cycle.

Before leaving Batu Lintang, the women had sworn to each other that they would stay in touch. The adversity they had been through was a common bond. It was something that would link them together forever. Rachel had written and received letters, the words were marvellous to read but they had not been what she wanted. There was always something missing – it was not the same. Marjory Field would understand. She and Peter were up in York and although there was an open invitation for Rachel and Angelique to visit whenever and for as long as they wanted, but Rachel knew it would not work.

Not being sure what she was looking for, did not help. But she did know that she would not find it in Market Harborough or anywhere else in England. She was still as determined as ever to go back. The moment she set foot on Sarawak soil for the first time, she fell in love with the country and its people. Meeting Colin had perhaps introduced a complication that in retrospect she possibly could have done without ... for a little longer. She did not mean that in an unkindly way, she did love him, but if he had come along a little later, after the war, it would have been better.

Then they could be a proper family. In Sarawak there had been so much to explore but the Japanese had invaded and brought that pastime to a grinding halt. Therefore, there was still so much to see and do.

Was it that? Was it the fact that she had returned to England feeling incomplete? Her time in Kampong Punkit and Batu Lintang had been a different sort of adventure. It had been an exploration of the mind. No doubt if the war had passed her by, she might have been back in England for some time. Her contract would have come up for renewal in 1943 – now she thought about it, nobody from the bank came looking for her wondering why she had not bothered to renew her contract!

She smiled as she imagined Mr Pennington cross-examining Captain Oshida as to where his employee, Rachel Lefévre, might be and what he had done to her.

She had to go back. The Far Eastern Banking Corporation might not want her but there were more ways than one to skin a cat! She had so much to offer, there must be an organisation that would pay for her passage out to Sarawak.

After the liberation of Batu Lintang, everything happened so quickly, perhaps too quickly. She had not even had time to find out whether any of the many Sarawakian friends she had made before the war, were still alive. Because she had a young daughter, she found herself on Labuan Island and processed for repatriation before she had time to object. Perhaps she should have refused. Could she have refused? Could she have said, no, I want to stay in Kuching?

How would the authorities have reacted?

Then there was Sister Angelique, dear Sister Angelique. Did she survive? She would start today. She had to start today. Her current situation meant she was going round in circles and not getting anywhere, other than feeling more and more depressed. She wanted to go back and she would not stop until she had achieved what she wanted, no matter how long it took, and no matter under what circumstances, she didn't care.

She would go back.

Chapter One Hundred and Eighty-Seven

The doctor smiled as only doctors can.

"Another twenty-four hours, Mr Freemantle. Your skull is not fractured and as far as we can tell, there aren't any other complications. But with head injuries it is always best to err on the side of caution, which basically means observation ... hence another twenty-four hours." The doctor picked up the board from the end of the bed and nodded. "Everything tells me that the heavy bruising will continue to give you discomfort for a while but other than that, you're a lucky man."

"Thank you, doctor," Colin said. He was not too keen on staying in hospital for another day but it would give him more time.

Putting the millboard back on the end of the bed the doctor hesitated.

"Mr Freemantle, the wound to your leg, your thigh that is, the scar suggests that it was a bullet wound, am I correct?"

"Yes, but you must see so many of them."

"I do, I do, but the repair and healing process tend to produce some uniformity in scar tissue. I have never seen anything like yours before." The doctor was in his fifties, had thinning grey hair, but other than that he looked extremely fit and studious. "May I ask where it occurred?" he said.

"Borneo, Sarawak to be precise."

"Ah, you were there, were you? And your shoulder, that scar tissue suggests it happened at the same time, is that correct?"

"Yes. I didn't know it was possible to tell such things," Colin said.

"It is, it is." The doctor tapped his teeth with his pen. "So were you a prisoner-of-war?"

"No, far from it, I enjoyed a freedom that was unbelievable."

"So it wasn't the Japanese who ...?"

"No, it was two people who had no medical training whatsoever. They used drugs they made from jungle plants, patience and just a little tender care. One was a lady in her forties who learnt everything from her mother, and who passed her skills to her seventeen year old daughter." A picture of Aslah sitting by the entrance to the *bilik* the day he had woken up properly from his fever flashed into his mind.

"Remarkable," the doctor observed. "And where was this?"

"In Sarawak, and courtesy of the Iban, an inland tribal people with whom I spent nearly four years of my life. They became and to a great extent still are, my family."

"They did a wonderful job, Mr Freemantle, a really wonderful job."

The doctor turned to leave but stopped.

"Oh yes," he said. "When you were brought in you were wearing a money belt containing a considerable amount of cash. The belt is in the hospital safe, along with your papers. Both will be made available to you on request."

Colin had not given the belt a moment's thought. "Thank you," he said.

"And the police would like to interview you."

"That's understandable. Are they here now?"

"No, they have asked for us to let them know when you are ready to see them."

"I see."

"So, not for a while yet, they can wait. As I said, the bruising will still give you some discomfort, and to some extent, the bruising and swelling could hide something more serious. But I think in your case you'll be in the clear." The doctor nodded and left.

"But why?" Julia asked, the tears coming easily. "Why now? I don't have to be back at work until tomorrow. Why can't I stay here?"

"Julia, it was kind and considerate of you to come to the hospital in the first place," Colin told her. "Staying the night was also unexpected. But the doctor said I must stay in for observation for at least another twenty-four hours, I cannot expect you to stay any longer."

The tears that were streaming down Julia's face were quite bewildering.

"But I want to, there's no need for me to be anywhere else."

She was standing by the bed, her fingers on the back of Colin's hand. He slowly moved his hand away from hers but his naivety suddenly hit him like a sledgehammer.

"Julia, I am on my way to Market Harborough to see my ... my wife and child. I haven't seen my wife for a long time and I have yet to meet my daughter." Julia lowered her head. "I am flattered that a young and pretty girl like you is interested in somebody like me, but I am married and I love my wife."

Julia stayed still, her head still bowed, her hands in front of her.

"I am pleased that I was there to help you on the train, and that you have been here to help me after I was attacked. But this is where the incident comes to an end."

"But ... but, I thought ..."

"There was nothing to think, Julia. We have known each other for less than a day, and the circumstances were to say the least, unusual. Ordinarily you would have ignored me and I would have given you a sideways but admiring glance. That is the way it started and that is the way it must end," Colin said.

Julia picked up her bag from the chair and hurried from the ward without looking back.

Sighing deeply, Colin lay down against the pillows. He had needed to lie to the girl but maybe the lie was what he really wanted. Would he have travelled half way round the world to a country he did not want to be in, if it he really wanted something else?

The door opened and a different nurse came into the ward.

"Have the police been told they can see me?" he asked.

"Yes," the nurse said.

"When are they coming?"

"Oh, I don't know, sometime today I suppose." The nurse took Colin's pulse.

"The doctor said another twenty four hours …"

"He did."

"I can't stay here that long."

"Oh," the nurse said, a smile coming to her lips, "you have no choice."

"Can you keep me here against my will?"

"No … no, if I'm being truthful, we can't," the nurse told him, the smile disappearing.

"So I can leave now if I want to?"

"Well … well yes, but …"

"Then can you bring me my clothes and belongings, please."

As he saw Julia disappearing out of the ward, he made up his mind. Staying in hospital a moment longer was not an option. He needed to get a train to Market Harborough and he needed to see Rachel as soon as possible. He would go and see the police after which he would move on.

The incident on Rugby station was no more than that … an incident.

It was over and he had other things to do.

"I don't want to press charges," Colin said.

He was sitting in an interview room with a police sergeant, who, with pen poised, was waiting to take Colin's statement.

The sergeant looked just a little surprised. "I beg your pardon, Sir. Are you saying that you don't want …?"

"I don't want to press charges, that is what I am saying." Colin looked at his watch before adding: "They were young soldiers returning from a world war, she was a pretty girl, they flirted with her and I stepped in. They took offence and their pride was hurt so I paid the price. It was as simple as that."

"But they put you in hospital, Mr Freemantle. They deserve to go to prison," the sergeant said, his confusion obvious.

"Do they? I do not wish to give a statement, I do not wish to describe the soldiers and I do not wish to press charges."

To Colin his reasons were understandable.

He did not want anything other than the reason he had returned to England to occupy his mind. If the soldiers finished up charged with assault, there would be a court case, he would need to give evidence and it would all take a long time. He did not want any complications, and he hoped he had already put paid to the other one … Julia Danbury.

"This is most unusual," the sergeant commented.

"Unusual or not, that is the way I wish to proceed."

"All right, if that is the way you want it to be, Sir, but …" The sergeant closed his notebook. "When you were admitted to hospital," he said, "you were carrying a lot of notes in a money-belt round your waist, I presume it has been returned to you."

"Yes, it has," Colin told him.

"May I ask the origin of the money?"

Colin leant forward, shook his head and smiled ironically. "Because I don't want to press charges, I am now under suspicion for what … theft, is that right?" he asked.

"Not at all, Mr Freemantle, but the hospital …"

"… has returned what is mine, Sergeant. The money was, until two days ago, in an account in my name. I withdrew the balance and closed the account. If you want the details I am more than willing to give them to you, but I can assure you, you will find everything above board."

"I wasn't suggesting …"

"No, I am sure you weren't. Now, if there is nothing else you wish to pursue, I would like to be on my way."

"Of course, Mr Freemantle."

A few minutes later Colin left Rugby Police Station.

As he approached the main doors the soldiers who had assaulted him were being led from a different area.

They saw him as he saw them.

"Good on yer, mate!" the taller one shouted.

"Yeh," the other one added, "it were nuffin persnal."

Colin stopped and looked at them.

"*It* may have been nothing *personal*, but it could have resulted in both of you going to prison. However, *I* did what *I* did for purely personal reasons."

The soldiers did not say anything else.

It was the end of her first day.

Aslah was surprised how after a few hours she had welcomed the attention she was getting. Initially she did not seem to be able to concentrate on anything but Norah's blue eyes.

Coy-lyn and of course Dani, had therefore been on her mind as the morning progressed but as it became clear what was expected from her, her interest began to grow.

"I think we are going to make a good team," Norah told her as they stood on the veranda sipping cups of tea.

It was still dry but the clouds were ever threatening.

Aslah smiled, her eyes taking in the lines of the strikingly beautiful face she was looking at.

"You must excuse my English," she suggested, "I learnt it from a good teacher but not in a school."

"Oh, and who was your teacher?" Norah asked.

"My husband, Coy-lyn, he taught me English and I taught him Iban," Aslah told Norah, proudly.

"And he was obviously a good teacher, your English is excellent." Norah hesitated. "And your husband, Coy-lyn you said, why is his English so good?" she asked innocently.

"Because he is English," Aslah said, feeling a little confused.

"Your husband's English?" Norah repeated, her eyes opening in surprise.

"Yes," Aslah insisted, "and we have a son, Dani. He is with Fung's wife, Chao. She is looking after him."

"Oh, I see, or I think I see."

Norah appeared as though she had become a little confused herself.

"And where is your husband? Did you say his name is ... Coy-lyn?"

"Yes, he is Coy-lyn to me and always will be. His real name is Colin but I call him Coy-lyn because I could not say his name properly when we first met. My family call him Coy-lyn too." She paused. "He is in England at the moment. He ... he had to go to England."

Aslah could not say anymore so she asked Norah why she was in

Sarawak.

"Before the war my husband and I were in Hong Kong, he was on the administrative staff but fortunately we were on leave in England when the Japanese invaded. My husband, Jeremy, had polio as a child and couldn't get into any of the armed forces, but he was seconded to the War Office, so we spent the war in England. We lived in West Byfleet in Surrey … have you heard of it?"

Aslah shook her head. "No, I am sorry. I hope to go to England one day." For some reason she did not want to tell her new friend that up until a week ago she had spent almost her entire life living in a longhouse in the jungle. She did not feel ashamed or embarrassed but she just did not think Norah would understand.

"Surrey is a lovely county," Norah said. "But immediately after the Japanese surrender we couldn't wait to get back out to the Far East. We were asked if we would come and work for the re-formed Sarawak administration, agreed, and within a short space of time here we are. We've been in country for only a matter of weeks but we are already delighted to be here."

"Here it must be a lot like the land you called Surrey, it's beautiful. It can be hot and humid but once you become used to it you will hardly notice it."

"I'm sure I won't, but I must let this pale skin of mine see the sun," Norah said.

"Why?" Aslah asked. "It is so beautiful."

Chapter One Hundred and Ninety-One

As he stood on the market square across the road from Lloyds Bank in Market Harborough, Colin felt very nervous. In fact, he felt more apprehensive than before any of the sorties against the Japanese. His stomach was churning, and the steady throb in his head seemed to have become more intense.

The market was busy: the various vendors keeping up a steady cacophony as they attempted to sell their wares.

Their voices were an echo: the people around him seemed to be moving in slow motion.

All he could do was stare across the road at the doors of the bank.

Every now and again, a customer went in and a few minutes later came out. It was a wintry late-November day, but the sky was clear and in the sunshine, the temperature rose a few degrees.

With his hands thrust deep into the pockets of the trench coat he had bought before leaving Rugby, he lowered his head so his trilby hat shaded his eyes from the low sun. The headache had persisted but he had lied to the doctor when he had insisted on leaving the hospital. He had taken some of the pills he was given in case the headaches returned and the pain had been reduced to a background ache, but now it was as though his head was about to explode.

He could not go into the bank the way he was.

Reaching deeper into his pocket, he took out the pills and swallowed two more.

Ominously, his thoughts raced back to Leamington Spa and his meeting with Rachel's mother.

"Does she know you are looking for her?" she asked.

It was a question Elspeth Lefévre had repeatedly stated but in different ways. "No," Colin replied again, "I didn't know where she was for certain."

"Poppycock!" Elspeth said. "You knew this address so you could have written to her here."

Colin thought Rachel's mother had every right to be resentful. After all, he was the man who had made her daughter pregnant after which he had walked out of her life … or in his case, flown. She would be thinking he could have prevented the pregnancy in the first

389

place and more importantly, her daughter's incarceration by the Japanese. She would be asking why he had not insisted on taking her away from Kuching when the first opportunity arose. He wanted to tell her that if Rachel had gone with him it was more than likely that they would be dead.

Writing a letter was alien to Colin. He had not put pen to paper to anyone in over four years, so the option did not even enter his head. Anyway, even if he had written there was no guarantee it would have arrived at its destination. "Yes, I could have written, Mrs Lefévre. I do admit that," he said.

Elspeth Lefévre thought for a moment.

"All right," she said. "She's in Market Harborough. God knows why she wanted to go there, but that is where she is. She's working in a Bank, Lloyds I think, in the High Street. I'm not going to give you her home address, if she wants you to have that she will give it to you. And Mr Freemantle, if you do anything to upset my daughter and granddaughter, you will have me to answer to."

"I can assure you, Mrs Lefévre, upsetting either of them is the last thing I will ever do," Colin said.

"I should think not, young man."

"Thank you for telling where she is, Mrs Lefévre. I am not sure how things will turn but you will be kept informed."

Chapter One Hundred and Ninety-Two

Closing his eyes seemed to help with the headache but when he opened them again his vision was now blurred. He shook his head hoping it would help. Unfortunately, his vision and headache were the same.

"Are you all right, love?" a voice asked next to him.

Colin tried to focus on the woman who had spoken and he thought was tending the stall nearest to him. The table in front of her had only a few items on it – he could make out cups, saucers, plates and a few pots and pans.

"Yes … yes, I'm fine thanks. I've got a bit of a headache that's all."

"I've been watching you," the woman persisted. "Are you sure you're all right?"

"Yes, honestly, it must be the sun," he added jokingly, trying to smile.

"If you say so," the woman said but she was far from convinced. "Are you waiting for somebody?"

He could now see that the woman's expression had changed from concern to suspicion, a bit like the sergeant at Rugby police station. Maybe she thought he was with the black-market, or even a policeman checking to see if the stallholders were selling goods that were supposedly rationed.

"In a way," Colin told her. "Just trying to pluck up the courage to see somebody I haven't seen for a long time."

The woman's face softened again.

"A young lady is she?"

Colin nodded.

"Yes, she's a young lady. She works in that bank over there."

The woman eyed the bank entrance before starting to pack her goods away.

"Got to get on," she said. "The damn power's off tonight. Bloody cuts, you'd think the war was still on." She stopped what she was doing. "If you want my advice young man, love don't wait for no man. If she's worth it don't hesitate. If you hesitate she'll be courting somebody else afore you know it."

"Thank you," Colin said smiling, the headache easing a little and his vision clearing. "That sounds like good advice. You said the power is going off, at what time?"

"Seven o'clock or thereabouts, it allows those who are lucky enough to have the electric to get home from work and have their tea. Me, I'm all gas and in more ways than one my hubbie says."

The woman cackled.

"Sorry to ask you so many questions but I've only just come back to England and this is my first time in Market Harborough. Can you recommend a good hotel if I need to stay the night?" he said.

"There's the Three Swans Hotel up the High Street, that's the nearest. You should get a room there all right."

"Thanks. I'm sorry to have bothered you."

"You've been no bother young man. It's nice to have a chat at the end of a long day."

Colin turned to walk back up the High Street.

"The bank's over there, not that way," the woman said behind him. "The hotel will be open for a lot longer than the bank. It closes in fifteen minutes."

Colin smiled at the woman and nodded, then changed direction so that he could cross the road towards the bank.

"He's here again," Mildred Bryant said to Rachel's back as she was putting some papers in a drawer.

"Who?" Rachel asked without turning round.

"That man who was in here the other day who took a fancy to you – and you to him – he's over there by the door."

This time Rachel did turn round but the bank's lobby was gloomy.

She could see a man in a trench coat and trilby hat but his face was in shadow. He just stood there by the door. Because it was almost closing time there were only a few other customers in the bank.

"How do you know it's him?" Rachel asked, going back to her filing. She wanted to look round but decided not to be too obvious. Perhaps he had come in to see her again, more likely he has come in to cash another cheque.

"'Cos it is. He's coming over. Bet you I'm right," Mildred said.

"Rachel," the man said quietly.

"Mr Brasher I think …"

Rachel looked at the man on the other side of the grill. The file she was holding dropped to the floor. She felt her heart suddenly beat faster and harder.

"Colin?" she whispered.

The man smiled.

"Yes, Rachel, it's me."

"But … but … it can't be, you're …"

"I'm here that's where I am," Colin said.

"Do you two know each other?" Mildred asked.

Ignoring Mildred, Rachel just stared at Colin, her mouth was open and she suddenly felt weak at the knees. "It … it can't be, this … this isn't true, it's … it's night time and I'm dreaming. But …" She sat down. "What … I mean how … I don't know what I mean."

She laughed nervously. Colin took a deep breath.

"What time do you finish?" he asked.

"Finish … oh, yes, finish. Half past five," Rachel told him. "Is … is it you?" she asked again, her heart thumping, her palms moist. Wishing the partition between them could disappear.

"Yes, it's me," Colin said.

"And who is me?" Mildred enquired, not knowing really what to say.

Colin looked at her. "My name is Colin Freemantle. I have travelled half way round the world to see the lady sitting next to you but unfortunately there was no way of letting her know that I was coming." Although he was looking at Mildred, his words were for Rachel. "I hope by appearing suddenly like this I haven't shocked her too much," he said.

"I'm sure … sure you haven't, Mr Freemantle." Mildred glanced sideways at Rachel who was still staring at Colin, her mouth open. "Well not too much," she added. "You're looking pale, Rachel. I think you might be coming down with something. Why don't you get yourself off home? I'll tell Mr Prendaghast that you weren't feeling too well."

Rachel stood up.

"Thank you," she said. Her eyes were staring at the unbelievable.

She reached for her coat.

Having collected Dani from Chao, Aslah ran home as best she could through the rain and wind.

The roads were muddy and pot-holed but she was used to it now.

Abas arrived home before her. Aslah went to her bedroom, stripped off and put on a sarong and her favourite T-shirt – the one she was wearing when she nursed Coy-lyn. It was now almost threadbare and it had shrunk but it did not matter.

She changed Dani's nappy.

"So," Abas said in English as Aslah joined him, "did you work hard?"

He had a small stove on the veranda upon which he had put some water to boil. They had laughed when they realised there was a larger cooker in the kitchen but they were both reluctant to use it, preferring to cook on the veranda in the open air … and the rain.

"Old habits die hard," Abas had said quoting Coy-lyn, which was probably not the right thing to do.

Aslah squatted down next to him, arranged Dani on her lap and said, "It was not what I expected. The woman, her name is Norah, who I am to work with, is so nice. We talked a lot. She wanted to know all about the Iban, the *Dayaks*, the *Kelabits* and all the other tribal people of Sarawak. She asked lots of questions, and the more I told her the more questions she asked."

"With what purpose?" Abas asked pouring the water into a pot containing some tea leaves.

"It is all to do with giving help to the people who will have suffered during the war … thank you," she added taking a mug of steaming tea from Abas. "I must feed Dani."

"If they want help," Abas suggested.

"What do you mean?"

"Not all the people, especially those far into the jungle will want any help. They will just want to be left alone."

"Then they *will* be left alone. Nothing will be forced on them," Aslah said.

"On *them*, Aslah? You are talking as though you are not from there. We must never forget where we are from." Abas sipped his tea, his head turned away as he watched the rainwater streaming

395

from the roof … missing the veranda by inches.

"What is the matter, my brother? Why are you being like this? You wanted to come to Miri. We are so lucky to have Fung to help us find work, and of course Chao who is happy to look after Dani during the day. Is what you are doing not to your liking?"

Dani became restless so Aslah put him on the floor.

Abas looked at his sister. "War is a terrible thing," he said. "The people who are still alive do not know how lucky they are. Today I have seen what horror war brings, as if I didn't know already. I went two miles into the jungle with some others because there were reports that there was a mass grave in the area. We found it and I am not too proud to say that what I saw made me cry, Aslah. There were over thirty skeletons, some without skulls: others with their bones broken. There were children, and a man with us identified many female skeletons too. It was terrible."

"There is nothing you or anybody else could have done, Abas."

"That is what makes it more terrible," he said.

"But we are alive and we must make sure nothing like what you have seen ever happens again," Aslah said.

"You embarrass me, Aslah."

"I didn't mean to but listening to people today has made me feel more positive."

"That has to be a good thing," Abas told her.

Rachel and Colin were sitting in a teashop tucked away on the corner in an alleyway behind the old grammar school. The gas lamps on the walls put out a strange light, the shadows seemed slightly eerie.

There were three other people sitting at the tables.

After gathering her composure, Rachel had suggested they have a cup of tea before everything closed up because of the expected power cut.

"What do two English people do after not seeing each other for four years?" Colin asked, smiling. "Have a cup of tea."

Miraculously his headache had gone: it disappeared the moment he set eyes on Rachel. Even in her everyday work clothes, she looked more beautiful than he remembered her, a little slimmer maybe, but that was understandable. He had so many questions but they would have to wait. He had expected Rachel to be more skeletal, and her composure changed: her mother had said Rachel was not the same young woman who had gone away. However, she was as he remembered her … and he could not believe his luck.

"For the moment it might be for the best," Rachel said. "How did you find me?" she asked but then added, "of course, my mother. You have been to Leamington Spa."

Colin nodded, wanting to hold her hands but he must bide his time.

"I was there for an hour yesterday and came on here today."

There was no point in mentioning what had happened in between leaving Leamington and reaching Market Harborough.

"How was she?"

The small talk was necessary.

"Suspicious at first but then she relaxed."

"So you know?" As she asked the question, Rachel bowed her head, unable to maintain eye contact.

"I know about the hell you have been through. I know about the awful things you will have experienced and I know about Angelique." He could not stop himself, so he reached across the table and took her hands in his. Rachel did not resist but he saw the tears come to her eyes straight away.

"Don't," Colin said. "There is no need to cry."

"There is every need, Colin. I … I thought I would never see you again. I've done an awful thing."

"What can be awful now that we are together again?"

Rachel lifted her head, tears streaming down her cheeks. "I have told your daughter that you are still missing. She thinks you are dead."

"As you can see, I am very much alive," Colin said.

"But … but is the love we once had for each other?" Rachel asked, regretting her words the moment they were spoken.

"Well, that is for us to find out, isn't it? I didn't come all this way –"

"I know and that was a question that could have waited. I … I just can't believe that after all this time we are sitting here as though nothing had ever happened," Rachel said.

"We are sitting here because of what happened. If the Japanese hadn't invaded, well there –"

"You are pleased, aren't you?" Rachel asked.

"About Angelique?" She nodded. "I couldn't be happier," Colin said.

Colin understood why Rachel was being cautious.

"I couldn't be happier and I can't wait to meet her," he said. "The fact that we both survived the war is perhaps a sign that neither of us should ignore – it was fate. I really want to meet Angelique – our daughter – but only when you consider you are both ready. What you told her was understandable. I left you in Kuching to fend for yourself and in retrospect that was the wrong thing to do."

"Is that you talking or my mother?" Rachel asked.

Colin smiled. "Perhaps both of us but for different reasons," he said. "Would you like another cup of tea?"

He closed his eyes as Rachel's image suddenly became slightly blurred. He shook his head to try to clear his vision. He wanted to reach for the pills in his coat pocket but he did not want to alarm Rachel. He just hoped the experience would pass quickly.

"Another cup of tea is not going to give us the time we need to say what needs to be said," Rachel said. "I have no idea where you were during the war, you look well enough but there is so much to ask, and so much to tell." Rachel took her hands from Colin's. "I must go home shortly. Amy, the girl looking after Angelique, must leave by six o'clock."

"And now is not the right time?"

"No, Colin, it isn't. This morning when I said goodbye to Angelique I had truly convinced myself that I would never see you again but at teatime today there you are, back in my life. It is a lot to take in and to come to terms with. I've got to get used to seeing you again before I ask Angelique to do the same." Rachel reached for her bag.

"So what happens next?" Colin asked. "I am going to book into the Three Swans Hotel and I can be there for as long as necessary."

Rachel bowed her head again. "I don't know at the moment what needs to happen next. I have to take in what has already happened. I have prayed for this day for a long time, but now it has happened I am at a loss. I'm sorry."

"I understand," Colin said. "I knew what was coming, but you didn't."

"It's not easy," Rachel said.

There were a few moments of silence before Colin asked: "If there is somebody else perhaps now is the time to tell me. Is there?"

"And is there with you?" Rachel said, her eyes narrowing. "That question could only come from a man. I have been back in England for less than two months and men were and are not high on my list of priorities ... I'm sorry, what I mean ... well, I didn't know ..."

"I'm sorry," Colin said, kicking himself for being so selfish. Only when he felt she was ready would he tell Rachel about Aslah and Dani. On seeing Rachel again he knew that his journey had been necessary – not in vain – whether it had been the right thing to do from her point of view he had yet to find out.

Colin looked up as a middle-aged woman he had noticed had been watching them, got up to leave but rather than heading for the door, she came over to their table. "I'm an old busybody," the woman said, "but seeing you two sitting there and watching you I can only put two and two together. You are so lucky to have found each other again. There will be a lot of lost souls out there wishing they could have what you have found. I hope you don't mind me saying so."

"Not at all," Rachel said. "And thank you." The woman smiled and walked away.

"How on earth did she know that?" Colin asked.

Chapter One Hundred and Ninety-Seven

The lone candle on the washstand flickered.

There was a knock on the door and Colin eased himself unsteadily off the bed. He had another headache and he thought lying down would ease it. It seemed to have worked.

"Come in," he said trying to locate his shoes.

The door opened a crack.

"Mr Freemantle," a female voice said. "Lucy here … the chambermaid. There's a lady downstairs who would like to see you, if you please."

Colin went to the door and opened it.

The chambermaid, dressed in her black and white uniform, stepped back into the corridor, her head bowed and with her hands clasped in front of her.

She couldn't be more than sixteen, Colin thought.

"Does the lady have a name?" he asked.

"Yes, sir." She looked at a piece of paper. "Leafever," she said. "It's a Miss Leafever."

Colin smiled, not wishing to embarrass the girl by correcting her pronunciation. "Please tell Miss Leafever I will be down shortly."

The girl nodded. "Yes, sir," she said as she scurried away.

Colin went to the bathroom a little further along the corridor, swilled his face and straightened his tie.

It was nearly eight o'clock.

He had eaten a simple meal by candlelight in the hotel dining room. Not wanting to wander the streets of Market Harborough, he had retired to his room. He had also felt the headache coming on while he was eating. His vision had cleared soon after he left the teashop. As he watched Rachel walking down the High Street away from him, he really could not believe his luck. The way she walked had not changed – even under her winter's coat he could detect the slight sensual swing of her hips.

He had to give her time, and he did not know what to read into what she had said. Her mother had implied that she had become distant and not at all forthcoming with any detail about what had happened to her.

Her mother's patience, or so she said, had been sorely tested.

She had been sorry to see her daughter and granddaughter leave but it had – maybe – been for the best. She did hope though, that it was a temporary solution. At some stage, she prayed that both would return so that they could lead as normal a life as post-war England allowed.

Colin paused at the top of the stairs leading down to the ground floor. He felt that the next few minutes – or however long it took – could affect any number of people's futures.

His decision to come to England in the first place had already gone part way to doing exactly that, but he had not expected Rachel to come to see him this evening. Perhaps, having given his re-appearance some thought, albeit after only a couple of hours, she had decided what she wanted from the future … did it include him?

She was in the foyer. She looked up when she became aware that he was almost at the bottom of the staircase: she smiled.

He stopped.

She stood up, and after a few seconds of just looking at him she rushed across the foyer into his arms.

"Thank God you've come back to me," she said against his cheek and with tears in her eyes.

Chapter One Hundred and Ninety-Eight

"Would you like to have a drink?" Colin asked as they parted.

The smell of her hair, the softness of her cheek next to his and the way she rested her arms on his shoulders, took him back all those years. She was as intoxicating as ever.

"Bars aren't for women," Rachel replied, glancing over his shoulder.

"Who on earth told you that?" he said, laughing.

Not believing things had moved on so quickly, he said, "This is the Three Swans hotel, not a spit and sawdust pub."

"Oh, all right," Rachel said, feigning reluctance. "And before you ask, your daughter is being well looked after. Mildred from work is with her."

Colin stopped just inside the bar. "My daughter? Those words sound incredible."

"They are."

They found an empty table by a window.

"What would you like to drink?"

"A port and lemon, please, I think you can still get that."

Colin went to the bar and ordered the drinks..

He gave his room number.

Glancing round the bar it was difficult to determine how many other people were in the room, the promised power cut had happened and there was a single small candle on each table. The barman also had to operate by candlelight.

Taking the drinks over to their table, Colin sat down opposite Rachel.

"We have so much to talk about," Colin said sipping on his pint of bitter. He shook his head. "I just can't believe that we are sitting here in this hotel, in a town neither of us had probably ever heard of before, drinking as though the last four years hadn't existed. It really is incredible."

The bar was quite warm so Rachel had taken off her coat.

She was wearing a white blouse and blue-grey skirt. A simple gold chain framed her long slender neck. Colin could only guess what she had been through but he certainly was not going to press her for any details, not yet, and especially after what her mother had said. Although by looking at her he acknowledged she was slimmer, her face and hair looked so healthy, although there was hardness about her eyes.

"The last four years existed," Rachel said. "But what about you? You look so well. The tanned, blond, blue-eyed man I fell in love with and whose love …"

Rachel's words trailed off as she looked down at her glass.

"Give it time, Rachel. We are both going to need time." He waited a couple of seconds. "There is so much to tell and I've a feeling that you might not want to relive a lot of what you experienced, but just tell me one thing. Was it awful?"

"There … there were times when … no, I mean yes, it was awful but … but I'm having … no, it's too early. I will tell you but not yet."

"I understand," Colin said. He thought for a moment. "Tell me about Angelique. Who does she take after, you or me?"

"She …" Rachel looked up as a young woman stopped at their table. There was an airman in American uniform behind her, trying to pull here away.

"Come on Julia, don't bother these ..." the airman said.

"So this is your wife, Colin. Aren't you going to introduce us?" Julia Danbury asked, her speech slurred.

"Come on, Julia," the American airman repeated, still tugging at her arm. "Let's leave these good people in peace."

Julia Danbury jerked her arm away.

"Get off, Greg. I'm only being sociable." She was still slurring her words and her eyes looked glazed. "So, aren't you going to introduce me to your wife, Colin?"

"Who is this?" Rachel asked, looking at Colin.

Colin decided to bluff his way out of the situation: the questions would come later.

He stood up.

"Yes, I'm sorry. Julia this is Rachel and Rachel this is Julia."

The two women did not look at each other but instead they stared at Colin. The American took a step back and shrugged an apology,

"Did he tell you he spent last night with me, Mrs Freemantle?" Julia Danbury asked spitefully, this time looking at Rachel. "And when I say last night, I mean the whole night."

"Colin, what's going on?" Rachel asked, her expression communicating her confusion. "Who is this girl? And why ...?"

"Julia," Greg tried again. "Look I'm real sorry about this," he apologised. "She's had too many sherries."

"Greg, how dare you say that –"

"Julia!" This time the American managed to move Julia away from the table. "I'll get her home," he said. "Mr and Mrs Freemantle, I can but apologise again. If what she told me earlier is true, Mrs Freemantle, your husband was in hospital last night. Julia sat with him, that's all. I am sure your husband will tell you all about it. Please do not think anything untoward took place."

"He –" Julia started to say.

"Be quiet," Greg said firmly. "You've tried to cause enough trouble for one night. She goes like this if she drinks too much. Sorry."

Taking her arm firmly, Greg steered Julia Danbury out of the bar.

"What was that all about?" Rachel asked picking up her drink. "And what were you doing in hospital?"

"Yes, I'm sorry. I should have told you earlier. The American was right, that's where I did spend last night."

Colin told Rachel exactly what had happened. The only detail he left out was the fact that he was having intermittent but debilitating headaches and blurred vision: there was little point in complicating matters.

"So you told her you were married to put her off?" Rachel asked when he had finished.

"Yes," Colin agreed. "But …"

"And she thought I was your wife?"

"It looked like that. But there is …"

"It's certainly been an unusual day to say the least. Are you sure you are all right? You look all right. Being hit on the head like that, well …"

"Yes, yes, I'm fine. Look Rachel there is something …"

"Well if you are sure."

Rachel sipped her drink.

Colin was sure her eyes were telling him she did not want to know what else he was trying to say, so perhaps now was not the right time.

"Let's get back to Angelique, tell me about her," he said instead.

Rachel was reluctant to go into detail of the conditions under which Angelique was born. Although irreversibly etched into her mind, the details were too intimate to discuss with somebody she had not seen for nearly four years.

There would be a right time.

It was not now.

So she said, "Angelique is your daughter as much as she is mine, but she has had rather an unusual start in life to say the least. On the outside she looks as though she is as innocent as any other child of her age, on the inside though, she has witnessed the worst horrors of life and she is only just over three years old, but she talks and behaves as though she is a lot older." She paused. "I hope you understand that I just don't want to introduce another complication into her young life unless we are absolutely sure that we have a future together."

Colin looked at Rachel. "It is too early to decide that but I did come here to discover if you were all right. If I hadn't known about Angelique I would still have come to find you anyway. So, of course I understand. As you say, we haven't seen each other for four years. I have changed, you have changed and you in particular had every reason to want leaving alone. From what I have read and heard, I can only guess the horrors Angelique and you must have experienced. If and when you are ready to talk I am here, if I am the one you want to talk to that is."

Rachel stared at Colin for a few seconds.

"You've only been back in my life for a matter of minutes but I can tell you haven't changed as much as you think you have." She smiled but then she became serious again. "But I have, my mother will have told you that. I don't know which way to turn, if it wasn't for Angelique I think … no, I'm not going to go there." She looked at her watch. "I have not spent this long at night away from Angelique since she was born. I am worried that if she wakes up and calls for me and I'm not there she will be frightened. I must go."

A little taken aback, Colin hesitated.

"Of course," he said. "When can we meet again?"

"We mustn't rush any decision that needs to be made," Rachel said reaching for her coat. "We have to take things slowly." She stood up and Colin helped her on with her coat. "But I don't know how long you are in England for."

"As long as it takes," he said.

"I am going to Leamington Spa this weekend to see my mother. Maybe that is the next time we should meet. We will have more time and I will not worry if I leave Angelique with my mother."

"Can we travel together?"

Rachel shook her head. "No, Angelique will be with me. Even if you were in the same carriage and I knew it, she would sense something. Your daughter is very astute."

"Our daughter, and once again I understand."

"I will meet you in The Royal Pump Rooms at the bottom of the Parade mid-morning on Saturday."

"I'll be there."

"You tried to tell me something earlier. I will listen when we next meet."

"I'll be there."

"And to answer a question you asked earlier, Angelique has got your eyes."

"Thank you for telling me."

Chapter Two Hundred and One

As with Market Harborough, Colin once again marvelled at the lack of damage to Leamington Spa. Nothing he saw, other than the people, suggested the town had just survived a world war.

The town had obviously not been deliberately targeted, although Colin did appreciate that a jettisoned bomb could still kill, albeit indiscriminately. So maybe, other than providing fighting men and women, there was nothing that meant Leamington would have become a target. He did remember reading somewhere that a company called Borg and Beck produced its one-millionth sliding clutch in the town just before the outbreak of the war. The names implied it was a German company ... and it was. He wondered what had happened to the company, and some of its employees.

Whereas he was not aware of any damage, he was aware of the queues at all of the bakers' and the butchers' shops. The queues stretched for many hundreds of yards as people waited patiently for an egg or two, some processed meat and even potatoes. Colin smiled as he wondered what would happen if they had to fend for themselves as Anak and his family did back in the jungle.

As he left the hotel for his rendezvous with Rachel, Colin did marvel at the steadfastness of the people he saw. The war had been over for months and there were still harder times to come, but the people puffed out their chests with pride ... and smiled. They had managed to withstand the onslaught and nothing would defeat them now.

He had left Market Harborough to return to Leamington Spa the morning after his meeting with Rachel in the hotel. He wanted to get as far away from Julia Danbury as possible, he also wanted to remove temptation from his itinerary. Knowing Rachel was in the bank would have been too much of an invitation. He booked into The Angel Hotel on Regent Street in Leamington Spa and spent Friday walking the streets of the town. It was an overcast day but fortunately dry. He did go along Beauchamp Avenue but calling on Rachel's mother again was not an option.

He walked aimlessly through Jephson Gardens and Victoria Park, he even found his way to St Nicholas Park where he sat on a bench, ignoring the chill in the air, and allowed his thoughts to run wild.

He pictured Aslah, with Dani on her good hip, going about her day-to-day chores around the longhouse. He could see Abas fishing down at the river's edge, or returning from a re-supply run to Miri. Then there was Anak, his small but dominant frame everywhere for his people to see, his pride not yet ready to let him hand over to Abas. He could see and smell the jungle, feel the humidity, hear the birds, the rush of the river, but just as suddenly, he felt the cold again. He could hear the rustle in the branches above him, he could see the other walkers scurrying past, as a now numbingly cold late November day in England brought him back to reality.

What was reality? Where he was or where he ought to be?

If his conscience told him he ought to be with Aslah and Dani, why was he sitting in a park in Leamington Spa? Why had his heart missed umpteen beats as he had walked into the bank and seen Rachel for the first time in so many years?

He would have to tell her.

She knew there was something to tell. Once he had told her, their futures were no longer his to play with. Even if she understood, his future might not be with her.

Walking back to the hotel he felt the start of another headache coming on. He felt tired and the pedestrians who walked past him were a blur.

Rachel was a few minutes late for their next meeting.

Angelique had one of her rare bad nights resulting in Rachel oversleeping. Having travelled to Leamington Spa the previous evening, she had also stayed up late talking, which was something she had not done with her mother since her return. Now she felt she had to and maybe she wanted to. Colin was her past that was further back than Kampong Punkit and Batu Lintang. It was Kampong Punkit and Batu Lintang she could not talk about: maybe one day ... but not yet.

Colin was a subject with which she felt safe.

"So are you telling me that you didn't know he was coming to find you?" her mother had asked.

They had enjoyed a simple meal and were having a rare cup of coffee, the beans for which Rachel had been given by an American serviceman who had taken a fancy to her at the bank. "No, Mum, I had no idea."

"But he found you?" her mother said.

"Yes, on Wednesday. And thank you for telling him where I was, I know what you must be thinking. I –"

"Your father always used to tell me what I was thinking," her mother retorted. "He was often wrong too."

"I'm sorry, Mum, that was rude of me. I just thought ..."

"There is no need to apologise." She paused. "I may have been a little abrupt with your young man, my dear. His arrival was out of the blue and did rather take me aback."

Rachel could see that her mother was inwardly delighted that she was having a longer conversation. She became more animated and quite tactile.

"He's not my *young man*, Mum. He is a man with whom I was in love a lot of years ago. Neither of us is the person we were then."

"He is the man who made you pregnant. He is the father of your daughter, the man with whom you ... well ... perhaps that is getting too personal. You didn't tell us about him in your letters, dear."

"He didn't make me pregnant as you put it, Mum. Neither of us planned to have a baby, not before we married anyway ... and that was still a fantasy, but these things happen. And I didn't tell you about him because I didn't think you would approve. I love Angelique so much, but she was a mistake. Colin and I hadn't really discussed … and well, he was not the sort of man I thought you and dad would have wanted me to marry."

"The man your father and I wanted you to marry was the man you wanted to be with," her mother said. "We wanted you to be happy so why else do you think we let you go to that God forsaken country on your own?"

Rachel took a deep breath. "Sarawak is more of a God given than a God forsaken country, Mum. The people are some of the nicest you could ever hope to meet. They lead simple lives but they are so, so happy."

"If you say so, my dear, but are you happy with what has happened? Would you have preferred it if Angelique's father had not reappeared?" her mother asked.

"Mum, I spent every moment, every second as a prisoner of the Japanese praying that Colin survived the war. He did and I did. Tomorrow will determine whether we have a future together or not," Rachel said.

She just hoped she was right.

Perhaps Colin was her way of getting back to Sarawak … no, it was wrong to think like that.

"You are unhappy," Chao said.

Bowing her head Aslah did not know whether to admit that Chao had told the truth. She *was* unhappy and it was getting worse by the day. If the Japanese had killed her Coy-lyn she would still be in mourning. If he had gone away to his own country and she knew he would return, she would be missing him but her heart would be happy because she would know she had not lost him. He had been truthful with her and she thought she had done the right thing, but now she wished she had said what her heart had told her, not her head.

"You and Fung have given me a new life," she said. Dani was sitting on the floor with Chee who was playing a game with him. Aslah smiled at them before saying: "You have been so kind and that has made me happy."

"Fung tells me that you are doing well at your job, as is Abas, and you and Norah are getting on well," Chao said as she looked at Aslah sympathetically.

"Yes, she is a lovely lady. She was surprised to discover that I was married to an Englishman, I am not sure whether she still believes me or not."

"Why would you lie about such a thing?" Chao asked.

Shrugging, Aslah said, "I just suppose it is most unusual."

"There's nothing unusual about the product," Chao said, looking at Dani.

"Except for his blond hair and blue eyes," Aslah said. "Norah and I will be going upriver in a few days. I am going to show her my father's longhouse; she has yet to see one."

Aslah's felt her whole body stir at the thought of being back.

"That is good, and if it is possible I would like to go with you. Seeing your mother and father, and all the others again would make me happy."

"And them too," Aslah said. "I am sure they would love to see you. I will let you know when we plan to go."

"Thank you."

Aslah saw Chao indicate to Chee for her to take Dani to another room, and she guessed what was coming.

When the children had left the room, Chao said, "But you are unhappy, Aslah. You are doing everything you should be doing and more, but when you are not at work, when you come to collect Dani, I can see how unhappy you are. You used to be so full of life, even after you were shot and we all thought you were going to die, you were the one who told jokes, laughed at us looking so sad. From dawn to dusk you went about your chores with such enthusiasm, you were loving life and life was loving you. But now, you do not love life and the reason is obvious."

Aslah couldn't stop herself from bursting into tears. "I … I miss him so much," she said. "And … and I long to see him again: I want him to touch me and I want to touch him. I have tried everything to get him out of my head but he is always there. I can hear him laugh, I see him with Dani and I see him going down to the river: I see him everywhere. At night I feel him resting next to me, and when he is touching me and he is loving me." Aslah looked up, wiping the tears from her eyes. "I thought it would get better, Chao, but it is getting worse and worse."

"And your unhappiness is also getting worse."

"It is."

"Then we must do something about it."

"But what can we do?"

Chao nodded. "There may be something."

Chapter Two Hundred and Four

Her unblinking eyes stared at Colin.

With her lips slightly parted in shock and disbelief, she tried to understand. What he had told her had hit her like a sledgehammer. It was the last thing she had expected and now the last thing she wanted to hear.

She was literally speechless.

The previous night she had lain awake with her hands behind her head, thinking how in such a short while he had changed her life – again. This time it was so much for the better, and they now had so much to look forward too. It was a dream come true.

He had given her a new direction.

The unimaginable had become reality.

She knew what she wanted from the moment he walked into the bank the previous Wednesday. She had not been able to believe her eyes but as Marjory Field told her in Kampong Punkit and Batu Lintang, her heart would always lead her. It was as though her mind and body went through the most amazing transformation in just a matter of seconds. Every square inch of her skin had tingled with anticipation and delight.

She would not rush things but the outcome was clear.

She had talked openly with her mother, and although her mother had not said as much, Rachel had sensed approval. Her mother approved of Colin so if she were to tell her that they were going to get married she would be happy for them.

They would marry in England and as a family they would go back to Sarawak. Colin could get another plane – and if he called her Sammy II, there would no complaint from her – Angelique would go to school and grow up in an environment that would be so good for her. They would have a son, no two sons, no another son and daughter: perhaps just another two children would do.

In such a short time she had planned it all and …

Now her dreams were shattered and her heart thumped and ached with the pain.

They had been dreams: stupid, stupid, dreams.

If he were married, why had he come to find her? Even discovering that he was a father – for the second time – did not justify him leaving his wife with a baby, leaving her to fend for herself in the middle of the jungle. So, why, why, why?

No, that was silly, his wife would not be fending for herself but she would be alone, without him. Rachel had been on her own for more years than Angelique had been on this earth. Without him reappearing, they both would have survived. They had already lived through hell on earth. She would have brought Angelique up and if another man had come into her life that was the way it was meant to be, but it would not have been the end of the world if she had stayed on her own.

It did not matter that he had told her the marriage – conducted under Iban lore – was only recognised by the Iban. Had he not married her? Would it be different if there were no baby?

The numbness she was experiencing seemed worse than anything she had lived through in Kampong Punkit or Batu Lintang. The future that had kept her going in both of those awful places had been presented to her when she was least expecting it, but now it had been snatched away.

It was incalculably cruel. She felt at a depth she had never experienced before.

"I want to call you a bastard, but I can't," she said softly, unable to look at him. "I want to cry, but I can't. Thank God you haven't met Angelique." After a while, she did look at him. "Why did you do it? Why when you already had a wife and child, did you need to find me?"

"Because I have never stopped loving you," Colin said.

Chapter Two Hundred and Five

"We must not interfere," Fung said. "Colin left Sarawak with Aslah's blessing. I think she knew from the start that when the war was over he would have to leave."

"What do you mean *have to*?" Chao almost spat at him. "There was no *have to* about it. He and Aslah are married and they have a young son. There was commitment, responsibilities, or there should have been."

Chao picked up her bowl of rice, fish and vegetables and spooned some into her mouth. She had never bothered to go back to chopsticks after spending so long with the Iban.

Lim and Chee were in another room doing their homework ... she hoped.

Fung shook his head. "You were there, you saw the ceremony. The "

"Are you saying that because it was an Iban ceremony it shouldn't have meant anything?" Chao asked incredulously.

"No, that's not what I am saying but ..."

"Fung, there is no *but*. Colin made a commitment to Aslah, her family and their ancestors."

"All right, all right," Fung said sitting back in his chair. "But it was a war marriage, it was one of convenience. It –"

"What do mean *convenience*? There was nothing convenient about it. How can you say such a thing? And why are you defending him so much? He knew exactly what he was doing and he should have honoured the vow. He wouldn't have had to stay at the longhouse because he could have brought Aslah and Dani to Miri, Kuching, or anywhere else."

"But we don't know what commitment he had to this other woman. She was the mother of his child too."

Chao could tell that Fung knew he was not going to win, although he did feel somebody needed to defend Colin's actions. However, she was determined for him to see sense because he was a critical part of her plan, without him she would not be able to go ahead with it.

"They weren't married," she said, "unless he lied to us, and although I don't agree with what he did, Colin would not have lied.

417

Even when he found out that Rachel had a baby that was not a good enough reason to walk out on Aslah."

"He didn't walk out. You make it sound worse than it was," Fung reminded his wife.

"Worse? That poor girl's heart is breaking into little pieces. She is missing him so much. I am worried for her, Fung, worried. Her health is suffering, and I have no idea how much longer she can carry on like this. All I am asking is that you try to find out where he is so that she can write to him as his wife, to tell him what is happening to her."

Chao watched her husband closely. If he said he would not help she would have to find another way. She could not and must not raise Aslah's hopes only to have them dashed because her stupid husband would not see reason.

"I suppose there would be no harm in what you are suggesting. I do not know his address in England but there will be a record of Rachel's somewhere. The Australians handed over all the details of the repatriations that took place. I still do not think we should interfere though, and anyway writing to her could cause just more problems."

"We are not interfering and thank you for agreeing to do something. Aslah would not be writing to her, but to him. This Rachel would not open a letter to him even if it does go to her address. I think even if Aslah knows that something she writes will be read by him it will make her a little happier."

"But will it do the same for Colin?" Fung asked.

Chapter Two Hundred and Six

He could have withheld the truth from her so it was his choice to tell her, but for him there really was no choice. Regardless of what she now thought of him, he did not want to stoop to deception that in turn would have generated the need to lie. He could not have gone through with any commitment they might have made to each other without her knowing.

In the same way he told Aslah the truth, Rachel had a right to know it too.

He had expected no other reaction.

She loved everything there was to love about Sarawak. Regardless of whether they lived in the towns, the villages or deep in the jungle, he knew she loved the people from the bottom of her heart. She also loved the climate, the beaches, even the dangerous waters in which they used to swim. Now, though, she would be regarding that love as tenuous, it would be tearing her in two.

Half expecting her to walk away and out of his life, the fact that she was still sitting opposite him suggested that there was also still hope. He prayed there was hope.

What was he hoping might happen? His love for her was not in question, nor was his love for Angelique, although they had yet to meet.

However, if asked there was no way he could deny the fact that he also loved Aslah and Dani.

So was it a competition between the strength of the love he felt for a mother and his daughter and a mother and his son? On the other hand, was it more to do with where his responsibilities should really lie?

"I … I want to go for a walk," Rachel said. "I want to find somewhere where nobody else will bother us, and I want you to explain to me why you are here, why you are really here." Rachel put on her coat, picked up her bag and headed for the door of the café without another word.

They found a secluded bench in Jephson Gardens overlooking the River Leam. The clouds had cleared allowing a weak sun to give a little warmth. They sat a foot apart.

"I am not going to try to excuse what I left behind in Sarawak,"

419

Colin said slowly. "All I will say is that my life was saved by a magnificent group of people with whom I would spend all the war years. Aslah was the daughter of the headman. She, more than anyone else, was responsible for making me well. She nursed me day and night. I felt an obligation to her and her family. Her brothers became my brothers, when Babu died I lost a brother.

"It would be wrong of me to say that the obligation I felt went as far as marrying Aslah, it didn't. If I had said 'no', she and her family would have respected my decision. But I didn't say 'no'. Neither can I say that I regret my decision. Without Aslah to guide me I doubt whether I would have survived the war, I would have become reckless which would have led to only one result. What I can say, Rachel, is that I do not love Aslah as I love you. There are too many differences between us. If I had stayed I would have made her unhappy, she knew that too. That is why she let me go."

"And your son?" Rachel asked next to him.

"He was and still is too young to understand."

"No, I mean do you love your son?"

Colin looked down at his hands in his lap. "Yes … yes, I love my son, Rachel but … but if I stayed I would have finished up making him hate me. He would have seen how unhappy I was making his mother and he would have blamed me."

"And your wife is going to be happy without you being there, is she? Is he going to hate you any the less because you only left her to be unhappy?"

"I don't know."

"You do know, Colin. The difference is that you are not there to see the unhappiness you will have caused."

"I do understand what you are saying. I made too many assumptions," Colin said. "Discovering you were alive and that you had a daughter ... I suppose I just felt I had to find you."

"Maybe under the circumstances you did act impulsively," Rachel said, "but that won't change any of what you've told me, will it?"

"No, you're right," he said. "So where do I go from here?"

"That is for you to decide," Rachel told him.

"It can't be," he said. "Impulsive or not, I made my decision before I left Miri."

"And that was?" Rachel looked down at her hands.

"You," he said quietly. "Why else would I be here?"

"So are you now putting the responsibility of what happens next on me?" she asked.

"I have made my decision but it is of little consequence if you don't agree. So yes, I suppose you can be the only one who can decide."

"That is so unfair and you know it. Three days ago I had convinced myself you were dead and I was planning to go back to Sarawak, but out of the blue you appear and I think all my prayers and worries have been answered and solved. Then you hit me with this bombshell and expect me to ... if I say go, will you go?"

"Yes, I will."

"And not come back?"

"Yes."

Rachel stood up and walked slowly to the river's edge. "It's not as simple as that."

"If it were maybe I wouldn't be here."

Rachel turned to face Colin. "I love you Colin, I have never stopped loving you. I've already told you that it was the love I have for you that got me, got me and your daughter, through hell."

"There is a *but* coming," he said.

"Of course there is a *but* coming," she said. "If you had appeared in the bank without any complications then today I was going to tell you that I still love you. I have done that. I would also have taken you to meet Angelique and if you had asked me, I would have agreed to marry you."

"But?"

"But," Rachel said, her annoyance beginning to show, "but that was before you told me you were married with a son."

"I want to be with you."

"And you expect me to ignore what you have told me? You've cleared your conscience, I shrug my shoulders and we go back to square one? Is that what you anticipated happening?"

"You know it isn't. But I could not allow you to commit yourself to anything without you knowing what my situation was."

"Commit myself?" Rachel repeated, as her eyes opened wide in surprise. "Do you know the meaning of the word commitment? I was willing to do exactly that, but what would I be committing myself to?" Rachel turned back to the river. "Colin, I thought I understood why you are here, but I now think it would be best if you leave me to get on with the rest of my life without you."

"I will go if you really mean what you say. Do you mean it?"

Facing Colin once more Rachel replied with tears in her eyes.

"I don't know," she said.

It took Fung only three days to discover Rachel's address in England.

As he thought, the Australians had given the administration the details of all repatriated British citizens.

However, in those three days other events took a turn that meant certain plans were changed significantly.

On his return from work on the same day, Fung called Abas into his office.

"We know each other too well for me not to be straight with you," Fung said. "It's your father, he is seriously ill. Didaku came here this afternoon from the longhouse to find you. He has gone to get the doctor to take him upriver. Your father is evidently too ill to come here himself. I am sorry to give you this news Abas because your father is a wonderful man."

"Thank you, and yes he is a great man. But even great men are mortal," Abas said. "I must go to him. I will go and get Aslah and we will both go to him."

"Aslah does not know, Abas. I thought it would be best if this sad news came from you," Fung suggested.

"Thank you for respecting my standing, Fung."

Forty-five minutes later Abas, Aslah, Didaku and the doctor were racing against time to get back to the longhouse. Unfortunately, they were all too late. Indeed, it had been too late even before Didaku had left the longhouse to go to Miri. Abas and Aslah's mother told them that as well as being a great man their father was also stubborn and had refused all suggestions that he needed a doctor. She had finally over-ruled him but she had already known it was too late.

After a quick examination, the doctor decided that Anak had died from blood poisoning with complications. There was certainly no suggestion that any third party might be involved.

After a great ceremony of life and much heart beating, his family buried Anak in the exact spot he declared many years earlier. With further ceremony, Abas became the new headman. It was not the way he wished to succeed his father, but now he had little choice. The plans for his immediate future had to be changed, he could not be headman while living and working in Miri.

As Aslah was preparing to return to the town, he asked her to explain his absence and give his apologies to Fung.

"But how will I survive without you?" she asked, forlornly.

"You are already surviving without me, Aslah. Our father was so pleased that you decided to take Dani out of the jungle for a new life. That is what he would have said if we had got here before he died."

"But what about mother?"

"I will be here and all the other women will be here. She will be in mourning for many days. She too wants you to have this new life ... you must not let either of them down."

"Then I will go back but I will visit often."

"You are making the right decision," Abas said.

"Am I?" Aslah said.

"It is not only your future, my sister, it is also Dani's. He will be a great man, just like his father, and his ..."

"It is his father that makes me want to stay here with you," Aslah said.

Abas shook his head. "Time, my sister, time will pass and so will your longing."

"Time has done nothing but increase my longing," Aslah said.

After booking in to the Whipper-in Hotel in Oakham, Colin went straight to his room.

Without taking anything out of his bag, he pulled the curtains closed, took off his shoes and lay down on the bed with his hands either side of his head.

He moaned.

The headache had started as he was travelling by train from Leamington Spa to Oakham. It had begun as a dull ache but it had become so intense that his whole head felt as though it was going to explode. He had never felt anything like it before, even when he was badly injured all those years ago.

His vision was blurred and he felt nauseous.

"Do you need a doctor, Mr Freemantle," the receptionist in the Whipper-in asked as he booked in. "You look awful."

Colin managed to tell her that he did not need a doctor, it was just a headache and that it would go once he had rested. He had the pills and they had worked before, although he would need some more in a few days time.

"Well, dinner is between seven and eight-thirty," he heard the receptionist say behind him as he headed for his room. The pain was so bad he stumbled up the stairs and wondered if he would make it. He could remember little of the villages and towns he had passed through during his journey. Oakham station was a blur, as was the walk down Station Road and the High Street to the hotel. Having lived in the town for his early years he managed to make it alone, he knew every back street and alleyway extremely well. He had left Oakham behind seven years earlier having gained his pilot's licence.

Being orphaned at an early age – his father having died of pneumonia and his mother died only a few months later, probably from a broken heart – resulted in a strict aunt bringing him up. She was a spinster who seemed to dislike anything to do with men. Colin was initially too young to understand. The aunt, Aunt Edna, had died shortly after he had leased and started flying his first plane, Sammy … in Sarawak.

Before they parted in Jephson Park the previous day, Rachel had said that for the next week Colin was to be far enough away from

Market Harborough so that neither of them would be tempted to break the agreement. He spent one more night in The Angel Hotel in Leamington Spa before leaving it early the next morning for the station. He did not know how he should feel as he walked to the station, bought his ticket and boarded the train. If Rachel wanted a week, a month, even two months to think then that is exactly what she would have. Because she was thinking perhaps there really was hope, although as time passed it would make any decision that much harder. After he left Rachel, he chose Oakham because he needed to feel more secure, mentally. Oakham was not that far from Market Harborough but the distance was irrelevant.

His head started pounding after he made the decision to go to Oakham.

The dull ache began as soon as the train pulled out of the station and during the first part of the journey to Oakham, it got worse and worse. A sixth sense told him that what he was now experiencing was serious and it was not something that he was going to wake up from in the morning with everything back to normal. So there was something he had to do because a week, a month would possibly be too long.

He switched on the light by the bed and sitting at the desk in the room, he wrote a letter. Afterwards he put the envelope in the money belt before lying down again. The darkness helped a little. He hoped the letter he had written would never be read.

He drifted into a deep but troubled sleep.

Chapter Two Hundred and Ten

Normally the receptionist who was on the late shift would not have been concerned if one of the guests she had previously registered did not appear for dinner. But having seen the way Mr Freemantle looked when she first saw him, and when she watched him walk up the stairs to his room, she became a little worried when he had not come down for dinner by a quarter past eight this evening.

She called one of the waitresses from the restaurant and asked her to care-take the front desk while she went to investigate.

Going up to the first floor she went along to Mr Freemantle's room and, after listening at the door, she knocked lightly.

"Mr Freemantle, it's Penny from Reception, are you all right?" she whispered.

She waited before knocking a little more loudly.

"Hello, Mr Freemantle, it's Penny from Reception, can I come in?" she asked, raising her voice.

There was no response. Stopping and thinking what she should do, she went to check on the two bathrooms on that floor but neither was engaged. She went back to the bedroom door. She knocked again.

"Hello, Mr Freemantle, it's Penny from Reception."

Nothing.

Taking the passkey out of her pocket Penny went to put it in the lock but discovered the door was already open. She peered round the door into the darkness, having now assumed that Mr Freemantle had gone out and forgotten to lock his door. But she noticed in the darkened room that there was a shape on the bed.

"Mr Freemantle, I'm sorry to disturb you but ..." She went further into the room. "Hello, Mr Freemantle?" In the gloom she could see that he was still fully clothed.

She shook his shoulder gently but there was no reaction. Flicking on the main light she tried again, but there was still no response.

Reaching for the phone by the bed, she dialled 999.

"An ambulance," she told the woman who answered. "I need an ambulance at the Whipper-in."

Twenty minutes later an ambulance took Colin to the Cottage

427

Hospital in Oakham. Shortly after that, the same ambulance took him to the Leicester Royal Infirmary, the bell on the ambulance clearing the way as best it could.

Neither the Cottage Hospital nor the Royal Infirmary knew what had happened to Colin Freemantle only a few days prior to his admission, nor was there any sign that anything untoward may have happened. The only indication that he might be suffering from some form of head injury was the unequal pupil size below the closed lids.

Fortunately the young doctor on duty went with his instincts. "I want an X-ray of his skull," he ordered before moving on to the bleeding from of a drunk's nose.

In a side ward and an hour later, the doctor examined the x-rays.

"I need a second opinion," he said to the nurse next to him. "Can you go and find Mr Emmanuel."

Only ten minutes later the two men agreed that Colin had a fractured skull and there were small bits of splintered bone pressing against his brain.

Fortunately, there was no sign of a thrombus.

"Emergency operation needed," Mr Emmanuel said.

"This is kind of you and it should not be for too long," Aslah told Chao.

"Will you please stop thanking me? It'll be lovely to have you and Dani in the house. It is far too big for the four of us. Fortunately because it was used by Japanese officers as living accommodation during the war there wasn't a lot of damage." Throwing open the shutters in the large room she had allocated to Aslah and Dani, Chao said, "And anyway, your family did look after mine for quite a while." She smiled. "And it wasn't just for a few days."

"It is still kind of you," Aslah said, putting her case on the bed.

"We were so sorry we weren't there to say goodbye to your father."

Taking Dani from Aslah, Chao sat on the side of the bed and put him on her knee.

"It all happened so quickly and it is our custom to bury the dead within a day of them dying," Aslah said.

Aslah was still ashamed of what she was now taking out of her case. Although she had bought some second hand western style clothes, they were old and drab. She tried to hide a few of the items from Chao's view.

"Yes, I know from those who died when I lived with you." Chao saw the expression on Aslah's face. "I do wish you would let me help you with your clothes."

"No," Aslah said firmly, "I must pay my own way. If I rely on you too much I will never learn. It's getting used to wearing them that may take a little longer," she said smiling sadly. "I just think …"

"You could not stay in that place on your own, not just you and Dani. It wouldn't have been safe," Chao said.

"I know and that is why I am so grateful." Aslah could feel herself filling up. She closed her eyes to try to stop the tears.

Putting Dani on the bed, Chao took Aslah in her arms. "You are so unhappy, aren't you?" she said, stroking the other woman's hair. "Losing your father at a time like this is not what you needed."

"It is not only my father but Abas must stay at the longhouse. He is the headman now. I will miss him."

"Of course you will, but you must visit often." She held Aslah by the shoulders. "Right, let us get Dani fed and then we have a letter to write. Have you decided what you want to say?"

"I will tell him about my father, my move to Miri, Abas, the fact that I am now living with you, and of course his son, Dani. I must tell him all about Dani, the way he is growing so quickly, using small words, trying to walk." Excitement had replaced the sadness in Aslah's eyes. "But won't a letter take a long time to get to the other side of the world? He may have left long before it gets there."

"We will pay to have your letter sent by airmail, Aslah, it should only take a few days," Chao told her.

Aslah thought for a moment. "And I will tell him how much I miss him and how much I love him."

"Don't forget to tell him that you want him to come back to you?" Chao added.

"It's not just me, it's for Dani too. We both need him here."

"So, that's what you must write."

"How will we know if he ever sees it?" Aslah asked.

"Either you will get a reply telling you when he will be here … or maybe, one day you will wake up and he …"

Rachel and Colin had agreed to meet in the Pump Rooms at the same time on the following Saturday morning, exactly a week after they had said goodbye.

It was now approaching eleven o'clock and Rachel was worried.

She had spent the week only thinking about her future with or without Colin. At work, her mind had not been on anything else either. On the Wednesday evening, she had almost reached the point where she was going to include Angelique in her deliberations but she imagined what the conversation would be like:

"Darling, if I were to ask you whether you wanted your father to be part of your life and mine, what would you say?"

"But you told me that daddy was dead, Mummy."

"No, not really, I didn't say that. But he came into the bank a short while ago and when I left you with Grandma on Saturday, I went to meet him."

"But Mummy, if he is my daddy then ..."

Dismissing even the thought of discussing it with Angelique, Rachel had gone back to her own reverie.

Was it just a *yes* or *no* situation? Did she want him?

Of course she did, but that was before he had told her about his Iban wife and child.

How could he have done that?

But he had done it and there was no going back. Just seeing him again, though, had brought her out of her self-induced depression. The longing that she had endured for over four years had walked through the doors of Lloyds Bank in Market Harborough and back into her life. Her heart had missed a beat – well, a lot more than one beat – her skin had tingled and she wanted to be held, she wanted to be hugged, she wanted to be kissed and told that he was back and that everything would be all right from now on.

She had never stopped loving him and she never ever would, even if ... even if, what?

If she were to say *yes,* they still had a long way to go. They would need to rediscover each other and she would have to tell him everything, everything that had happened to her at the hands of the Japanese. Moreover, she would want to know everything, everything that he had done since he flew away on that fateful day.

Nevertheless, his wife and son would always be at the forefront of her mind. If she were to say *no* he would walk away and out of her life forever. He would not be walking out of Angelique's life because they had never met. Would he go back to his Iban wife, to his Iban son? What would he do?

He was not the sort of man who would ignore the fact that he had a son, he would need to see him: he would need to see him growing up. But the same could be said about Angelique, she was as much his daughter as his son was his son.

What could she do? What should she do?

Was there anybody who could help – Marjory, Marjory Field? But there wasn't time. She needed more time.

Her mother?

She knew nothing of his real circumstances and she certainly would not approve of him taking a native wife. Marrying someone who lived in a longhouse by a river in the jungle … well the reaction from her mother would beggar belief. As for having a baby with such a woman … how could he?

All of that apart, where was he?

She had no idea where he had gone for the previous week.

"The operation appears to have been a success," Mr Emmanuel told the matron. "He's a lucky man. If we hadn't caught it when we did he could have died or had irretrievable brain damage but we're not out of the woods yet. What do we know about him?"

"Bit of a mystery man, doctor," the matron told him.

"But what do we know?"

"His name is Colin Freemantle and his papers suggest he's only just come back into England from a place called Sarawak."

"What was he doing there, was he in uniform?"

"There's nothing to say whether he was a soldier or the like. He was wearing a money belt with nearly £5000 in it and a letter addressed to somebody called Lefévre, a woman called Rachel Lefévre ... the money could take some explaining," the matron said solicitously. "His clothes are new. But other than that he's a complete mystery. His other possessions are still at the hotel in Oakham."

She looked down at the mystery man in the bed, his head heavily bandaged.

"Do you think we ought to involve the police?"

"Do you suspect something?" Mr Emmanuel asked. "Do we have any reason to contact the police?"

The matron shook her head. "No, I've no reason to suspect him of any wrongdoing, but if ..."

"He's had quite a hefty blow to the back of his head and quite recently, but there wasn't any evidence that he'd been treated by anyone. The blow would almost certainly have rendered him unconscious. As you say, he's a bit of a mystery."

Mr Emmanuel thought for a moment.

"Can you contact the hotel ... in Oakham did you say?" The matron nodded. "And tell them what has happened. He'll be in here for another week or so after his operation and there's nothing to say he'll regain consciousness when the anaesthetic wears off. Suggest to them they box up his possessions and put them somewhere safe."

"Yes, Mr Emmanuel."

Penny – the receptionist who was on duty at The Whipper-in the evening she discovered Colin lying on his bed unconscious – had spent the previous night and most of the next day worrying whether she had done the right thing.

When she came back on duty at three o'clock the following afternoon she telephoned the Cottage Hospital to ask whether Mr Colin Freemantle was still there. After discovering that he was in the Royal Infirmary in Leicester, she went up to his room.

His bag had remained packed, so after she had gone through it to see what was there, it was quite easy to put in his shoes and the box of tablets that was on the bedside table.

She took the bag down to Reception.

After telling the chambermaid to change the top sheet only in his room, she marked the room as vacant.

If she heard no news within a week, she would contact the hospital in Leicester.

These distractions were annoying to say the least. It was hard enough trying to please all their guests all the time.

But then again Mr Freemantle had seemed a nice man – not that she had the opportunity to speak with him at any length.

She wondered what might be wrong with him – she hoped it was nothing too serious.

Having waited another hour, Rachel went from being frantically worried to being desperately disappointed. Telling him that she needed a week was an indication of what her decision was going to be – if she were going to say they did not have a future together she would have said so straight away – wouldn't she?

She walked slowly back up the Parade towards Beauchamp Avenue.

The other people around her were irrelevancies.

There was no longer a decision to make.

He had made it for her.

Was it her fault?

He had come to find her, he had found her, she had prevaricated, and now he had gone. It was as simple as that. He had been honest with her. There was no need for him to tell her, he could have let their relationship rediscover the magic that had existed so long ago and she would have been none the wiser. Even going back to Sarawak as a family … no, returning to Sarawak would not have been possible.

Being totally honest, though, was in his nature.

His honesty was one of the reasons why she had always loved him.

Was it now too late?

If she could find out where he might be, should she try to contact him? If he were the man she really thought he was, would he have just left her sitting in The Pump Room waiting for him?

She stopped suddenly in the middle of crossing Regent Street.

Her hand flew to her mouth.

No, no, he would never have done that willingly. Regardless of what he had told her, he would have known just how worried she would be so there was no way he would not have got a message to her.

She jumped at the sound of a car horn and ran across the road to the pavement.

No, he most definitely would not leave her sitting there. Something must have prevented him from keeping their appointment.

Rachel started running and she did not stop until she reached her mother's house. She burst through the door and shouted: "Mum, has there been a telephone call for me?"

Her mother came out of the kitchen drying her hands with Angelique by her side, her doleful eyes suggesting she knew more than she should have done.

"No," her mother said. "No, there have been no telephone calls. Why, what is the matter? Didn't he meet you?" she asked.

Angelique looked up at her grandmother and then across at her mother. "Mummy ..." she started to say.

Was her disappointment that obvious, Rachel wondered. "I ... I thought he might have rung while I was out," Rachel said quickly but full of confusion.

She knew that Angelique heard and understood almost every word, which often resulted in some penetrating questions on occasions.

"No, no one called," Elspeth said and mouthed, "Sorry," so that Angelique did not see her do it.

"Oh, that's a pity. I thought ..."

"Didn't who turn up?" Angelique asked her eyes as inquisitive as the question.

"A friend, darling. I went to meet an old friend."

"Do I know your friend, Mummy?" Angelique asked.

"No, darling, and you ..."

Chapter Two Hundred and Fifteen

As Angelique got ready for bed later that evening, she asked: "Who was the friend you were going to meet today, Mummy? Was it a man?"

In anticipation of the expected question, Rachel had given her answer a lot of thought. "Yes, it was a man," she said. "It was a man I knew many years ago before the war. We thought we could perhaps revive an old friendship ..."

"Revive, Mummy. What does *revive* mean?"

"It means to go back many years to try to relive those years again, darling."

Angelique thought for a moment. "Did you love this man, Mummy?"

"Yes, darling, I did."

"Like you loved daddy?"

Although she had anticipated the question, Rachel did not expect Angelique to make the connection with her father. "I loved your daddy more than life itself, darling," she said, as she closed her eyes. The predictable tears were welling up yet again. Yes, she really did love him and more than life itself.

"Don't cry, Mummy."

Rachel felt the softness of Angelique's fingers against her cheek.

"I'm not crying, it's just that ..."

"Is daddy in heaven, Mummy?"

The lying had to stop.

Angelique's father was alive and she had to know. Rachel picked up her daughter and carried her over to the bed.

The room was cold.

"Come on, into bed with you, you'll be nice and warm in there." She pulled the eiderdown up to Angelique's chin. "Darling when I said your daddy was missing after the war, I didn't tell you the truth. I didn't want you to be upset if one day we discovered that he had been killed."

Her eyes wide in anticipation Angelique asked: "So where is he?"

"At the moment I don't know, darling."

"But ... but are you saying that maybe one day I might meet him?"

"One day, darling, yes, that is what I am saying."

Angelique lifted herself up so that she could hug her mother.

"I will love him the way you love him, Mummy."

"That would be nice for all of us, if you could. Now you must go to sleep, darling. It is late."

Blowing out the candle Rachel looked down at her daughter in the gloom.

"Was daddy the man you hoped you were meeting today, Mummy?"

"Yes, darling, it was but he was delayed."

"So maybe tomorrow, or next week? Will you meet him then?"

"Yes, maybe tomorrow or next week. Good night, darling."

"Good night, Mummy and good night Daddy wherever you are."

This time Rachel could not hold back the tears.

As she left the room, the tears were streaming down her cheeks.

Had she said too much?

There were bound to be more questions to which she currently did not have the answers.

"I've told Angelique that her father is alive."

Rachel's mother stopped eating. "Was that wise?" she asked.

"I couldn't lie to her any longer," Rachel said.

"You hadn't lied to her, you'd been protecting her," her mother said.

"Protecting her from what, Mum? She's just over three years old and she's seen more horror in her young life than everyone else sees in a lifetime, if at all."

"You have never told me about the horrors either of you saw, or suffered," her mother said.

Rachel slowly put her knife and fork on her plate.

"Mum, I am really, really sorry for the way I have been, the way I have treated you. I have been horrible to you especially as you lost dad when I wasn't here for you," Rachel said. "I think when you told me what had happened I was just grateful he didn't suffer."

"Losing your father was, at the time, the lowest point of my life," Elspeth said. "Having you return when I thought I had lost you as well was the highest point. I could not expect you to come back from years of imprisonment and brutality the same Rachel who went away. You know I never wanted you to go in the first place but you and your father got your way. You are here, little Angelique is here: having you both under my roof is like being given a new life."

"Thanks, Mum, that was a lovely thing to say." Rachel reached across the table to touch the back of her mother's hand. "Adjusting to this normal way of life –"

"Normal?" her mother said, interrupting. "This is not yet normal. When rationing stops we may be approaching normality."

There were a few seconds of silence. "When Colin appeared on my doorstep I was suspicious," Elspeth said. "When he told me who he was I was upset. But the more I spoke to him the more I saw what you must have seen in him. I cannot condone what he did to you, either making you pregnant or leaving you the way he did. I …"

"Mum, it takes two to make a woman pregnant. We both knew what we were doing at the time, or so we thought. I am as much part of Angelique as Colin is. As far as the way he left me, I was the stubborn one. It was me who refused to go with him, not him who refused to take me."

Elspeth stared at her daughter. "Against total adversity you have grown into a fine young woman, Rachel, and you have become an equally excellent mother. I would have to be totally blind and deaf not to realise that. It is also evident that you are deeply in love with Angelique's father. You haven't said as such but I can tell. So he didn't appear today, but for what reason?"

"I have no idea, Mum. What I do know is that if for whatever reason he couldn't make it, he would have let me know."

"You are absolutely sure of that?" her mother asked.

"Totally and utterly, Mum. Something has happened, I know it."

"Then for you and because of what you have now told your daughter we must find out if you are right."

"But where do we start?"

"I suggest the beginning might be the best place."

"And where is that?" Rachel asked, not sure herself.

"For a start there are things you have not told me."

Rachel allowed a wistful smile to cross her lips. "I don't know who is more astute, Mum, you or Angelique."

Chapter Two Hundred and Seventeen

Come the following evening Rachel had told her mother about her relationship with Colin, the Japanese invasion, her internment in Kampong Punkit and Batu Lintang, and her repatriation.

She described the friends she made and why she had called her daughter Angelique. The humiliation she felt when stripped half-naked in front of the Japanese soldiers in preparation for the lashings. She relived the time she was in solitary confinement, a time when she first thought she might be pregnant. Telling her mother about the degradation, the embarrassment and the acceptance that life was not going to change unless she and the others adjusted to the terrible, inhuman conditions, was not easy, but it was something she now felt she had to do.

She explained how the move from Kampong Punkit to Batu Lintang drove them to a new low. How the inhumanity of their captors was set against the determination of many of the prisoners to survive, and as time passed how the body and mind adapted to the hellish environment.

Her mother listened.

She sat opposite her daughter and granddaughter and listened, not believing some of the gruesome detail but accepting everything had to be the truth. She witnessed a three-year old child nodding as her mother described some of the most harrowing and ghastly of circumstances, and there were occasions when that same three-year old child gave her own simplistic account of what they had experienced.

Rachel knew her mother was not an emotional woman. She was from a generation that considered it socially inappropriate to be too expressive about one's feelings, but listening to the stories and events portrayed by all she had left in the world, even she was brought to tears.

On seeing her grandmother cry, a three-year girl had gone to her and said, "There, there Grandma, it wasn't that bad and we are here now."

When Rachel had finished they sat in silence for minutes. Eventually Elspeth said, "You poor, poor children. Nothing could have prepared me for what you have told me but I do thank you for

441

telling me. I understand now why you couldn't say anything when you first came home."

"If it hadn't been for Colin, Mum, I wouldn't be saying anything now. He came for me, he made everything worthwhile again and now I have let him down."

"You cannot say that, Rachel. There has to be a reason."

"Then as I asked you last night, where do we start?"

"We have already started," her mother said. "We now carry on. I will ring the bank in Market Harborough tomorrow morning to say that you won't be in for the foreseeable future."

"But I will lose my job."

Her mother shrugged and smiled.

"So? You're not enjoying it and your father left me more than enough money to look after the three of us for many a year to come."

"Do you mean that, Mum?"

"I am a little disappointed that you have to ask, my dear. Of course I mean it." Her mother smiled. "And as far as what we should do after that, I suggest we get on a train and go to Oakham. That is where you said he was from, didn't you?"

"Yes."

"Then that is where we will go."

"But …"

"Trust me," her mother said. "I know I am right."

Chapter two Hundred and Eighteen

Their journey to Oakham did not happen as planned.

Angelique woke up on the Monday morning with a sore throat and a temperature. Rachel and her mother put it down to all the excitement and discovery.

The doctor put it down to the time of year.

"Keep her in bed, give her one of these pills three times a day, lots of fluids and if there is no improvement by the end of the week call me again."

Nonetheless, as the days passed and there was still no contact from Colin, Rachel became even more convinced that something must have happened to him that in turn prevented him from appearing at the appointed time on the previous Saturday. He would not just have left things up in the air. There had to be an explanation but other than something happening to him, she could not think of another reason.

That was until the post arrived on the Friday morning.

"There's an airmail letter here for Colin," her mother shouted from downstairs.

Rachel was giving Angelique an early morning bath.

Angelique was almost back to normal and they had decided that if she were still all right the following morning they would go on a day trip to Oakham. It wasn't far and although the weather wasn't at its best, if they wrapped up they would be all right.

"For Colin? Does it say who it's from?" Rachel, suddenly excited, shouted back.

"No," she heard her mother say. "It's an air mail letter but the post mark is smudged."

"I'll be down in a minute."

Rachel quickly dried Angelique before rushing downstairs.

My Coy-lyn

The letter started.

The flap on the envelope was had become unsealed and as Rachel and her mother reasoned, without reading its content they had no idea how important the letter might be. It might give them some idea as to where Colin was. Even so, Rachel felt guilty as she withdrew the single sheet of paper.

I must start with some sad news. My father died last week. He died peacefully in his sleep but regretfully neither Abas nor I were with him. When we buried my father, I said some words from you as you told me that was your custom. He would have liked the words I used because I know how much he thought of you.

I am not at the longhouse anymore. Soon after you left and before my father died, Abas and I went to live in Miri. *Fung and Chao have been absolutely marvellous. Abas and I were given jobs with the Miri administration. I work with a lady of my age called Norah and she is a nice person. I think of you and Dani every time I look at her because she has the same blue eyes you two have.*

They ...

Rachel stopped reading.

She could not break into Colin's privacy any further.

The letter was not going to help them find him – that was just an excuse to read it – but it was going to play on her conscience. She had started reading a letter from Colin's wife and she had no right to do such a thing ... she did not care that their marriage was conducted under tribal lore, it was still a marriage generated by their love for each other and from which a son had been produced.

Putting the letter on the kitchen table, Rachel wished she had not started reading it. Of course there had been temptation but for some misguided reason she thought it might give a clue as to where he was now.

It had been wrong and Rachel felt guilty.

"What does it say?" her mother asked.

"It's from his wife," Rachel told her mother. Telling her mother about Aslah and her son, had been the hardest part in many ways, and to that point her mother had not passed comment, although her disapproval had been written all over her face.

"I don't agree with you calling her that but …" Elspeth turned from the sink where she was washing up the breakfast dishes. "Why have you stopped reading?"

"I can't, Mum. It's a personal letter."

"What harm will it do? We can seal it again."

"Mum, that's an awful thing to suggest."

Elspeth dried her hands on the tea towel. "Rachel, do you or don't you want Colin to be with you and Angelique."

"Yes, you know I do," Rachel said. "I told you. I've been stupid, I shouldn't have waited and now look what's happened."

"We don't know what's happened yet," her mother said, joining her daughter at the table. "In that letter is what you are competing with. If you really want him you will find out what you are up against. I certainly don't approve of what he did, but that's no longer the point. I –"

"From what he's said I am not *up against*, as you put it, anything or anybody."

Rachel turned her head as she heard a noise. As she listened she realised she could hear Angelique in the front room scolding one of her dolls for not washing her face.

"Then there is no harm in reading the letter, is there?" Elspeth suggested.

Rachel hesitated but reluctantly reached for the envelope.

They have been so kind.
Fung really did get both of us jobs but after father died Abas felt

he ought to stay at the longhouse for the time being. I am living with Fung and Chao now. They said that they lived with my family for so long, why can't they be allowed to repay some of what they owe? They owe us nothing.

Dani is growing up so fast. He is almost one year old now, but of course, you know that. He is nearly walking and I am sure he called me Mummy the other day.

Coy-lyn (I should write Colin but Coy-lyn was my name for you from the start) I know why I let you go. You loved somebody else before you came to my family, and I had to respect that when the time came, as I always knew I would have to.

But now, now I wish that I had not been so understanding because I am missing you so much. I lie awake at night and wish you were by my side. I miss your gentleness with me, your fingers making my skin tingle with happiness. I wish now I had fought for you rather than let you go. At the time I thought I was doing the right thing, but now ...

Once again, Rachel dropped the letter onto the table.
"I can't read any more, Mum."

Elspeth picked up the letter and with Rachel looking at her disapprovingly, she turned the page over so she could read it from the start. She frowned as she read and a couple of times she peered at Rachel over her glasses.

Once she had finished the letter, she folded the sheet of paper and put it back in the envelope. Holding the envelope between her fingers, she then pondered as to what she should say.

Looking across at her daughter, she smiled.

"She seems a pleasant young woman," Elspeth said, still smiling.

Picking up Rachel's hand in hers, Elspeth closed her eyes.

"I can only guess what you are thinking ... your mind and heart will be in conflict, my dear. You have told me everything Colin told you about his escape into the jungle, and the reasons why he went through the ceremony of marriage to this girl. There will be a lot he hasn't told you though." Elspeth opened her eyes: her daughter's head was still bowed. "Look at me Rachel, please."

"I know what you are saying, Mum, but –"

"Your father and I often discussed what we would do when the other one died, we even found reason to laugh about it because neither of us ever came to terms with the fact that one day it would happen. When it did, and I thank God he didn't suffer, all I could think about was the day I gave birth to you. It seemed like yesterday, I could remember every second of the day you came into this world. But I also appreciated just how short life is.

"Your father was engaged when he and I first met but that did not stop me from going after him, even though I knew if I won in those days he could be sued for breach of promise, but he wasn't. I was determined that I would succeed in drawing him away from this girl. I saw a photograph of her and she was pretty but that made me even more determined. I did win his love but I'm not sure the other girl knew I existed, so you could say the fight for your father's affections was unfair. Anyway, he broke off his engagement to be with me. I didn't have a conscience; in fact other than as an adversary I never gave the other girl a second thought.

"You and Colin love each other. You were together before the war. When he left you in Kuching ..."

447

"I've told you, he didn't leave me, Mum," Rachel reminded her mother.

"All right, when he flew away from you, you were carrying his child. From what you have told me, Rachel, if he had known you were pregnant you would not be faced with this emotional conflict.

"War is cruel, and as this other woman says, she knew that there was no future in their relationship regardless of the ritual they went through and the existence of a child. His first loyalty was to you, and that is why he came back to find you. If you want him you must fight for him."

"But, Mum, he is married to Aslah," Rachel said. "She is the mother of his son and she now much regrets letting him come to England."

"Your father had asked his fiancée to marry him when he met me, my dear."

"But Mum, the comparison is so tenuous. I –"

"If you want him, my dear, you will fight for him. He is here somewhere, so is your daughter. Life is too short."

Rachel looked at her mother and shivered.

She pictured what she thought Aslah would look like.

She imagined Colin with her and she wondered if, regardless of what her mother said, she should give him up and let him go back.

"What made you suggest Oakham, Mum?" Rachel asked when they were settled on the train, wondering why she had not posed the question before.

The letter, of which she had read no more, was in her bag. Angelique was by the window, her nose pressed against the area cleared of condensation. Rachel noticed that whenever they travelled by train, Angelique took in every yard of the way. She just marvelled at the scenery even in early December. She pointed out things every now and again, and of course, there were the inevitable questions.

Elspeth looked over her glasses at her daughter.

"I do dislike these horrible, smelly trains," she said.

There were another two people – a middle aged couple – in the compartment but they just smiled politely.

"Why Oakham?" Elspeth said, repeating Rachel's question. "Well I would have thought it obvious. It was where he was born and brought up, or so you tell me he told you. He's been out of the country for so long, it's the homing instinct. You wanted time, which was maybe not the best ploy in retrospect, and he needed to find somewhere to wait. Where better than in a town that he knew? A town where perhaps he could feel a little more, how can I put it? Perhaps a little more secure, that's it, secure."

"I can't doubt your logic, Mum, because if I did I wouldn't know where to start. It would be like looking for a needle in a haystack," Rachel said.

An hour and a half later, the train pulled into Oakham station. Once on the platform, Rachel asked: "And where does your logic suggest we start looking, Mum?"

Angelique looked up at her mother and grandmother.

"Well," Elspeth said, "he told you his parents died when he was a young child and that he was brought up by an aunt, who is also dead, correct?"

"Yes, Mum."

"He may have gone to a school friend's, but I doubt it, and not after all this time. He had and maybe needed a week to sit and think."

Elspeth looked up and down the platform until she spotted what she was looking for.

"Young man," she said in a raised voice, waving her umbrella at a man in railway uniform. "Come here, please," she ordered.

The man, who walked with a limp and was probably only twenty or so, went over. He looked at Elspeth Lefévre apprehensively.

"Yes, Ma'am," he said.

"Are you from here?"

"What Oakham?"

"Where else?"

"Yes, Ma'am. I work her and live here."

"Recommend an hotel to me and my daughter."

"The Whipper-in," the man said without hesitation.

"And why do you recommend this Whipper-in," Elspeth asked.

"Well … well," the young man said, this time looking at Rachel and smiling. "It's not the only hotel in Oakham, but it is probably the best. Lots of character, good food – even with rationing – and it's … well, the sort of hotel I think you would like."

"The Whipper-in it is," Elspeth said. "Can you give us directions please?"

"Yes, Ma'am," the young man said, looking relieved. "Of course I can."

"I've never stayed in a hotel before, Grandma," Angelique said looking around the reception area.

"*An* hotel," Elspeth informed her granddaughter. "It is *an* hotel, because the *aitch* in hotel is silent."

"All right," Angelique said, exchanging her confusion with her mother, who shrugged and smiled. "*An* hotel. I've never stayed in one before, have I, Mummy?"

"No darling, you haven't and we might not be staying in this one unless we can justify it."

"Young lady," Elspeth said to the woman behind the reception desk. "If we find it necessary to stay in Oakham overnight, do you have rooms available?"

The receptionist lifted her hand to her mouth to cover her amusement ... Elspeth didn't notice but Rachel did and under the circumstances she felt like saying something.

"Yes, we do have rooms available, Madam. Would it be a twin and a single?" the receptionist asked.

"That would be satisfactory, yes. However, before we register we would like to enquire whether you have or did have a young man staying here last week –"

"Week before, Mum," Rachel said, correcting her mother.

"Oh, yes, of course sorry, the week before. His name is Colin Freemantle."

The receptionist frowned. "That name does ring a bell," she said, turning the register's pages over.

Elspeth looked at Rachel and smiled.

"We may be in luck," she said.

"Yes," the receptionist informed them. "He registered two weeks ago ...well two weeks ago yesterday. Let me see, it seems he was here for just one night. I remember seeing the name when I checked the register when I came on duty last week."

"One night?" Rachel asked. "Are you sure?"

"Well yes, although it appears he had originally booked in for longer. The dates have been changed."

"Let me see," Elspeth reached for the register.

"It's not hotel policy to allow other guests to see –"

451

"What poppycock," Elspeth said. "It's a matter of – "

"Mum," Rachel said, holding back her mother's arm. "This young lady is right and we've no right … but," she said turning towards the receptionist, "it's rather important, you see. We are looking for Mr Freemantle and we thought he was still here."

The receptionist eyed Elspeth who was becoming impatient. "He was booked in for a week but he left after only one day."

"And you have no idea why?"

"No, I'm sorry. I've been away on holiday and only returned a week or so ago." At that moment, one of the chambermaids came down the stairs. "Lucy, can you come over here?" the receptionist called. The chambermaid joined the group. "Do you remember a Mr Freemantle who stayed here a fortnight ago yesterday? He –"

"Oh, yes," Lucy said eagerly. "He was the one who was taken to hospital. There was an ambulance and a lot of fuss. Penny was on reception that night."

"Hospital?" Rachel said.

"Yes," Lucy said, "rushed in he was."

Rachel closed her eyes as a shiver ran down her spine.

They found their way to the Cottage Hospital only to discover that it had been, to some extent, a wasted journey.

"And what precisely was wrong with him?" Elspeth asked the two nurses with her usual authority.

"I'm sorry but we can't discuss a patient's condition without their permission, unless we are speaking to close relatives," one nurse responded, while the other one nodded in agreement.

It was Rachel's turn to speak.

"This little girl," she said, "is Mr Freemantle's daughter and I am her mother, do you need any closer relationship than that?"

"So you are Mr Freemantle's wife?" the older nurse asked, not thinking that Rachel's wording needed questioning any further.

"Precisely," Rachel said.

"You should have said so straightaway, but in that case could I ask you to wait a few minutes so I can find somebody who can tell you what you want to know?"

Without waiting for a reply the nurse hurried down the corridor.

Minutes later a young female doctor appeared.

"You are fortunate," the doctor said, moving towards them with an outstretched hand, "in that I was here when Mr Freemantle was brought in. Suffice to say we did not have the facilities to look after him and he was sent immediately to The Leicester Royal Infirmary."

"May we enquire why?" Rachel asked.

Since the discovery at the Whipper-in, she had not known what to think. Why would somebody, and especially Colin, be whisked away from the hotel to hospital? Food poisoning? Appendicitis? Malaria?

He had been living in the jungle for years so it could be anything.

"We believe he was concussed but with complications," the doctor told them.

"Concussed?" Rachel repeated slowly. "Oh my God, of course!"

She looked at her mother but at the same time she wondered why she hadn't thought of it before.

"You sound as though you might know something about it," the doctor said.

Rachel nodded and looked at her mother. "The day he came to see you and he caught the train from Leamington to Market Harborough,

Colin was assaulted on Rugby station by a couple of soldiers, he was knocked out. He was admitted to hospital in Rugby but he said there was nothing seriously wrong."

"Perhaps they were mistaken, he –" her mother started to suggest.

The doctor interrupted. "What you have just said could be important. Obviously we had no knowledge of this assault but it does explain the way he was."

"And you discovered nothing further?" Rachel asked.

"I'm sorry to repeat myself but we don't have the facilities."

"We must go to Leicester," Rachel said looking at the doctor.

"Of course you must. When you get there tell them everything you know about what happened to your husband on Rugby station. I would tell them but the telephones are down," the doctor advised.

"I will," Rachel said, the anguish rushing through her entire body. "God, why didn't I think of it before?"

"Why did you say you had a husband?" Angelique asked as they left the hospital.

Chapter Two Hundred and Twenty-Four

Reaching The Leicester Royal Infirmary just before twelve o'clock the following day, Rachel, her mother and Angelique had travelled to Leicester courtesy of the Great Central Railway and taken a taxi from Leicester Central Station to the hospital. The need to stay in Oakham for one night had not been their decision, various connecting trains had been cancelled – to conserve fuel – and so there was little choice but to stay.

Angelique, who had been told what was happening, did get her first night in *an* hotel. She told her mother at breakfast the following morning that from now on she would call all hotels *Anne*.

It was a light moment that temporarily lifted heavy hearts, and allowed Rachel to try to answer Angelique's question. For once, she was not sure her daughter understood.

Rachel lay awake for most of the previous night. Her thoughts went back to the evening she woke suddenly after she fell asleep in the chair in the house in Market Harborough. She knew that something had happened. When Colin told her about the incident on Rugby Station, she dismissed it when he also told her that he was all right. She should have done something about it there and then. She was more concerned at the time about the intervention of a silly girl who had drunk too much sherry. She rejected Julia Danbury's involvement straight away as a childish immature girl getting an immediate crush on a man who had protected her.

Nevertheless, her conscience would not let her reject what she now knew as being the cause of Colin's hospitalisation. In the taxi from the Central Station to the hospital and due to the need to follow a detour, the driver had to pass the remains of the gas works in Aylestone Road.

"German bomber raid on 19th November 1942," the driver said. "The only real raid the residents in Leicester suffered although we did have nearly two hundred air raid alerts. On that day bombs and mines were dropped, they fell in a line from Aylestone Road to the Great Northern railway station in Belgrave Road some four miles away to the north. A lot of damage was caused and one hundred and two people were killed. Bloody murder, that's what I call it. It was like hell on earth for a while."

Rachel could not stop the immediate anger the taxi driver's words caused in her. She thought of the thousands of poor souls, the walking skeletons, the soldiers bayoneted or beheaded because they had failed to do something as simple as bowing low enough. The daily ceremony towards the cemetery on the hill as others carried those who had died of malnutrition, disease and beatings to their final resting place.

With one actual bombing raid in six years, the people of Leicester did not know what suffering or war really was. They certainly did not know what the real hell was like.

Rachel knew she needed to control her temper and she had to readjust.

After arriving at the hospital, it was evident that the female doctor they spoke to at the Oakham Cottage Hospital had managed to ring ahead because Elspeth and Rachel Lefévre were expected.

A nurse led them down an austere corridor to a sparsely furnished room, and she told them to make themselves comfortable. "Somebody will be with you shortly," she said, "but we are very busy."

"They can work wonders nowadays," Elspeth said once the nurse had left. "They have had so much more experience because of the war."

"I'm sure you're right, Mum, but if only I had done something when Colin told me what happened."

"It might not have changed anything," her mother suggested.

"I understand you are Mrs Freemantle," the consultant said, holding out his hand. "My name is Emmanuel, I am a consultant neurosurgeon and I operated on your husband."

"You're not Mrs Freemantle, Mummy," Angelique said, innocently. "You're like me, you're Miss Lefévre, and Grandma is Mrs Lefévre."

The consultant looked confused. "I'm sorry," he said. "I was told to expect Mrs Freemantle, her mother," he added looking at Elspeth, "and Mr Freemantle's daughter." Mr Emmanuel squatted down. "Are you saying Mr Freemantle is not your father," he asked, smiling at Angelique's shyness.

"He is my father ... I think," Angelique whispered, solicitously. "Mummy ... Mummy told me but ... but mummy isn't married to him ... not yet ... I think."

The surgeon looked up and allowed a smile to cross his lips. "In a situation like this I'm afraid I can't ..."

"Angelique is Mr Freemantle's daughter, Mr Emmanuel, and I am her mother."

"So what your daughter said is exactly as things are?" he asked.

"Yes, that is right."

"Ah," he said. "That explains something that I will mention in a minute. Do I take it various assumptions have been made down the line and not denied to save confusion?"

"Precisely," Elspeth informed the consultant. "There was little point ..."

"I see and I understand," Mr Emmanuel said. "So that clarifies something but before mentioning what it is may I ask you to sit down? I need to apprise you of where we are with Mr Freemantle's condition."

After they sat down the consultant said, "Mr Freemantle is still unconscious. If I may be blunt, he is lucky to be alive. I understand now that he was hit rather heavily on the back of the head just over two weeks ago."

"Yes," Rachel told him, and described what had happened on Rugby station.

Mr Emmanuel nodded. "His injuries are commensurate with a

heavy blow with a blunt instrument. Sometimes such an injury can result in bruising on the surface and swelling inside which can disguise obvious signs of a fracture. However, with sufficient force and at the right angle, such a blow can cause the ..." He saw Angelique's eyes staring at him. "I'm sorry," he said, "perhaps you'd prefer it if I asked a nurse to take care of your daughter?"

"No," Rachel said hurriedly. "She has seen far worse than a fractured skull. Her innocence was taken away from her long ago. Please continue Mr Emmanuel."

"Her innocence?" he asked, frowning.

"When my daughter was born I was a prisoner of the Japanese in Sarawak, and then my daughter spent the first three years of her life in an internment camp."

"Right, yes, you need say no more." He paused as he smiled at Angelique. "Such a blow can cause a fracture and small fragments of bone on the inside of the skull to become detached. This is what happened to Mr Freemantle ..."

"Shouldn't such a fracture have been detected straight away?" Rachel asked.

Mr Emmanuel nodded. "Yes and no, it depends. As I said, bruising and swelling on occasions can hide something like this. X-rays are all well and good but they are not full proof, and there is always the possibility of human error."

"Let's not prevaricate and go looking for too many excuses," Elspeth said. "What condition is he in?"

"I don't know," Mr Emmanuel told them.

"You don't know, but …"

"I admit," the consultant said, looking at Elspeth, "it is worrying that the hospital in Rugby did not detect the fracture straight away but looking for excuses apart, X-rays are not foolproof. I am aware that Mr Freemantle was found unconscious but I don't know what other symptoms he may have experienced. He, undoubtedly, would have been aware that something was wrong but he unfortunately chose to ignore the warning signs." Mr Emmanuel clasped his hands in front of him. "I won't know of any short or longer term damage that may have been done until he is conscious."

"What damage are you talking about?" Rachel asked.

"There could be none, none at all, but on the other hand there might be physical effects like the movement of his arms and legs, extreme tiredness and speech difficulties. There could be a loss of memory, and emotional and behavioural effects. However, I do not want to paint too dark a picture."

"Thank you for being honest with us, doctor … I mean, Mr Emmanuel," Rachel said. "Is it possible for us to see him?"

"It is but only for a few moments and," he looked at Angelique. "I'm afraid I couldn't allow your daughter in with you."

"I understand."

"Mummy, I …"

"No, Angelique, you will see your daddy when he is better," Rachel told her daughter.

"But Mummy!"

"Angelique, no. Please, darling, please try and understand."

"I will stay with her," suggested Elspeth. "You go and see him first."

"Before I take you through, Miss Lefévre, there is the other matter to which I referred earlier." Mr Emmanuel withdrew an envelope from his inside pocket. "Mr Freemantle was wearing a money belt under his clothes and as well as it containing a considerable amount of money, there was also this envelope addressed to you. You can perhaps understand now why I was a little cautious when we first met, especially when I thought you were Mrs Freemantle."

459

Rachel took the envelope. "Thank you and yes, I understand. It is a long story Mr Emmanuel but one that has no relevance to what is happening here. Colin has only recently returned to England after the war. When he came back I hadn't seen him for nearly four years, and his daughter has yet to meet him."

"Once again I also understand, Miss Lefévre. May I say your daughter is an incredible little girl? To have come through what I can only guess was a horrendous experience, is quite remarkable. You are both looking healthy now." He shook his head, his eyes searching Rachel's. "Quite remarkable. Your daughter is so eloquent for her age."

"Yes, we were the lucky ones, there were others who … well I am sure you understand what my daughter went through," Rachel said. "She had to grow up very quickly."

"And she certainly did that. Now if you would like to come with me?"

Glancing towards her mother and daughter Rachel smiled.

"I won't be long," she said. "And I'll give your daddy your love."

Elspeth nodded whereas Angelique folded her arms and pouted.

"We'll be waiting," her mother said.

For once Rachel was pleased Angelique was only three.

"Tell him how much I want to meet him," Angelique added.

Chapter Two Hundred and Twenty-Seven

Sitting by his bed, Rachel picked up Colin's hand.

He looked as though he was asleep and there was no reaction to her touch. There was a bandage round his head and a tube hanging from the corner of his mouth. Mr Emmanuel and the nurse, who had gone into the ward as well, had left after informing her that she had five minutes.

Rachel brushed her lips against Colin's. "Why now?" she asked. "Why now?"

Taking the envelope Mr Emmanuel had given her from her bag she slit it open and held the single sheet of paper in front of her. He had used Whipper-in notepaper. She smiled when she realised she had never had a letter from him before, in fact she did not think she would have recognised his handwriting.

She started to read.

Friday 1st December 1945

Darling Rachel,

You will understand why I won't be able to write much, you will also be cross because I wasn't entirely honest about how I felt after the incident in Rugby. I am in my room in the Whipper-in in Oakham and I know from the way I feel I won't be able to meet you next Saturday.

My head is splitting in two, my vision is blurred and I feel sick.

In the morning, I will go and see a doctor.

I think I know what your decision is going to be which means I now regret putting you through the trauma of the last week. I shouldn't have come to England, and I shouldn't have bothered you, not after so long.

I am so sorry that I will never meet Angelique but it is better this way, but please tell her that I love her as much as I love her mother. I am sure she is just like you.

The hospital, if that is where I am, will find a money belt on me that will contain over £4500. It is yours to do

461

with as you wish. I have enough in my wallet to pay for my journey back to Sarawak, if that happens.

I have always loved you and always will, but under the circumstances that is not enough. I will not trouble you again.

I hope you and Angelique have the happiest of lives and that one day you will meet somebody who will make you even happier. I understand why you were so hesitant. I should never have put you in that situation in the first place.

My feelings for you, though, will never change. I am sorry for putting you through all of this - it was not necessary. If I am not as ill as I think and I'm allowed to leave hospital, I will post the money and this letter to you before I return to Sarawak.

However, if you are reading this letter with me near you, then I'm sorry to put you through even more heartache.

Please say goodbye to me and when I recover I know I can leave with your blessing. I wish you and our daughter, Angelique - a lovely name - all the happiness in the world.

Colin

Chapter Two Hundred and Twenty-Eight

"You stupid, stupid man," Rachel said through her tears. "If I didn't want to be with you, you would have known straight away." Her fingers caressed the hairs on the back of his hand. "We were survivors, so why after what we have been through does it come down to this? We both fought the Japanese in our own way but now you are here because of stupid male pride."

"Miss," a female voice said behind her, "Miss, it's time I'm afraid. Mr Emmanuel said five minutes."

"Yes, of course," Rachel said dabbing at her eyes with a handkerchief. She lifted Colin's hand to her lips and kissed it. "You," she said, "stop this nonsense and come back to me. Your daughter needs a father and I need a husband should you ever get round to asking me."

"Miss!"

"I'm coming!" Rachel said impatiently. "Please," she added quietly, letting go of Colin's hand, "after what we have both been through we can't lose each other now."

She bent down and brushed his lips with hers after which she put the letter in her bag and left the ward.

Elspeth took one look at her daughter and decided that the obvious questions could wait. Rachel was pleased when she saw the understanding smile on her mother's face.

Little Angelique was not so observant.

"How was daddy, Mummy?"

"He was fine, just fine," Rachel said as she fought to control the deepest of sighs, and her tears. "Just fine."

She felt herself shudder.

"Then why can't I see him?" Angelique asked.

"Because, darling, he is sleeping. Before he closed his eyes he asked me to give you his love and to tell you how much he is looking forward to being with you."

"Did ... did he really, Mummy?"

"Yes, darling," Rachel said as she turned to her mother.

She regretted the lie straight away.

"Mum I think ..." She stopped as Mr Emmanuel came into the room.

"I'm sorry I could only allow a short time, Miss Lefévre, but in cases like this we …"

"That's all right, I understand." Rachel reached into her bag for Colin's letter. "You'd better read this."

She handed the letter to Mr Emmanuel and after reading it the consultant nodded. "I thought that would be the case. As I gave you the letter I know it is authentic, therefore his request is also genuine. If you would care to come with me I will give the belt and the money, I see little point in involving people who would only complicate matters."

"I do not want to get you into trouble," Rachel said. "We aren't married and I have no right to –"

"This is between you, me and Mr Freemantle. Nobody else need ever know."

"Thank you," Rachel said.

"Where are you going, Mummy?" Angelique asked.

"Don't bother your mother –" Elspeth started to say.

"No, Mum, she has a right to know." Rachel knelt down and took Angelique's hands in hers. "Your daddy has given us enough money … well, let me just say it'll keep us going for a long time."

Previously Rachel had little choice but to be as truthful with Angelique as circumstances allowed. There was now no point in lying – or withholding the truth – when the evidence was there, in front of her eyes.

Angelique had been part of the absolute squalor, the deprivation and the humiliation.

Seeing soldiers beaten with rifle butts was part of her education about life.

She had also seen men bayoneted, and on one occasion when Rachel was not quick enough, Angelique had witnessed a beheading.

Rachel remembered seeing her daughter standing there with her eyes like saucers as she tried to comprehend what she had just witnessed. Before Rachel could get to her, Angelique had turned away from the horrific scene, walked across to her mother, taken her hand and she had never said another word about what she had seen.

Ironically, Suga had demonstrated unexpected and rather bizarre behaviour towards Angelique and the other young children. Although they did not get any extra rations, he did on a couple of occasions take the children for rides in his car and give them sweets and chocolate.

Suga ignored the mothers' protests.

Rachel marvelled at her own mind and the way, within reason, she had been able to reach out to the future rather than dwell in the past. There were flashbacks – like the one with Suga and the children – because anybody who had experienced such horror was bound to have flashbacks. There were occasions when she woke up with her body covered in perspiration, as she relived the dreadfulness of internment. Nevertheless, if she thought her own control and ability to cope was a marvel, then her daughter, not yet four years old, was a miracle. What she had been born into and lived in for three years had for her been normality.

That was life; she did not know anything different.

It was what she was experiencing now that was unusual. Rationing meant nothing to either Rachel or Angelique and being able to sleep in a bed, have a wash using soap, even a bath, being properly clothed: they were all luxuries, sheer magnificence.

What Rachel could not get her head round though, was what she had seen lying in Leicester Royal Infirmary and what her daughter needed protection from: her father, who had lived with and fought alongside the Iban in Sarawak, had been attacked in his own country by two of his own countrymen.

All he had done was protect a young girl.

Julia Danbury had not been an invading army whose soldiers thought nothing of mass murder: who got absolute enjoyment out of seeing their fellow human beings suffer the most horrific torturing techniques and the most gruesome of deaths.

Rachel needed to talk to her own mother: she needed to discuss, seek her mother's advice as to what she should do – but not in front of Angelique.

Why?

The child knew that her father was in hospital, and she knew that people in hospital were there because they were ill or injured. So why did she need to protect her daughter from what was obvious? It was because of what Mr Emmanuel said to Rachel when he took her to his office to get the money belt from his safe.

"Miss Lefévre, I think you must prepare yourself for the worst. I hope and pray I am wrong but I cannot even start to raise your hopes."

How could she discuss that in front of Angelique? She needed to know that her father was going to get better and that they were going to be a proper family.

The opposite should not be an option.

After leaving the hospital, Rachel suggested they should find somewhere to have a cup of tea and maybe a biscuit.

Close by there was a teashop in Jarron Street and a bank just down the road.

While her mother and Angelique went into the teashop, Rachel went into the bank, opened an account and deposited the money that had been burning a hole in her bag. The young male cashier with whom she conducted the transaction had called the manager when he discovered how much was being deposited.

The manager had taken Rachel into his office and asked for an explanation.

Rachel told him the truth and it took over fifteen minutes.

The manager, who was a young man and the opposite in every other way to Mr Prendaghast in Market Harborough, listened patiently. At the end of her narrative, he said, "Miss Lefévre, I am sure there are going to be many, many exaggerated stories and a lot of untruths told about the last six years of human failing, but I doubt if anybody could make up what you have just told me." He smiled. "It has to be true. Consider your money deposited."

It was nearly thirty minutes later when Rachel joined her mother and daughter in Mollie's Tea Shop. There were a few other people at the tables.

Rachel sat down, asked for a fresh pot of tea, and looked at her mother.

"Sorry that took so long but I would have been equally cautious had somebody come into the bank in Market Harborough with that amount of money for deposit." She glanced at Angelique and saw something in her daughter's eyes that worried her. "And you two?" she said turning back to her mother. "What have you been talking about?"

"Angelique has been asking some searching questions, haven't you dear?" Elspeth said, looking at her granddaughter.

Angelique did not react.

"What sort of questions?" Rachel asked.

"She wanted to know why you and her daddy aren't married. She wanted to know if you and her daddy are going to get married and are you all going to live together. She wanted to know why you wouldn't let her see her daddy in hospital."

"And you told her?"

"The truth," Elspeth said.

Looking at Angelique, Rachel tried to see beyond the adult eyes in such a young head.

She realised she had made another mistake.

The truth should have come from her.

She should have been more open and honest with her daughter from the moment she asked about her father. The bond that had developed since Kampong Punkit, the invisible umbilical cord that still connected one to the other, was still strong but now strained, but hopefully, it would never break. "I'm sorry, darling," Rachel said. "I should have told you everything. There will be no more secrets."

Angelique looked at her. "Grandma said you were protecting me, Mummy."

"That is kind of grandma, because that is exactly what I have been doing," Rachel said.

"But now I know that daddy is very ill, there is no need to protect me anymore is there, Mummy."

"A mother must always be there to protect her daughter," Rachel said looking from Angelique to her mother. "The trouble is you never really begin to appreciate your own mother and father until it is too late."

"But grandma is here with us," Angelique said.

Sarawak, Borneo June 1963

Chapter Two Hundred and Thirty-One

In the terminal the young man became a little concerned when Angelique was not one of the first to appear from the aircraft. He could see all the passengers filing down the steps from the doorway but there was nobody who looked remotely like his sister.

Then he saw her.

For some reason she had delayed getting off the plane.

She stood on top of the steps, putting on her sunglasses as she surveyed the terminal buildings. He nodded as he saw her take a deep breath and smile. It was a mannerism that really said, "I'm home."

She was back where she belonged and he was there to meet her.

He also wondered why she had waited until last to leave the aircraft.

He smiled again.

Even from over one hundred yards away it was obvious that she was as beautiful as her photographs had suggested. She was tall, blonde, and English. He hoped that when she saw him he would live up to her expectations.

Since arriving to meet Angelique, he had seen others talking and pointing. He was used to it. Seeing a local – or somebody that they thought was a local – who was over six feet tall, had blue eyes and bleached blond hair wasn't an everyday sight. If somebody stared he either stared back until they averted their eyes, or he completely ignored them: it depended on his mood.

After he saw her disappear into the building, he backtracked from the viewing area so that he was waiting impatiently on the other side of customs and immigration. He realised he was hopping from one foot to the other like a schoolboy.

It was a long thirty minutes.

Once again, she was almost the last to appear.

"Angelique?" he asked, reaching for her case.

"Dani?" Angelique said, her face breaking into the broadest of smiles. Dropping her case, she put her arms round his neck and kissed him on both cheeks. "It really is wonderful to see you."

469

Without thinking Dani picked Angelique up and swung her round and round almost colliding with one of the other passengers.

"This is absolutely fantastic," he said. He lowered her to the floor but kept his hands on her hips. "Hello to the sister I have wanted to meet for so long."

"And hello to the brother who is more gorgeous than his photographs ever suggested."

They hugged each other again.

"So," Angelique said after they had regained their composure, "what happens now?"

"Our flight tomorrow is at eleven o'clock," Dani told her. "We fly into Bandar in Brunei and pick up my jeep which I left at the airport to drive south, over the border into Sarawak and then to Miri." He picked up his sister's case. "It'll be a long and rough ride so tonight we're staying in a small hotel down by the river, you'll love it," he said.

"Am I really here?" Angelique asked.

Dani nodded. "I can't believe it either, but yes, you are really here."

"And your mother?"

"Tomorrow, Angelique. You will meet my mother tomorrow," Dani told her.

An hour later Angelique unfastened the slatted doors that opened onto the small balcony and agreed that Dani was right.

She let the breeze from the river play with her nakedness.

"I do love it," she said to herself. "I love everything about it."

The shower had creaked as it had spluttered lukewarm water onto the suds in her hair and over her body.

Angelique had smiled because she had expected nothing else.

It was all so wonderful.

The welcome note in her room told her that the hotel had only six rooms and a small restaurant, which meant the owners – a Chinese couple – could look after their guests personally. They hoped she had a wonderful stay and one day she would return.

Fifteen minutes later and as she sat with Dani at a table in the restaurant which overlooked the river, she was still loving every minute of what she was experiencing. The fans were whirring above her, she could feel the perspiration running down between her shoulder blades but the ice-cold beer in front of her was the most welcome of sights and tastes – nothing else mattered.

"This really is the most incredible hotel I have ever stayed in," Angelique said, looking around. "It's so quaint and unpretentious. It's the best *Anne* I have ever seen."

"The best what?" Dani asked, laughing.

"The best *Anne*," Angelique said, shaking her head and laughing with him. "Oh, it's a long story, and we have so much to talk about. But this really is a lovely place."

"Thank you. It's my first time here too. It was recommended to me by a friend in Miri."

Angelique took another a sip of her beer.

"That's good," she said before thinking for a moment. "Your mother, Dani, she really is happy that I'm here isn't she?"

"She was the one who suggested you come in the first place, remember."

"But that was two years ago, she may have changed her mind," Angelique said.

"Why? She read all your letters and she wants to meet you as much as I did."

Dani paused while their meal, which was a rice, fish and vegetable mixture, was placed on their table. The contents of the various bowls took Angelique back eighteen years but its presentation, content and taste were now rather different – and delicious.

"She's been rushing around for weeks making sure the house is perfect in every way," Dani said as he spooned some rice into Angelique's bowl. "The fish is Snapper. I think you'll like it."

"I'm sure I will." Angelique helped herself to the fish. "There was no need for her to go to all that bother. I'm just so delighted to be here."

"The old Batu Lintang camp, or what's left of it, is just across the river," Dani said after a short silence and pointing out of the window. "Do you remember much about it?"

"Dani," Angelique said, ignoring his question and her expression serious, "you haven't asked after your father."

Dani put his spoon down quietly.

"If I were to ask, Angelique, I would be asking how our father is, not mine."

Angelique had not known when she should raise the most important matter that needed explaining, all she did know was that it had to be broached before she met Dani's mother.

She had to know how Aslah would react when told the truth.

So the air had to be cleared with Dani first.

"You know the idea that you and I should exchange letters was originally suggested by my mother, but it took a while for your mother to agree," Angelique said.

"I know and she regrets that now, believe me."

"We are brother and sister and when I sat down and composed that first letter, I was eight and you were nearly seven." Dani nodded. "It took months for a reply to arrive and I was worried but when it did arrive and although it was short in words, it was in your own handwriting and it was marvellous. You'll never know the thrill that gave me."

Dani smiled. "And it was the beginning of an exchange that was going to go on for the next thirteen years."

"Yes, thirteen years," Angelique repeated. "In all your letters you always sent your best wishes to your father and your love to me. My mother explained the resentment you must have felt towards her but I never really understood. But more recently, and after your mother suggested I ought to visit Sarawak, you included my mother with your best wishes – that was lovely."

"Yes, and I'm sorry if I upset you but –"

"No, Dani there is no need to apologise but the truth must be discussed before we continue with our journey in the morning," Angelique said.

"Angelique, I knew that we would need to discuss this and I have given what I need to say a lot of thought. But is the first evening after we have met each other the right time?"

"We will be in Miri and with your mother tomorrow evening?" Angelique asked.

"Yes."

"Then we need to discuss it further this evening. I need you to know the truth, because it is not what you believe has been happening on the other side of the world for so long."

Dani looked at his sister.

He was so proud to be sitting with her.

He knew from the moment they embraced at the airport they were the centre of attention. It might be 1963 but seeing a white girl with a local was still unusual, and rightly or wrongly frowned upon by some people from both cultures.

Using the word 'local' would have confused a few people because they might question why he had blond hair and blue eyes. He wondered if their critics had known that they were brother and sister, their disapproval would have increased.

He chose the hotel they were in for that reason.

The owners were Chinese and were unlikely to ask any questions. If they had stayed in one of the larger well-known hotels, they would not have had the privacy they needed.

"This is going to sound rather strange," Dani said, "but I feel I have misled you for all the time we have been writing to each other."

"You've misled me?" Angelique said. "I don't understand."

Dani put his spoon down and reached for his sister's hand. "I knew about you before your first letter arrived," Dani said.

"Knew about me?" Angelique said, "but how did you …?"

Chapter Two Hundred and Thirty-Four

"Look at me, Angelique. I am probably the tallest Iban in Sarawak. I have blue eyes and blond hair. Even when I was young, I knew I was different. My mother waited for the question she knew was going to come one day and when it did come, she didn't lie. She told me about how my father came to live with the Iban after the Japanese invasion, she told me what a great warrior he was and she told me that she saved his life, but she also told me how she fell in love with him the first time she saw him."

"So you know –?"

"Let me tell this in my own way," Dani said before carrying on. "My mother also told me that she was responsible for the Iban marriage between her and my father. According to my mother, she left my father little choice but to go through with a ceremony he knew nothing about and didn't understand.

"When I asked why, if they were married, he wasn't still living with us, she explained that she had been so unfair to him. Before they were married, a Chinese woman called Chao, who was also living with my mother's family – that is all another story which I will tell you one day – advised her that if she did get married, after the war my father would almost certainly leave."

"Because of my mother?" Angelique said.

"Yes," Dani replied. "My father had confided in Chao's husband – his name was Fung – that he had an English lady-friend with whom he was in love and that after the war … well, you know the rest." Dani paused for a few seconds. "A month after he left for England, my mother was so unhappy she wrote to him but the only address she had access to was where she believed your mother was living."

"Yes, my mother told me," Angelique said, nodding.

"She was worried when she didn't get a reply but in January 1946, she received a letter from your mother. In this letter, your mother explained about you, when you had been born and where. My mother, being the woman she is, was distraught but not only for herself, but also because your mother's experiences were equally distressing.

"She could not believe the circumstances under which you were born and you both lived for so many years. But on receipt of your mother's letter my mother knew that your father would never return to Sarawak. So you see, Angelique, I have misled you and I am so, so sorry." Dani took his hand away and sipped his beer. "I have known of your circumstances from the beginning and I am embarrassed that I didn't wish your mother well from the start, but I suppose inside my young head I resented her being with my father."

"You have not misled me, Dani," Angelique said, reaching for her brother's hand again. "If anything the reverse is true, and that is why you need to know the truth before we see your mother tomorrow. Having listened to what you have just said I have difficulty in believing that you do not still hold a grudge towards my mother and me. You have spent so many years thinking that your father was living in England with my mother and me and not giving any thought to you and your mother."

"Yes, that is what I thought and perhaps my mother too, but she never said as much. When I was old enough to understand she explained that after the war she accepted that either your mother or she had to lose and unfortunately, but not unexpectedly, we were not the lucky ones."

Angelique closed her eyes as she felt the tears well up. "Dani, nothing … nothing could be further from the truth," she said, lifting her napkin to her eyes.

Chapter Two Hundred and Thirty-Five

Through her tears, Angelique could see her brother's confusion.

"What do you mean?" he asked.

Taking a deep breath Angelique said, "Can we have another drink before I tell you?"

"Of course."

With their plates cleared away and two more bottles of ice-cold Tiger on the table, brother and sister looked at each other.

Dani poured the drinks and sat back.

"Are you ready?" he said.

Angelique nodded. "When … when your father discovered that my mother had spent the war as an internee suffering at the hands of the Japanese, he was understandably, like your mother, upset. But, and this is a big *but* Dani, it is something he could have coped with because my mother had survived the war. She was back in England and, once she had recovered, would be able to make up for the years she had lost.

"What he hadn't allowed for was me. Finding out that he had a daughter threw him into such a quandary he didn't know which way to turn. He not only had a son, you, here in Sarawak, but he also had a daughter, me. By then I was three years old. On the one hand there was your mother and you whom he loved so dearly and here was my mother and me. He was completely torn in two. Whichever way he turned he would have to live with his conscience. If he'd stayed with your mother and you, he would have forever been worrying about my mother and me, if he left you and your mother, well, he would be no better off.

"He went to England because we were the unknown elements in the equation for which he couldn't find an answer, but which he needed to find. He had not seen my mother for four years: she had been through hell and had me into the bargain. Perhaps I only added to her idea of what the real hell ought to be."

Angelique smiled ruefully but Dani did not respond.

"He had no idea," she continued, "whether my mother was the same woman he had loved before the war, but I was the product of that love and yet he had no idea I existed until then. Yes, your father left your mother and you, but he would not have done so if he'd believed that you would not be well cared for while he was away. That sounds as though he had always intended coming back to you. He may not have known that when he left but deep down that is what he felt, because in the end that is what he decided he must do."

Dani shook his head. "Are you saying that after meeting your mother and you, he always intended coming back to us, here? I can't believe –"

"Yes, Dani, that is exactly what I am saying because it is what he decided."

"So why didn't he? Where has he been for the last eighteen years? Why has he been with you?"

"I will answer your question in a minute, Dani."

Angelique took a sip of beer followed by another deep breath.

"Your … your father had to find my mother and me ... he had to know that we were well and safe. If he hadn't been able to clear his conscience in that way his life with you and your mother would never have worked."

"So I must ask again, why isn't he here, why isn't he in Miri with my mother?" There was no spite in Dani's question, just the need to know. "He is still in England. He is with your mother so he is not here."

"He *is* in England, Dani," Angelique said, "but he is not with my mother. He never has been because as you have been without a father for all this time, so have I."

Dani's brow furrowed again and he tilted his head to one side. "I'm sorry, I don't understand. What do you mean? If he hasn't been with you and your mother where has he been?"

"Before I tell you Dani, you asked me a while ago whether I remembered anything about Batu Lintang Camp. I am twenty-one years old and the last eighteen of those years have gone by so quickly it scares me. Yes, I remember Batu Lintang. Something like that can't help but be permanently etched onto the mind, even one as young as mine was at the time.

"My mother always jokes that when I left that camp I was physically only three years old, but in my head I was many years older. I knew nothing else. In my young mind, rags and lice, stale foul-smelling rice and weevils were what life was all about. The bags of bones that were once men *were* real men to me. The women who cried every night, some of whom never woke up in the morning, were wives, mothers and sisters. I saw a man kneeling in the dirt just before he was beheaded ... I saw the blood shoot in jets from his neck as his head rolled in the dirt … and I was so young.

"In my undeveloped mind I thought what I was witnessing was normal. There was no heaven or hell because I didn't know there was an alternative to the nightmare I was part of. No matter how much my mother tried to protect me, she could not hide what was going on all around us all the time. It was hell Dani, I know that now, but at the time it was life."

Angelique paused, sipped her coffee and said, "But, I would willingly live through it all again if it meant I did not have to answer your question. If I did not have to tell you what you need to know.

"Yes, as I … I said earlier you have been deceived but it wasn't by your father. My mother and I have deceived you. At the time we thought we were protecting you and your mother, now I know what we did was tantamount to betrayal."

"I still don't understand," Dani said.

"And I wish you didn't have to, Dani, because soon after your father arrived in England and after he'd found my mother, he was on a train and he stood up to a couple of soldiers who were pestering a young girl. The soldiers wanted and took their revenge, they waited until the time was right and they attacked him, knocking him unconscious. He was taken to hospital but he was allowed to leave too soon. No sooner had he met my mother but not me, he was readmitted to hospital. Although he was operated on immediately, it was too late the damage had already been done.

"I never heard my, your, father speak, Dani. I never heard him speak and I never saw him walk. I never felt his arms around me, I never heard him tell me he loved me, I never saw him do anything that suggested he recognised my mother.

"Until recently he has been in a home not far from where my mother and I live. We visited him regularly but he never knew we were there. We sat with him, held his hand, talked to him, read him your letters and told him at every opportunity that you and your mother loved him as much as my mother and I loved him."

"You said until recently," Dani almost whispered as though he knew what he was about to be told.

"The man who loved us, our mothers, you and me, died three months ago, Dani."

Angelique looked at the tears in her brother's eyes before she carried on.

"For the last eighteen years he was in a coma. He wasn't attached to any machines that we could have turned off. His heart and lungs continued to function and therefore there was always hope. Every time we went to see him, we prayed for him to regain consciousness but our prayers went unanswered.

"My mother and I know now that we were wrong to hide the truth from you and your mother, but what your mother told you from the outset was the truth. We did what we did for the best possible reasons, we wanted to protect you from the truth the way my mother tried to protect me in the Batu Lintang internment camp.

"We wanted you to think your father was happy where he was, not in a coma and fighting for his life. You may be wondering how I am able to tell you all of this without showing the emotion you might expect. Dani, when he died it was a Godsend. He'd known nothing of the last eighteen years of his life, so he knew nothing in death. He is far better off where is now."

Dani closed his eyes and bowed his head.

"After he was admitted to the hospice –" Angelique started to say.

"What … what is a hospice?" Dani asked in a monotone, his head still bowed.

"It is a type of hospital where people go when they are terminally ill. Hospices provide the best conditions for such people to live out their final days."

"Or in our father's case, many, many years," Dani said.

"That is so." Angelique squeezed her brother's hand. "While our father was fighting for his life, my mother spent a long time trying to track down any distant relatives there may have been but without success. But when she went into a particular solicitors in Oakham that our … Dani, I can't keep on saying *our father*, it sounds so biblical."

This time Dani did look up. "What about *dad*, that's what we would both have called him."

"Dad it is," Angelique repeated, smiling. "Anyway, dad was a lot better off financially than he ever realised."

Angelique explained the background to their father's upbringing.

"This aunt died," she continued, "after he'd come out to Kuching in 1937 but she left behind a considerable inheritance for him. He didn't know anything about this inheritance, maybe all the correspondence from the solicitors got lost in the build up to and during the war.

"My mother went round all the solicitors in Oakham – not that there were many – to see if anybody knew anything about him or this aunt who brought him up. She found one in the High Street and they were glad to see her. That is how she found out about the inheritance.

"She explained to the solicitors the background to why she was there and whether they could help. Well they could and after so long they were rather pleased to blow the dust off some old files. I won't bore you with the details Dani, because I do not understand them myself, but over the years these solicitors have been in and out of court on behalf of all of us.

"Only a few months before dad died my mother and yours, were given rights of access to dad's inheritance when he did die. Our mothers' share of dad's own inheritance means they are rich women."

Taking his hand away from his sister's, Dani said, "Money? What good is money when you would give anything to be able to relive so much of your life?" he said.

"You mustn't feel like that," Angelique said. "There is nothing you could have done even if you had known."

"I feel as though I have let you down, let my mother, your mother, down. I was so selfish," Dani said. "I should have sensed that a man my mother loved could not treat us the way I believed he did. I feel so ashamed."

"You must not start chastising yourself, Dani. In many ways, my mother and I should feel selfish and ashamed, not you. The circumstances meant that withholding the truth from you was that much easier."

Dani shook his head.

"I was expecting none of this but also I did not lie when I said I wanted nothing more than to meet my sister from the other side of the world." He smiled for the first time since Angelique had told him the truth. "What happens next?"

"It is happening as we speak. My mother is waiting in England for a telegram from me to say that she can go to Heathrow airport to start her journey to Sarawak. She needed to know that by coming here she would be welcome."

"She is coming here?"

"She has always wanted to return but while dad was in the hospice she wouldn't leave him. I think I said earlier, but then again maybe I didn't – my mother never re-married, in fact, she never married at all. I –"

"Neither did my mother," Dani said.

"I didn't think so, from what you said earlier. My mother dedicated the last eighteen years to dad, praying that he would come back to us, and when I say us I mean all of us. So now she wants to bring dad's ashes –"

"Ashes, what do you mean?" Dani asked.

"Dad was cremated, Dani, and my mother has his ashes ready to bring to Sarawak. She thinks that had he ever written a will he would have asked for his ashes to be spread on the river he loved so much."

"And where is that?" Dani asked.

Angelique smiled. "Your eyes tell me that is an unnecessary question. The river where your uncles – his brothers – saved his life and the river that gave your mother, his wife, and family the source of life."

"It is a ritual you may have to explain to my people," Dani said but he was smiling too.

"Your people?" Angelique asked.

"The Iban," Dani said proudly. "Do not let these blue eyes and blond hair deceive you. I will never be anything else."

Angelique nodded and smiled.

"I understand," she said. "So you see, Dani, after the war your mother was right, somebody had to lose. At first, it was you and your mother. After coming to England, it was my mother and me, but in reality, there was only one person who lost everything, and that was dad. When that soldier hit him on the back of the head just because he protected a young girl, he became the loser and as he fell I think he might already have known everything was coming to an end."

Epilogue

Long Lohang, Sarawak, Borneo June 1963

Standing on the bank of the river a few feet from where he had washed his healing wounds, fished and allowed his thoughts to govern his and their futures, the two women held hands.

There was nothing false about the way they were, they needed to share his leaving in the same way they had shared his mind and his body when he was alive.

They watched as his son and daughter fifty feet out into the river leant over the side of the prau and together they lifted the urn to let their father's ashes fall onto the surface of the water. As they watched the current sweep him away downriver, they bowed their heads.

It was right that they were the ones to enact what they all knew he would have wanted.

Abas, the headman, twisted the throttle on the outboard motor and the prau's bow slowly shifted so that it was pointing towards the others.

As well as Aslah, Dani's mother, Angelique's mother Rachel, Fung and Chao, Lim and Chee – the Chinese family who had meant so much to him and all the others – the bank was many deep in people from the Iban longhouses up and down river.

A stranger would have viewed what they saw with bewilderment, but for those who knew, it was the conclusion to what had started with the threatened Japanese invasion of Sarawak in 1941.

Everyone watched in silence as the fast flowing river took his ashes downstream toward Miri and the South China Sea. Although a generation later, they understood why Colin Freemantle would be part of their lives for years to come; in fact, his name would become included in their folklore.

His son and daughter climbed out of the prau and each in turn embraced the two women who could now get on with the remaining years of their own lives, renewed hope in their hearts.

Rachel smiled understandingly as she looked into her daughter's ice blue eyes, and Aslah did the same with her son.

Colin Freemantle's son and daughter took hold of each other's

485

hands, lifted their heads proudly towards the jungle's canopy before embracing in front of all who were present.

Rachel gripped Aslah's hand in hers and the tears came to both women at the same time. They had been so strong to that point but seeing their son and daughter embrace they could no longer hold back their own emotions.

It was the culmination of so many years for both women, perhaps now they could find the strength to move on.

Abas, the headman, watched from just a few yards away and he too was in mourning. He had lost his remaining brother and dear friend.

The flight in the silver bird would never happen, not now, not with Coy-lyn.

Nevertheless, as with the others, now he could move on.

There was much to do.

The war against the Japanese was many years in the past but now there was another threat looming on the other side of the mountains, a threat that could have an even more profound effect on the future of his people.

The Iban.

THE END

King George VI"s Speech to the Nation at 9pm 15th August 1945

"Three months have passed since I asked you to join with me in an act of thanksgiving for the defeat of Germany. We then rejoiced that peace had returned to Europe, but we knew that a strong and relentless enemy still remained to be conquered in Asia. None could then tell how long or how heavy would prove the struggle that still awaited us.

Japan has surrendered, so let us join in thanking Almighty God that war has ended throughout the world, and that in every country men may now turn their industry, skill, and science to repairing its frightful devastation and to building prosperity and happiness. Our sense of deliverance is overpowering, and with it all, we have a right to feel that we have done our duty.

I ask you again at this solemn hour to remember all who have laid down their lives, and all who have endured the loss of those they love. Remember, too, the sufferings of those who fell into the hands of the enemy, whether as prisoners of war or because their homes had been overrun. They have been in our thoughts all through these dark years, and let us pray that one result of the defeat of Japan may be many happy reunions of those who have been long separated from each other.

The campaigns in the Far East will be famous in history for many reasons. There is one feature of them which is a special source of pride to me, and also to you, the citizens of our British Commonwealth and Empire to whom I speak. In those campaigns they have fought, side by side with our allies, representatives of almost every unit in our great community – men from the Old Country, men from the Dominions, from India, and the Colonies. They fought in brotherhood; through their courage and endurance they conquered. To all of them and to the women who shared with them the hardships and dangers of war I send my proud and grateful thanks.

The war is over.

You know, I think that those four words have for The Queen and myself the same significance, simple yet immense, that they have for you. Our hearts are full to overflowing, as are your own. Yet there is not one of us who has experienced this terrible war who does not realize that we shall feel its inevitable consequences long after we have all forgotten our rejoicings of today.

But that relief from past dangers must not blind us to the demands of the future. The British people here at home have added lustre to the true fame of our Islands, and we stand today with our whole Empire in the forefront of the victorious United Nations. Great, therefore, is our responsibility to make sure by the actions of every man and every woman here and throughout the Empire and Commonwealth that the peace gained amid measureless trials and suffering shall not be cast away.

In many anxious times in our long history the unconquerable spirit of our peoples has served us well, bringing us to safety out of great peril. Yet I doubt if anything in all that has gone before has matched the enduring courage and the quiet determination which you have shown during these last six years.

It is of this unconquerable spirit that I would speak to you tonight. For great as are the deeds that you have done, there must be no falling off from this high endeavour. We have spent freely of all that we had: now we shall have to work hard to restore what has been lost, and to establish peace on the unshakeable foundations, not alone of material strength, but also of moral authority.

Then, indeed, the curse of war may be lifted from the world, and States and peoples, great and small, may dwell together through long periods of tranquillity in brighter and better days than we ourselves have known.

The world has come to look for certain things, for certain qualities from the peoples of the Commonwealth and Empire. We have our part to play in restoring the shattered fabric of civilisation. It is a proud and difficult part, and if you carry on in the years to come as you have done so splendidly in the war, you and your children can look forward to the future, not with fear, but with high hopes of a surer happiness for all. It is to this great task that I call you now, and I know that I shall not call in vain.

In the meantime, from the bottom of my heart I thank my Peoples for all they have done, not only for themselves but for mankind.

Printed in Great Britain
by Amazon